GAV

Stephanie Merritt was born in 1974. She has written for a variety of newspapers and magazines and is currently Deputy Literary Editor and Comedy Critic of the *Observer*.

STEPHANIE MERRITT

Gaveston

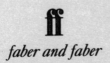

faber and faber

First published in 2002
by Faber and Faber Limited
3 Queen Square London WC1N 3AU
This paperback edition published in 2003

Typeset by Faber and Faber Ltd
Printed in England by Mackays of Chatham plc, Chatham, Kent

A CIP record for this book
is available from the British Library

ISBN 0–571–21065–1

2 4 6 8 10 9 7 5 3 1

And it is always past before we can know it.
Just as our individual lives, which we see
In daunting or luring prospect, minute by minute,
Make little sense until we are seen by others
As completed fact or anecdote, not likely
To slip out of character, palpably there.
Is this, then, our chance of eternity?
And what would you, what can you, say of it now?

John Fuller, *History*

For Arnold Kemp
1939–2002
much-missed friend

Prologue

It was hardly what he would have wanted.

You might have mistaken the crematorium chapel – wedged between the corrugated roofs of the industrial estate – for another warehouse, but for its mock-Gothic mullioned windows and a discreet sign pointing to the Garden of Remembrance (No Dogs) and Patrons Only car park. Coils of barbed wire topped the high fencing that separated the garden from the railway line; the garden itself was made of gravel, and remembrance was constantly interrupted by the thunder of passenger jets taking off from the adjacent airport. It was a dismal place to take your final bow, chosen solely because it offered – in theory – the twin advantages of distance and anonymity.

In fact, the car park had been crammed since the early morning with transit vans, freighted with rotating satellite dishes and aerials and decanting reporters, photographers, technicians, loops of cable, sound engineers and cameramen in baseball caps into the chapel's forecourt. Any attempt at solemnity on the part of the arriving mourners had been thwarted by the noises of the news industry: instructions barked through static into phones; small bleepings of pagers and cameras in counterpoint; the rallying shouts of men in headphones. The reporters shared cigarettes and watched the door, barred to them by ranks of titanic security guards, while they scuffed bored patterns in the gravel and waited for the congregation to emerge. Flanking the steps were two rows of photographers, glancing at the sky and swearing, or cupping anxious hands around their lenses to guard them from the film of drizzle already settling in silver beads on their hair and on the nylon fur of the booms. Others climbed the railings or perched on the bonnets of vans for a better vantage point. Beyond the perimeter fence a further row of vans lined the grass verge, where a knot of crop-haired protesters piled against the gridded gates, shouting and brandishing placards bewailing bigotry, hypocrisy, the evils of global capitalism.

The glass of the chapel windows rattled against the frames with the wind. Inside, the congregation shifted in their seats as the service progressed with terrible slowness and inappropriate sentiment. *They shall hunger no more, neither thirst any more; neither shall the sun shine on them, nor any heat . . . He that overcometh shall inherit all things . . .*

Finally, the double doors eased open, releasing a blast of doleful chords, and the crowd in the yard surged eagerly to the foot of the steps, jostling into a scrum of whirring shutters and flash-bulbs. For a moment he stood motionless, framed in the proscenium of the door, eyes visored by his mirrored sunglasses. A short pause, then the babble of questions began – 'Is it true –?', 'Was this an accident –?', 'How do you explain –?', 'And the divorce settlement –?' – the spiky microphones pushed into his face, the scratching of gravel as they hefted the television cameras aloft and elbowed to the front. With a forced dignity, he drew his head up, adjusted the black coat draped across his shoulders, then strode through the mob to the waiting car. The security Neanderthals, two before and one behind, shoved the more persistent journalists away, but many stepped back instinctively, as if guiltily impressed by the composure of this tall, dark-browed man who had paid a wage to at least half of them at one time or another.

I watched all this from the shadows of the chapel porch, one hand in my pocket turning over the engagement ring Piers had given me until the metal grew warm. My uncle was folded into the car by his minders, and it pulled away through the gates with a squealing of tyres, pieces of sky flashing in its tinted windows. The nimbler film crews scampered in pursuit, and behind them the protesters, still baying

2

their slogans; for a moment the crowd fell on the car as it snagged on the speed bumps and then muscled free.

People muttered past me through the doorway, darting quick, curious glances. I felt a hand on my shoulder.

'Hard to believe it's still August.' Oliver allowed a little shudder for emphasis. It was the sort of remark you make at funerals. 'You shouldn't be hanging around here. They'll be back for you.'

'I suppose.'

'I'm telling you. You know the press. Vermin after carrion.' He produced a small laugh through his nose. 'Come on, then.' Steering me back into the shadows of the emptying chapel, he led me through the lobby to a side door. 'I parked round the back. You don't want to get caught up in that lot, not now.'

We drove back along the motorway in silence, the light fading behind sulky clouds. Oliver was jittery, as if he had drunk too much coffee; he drove too fast, drumming his fingers on the wheel, glancing often at me or in his mirror as though he expected to be followed. I stared unseeing at the blurry landscape, eyes parched, too tired to speak.

'Edward looked terrible,' Oliver commented, after some time.

'Yes.'

'I mean, I suppose he would – but you never think of Edward as having any feelings.'

'Yes.'

'He must have done, though, mustn't he – in his own way? Loved him, I mean. Poor Edward. Never thought I'd hear myself say that. Maybe it's all for the cameras. Edward always seemed so –'

'Olly –'

'What?'

'Leave it.'

'Sorry.'

We drove on in silence.

'You should get away, Gaby, you know.' A car behind hooted twice as he pulled into the outside lane without indicating. 'For a while, until this all blows over.' He pushed his glasses up on to the bridge of his nose and glanced at me again.

I shrugged. 'Where would I go?'

'I don't know. To France, to your mum's? I just think you need a break. It's not over yet.'

I turned away.

'I don't understand. Why now? When they must have known –'

'Timing,' Oliver said, brusquely. 'Saving it for the silly season. We have to sell papers. It would be ungallant of me to remind you that I did try to warn you.'

'You didn't tell me anything.'

'You wouldn't listen.'

Nearing London, the lanes of traffic began to slow and clot. I watched the crash barrier undulating past the window.

'How do you mean, not over?'

'Don't know, just – I think there could be more to come out. It might be better if you were – out of reach.'

'I'll think about it.'

After some moments, he asked, 'Do you think it was an accident?'

'No,' I replied immediately. It was not the first time he had asked me this.

Oh, Piers. How did I so misunderstand you?

The silence thickened uncomfortably, and the car began to grow stuffy. Rain landed in fat pellets on the windscreen; Oliver clicked on the headlamps.

'Do you want to stop off somewhere?'

I shook my head. 'No. Let's just get home.'

'Your home?' He looked surprised. 'Do you think that's wise?'

'No. I meant your home.'

4

'They'll find you sooner or later.'

'Later would suit me.'

Innischonnell Hall, Argyllshire. September.

There was a neat irony about Oliver's quite genuine efforts to protect me from the press. His concern and discretion had got me through the long afternoons in hiding after Piers's death, while we waited for the results of the inquest and my uncle's wrecked face was slapped over the front page of every newspaper he didn't own under gleefully mocking headlines. Everything was skewed, then, during those days; only Oliver was a constant. It never occurred to me that he might be part of it.

From my desk here I can gaze out across the grounds as far as the forest, over the spires of the dark pines that run down almost to the edge of the water. Behind the Hall, the bulky shadows of mountains pile up against the sky. Loch Awe lies quietly, three miles to the east, guarding its scattered ruins; the late September wind that gusts round the house and batters the Virginia creeper against the windows comes straight off the sea, from the west, and the air tastes clean, salt and bitter.

It was Oliver who suggested I try Innischonnell Hall when my uncle disappeared after the funeral. Innischonnell is the seat of Sir Rory Campbell, Sixth Earl of Orchy, whose crest looms over the entrance hall and the mantelpieces: a field of argent, with a tower in canton, surmounted by a helm and mantling and supported by two stags rampant; beneath it the motto *Meum Protego. I Defend What Is Mine.*

Sir Rory is away from home at the present, so Moira informs me importantly, training flat horses in Ireland (she refuses to smile when I ask if they don't fall over), but I am welcome to stay for as long as I need. There are no questions, and my welfare has become part of her bustling routine as she moves in her own accustomed ways around the Hall, flapping a cloth at those few rooms not swathed in dust sheets, wrinkling her nose critically ('Ye'll ruin your eyes, all that reading. Young lassie like you.'). But she, of all people, should understand how I have come to value the solitude of the Hall, its creaks and strange echoes, its isolation and resolute blind eye to the outside world; the purging weather and my long walks along the shore of the loch; the absence of visitors and, especially, of television and newspapers. Moira herself is reassuringly dour, but there is always a pot of stew hiccupping on the stove when I crash through the door in the evening, wind-blown and raw, with the dog lolloping its trail of mud through the kitchen. Moira disapproves of me in a well-meaning way; she finds me too pale and skinny, too much given to moping and reading, all of which could be remedied, in her view, by a good solid meal and a bit less time brooding on ye'self, lassie, ken – but she never asks about my uncle, nor how we both came to be there at this time.

'This has always been a good place to get away from everything,' was the nearest she ever came to hinting. 'Sir Rory always pops back when it gets a bit much and he wants a wee bit of quiet.'

And so she tells me stories, of the Hall in younger days, and I tell her a few fished-up childhood memories, and the evenings grow gradually colder. Every morning I bring in fresh logs from the disused stables.

'Always writing, you are,' she sniffs in the evenings, as though this were self-evidently unhealthy. 'What is it you write up there, all these nights?'

So I tell her this: it's a story. The story of a man I once knew, unlike anyone else, and I'm writing it because now, finally, I think I have understood.

'Ye'll be stopping a wee while yet then. Your sweetheart, was he?'

'I thought so. Once.'

'And what happened to him, now?'

I pause for a moment, not quite trusting. She must know.

6

'He died.'

'Young, was he? An accident?'

'Yes. I suppose –'

She hesitates too; wipes her floury hands on her skirt. 'Och, well, comes to us all one time or another. Six years come December, my Robert's been gone, and there's not a day I don't think of him. But only the good die young, they do say. I'll see you in the morning – if we're spared.'

We have this sort of conversation most nights, Moira and I, as we eat our evening meal; unwilling to edge any closer to intimacy and lacking the energy to talk of much else – but both, in our separate ways, needing the reassurance of company. I even begin to look forward to it.

The story I am telling has several versions. That is to say, it has several beginnings. Were Oliver to recount his version, or my uncle, or, if the dead could speak, Denham Dowland or even Piers himself, we would have to begin years earlier, and in other countries. And gradually these separate beginnings would begin to run close to one another, like railway tracks, until they all converged at the same point – the death of Piers Gaveston.

And I have their stories now. But I must begin with my own. It starts nearly two years ago, on a bright, freezing January day in a fenland town, before Edward's overtures, before Piers came out of exile, before I became, unwittingly, part of their story.

PART ONE

Chapter I

The sun sat low in the sky, its light weakened by a thin drift of cloud leaking across the blue. Frost glazed the roofs and window sills and the brittle branches of the trees; it crackled underfoot on the tarmac. Between the buildings of the Livingstone Site, wherever the paving slabs dipped and buckled, small puddles had acquired a delicate skin of milky ice, causing more than one cyclist to slip and slither before they reached the safety of the bicycle racks on the far side of History.

The Livingstone Site was named, not as homage to the pioneering spirit of the famous explorer, as new students often imagined, but as a tribute to a Mr Bernard Livingstone, the stolid, bespectacled burgher whose generous bequest to the university had funded the site's construction and whose unimposing portrait decorated the foyer of the main hall. That had been in the early sixties, and the Livingstone Site enjoyed all the benefits of that period of British architecture. On a good day, if the sun was out, it looked like an experimental housing project. In gloomy weather it resembled a blighted suburb of pre-democracy East Berlin. The cluster of buildings housed the libraries and lecture halls of what the university arcanely insisted on calling the Liberal Arts – Literature, Philosophy, Classics, History, Languages (Modern), Languages (Ancient), Music and Art History – and boasted a dimly lit faux-Chaucerian cafeteria named The Tavern, a grotto of formica tables and chemical coffee. Adjacent to The Tavern was Philosophy and Literature, a pebble-dashed block poised alarmingly on fat concrete stilts. Among these pillars small bunches of students in identical jackets huddled round cigarettes as if to ward off the cold,

11

rubbing their hands furiously, their breath fogging in the sharp air.

Far above them, in a fourth-floor seminar room, Dr George Fenton stood by the wide window, hands clasped behind his back, surveying the construction work. The ring of metal on metal echoed across the site, where the huge glass dome was beginning to take shape out of what had once been the car park, its naked triangular girders poking rudely above the roofs of the surrounding libraries. Two tall cranes bowed towards each other, etched in crisp right angles against the sky, like herons in a mating dance. The new building more closely resembled a giant biosphere or nuclear research laboratory than part of a great and ancient seat of learning; in its present state of undress, it glittered brazenly under the cold light. Ainsley Ryerson – now Lord Ryerson of Crouch End – had been quoted in *Architecture Today* as saying it was possibly his finest conceptual work to date; finer even (and these were his own words) than his globally fêted Ludwigshafen Museum of Furniture and Social Development.

George gazed with a nostalgic sigh beyond the cranes and girders to the spires of the old colleges, heraldic emblems fluttering defiantly on their battlements.

'Think of it' – he unclasped his hands and tapped a finger against the glass, his back still to the room – 'think of it as a kind of cultural renaissance.'

From behind him came a nasal exhalation that might have been tinged with sarcasm.

'Or – no, better – think of this view as the embodiment of progress, as a visual metaphor for the future of arts scholarship. Behold, to your right, ladies and gentlemen, the spires of St Dunstan's College, circa 1300. To your left, the soon-to-be-completed Faculty of Cultural Studies, circa thirteen and a half million –'

'And the rest.'

Cheerfully in character by now, George ignored the interruption.

'You see' – he flung his arms wide – 'the ancient beside the trenchantly modern, each with its own values, a shifting sky-line, if you like, but maintaining a cohesive –'

'*George!* Absolute flim-flam, and you know it! It's not the end that's the issue, it's the means involved. This is sheer bloody bare-faced capitalism, is what it is, and let's not dress it up as progress.' The heckler, Dr Miles Park – a large, belli-cose historian with thinning hair and surprised eyebrows – slapped a hand forcefully on the table and glanced at his col-leagues for support.

George sighed. 'This is the age we live in, Miles.'

'That doesn't make it *right*! Not here. We shouldn't treat learning like a commercial enterprise.'

'Of course, your own scholarly asceticism is the talk of West Eleven.'

Dr Sara Croft smiled a thin, feline smile; Miles Park nar-rowed his eyes. His most recent book, a rather pedestrian and tortuous history of the Balkan states, had sold to a shameless-ly commercial imprint for an advance rumoured to be approaching the six-figure mark and was currently topping the paperback bestseller lists, to the astonishment of his col-leagues, most booksellers and critics, and especially to the chagrin of Sara Croft, who had confidently dismissed it in the modern history issue of the *London Review* – though some suspected her defamatory epithets were more *ad hominem* than she cared to admit ('conservative, obnoxious, self-con-gratulating, meretricious and inelegant').

'I'm talking about the university, Sara. This is wholly inad-missible. It flies in the face of every principle of free education.'

'But Miles,' George turned to face the room, leaning against the window and folding his arms, 'the university has always relied on donations, it simply couldn't exist without them. This is merely an extension of the same idea.'

Miles Park was shaking his head vigorously. 'A gift is one thing. We're talking here about corporate investors retaining a degree of control over the end product, as I understand it –

13

correct me if I'm wrong – but the new faculty won't even belong to the university. Whatever name you want to give it, it's effectively privatisation.'

'Nonsense, of course it will be a part of the university – the investor will be, I suppose, a sort of absentee landlord.' George moved around the table to stand in front of the whiteboard on the far wall, which bore the word 'KANT' in smudgy green letters. 'You know we've been obliged to look for alternative investment since the money ran out for the project?'

'I thought we'd been promised some of it from the D of E?' Park frowned.

'Not nearly enough, and persuading a coprporate sponsor that he'll get the right kind of returns is not so easy as you think, not for the kind of money we need. That's why, when we were approached –'

'Who's we?'

'Ah – we. Yes.' George removed his glasses, considered them for a moment and put them back on. 'The – ah – Vice-Chancellor and – ah, so on. Indirectly. Anyway. We were approached by an investor who agreed to put up the money for completion of the building, together with money for a Chair, with the proviso that the investing company make up the greater part of the Faculty Board. It's a sort of long-term loan, in effect.'

'But that's ludicrous! And it's obvious that private finance will, in a very few years, have cost the university far more than it ever would to put up the capital up front and keep the new faculty on the same footing as the rest.'

'But the capital doesn't exist up front any more, Miles, that's the whole point of finding an investor. The university will pay back what it can afford over the stipulated period, together with the money raised from additional tuition fees, and the investing company will shoulder the running costs. You can't deny that this is the kind of expansion the university needs to keep its foothold.'

'I bloody can! It's nothing but a giant publicity stunt – we'll become part of a brand name! Whatever happened to the objectivity of scholarship?'

George sighed.

'It's a luxury we can no longer afford.'

'But look, here's the crucial question,' Sara Croft leaned forward and pointed an accusing finger at George. 'Does this mean that the teaching staff will be in the employ of the investors or the university?'

George tugged at his beard. 'The university, in theory. But it's all rather complicated – it will be run as a business, but in a very invisible way, you see, so that staff will be paid by the company but appointed by the Faculty Board –'

'The majority of which are representatives of the investors,' Park interrupted. 'And forgive me, but they'll be business people, won't they? What do they know about running a university department?'

'And can this Faculty Board also fire people at will?' Sara Croft narrowed her eyes.

'Well – that's a matter to be discussed with the unions.'

'Listen, right.' Dr Jake Lennox folded his legs beneath him in an approximation of the lotus position, his earrings chinking gently as he moved. He was never at his most charming in meetings, particularly ones that began in the morning. 'It's a preposterous idea, granted. It's preposterous that the students should have to pay extra tuition fees to study at this faculty, but George is right – it's the way things are going. Has to be – ten, twenty years time, I reckon, maybe not even – government funding'll be a thing of the past and all our universities will be privately run, like the States, right? And I don't agree in principle – of course I don't – but I am convinced that the university needs this faculty like a shot in the arm – it's stagnating visibly, and without this, in ten years' time it won't be worth working here. Plus' – he hugged his knees, cocked his head and looked around the table – 'if your estimates are right, George, it means I'll be earning two and a half times my present salary to teach what I already teach –

15

but with better resources, in a nicer building and without interference from the traditionalists. And if that means I could be fired any day just like any other company – well, I'll live with that.'

'Jake is positively salivating at the prospect of stuffing all those impressionable young minds with unintelligible theories, aren't you?' Sara Croft tapped her tapered aubergine nails on the table and smiled, gently mocking.

'Well, you must be excited too, admit it. You get to staff a whole department of your own for Periods.'

'There is more to Women's Studies than that, Jay, as you know.' Sara pursed her lips. 'There will also be a course on eyeliner.'

'When you've finished flirting –' Miles Park hunched his shoulders irritably.

'That wasn't flirting, Miles.' Sara smiled acidly. 'You really should get out more often.'

'The enhanced media links will mean splendid opportunities for exposure,' George said, with a sly smile in Miles Park's direction. 'Television, and so on.'

Miles twitched his head, unimpressed.

'My agent sees to all that –'

Sara Croft sniffed unnecessarily; Jake Lennox hummed 'They're gonna put me in the movies . . .' under his breath. Miles Park glowered at both of them and muttered something indecipherable.

'I was wondering –' I stopped abruptly; the four of them swivelled together to regard me with a mixture of curiosity and suspicion. The position of Graduate Student Representative on this Faculty Board was something akin to the role of a court clerk; you kept your head respectfully bowed, and made careful notes, and certainly didn't expect to speak unless you were spoken to. Student representatives were desirable accessories, indicating a commitment on the university's part to democratic rule, but were in practice decorative rather than functional. (The Undergraduate Representative was evidently still in bed.) I had agreed to take on the position when George asked me the previous autumn partly because I knew he wanted an ally, and partly because I liked the idea of being a Trojan horse – privy to all the planning and decision-making while nursing a deep-seated suspicion of this proposed modernisation and its unknown consequences.

'Gaby.' George folded his hands together and beamed. 'You haven't said a word. What is it?'

George Fenton's appointment as Chair of the new Faculty Planning Committee had been greeted with mild surprise. George was amused rather than outraged by the pseudo-science of contemporary literary theory, and continued to teach literature first and foremost as a love of books. He had been raised a Catholic and still guarded a covert reverence for the mystical, though outwardly he watched life as if it were a comedy of manners. He had been a theatre critic for twelve of his sixty-three years, a travel writer for two, and a well-regarded academic for nearly thirty; he had produced six volumes of poetry (five now out of print), two novels and countless books of literary criticism, and was a frequent contributor to the broadsheet press. In spite of his quite deliberately tweedy exterior, however, George commanded a surprising amount of respect in some unusual spheres, and in this lay his value to the hopeful modernisers, and the source of my present anxiety. George Fenton, in another life, might have made an excellent spy.

I cleared my throat.

'It's just – I was wondering – who is this new investor?'

'Exactly! *Exactly*!' Miles Park banged his palm on the table emphatically, shot me a grin of encouragement and jabbed a finger at George. 'That's exactly what we need to know! What do they get out of it? I mean – they might also be sponsoring dam projects in India for all we know –'

'They might be Colombian drug barons!' Sara Croft chipped in with snide enthusiasm.

'Muscovite Mafiosi!' Jake suggested, eyes wide.

Miles Park sighed. 'It would be so nice if for once you could take this a bit seriously. It is, in fact, a big deal. The future of scholarship is at stake, and if that doesn't bother you, on a more immediate level, your careers and mine are about to come under the control of some corporate masters about whom we know nothing, and who's to say they won't start dictating the content of what we teach? Or taint us by association? So. George?'

The heads swivelled expectantly back towards George. Out in the building site, a drill struck up a dull whine. George squinted at the window, removed the lid from his pen, stared for a moment at the nib as if it might hold the secret, then replaced the lid carefully, laid the pen down in front of him and looked up at us with a calm smile.

'Oh dear. I'm afraid it's not really official.'

'What?'

George's reassuring smile was a little unnatural.

'Yet. You see, the contracts are not entirely signed and sealed. The party in question is understandably afraid of the press getting hold of this before the time is right.'

'If it's not finalised, what's that bloody banging and hammering out there all about?' Jake Lennox waved an arm wildly at the window. 'They're not working for tea and sandwiches and the sheer love of it. And Christ, we're on the inside, surely we should – I mean, we're hardly going to sell our stories, are we?'

Sara Croft looked at him sideways.

'No, no, the money is in place, be sure of that, the building will be finished. It's simply that – the *wording* of the agreement, you understand, it's rather complicated – a question of semantics, which you ought to appreciate, Jake, the lawyers are crossing t's and dotting i's, a great deal of that must be done and it may take some weeks. And publicity must be carefully timed. But!' – George clapped his hands together brightly – 'we needn't concern ourselves with that side of it. Our business now is getting down to the course content.'

'So you're not going to tell us?' Park stuck out his chin.

'Well' – George scratched his beard – 'that is one way of putting it. It's an investor with . . . significant media interests. But look, it's not so important. I'm rather embarrassed but I have signed a confidentiality agreement, otherwise of course I'd let you know. The announcement will be made very shortly, I promise.'

For the first time since I had spoken, George's gaze latched briefly on mine. Then he looked quickly away.

'Now,' George continued, smiling, 'I hope to have individual meetings with all the senior lecturers in the next couple of weeks to discuss the teaching and research programmes. Of course that will be more straightforward once the new professor arrives, since I'm sure he'll want to –'

A chair squeaked indignantly on the vinyl floor. Miles Park leapt to his feet, pointing his finger at George.

'Now this really is beyond a joke!'

Sara Croft folded her arms and gaped; Jake Lennox leaned his elbows on the table and flicked anxiously at his eyebrow ring.

'Ah.' George's smile was beginning to strain at the edges. 'I wondered if this might cause a bit of bother.'

'Come on, George!' An affronted scarlet blotch was developing on each of Park's cheeks. '*A bit of bother*? You just said "the new professor". How can there be a – I mean, you can't just – there's been no consultation, no approval – if the money for the Chair isn't even officially finalised how can you possibly have appointed – I just can't –' He slumped back into his chair, breathless. 'It's not true, is it?'

'*He*. You said "he".' Sara Croft's face was stony.

'I – ah –'

'Who appointed him? Were any women considered for this job?'

'Were any of *us* considered for this job?' Lennox cut in.

George didn't answer.

'What's he written, then?' Miles Park demanded, after a

19

short pause, in a voice that suggested if it hadn't sold over thirty thousand copies, he was clearly a paper tiger.

'He's been very involved in film.'

'Oh, *film*. For fuck's sake. So this is the way we're going.'

'Miles, please. Everyone.' George laid his hands flat on the table and allowed his eyes to coast slowly around the group. 'I know that this Chair was of great importance to all of you – Gaby excepted' – he waved a hand briefly at me – 'and to others. But – this is the point – the professorship here is very much a sinecure, a public role. We are the ones who will determine the direction of the faculty. But it was felt necessary to appoint someone – how shall I put it – media-friendly.'

'So what is he – a pop singer? Soap star? MTV video jockey? *Jesus!*'

Park balled his hand into a fist around his pencil; Sara Croft held up a hand to halt his tirade.

'You *said*' – she turned to George, enunciating crisply – 'any appointment had to be approved by the Faculty Board. But the Faculty Board hasn't yet been established. So who approved this appointment, eh?'

George looked at her; looked at me; looked at his watch.

'It's rather convoluted . . . Look, I'm so sorry, we'll have to go over this later – it's five past eleven, you must excuse me.' He laughed briefly, shuffled his chair back, bunched the sheaf of papers under his arm and made a dash for the door, pausing on the threshold to gesture vaguely. 'Of course, I'll be around, you know – if anyone wants to talk further – otherwise – same time next week.'

'George, could I just –' I half-rose, but George was already bounding down the stairs with unseemly haste.

'Not now, Gaby,' his voice floated up, 'I'm late. Another time, another time.'

Sara Croft came to stand beside me in the doorway, staring in disbelief at the empty landing. She folded her arms.

'He's so slippery sometimes.' She glanced at me. 'Never a straight answer. Do you know anything about this?'

'No.' I frowned.

'Sure?'

'Of course I'm sure.'

'I think we could all hazard a guess.'

Across the room, Jake Lennox and Miles Park leaned against the window facing the construction site.

'How *dare* they appoint a fucking Chair without giving any of us the chance to apply? It's fucking outrageous!' Lennox pressed his forehead to the glass.

'Well, it's exactly what I said would happen – he who pays the piper. Clearly these shadowy investors want their own man on the inside, it's as simple as that.' Park tapped a knuckle on the window. 'This whole thing's getting a bit too self-regarding, if you ask me. I mean, look at that – typical Ainsley Ryerson attention-grabbing – pretty on the outside, it'll take a lovely photo, but impractical as buggery to work in, you can be sure. Looks like somewhere you'd carry out illegal genetic experiments.'

'Still. Eight screening rooms, though, Parky, eight fucking screening rooms – imagine that. And an editing suite.'

'Hmm. And a whole floor with on-line access to every archive in almost every major public library across Europe and North America. Imagine *that* – the history of the world at the click of a button. If it works.'

'The book will become a thing of the past.'

'Oh, I think not. Not according to last Sunday's bestseller lists in the *Enquirer*.' Miles Park smiled fatly. Jake Lennox ignored him.

'I wonder, though.' He sighed faintly.

'What?'

'Well – what price we'll have to pay. Compromise. There's millions gone into that and you don't get something for nothing.'

'They're buying reputation.'

'Huh.' Jake took a step back, hands sunk deep in his pockets. 'Must say I'm dying to meet this new professor. He'll be some clapped-out arts show presenter who's fallen from grace with the BBC and failed to get his contract renewed.'

'Oh no, no – you can bet he's a corporate lickspittle – some aspirant little queen in thrall to the company, and we'll all have to kow-tow to him or risk losing our jobs. I hate him already.'

'Whereas I'm sure he'll take an immediate shine to *you*, Miles.' Sara Croft picked up her leatherbound notebook and tucked it into her bag. I shrugged on my coat. 'Are you disappointed that they failed to recognise you as the obvious choice for professor?'

'No more than either of you.' He jabbed a finger at Sara and Jake.

'My money was on George, for the record.' Jake Lennox shook his head. 'And I'd have been happy with that. I admit I'm amazed.'

'George is playing a strange game, that's for sure.' Sara Croft nodded. 'I didn't expect him to let go of the reins so easily. Well, we'll have confirmation soon enough.' She slipped me the same sneering look.

I pretended not to see it; I had my own suspicions about George's games.

The meeting appeared to be over.

Chapter II

As the new faculty continued to swell like a bloated jellyfish above the Livingstone Site, I was struggling through the winter of the third and (in theory) final year of my doctorate in the grip of a growing ennui.

I had begun this work because, a few years ago – when I was nineteen, perhaps, or twenty – George Fenton had recommended to me a book written by an eminent historian at the university. It was an account of the Dissolution of the Monasteries. The author was a Catholic but even accounting for a certain bias, it stoked in me a kind of righteous fury as I understood, for the first time, the fragility of our hold on the past and how suddenly it can be destroyed. Since I was a child, I had been fascinated by the early history of England: its ruined churches, abbeys and castles, but especially its books, chronicles and records. I loved the stiff crackle of manuscript pages between my fingers, the exquisite, devoted detail of the illuminations, the smell of manuscript archives – vellum and old leather; and on reading the Dissolution book, I felt a new, terrible grief at the loss of all those libraries, all those beautiful books burned, or torn and scattered in the dirt. I had decided then – and partly for want of a more concrete ambition – that I could do worse things with my time than set out to preserve some of our past, and hand on to others a love of its treasures, as George had handed it down to me.

Scholarship is essentially detective work, inspired by a belief that there are pieces of the puzzle yet to be dug out and interpreted; that our understanding of the past is susceptible to change or revision at any moment. In the early days I dreamed of being remembered as someone who caused just such a change of direction. Some unplundered crypt or private library, I felt certain, some antiquarian bookshop in a forsaken market town, some monastic attic or bricked-up hiding place, would one day yield the thing – a map, or manuscript; a letter, an etching or a printer's catalogue; perhaps just a translator's footnote or unobserved piece of marginalia – but of such profound importance that it would alter the map of the past altogether. How I imagined I would make this remarkable discovery, since I spent little time truffling around monastic attics, I have no idea, but I was convinced the lost manuscript was waiting for me somewhere. These were the things I cared about, then.

Of course, the minute you begin work on your thesis, all this bright optimism is knocked squarely on the head. You will be informed that you are expected to produce 'an original contribution to scholarship'. This means that instead of writing about the work that interested you in the first place – in my case, the twelfth-century chronicles of the Arthurian myth – you are obliged to wander further and further into the murky hinterland of secondary sources to find something that has not yet been said, distracted by increasingly resentful ferretings into minutiae, while trying to ignore the frustration and boredom that are quietly shunting your enthusiasm to one side.

Every morning I would leave my house in the south of the town at a quarter to ten and make the twenty-minute walk to the Livingstone Site or to the Manuscript Room of the University Library, where I would install myself in an airless crevice between book stacks and sift through unread and unreadable articles in back numbers of the *Journal of Arthurian Studies*; articles with titles that seemed to become increasingly silly with each issue, as if competing for some trophy of supreme pointlessness. 'Exhuming the Word: Semiological Absences and Dialectical Divergence in the *Gesta Regum* and Related Tracts'. 'The Bleeding Lance: A Gay Scottish Rereading of the Grail Sources and Later Appendices'. Or 'Not Worth a Bean: Amanuensical Interpolation and Partisan Interpretation in Wyclifite Appropriation of Higden's *Polychronicon*.' All of which might be reduced to the same fundamental formula: 'Desperate for Tenure: A Meaningless Rehashing of a Subject on which Everything Has Already Been Said but Necessary to Secure My Degree/Teaching Post/Continuing Academic Status/ Chances of Reviewing for the *TLS*.'

George knew very well that these detours were merely excuses to delay the business of writing – a prospect that sparked a very real panic, largely because I had no idea where I would go when the thesis was finished. I had already been told, regretfully, that neither the Faculty of History nor the Faculty of English could afford another Research Fellow in the near future, and moving somewhere else was difficult to imagine. After six years, the university had become the only home I knew.

Occasionally, on Mondays, I would take the train to London and have dinner with my uncle Edward's godson and my friend of some years, Oliver Dowland, now chief political correspondent of the *Sunday Enquirer*. Despite our very different worlds, Oliver remained a willing confidant.

'You should get out of there if it's not challenging you any more. Why don't you call some of your dad's old friends, see if you can get someone to open some doors?' he would suggest. 'Or I can make some enquiries . . .'

To which I would give the standard reply: 'I don't want to be given a job as a favour. That's not my ambition. Anyway – it would always come back to Edward.'

'Well, what is your ambition? To write the definitive book on the Arthur legends, get published by the No Hope Press and end up giving talks to mad people at Welsh historical conferences? I'm not suggesting you go to Edward, although I bet he'd help you out if you wanted.'

'Don't be stupid.'

'I think you're afraid of change.'

'Of course I'm not. But I don't want to be anywhere near his world.'

25

'I'm afraid he's hard to avoid.'

And Oliver would shrug, uncomprehending, immersed as he was in the blare and chatter of the present.

On the other hand, I could not deny that I liked my position in the university. Here I could be someone – not because of my uncle's name, but for my own sake. After six years people knew who I was. Some of the older fellows had known my father, and spoke of him almost reverently: Richard Harvey, the publisher responsible for discovering some of the late century's eminent novelists – Stuart Graham, C. S. Hughes, Ismail Awenat – and it pleased me to be recognised as his daughter. Occasionally, passing through the college bar or the Library café, I would sense nudgings and pointings from some of the undergraduates and would know whose name was being whispered, but since my clothes and bearing spoke so little of money or celebrity, and since the university and my place in it was so far from my uncle's court, the relationship was quickly forgotten. Until the new faculty arrived.

A week after his enigmatic performance at the meeting of the Faculty Planning Committee, I had still not managed to track George down. His set of rooms at St Dunstan's College announced permanently that 'Dr Fenton is OUT' in the sliding panel beside the studded oak door; his telephone clicked always to his antique answering machine: *This is George Fenton's answering message thingy, not sure if it's working. Try it anyway, though, why not* . . . I left messages with his secretary and his wife, but heard nothing back; I spotted him in the distance once, wobbling over the cobbles on his bicycle, and chased after him, calling, but he appeared not to hear and rode blithely away.

The frosty mornings gave way to days of chilly rain that squalled across the fields to batter morosely against window panes or to needle its way inside your coat. By mid-afternoon, dusk had crept over the town; steam rose into the gloom from the ventilation shafts of the pubs and cafés, and the puddles shimmered with rainbow rings of diesel under the street lamps. Slithering down the narrow back stairs of our terraced house on one such evening, I wrestled with my stubbornly buckled umbrella, paused, and launched myself through the spray from the blocked gutter and into the thick warmth of the kitchen.

It smelled of curry. A pair of wet boots stood in the centre of the floor; through the archway to the sitting room the flickering blue light of the television illuminated a thin ceiling of smoke. Bobby sat on the arm of the settee, hunched forward over a plate, big-eyed and unblinking in the screen's glow. He almost looked up.

'Hey.'

'Hey.' I shook off my wet coat and hooked it over the top of the door.

'I was just going out,' he said with his mouth full, eyes still fixed on the screen. He was wearing a Ry Cooder t-shirt and jockey shorts.

'Right.'

'Any minute.'

'Did you post the gas bill?'

'Oops.'

I sighed, and picked up an ashtray whose contents towered and flowed over a coffee-ringed edition of the *Historia Regum Britanniae* and the sports section of last week's Sunday paper like an installation at the new South Bank Gallery.

'Oh. Thanks. Hey, you got plans tonight?'

'No.'

'Want to come for a beer with the guys?'

'Which guys?'

'The Middleton Program guys.'

I mimed poking a finger down my throat.

'They're not so bad. Okay – they're a little preppy, but they're not all assholes. Oh, come on, Gab. Have some fun or something. Come to the pub.'

'If only the kind sponsors of the Middleton International Program knew they were paying thousands of dollars a year for you to watch *The Good, the Bad and the Ugly* in your pants all week.'

'I'll have you know' – Bobby rested his plate gingerly between his legs and waved a fork defensively – 'I met with my thesis supervisor at nine o'clock this morning, before you were even out the shower. I am *spent*. Since you're standing up, babe, you could throw me a beer.'

The kitchen tiles were disturbingly tacky.

'What's this stuff on the floor?'

'Garbage juice.'

'What?'

'Garbage juice. Or bin juice, as you would say. You know. It's, like, the stuff that sweats out of garbage bags.'

'Nice.'

The fridge offered six cans of defiantly American lager, two pears and a crumpled tube of cheese spread.

'Oh yeah' – Bobby half-stood – 'your asthmatic Darwinian Christian called.'

'Oh? What did he want?'

For a few weeks I had been going out with Paul, a junior fellow in Evolutionary Biology from a neighbouring college; he had come to the house once and immediately asked Bobby to put out his cigarette as it bothered his asthma. Bobby had been stunned into obedience, but had subsequently claimed, with a sly grin, that a friend of a friend had seen Paul handing out leaflets entitled 'Why You Need Jesus!' in the Market Square on a Saturday afternoon. I wasn't sure whether to take this seriously.

'Did George call at all? George Fenton?' I squeezed a blob of cheese on to my finger and sucked it.

'Don't think so. Oh, but – oh my God!' Bobby suddenly stabbed his cigarette in the air with animation. 'I totally forgot! The Dark One called!'

'*What*? He called *here*?'

28

'I shit you not,' he said solemnly. 'Well, okay, it wasn't in fact the Dark One himself, in person. But you have to call him back, really urgently. How did I forget that?' He bounced the heel of his hand against his forehead.

I slumped down on the cushions and reached for a cigarette, tucking my legs beneath me. Before us a tiny Clint galloped across a plateau of lurid orange.

'I have a hangover straight from Satan,' Bobby remarked, peering into the fridge.

'When did he call?'

'Satan?'

I sighed. 'My uncle.'

'There's a difference? This afternoon some time, I don't know – about three, I guess?'

'What exactly did he say?' I scratched anxiously at the wheel of Bobby's lighter with my thumbnail.

Bobby lolled against the archway, beer in one hand and a pear in the other.

'Well, it wasn't him, like I said. It was a fat guy.'

I frowned. 'How could you know he was fat?'

'He had a fat guy's voice. English and sticky, like everything was sarcastic. "Oh, Mr Mailer, *would* you kindly pass on a message? Thank you *so* much, you're *so* kind, I'm *much* obliged". Etcetera.' He bounced the pear off his forearm and caught it.

'Hm. Roger.' It was a passable imitation. 'So I have to phone him?'

'Yes! He*llo*? How many times – get on with it!' He bounced the pear again.

'But why?'

'Who knows?' He bounced the pear again. 'They tell me nothing. I'm just the errand boy.'

'Will you stop doing that? I have to make a phone call.'

'It wasn't making a noise.'

'I have to concentrate.'

'Jeez! Would you relax.' Bobby wandered away, shaking his head.

One hand hovering over the telephone, I fumbled in my address book for the embossed card tucked away in the back flap behind the street map of Paris and the Celsius to Fahrenheit conversion chart. It had been nearly two years since I had seen my uncle in the flesh. I lifted the receiver, halted, and replaced it again, flicking the card between my slightly wavering fingers. This required some mental preparation.

'I – uh – I think I'll do it later, in fact,' I announced to the empty room, as if I ought to explain.

Climbing the stairs slowly, I found Bobby in my room, contemplating his square-jawed reflection in my desk mirror.

'What do you want?'

'Did you call him?'

'Not yet. I've got some things to do first.' I switched on my computer purposefully.

'Look, uh' – he pinged the ring-pull of his beer can a few times and faced me with the lowered eyes of a supplicant – 'I have a little favour to ask.'

'Go on.'

'When you see him – uh – I know he's busy so, you know, but – I really really would like to interview him.'

'I know. You've said.'

'Yeah – I'm looking at a lot of stuff in the library right now about the company he worked for in New York, you know, in the seventies. Lockhardt and North.'

'Who?'

'Uh – they were closely involved in exports during the time of the Nixon legislation over the Twin Pillars policy.'

I shrugged blankly.

'It was a new ruling over arms trading to the Middle East, right? So I checked out some biographical info about him on the wires – the unofficial website – and it seems he did a lot of travelling, so he might have been out in Iran around seventy-two.'

'I think he was in Jordan for a bit. I don't know about Iran.'

'Could you find out?' Bobby leaned against the wardrobe, offering up a pleading smile. 'It's just – my research really sucks right now, you know what I'm saying? I'm kind of stuck. It would make so much difference if I could just talk to someone who was there, get some first-hand stuff, make it live a little.'

I shook my head.

'Bob, he absolutely won't. He never talks about those days and he hates people trying to do profiles. There must be other people who were out there, why don't you talk to them?'

'Because I don't know anyone who's related to them.' He sighed. '*Please*, Gab, come on. I'll take you to my father's house in Bermuda some day.'

I smiled. 'I live for that day, Bob. Look – I'd love to help, but – you don't understand.'

'When you see him, though –'

'I'm not going to see him.'

He looked aghast. 'You're shitting me? Why not?'

'Because we don't talk. You *know* this.'

Bobby plumped down on my bed. 'Yeah, but. Everyone's like, "Oh, I don't talk to my family." I say it all the time. No one means it.'

'I mean it.'

'But why?'

'Long story. We just don't. And I couldn't – I really couldn't, ever, ask him to do me a favour. Not even for you. Sorry.'

He shrugged, resigned. 'Listen, Gab, it's cool to be independent and whatever, but you never know when it'll be payback time. You shouldn't deliberately piss off the people you might one day need to call on – golden rule. That's the way the world turns if you want to get on, right?'

Bobby spoke from experience. His father was the president of a considerable financial law firm in Manhattan that had partially bankrolled the last successful election campaign for the Republican senator, though it was fair to say that Bobby's father held some unorthodox principles. On Bobby's twenty-first birthday, his father had sent him alone to Vegas with five thousand dollars, to make a man of him. Bobby had returned after a week with eight thousand dollars and a minor venereal infection and was judged to have qualified.

'I don't get it.' He shook his head, leaning back against the wall. 'I wouldn't have thought you'd be scared of him, it doesn't seem like you.'

'It's nothing to do with being scared.'

'What's he like?'

'*Like?*'

'Yeah – you know. Personally. As a person.'

I considered this.

'I have no idea.'

Sir Edward Hamilton-Harvey was a myth and a mystery. So much was agreed by fawning acolytes and embittered enemies alike, though these positions were themselves frequently and swiftly reversed. His photograph was never off the front pages for long, yet he could, when he chose, jog through Hyde Park or attend the theatre generally unrecognised; he managed to be both distinctive and forgettable in appearance, an imposing presence or a part of the scenery. It all depended on what the circumstances required. A tall, sturdy man of indeterminate middle age, with boisterous black hair, silvering, in a rather contrived fashion, with perfect symmetry at each temple – perhaps the origin of his tabloid sobriquet, the Dark One; turbulent eyebrows, a Caribbean tan, a nose like Dante's and a smile that always appeared faintly mocking. He changed his beliefs with the same reliable fickleness with which he swapped the editors of his several newspapers, always to his own advantage; focus groups of all political colours sought his advice and his favours. He believed loudly in the family, in core values, in the three R's, rural conservation, the right to blood sports and the nation state. He was also known, if the need arose, to believe in a federal Europe, the welcome of asylum seekers and the abolition of grammar schools. He dined with prime ministers. He had his suits made by Bertolini e Ricci in Milan. He never gave interviews, never wrote his own speeches – in fact, never *gave* his own speeches – yet his opinions were dispersed throughout the world's press almost daily. Pundits and leader-writers admired and deplored him in equal measure. But how much did anyone really know about Sir Edward? What could the public – the viewers, the readers, the consumers, the fans, the nameless millions who so freely offered their opinions to pollsters – claim, with any certainty, to know of the man who had come third in a recent BBC documentary on The Hundred Most Influential People in England?

Most people would know that his total assets flickered into billions, at least on paper, since every profit was immediately whipped away for the next acquisition, the next expansion and investment. They could tell you that his empire comprised, at present, the following: the *National* and *Sunday Ledger*, the country's biggest-selling broadsheet newspapers; one tabloid; a satellite television network whose beams snaked their way across most of western Europe; a magisterial publishing conglomerate with a New York arm and attendant multi-media subsidiaries; an international film distribution network; one men's lifestyle magazine title; one upmarket travel magazine; a chain of retail outlets in which to display his papers, books, CD-Roms and videos, and a first-division football team on the verge of being promoted. They might also know that the above had led to several investigations by the Monopolies and Mergers Commission, from which he always emerged ruffled but unscathed.

Most people would almost certainly be aware that Sir Edward was happily married to Isabelle – 52, ash-blonde, immaculate, a testament to the restorative powers of HRT – and had sired one son, Toby, a gaunt, handsome boy with dark-ringed eyes who was infamously expelled from his public school and now passed his time breathing in Colombia's finest and deflowering the daughters of the fringe aristocracy while claiming to work in web design. They would also know that Sir Edward was pleased to be considered a bold and generous patron of English arts. He made lavish donations to opera houses, theatres and galleries; he established grants for promising young directors and experimental performance artists who did unusual things with supermarket trolleys; he had even, briefly and under another name, sponsored a literary prize that was consistently, for the three years of its existence, won by his own authors, before this was rumbled by a rival newspaper.

Fewer people would have taken the trouble to look further back into Sir Edward's history. Those who were tempted might feel daunted by the one attempt at an unauthorised biography that had foundered in a messy libel case, leaving the publisher in question effectively bankrupt and the author blacklisted. Consequently, fewer people would know that Sir Edward first made his money selling US arms to the Middle East in the 1970s. Sir Edward himself, if interviewed on the subject, preferred to gloss over this episode with a dismissive waft of his hand, declining to comment on the morality or otherwise of commissions he had nestled snugly in off-shore accounts; not that there was anything intrinsically *wrong* in what he did, you understand, he was an ambitious young man keen to make his way in the world, it's just that people (here he would sigh) insisted on smudging the issue, they made 'arms dealer' sound so grubby, when in fact he was a sales consultant, and goodness knows it was the lifeblood of the economy in those days. He was also disinclined to remark on the origin, in those days, of his friendship with Denham Dowland, his clear-skinned, stiff-suited young colleague, an Old Etonian and fluent Arabist, who had, in the intervening thirty years, bloated into the claret-faced, paunchy, opinionated Secretary of State for Defence, the lone architect of 'ethical' foreign policy in the former Cabinet. Denham Dowland MP (Con, south-west Surrey), whose parliamentary career had begun in braying for the reinstatement of capital punishment and ended twenty-five years later in a carbon monoxide-filled Saab 900 in his driveway in Virginia Water, had always been Sir Edward's right-hand man. Sir Edward passed up few opportunities to say how much he was missed. Many had been the questions tabled in the Commons, many the donations, many the drafts of White Papers slipped across knees under the tables of the Garrick; Sir Edward was finding it less easy to achieve the same degree of intimacy with members of the new Cabinet. The recent referendum in favour of a devolved English parliament had been a particular worry. The Left speculated on the possibility of the imminent English elections inciting a renewed surge of nationalism. As Sir Edward's empire was taking on global dimensions, his country, it seemed, was shrinking by the day. Denham would have known what to do. 'Denham was like a brother to me,' he had pronounced on *News at Ten*, a manly quaver in his throat, on the day the former minister's suicide was announced.

Sir Edward's strength of fraternal feeling may have stemmed from the fact that his real brother had been something of a liability. Richard – my father – had been the only one not to buy wholesale into the myth of greatness and enigma with which Sir Edward surrounded himself. Further, Richard had had a mischievous sense of humour, and might well have found it funny to remind the world that Sir Edward was in fact born Nigel Edward to the Reverend and Mrs Ken Harvey of Marlow, or that, despite his gaudy string of honorary degrees, Sir Edward had no education beyond his meagre handful of O-levels, or that he suffered from dyslexia and was bullied at school, or that as a child he was given to putting on his mother's dresses and miming the songs of the Andrews Sisters into a wooden spoon. Edward's nerves had been sorely troubled by the thought of Richard divulging material of this sort – or indeed worse – to over-curious members of the press. He solved the problem by buying up the

35

publishing house where Richard had been an editor for nearly twenty years and at once appointing him Publishing Director, forcing his brother's loyalty and effectively blasting his reputation for integrity. Whether Edward knew of the cancer that was already gnawing at my father's insides when he squeezed him into this compromise remains unclear. Experience of Edward's character suggests that it would have made little difference.

And this was why I couldn't forgive him.

Chapter III

'You may find the time has come for you to show a bit of respect. Family is family, after all.'

Roger Mortimer paused between the towers of the bridge and nodded ominously, his jaw rippling slightly with the movement. He rested his hand on the balustrade for a moment and squinted over the river, still nodding.

The Thames swirled onwards beneath us out towards Docklands, sludgy and indifferent, crested with the yellow froth a tug had left in its wake. Gusts caught the surface of the water and whipped its smells upwards; sewage, chemical effluent, weed, diesel, eddying together in the air with the yelping gulls. Behind the roofscape of the Embankment, clouds the colour of graphite heaped and churned in the fierce wind. Roger rummaged in his ear with a forefinger, briefly considered his findings and carried on walking.

The strength of the wind over the river had caught him unawares; the unguents that slicked down his unruly hair were suddenly inadequate to the task, so he scurried along, two steps ahead of me, one hand clamped to the top of his head. I trudged along behind like a reluctant child on a school trip; sporadically I caught odd words shouted backwards over the grumble of traffic. Crossing the river always took longer than you thought.

The invitation was not a matter of choice. I was on my way to have lunch with my uncle.

It was our third attempt, almost a month since he had first called me out of the blue. Our first and second dates had been cancelled in favour of meetings in Geneva and Brussels with brokers, ambassadors, consultants and people of far more importance than a half-forgotten niece who had twice made the hour-long train journey only to find on arrival that Sir Edward was not, after all, in London until the following week, awfully sorry. But he was known to keep people waiting for weeks to see him, so all was not lost. Roger Mortimer – neither quite a Press Secretary nor a butler, but a factotum and consummate sycophant embracing elements of both – assured me that this time Sir Edward very much intended to be here if he possibly could. Which was a relief; if the idea of lunch with my uncle brought on a dank foreboding and choppy gut, the prospect of a third lunch alone with Roger and his oozing smugness might have inspired me to leap the balustrade there and then.

The restaurant of choice was not new but was just then enjoying a resurgence of popularity among those who lunched as a serious pastime.

'Dario!' Roger cried, waving with excessive familiarity at an Italianate gentleman in a flawless suit, as we emerged from the tall frondy ferns that guarded the entrance of La Rive Sud into the burble of conversation and clinking utensils. The man dipped his silvered head almost imperceptibly and turned away to continue his conversation. 'Director of the new South Bank Gallery,' Roger confided in a whisper designed to carry as far as the window table and beyond. 'Marvellous man, very important.'

A fine-boned waiter took my jacket; another, of equally delicate beauty, pulled out my chair; a third eased a wine list into my hand. All the waiters possessed the same effete, southern-European elegance and artificial, silent grace.

'Do you know what you're going to do?' Roger asked, his eyes slurping greedily over the menu.

'What do you mean?'

'With your life. Your career prospects.'

'Well – I'm still writing, after that, I haven't really –'

'I thought of doing a PhD myself, once, you know.'

'Yes, I know. You've mentioned it.'

'Thomas Mann. Wasn't to be, wasn't to be. And shall I tell you something else?' He leaned forward, pinning me with his little watery eyes.

'Please do.'

'Best decision I ever made. Because it forced me out into Real Life. You see? Look around you.' He embraced the restaurant in a sweeping gesture. 'Infinitely more rewarding. Real Life.'

I looked; beyond the sparkling coloured wall-mosaics and effulgent foliage, all I could see were clusters of port-faced, guffawing men and aggressively tailored, bored women being fawned on by limp staff. Wagner raged and thundered at a discreet volume from somewhere overhead; vintage wines tinkled into the very best crystal.

'Knowledge and experience, Gabriele, are very different things, and there comes a time when a person has to think seriously about putting something back into life.'

'And this is your way of contributing to the community?' I imitated his gesture, fighting to squash a smile.

'My meaning' – Roger sighed with forced patience – 'is that I came out of the cloisters, so to speak, into a world where decisions are made. Where your daily tasks matter to vast numbers of people. Not a selfish world, everyone wrapped up in their own research, Gabriele, but a world that affects the society we live in, for good or perhaps, who knows, sometimes for ill, who am I to say, but nevertheless, one with a vision.' He nodded a full stop, satisfied with his homily. 'But we just never know when our lives are going to be turned upside-down, do we? An act of God, perhaps, or the next best thing.'

Roger permitted himself an indulgent chuckle. I didn't like the suggestive width of his smile, a great crease in his chubby face.

'Why am I here?'

'That, Gabriele, is a question I would have supposed you to dwell on in the privacy of your own study. I cannot answer it for you – greater minds than yours or indeed mine have wrestled with it endlessly and to no –'

'Oh, Roger, shut *up*. I mean why does Edward want to see me all of a sudden?'

'Sir Edward,' Roger began gravely, drawing himself up, 'is a man who cares deeply about family.'

With impeccable timing, Sir Edward chose that moment to stride through the pot plants.

Ignoring family, he crossed purposefully to the window table, where the silver-haired gallery director leapt immediately to his feet and effusively they clasped hands, clapping each other heartily on the shoulder, each trying to out-smile the other. They remained in this attitude for some minutes, apparently in earnest conversation, while Roger watched in admiration.

Edward finally disengaged himself.

'Roger,' he bent subtly, resting a hand on his lieutenant's shoulder. 'Get a bottle of something nice sent to Dario's table, will you? Just a gesture. Surprised you haven't already.'

Roger bowed his head sheepishly and half-rose, then appeared to remember that he was not in fact the waiter, and beckoned one with a peremptory flick of the hand.

Edward sat down, picked up a menu, glanced over it, replaced it, swept his gaze around the room and popped an olive into his mouth.

'Self-serving hypocrite and thick as shit in a bucket, but his wife is big in the DTI. So you have to, don't you?'

Finally he removed his glasses and looked at me.

'So.'

'So,' I repeated, stupidly.

'Let me look at you.' He tilted his head to one side, then to the other, as if deciding whether to invest in me. 'Are you happy?'

'What?'

'Happy. You know. *Are* you?'

'Well, I don't really –'

'You see, I am a man,' Edward raised his voice just sufficiently to make this speech available to his fellow diners, my happiness or otherwise now secondary to whichever point of his it had been prologue to. 'I am a man who cares deeply about family. Deeply. Family, in my experience, is what gives our lives shape and meaning. Family is past and future, roots and – ah – hmm. Bottle of Krug, I think – no, hold on – Roger, is this one of my not-drinking weeks?'

'Well, it was, but we swapped it if you remember, because of the French Embassy do on Thursday.'

'Ah. Excellent. Krug it is, then. Irritable bowel syndrome,' he added in lower tones, patting his stomach. The sommelier, lately canted over our table, backed away discreetly. 'It goes, it comes back again, it goes, it comes back. Bloody inconvenient. It's giving me a break at the moment, but you can't be too careful. That's why we have a little detox every now and again, don't we, Rodge? No cheese, no coffee, no bloody *booze*. Raw juice. If there's one thing I hate it's a bloody tisane. But not today. Mind you, I've lost eight pounds. Where was I?'

'Family,' Roger prompted.

'Yes. Experience has taught me that you can work hard all your life, you can build an empire the size of – well, mine, for the sake of argument – but without family, what's it all for? Without family, we're no better than a – than a –' he snapped his fingers.

'– candle in the wind?' offered Roger brightly.

Sir Edward rolled this around his head as if tasting it.

'Precisely. That's rather good, actually. A candle in the wind. But I am saddened. Why am I saddened?'

I shook my head, needlessly; Edward was playing to the gallery.

'My own family is in a sorry condition. My parents are gone. My brother is gone. My son is an inexcusable waste of space. My one comfort is that my brother's only daughter has inherited Richard's brains, the famous Harvey good looks and, I sometimes dare to hope, perhaps a modicum of my business sense. She' – he gestured magnificently across the

41

table – 'she is my one remaining blood relative with potential. With a future. So you see – crab bisque, I think, to start, and what is the fish – oh, very good, no, with the *beurre citron*, I think, thank you – spinach – it pains me that my brother's daughter, my own family, should live in a squat in the arse end of nowhere, doing nothing of note. I worry about you. Endlessly.'

'You don't need to –'

'It looks bad, you see. You're my niece, and we see each other so little.'

'Looks bad to whom?'

'People. I promised Richard I would look after you.'

'I don't need looking after. And I don't care what people think. Not that I'm not grateful, but I – well, I'm nothing to do with you, really. With respect.'

My uncle leaned back and considered me from under the shelf of his eyebrows.

'You wound me. You see, I look at you, Gaby, and I think to myself – where is the gaiety of youth? Where is the recklessness, the *joie de vivre*? I don't see it. Instead I see someone wasting their best years locked in a dusty attic poking through a load of old dust. Look at you – you're a nice-looking girl and yet you dress like a bloody barrow boy. Show yourself off a bit. Tell me, Gaby, what do you dream of?'

'Sorry?'

'Before you fall asleep, what do you think about? Do you dream of the future? Do you know what it means to have a passion? Do you know who you want to be, hmm? Or do you, like most people, shuffle through life without a moment's reflection, accepting what comes your way, hiding from change, locked in with your manuscripts and your nice, sensible biologist?'

'How did you –?'

'I'm a database of knowledge, Gaby, my eyes and ears roam the globe.' He glanced at Roger with a questioning eyebrow; Roger gave a tiny shake of the head. 'No, that doesn't work. Stretch a metaphor too far and it'll ping back in your face, Roger always tells me, don't you? My eyes and ears are – anyway. George Fenton tells me you're a very promising scholar. But I could have guessed that. Got your father's brains, as I said.'

I felt a cold tug in my stomach.

'George? When –?'

'Oh, I see a bit of George, now and again. We had a charming dinner, must have been a month ago now.' He laughed, unconvincingly, through his nose. 'He's a talker, old George, eh? Told a fantastic story about a monk in – when was it, Roger? Medieval times, in – ah – Italy, I think, and this monk – oh, can't remember, anyway, very funny, it was. Something about shagging a donkey. We were all –'

'*Why?* Why were you having dinner with George?'

From the inner reaches of Roger's jacket something began to chirrup the Queen of the Night aria from *The Magic Flute*.

'ROGER!' My uncle banged his hands forcefully on the table either side of his plate, causing his sea-bass to flop briefly into the air. Everyone looked up. 'Haven't I told you to switch that thing off when we're eating? Have you no bloody manners?'

Roger shamefully extracted the offending telephone and glanced at the screen. His lip curled into a grimace.

'You might want to take it. It's from Buenos Aires.'

An unusual cloud crossed my uncle's dark eyes. It might almost have been fear.

'Would you excuse me for a moment?'

'Why was he having dinner with George?' I hissed to Roger, jerking my thumb at my uncle's empty seat.

Roger shrugged. 'They were at school together.'

'I know. But I didn't think they were that close.'

'He likes to keep up with old friends.'

I picked at my fanciful vegetable sculpture and waited for my uncle's return.

After eight whole minutes of my having to listen to Roger

43

engaging with his lunch, my uncle reseated himself, a beatific grin spread across his face.

'All's well,' he said cheerfully. 'Now, where were we?'

'George,' Roger suggested.

'George!' Sir Edward cried happily, spreading his arms as if George had at that moment walked in. 'Of course! As you know, Gabriele, I am a man with many ideas.'

I duly nodded.

'Some time ago, I had a particularly good one. Inspired, you might say. I decided I should share it with George, he being an old friend, you see, and quite uniquely placed to appreciate my vision.'

My uncle looked at me expectantly, as did Roger.

'What was your vision?' I asked, as I was meant to.

'My vision, my *grande idée*, is that history is dead.'

'That's been done.'

'Not like this. Hear me out. Let us imagine, for argument's sake, an ancient university, not unlike, perhaps, the one that provides you with food and shelter. An ancient university with seven hundred years of history, give or take. It depends on its history, on its traditions, and on the strength of these it manages to perpetuate a certain reputation. But what of the finished product? Does it perform?'

'*Perform*?'

'Like every other institution that relies on what it has been, it fails to realise that history is becoming a rapidly devalued currency. Or, to put it another way, if its graduates come out with no professional skills and a smattering of Latin verse, who gives a monkey's arse what happened there in 1500? You see where I'm heading?'

I saw exactly where he was heading. The tight knot in my gut burst suddenly, a sensation like cold jelly oozing through my insides.

'I knew it was you.'

'Shush! Let me finish.' Sir Edward held up a hand; his audience, now consisting only of Roger and me, shuffled in their

44

seats while he carefully removed a section of sea-bass verte-brae from his second molars. He lowered his voice. 'What this hypothetical university would need, in such circumstances, is something that would make it great again. Its traditions, its reputation – dead as a doornail. Worthless. No longer an incentive. But what if' – he paused, his eyes and chin gleam-ing – 'it could be reborn? What if it could boast the greatest faculty of arts scholarship in the country? No – in *Europe*, why not? What if all students graduating from this faculty were guaranteed a job somewhere in a related media industry, if the people teaching them were not stale academics but real professionals – newspapermen, film-makers, writers, televi-sion producers, advertisers? It would be unique – young peo-ple would be climbing the gates to get in, they'd be prepared to pay anything, and you'd have your pick of the very best. Half degree, half training-scheme, theory and practice, high culture, which it unquestionably has in spades, wedded to popular culture, where the money is, you see. From the industry's point of view, you recruit only from that pool and you guarantee you're getting young people who know how to do a job, so you don't waste their first year in employment teaching them how to use a buggering fax machine. Cross-fertilisation, industry and education. The university that could offer facilities like that would be the most sought-after in the country. It would pull in revenue like there's no bloody tomorrow. The faculty would have the prestige of the univer-sity's name and the decoration of its history, bolstered by real business know-how and proper investment. It would be a beautiful, beautiful – ah –' he snapped his fingers again.

'Symbiosis,' said Roger.

Sir Edward beamed. 'Exactly.'

I shook my head.

'You're incredible.'

'Thank you.'

'You can't just buy the university! Who do you think you are?'

'Gaby, Gaby. You can buy anything that's desperate for money. Money makes dreams come true. What better investment could there be than the education of our young people? We're talking about a one-hundred-per-cent graduate employment rate.'

'That's not just what it's about. You don't care about education! What about all the other arts faculties, the original ones? What about Classics, or Medieval History, or Anglo-Saxon poetry?'

'They will continue, as they always have, until the funding dries up.'

'But they'll become second-rate qualifications!'

'They're already second-rate qualifications. What possible use is Anglo-Saxon poetry in the modern world? It's a question of reading the times accurately, adapting to them.'

'But the whole point' – I could hear my voice getting squeaky – 'the whole *point* of university education and research is not about being *useful*. Rubber gloves are *useful*. Scholarship is about the preservation of our history, our culture, the furthering of knowledge!'

'My, you do sound pompous. Knowledge and history butter no parsnips, as my old mother would have said.'

'That's what I told her.'

'Don't interrupt, Roger. Listen, Gaby, I'm doing you a big favour. Believe me, within ten years every university in this country will be privately run, I'm reliably informed by people in the Department of Education who know these things. This is the road we're travelling, like it or no. But this will be the flagship. The model. It will spawn hundreds of poor imitations up and down the land, but it will be the greatest of its kind. If it works, I have an option on investing in the Faculty of Management Studies. And the Faculty of Law. We've begun on this road, and it's no use trying to turn the clock back. And you will benefit enormously.'

'So we have the prospect of a university which only trains people for lucrative jobs? Is that your vision? To demolish seven hundred years of tradition? What about Art? Haven't you persecuted high culture enough?'

Edward pulled out a plump Montecristo Number 4 and a pair of clippers from his inside pocket and tapped the cigar briskly on the table.

'God, you're so like Richard sometimes. Art. What does that mean? Whatever you call art is profit-driven these days as much as anything else. Globalisation. Market forces. I've said – tradition is meaningless. Nice enough in its place, I have no objection to a bit of harmless pageantry, bit of dressing up, New Year's gongs, for goodness' sake – I'm not going to start suggesting we get rid of all that. But it's all got to be modernised. Ideals are charming things to have, but also meaningless, as I often used to tell my unworldly brother. I invest in the future. I imagine it, and then I build it. And arts funding is in crisis, as this government never tires of reminding us. The only future for the arts is private investment, and that goes for your university, whatever you may feel about it. And the pay will be good. There'd certainly be a teaching job for you there, if that's what you wanted. George speaks very highly of your talents.'

His face disappeared behind a curtain of blue smoke.

My jaw tightened.

'This is exactly what you did to Dad.'

'Not this again, please.'

'You have to buy us all, don't you? I don't want your job. I'm a literary historian, how would I teach Cultural Studies? I don't even know what they are.' I paused, breathless. The immaculately brushed gallery director was staring at our table with some alarm.

'Keep your voice down, please, Gaby. And steady on the champagne, you're getting emotional. Let me explain this to you just one more time. Your father was delighted with the difference my investment made to his list. Do you think he would have hung on to half his authors if I hadn't bought Lexicon? Of course not. He'd already lost Awenat, Stuart

Graham's agent was about to move him, the money was shocking – everyone knew that.'

'It had a reputation. He cared about that – so did his authors.'

'Does reputation pay the mortgage?'

'You crushed him. He lost all his – spirit. He hated working for you. That's why he was –' I stopped, biting my lip.

My uncle ran a finger slowly around the rim of his glass and watched the tendrils of smoke twisting upwards to the lights.

'Gaby. Richard had cancer. It's terrible, but it happens. That's why he was not himself those last couple of years. I've made a few mistakes in my time, I admit, but your father's illness, I must protest, was not my fault.'

He tipped his glass back, noiselessly swallowed its contents, and stood.

'Apologies, but I'm expected elsewhere. I'm sorry if this has upset you, I supposed you'd be pleased. I thought you cared about the university. And I wanted to see you again, it's been a while. Thought I could explain in person. Tell me' – he hesitated, crushing out his cigar with a flurry of sparks – 'do you see much of Olly Dowland these days?'

'From time to time.'

His eyes narrowed, almost lost in his knotted brow. 'I'm not sure, you know, that Oliver is the best company for you. There's something – I mean, God knows I was fond of his father but' – he leaned closer, tapping his temple – 'there's a history of it in that family. Even Toby thinks he's becoming strange, Olly, and Toby's brain is as addled as his nose.' He shrugged. 'Well, your friends are your business. But I do feel responsible for you.'

'You don't want me talking to Olly because he's a journalist.'

'I hardly walk in fear of journalists, Gabriele – I own most of them. Besides, Oliver hasn't got the balls he was born with – he wouldn't dare write a thing about me under his own by-line. No, I just think he's – unhelpful.'

A beautiful waiter held up my uncle's coat by the shoulders like a matador's cape.

'Just one thing –'

He paused, half in one sleeve. 'What is it?'

'The new professor – I presume he's yours as well?'

He gave a curious laugh, which stuttered into a coughing fit.

'Mine?' he said, when he had recovered. 'What a strange thing to say. My placement, you mean? He's – ah – he's a remarkable character. You'll like him. Oh yes, you'll like him a lot, I guarantee. Which reminds me –' he fished in an inside pocket but retrieved nothing. 'Oh. Thought I had one here. I'm giving a little reception to celebrate my new partnership. Next month. I'd be delighted if you'd come.'

I'd rather have extensive root canal work without anaesthetic.

'I'll think about it.'

'She'll *think* about it, Roger. That *is* gracious of her.' He buttoned his coat and then, suddenly, leaned down over me until his face was inches from mine and banged his palm on to the table. 'Passion!'

'What?'

'Don't say what. Passion, Gabriele. *Passion*! Have you ever known what that means?'

'Of course,' I said, affronted and slightly puzzled.

'*Have* you?' He gave me a long look. 'I wonder. I do wonder.'

He turned abruptly to Roger. It occured to me, not for the first time, that he might not be entirely sane.

'I want a driver outside Millbank at 5.30 – not the one with the moustache, mind, he doesn't know his arse from his bloody elbow.'

Sir Edward swept out, leaving the ferny fronds trembling in his wake.

Chapter IV

The Crown and Dragon was built in 1872 in dark red brick
with leaded window panes, later replaced by gaudy Art Deco
colours, and had stood squatly in the same corner of
Clerkenwell for nearly 110 years before it was dwarfed by the
six-storey offices of the *Daily* and *Sunday Enquirer* that now
supplied its total clientele. In all those years it had remained
true to the original modus operandi of the working man's
pub: no concessions to the school of organic Uruguayan
lager, Plexiglas furniture and live salsa that had infiltrated
most other establishments in the area over the last decade;
nothing to suggest urbane young professionals or wholesome
families might want to venture through its frosted doors. The
Crown was always half-lit and smoggy; the ash0trays overflowed; varnish flaked from the wooden panelling unconvincingly bedecked with horse brasses; the stains on the
carpet and upholstery had long replaced (and to an extent
improved on) the original patterns. Clive, the landlord, could
be found most evenings with his forearm hooked around the
London Pride pump, a tea-towel draped over his shoulder,
opining matter-of-factly on how the gays/blacks/asylum
seekers/bloody pinko government were ruining the country;
the left-liberal broadsheet hacks who slumped in a row along
the bar, soaking up the bitter, and who privately thought the
bloody government wasn't nearly pinko enough, rarely bothered to disagree, since Clive operated a generous credit system together with a selective lock-in policy and it was as well
to remain on his good side. The Crown also flouted every
principle of democracy by not having a jukebox. Instead, a
veteran cassette player behind the bar spooled Clive's choice
of background music through two asthmatic speakers, which

usually meant The Searchers and The Dave Clark Five or, on Fridays and other special occasions, Edith Piaf. Clive was a man of catholic tastes.

It was in the Crown that I found myself on the afternoon of my lunch with Edward.

Oliver Dowland leaned across the table, propped his chin on his hands, fixed me thoughtfully with wide, earnest eyes the colour of strong tea behind silver-rimmed glasses, nodded, and said: 'Mmm.'

This was Oliver's tactical weapon, colleagues would whisper enviously; it was what made him such a successful journalist. He was an excellent listener. Oliver listened as though you were the most extraordinary person he'd ever met, as though you were telling him a story so unique, so riveting, so witty, he simply couldn't bear to interrupt. It was disconcerting; if you made a point that expected a response, you would find none, and to diffuse the embarrassment of silence, you would take up the conversation again yourself, babbling furiously, blurting out things you shouldn't, just to fill the gaps. And every now and again, Oliver would say, 'Mmm,' without ever taking his eyes off you.

He also drank non-alcoholic lager, a trick that had tripped up more than one parliamentary aide and purveyor of spin who had imagined him to be matching them pint for pint. But his skill was in the posture he adopted for listening: brow slightly creased, head just a touch to one side, the carefully timed nod of sympathy. He looked so inoffensive; twenty-nine, but he could have been twenty-one; his appearance understated, everything about him an unthreatening shade of mid-brown (except his skin, which was startlingly pale); his thin frame softened by woollen fabrics in muted colours. Oliver looked like a serious young man you could trust.

His advanced listening skills were copied from the Jungian therapist in Belsize Park on whose floral sofa bed he spent four fifty-minute sessions a week probing his unconscious.

This had begun of necessity after the trauma of his father's suicide and had blossomed into an almost religious devotion; Oliver believed that society would be a more organic place altogether if psychoanalysis were provided as a matter of course on the National Health. He was offended by the word 'shrink', as he was by my suggestion that too much self-examination could easily topple into self-absorption. 'How can we hope to understand one another unless we first understand ourselves?' was his insistent defence. He also had a habit of saying, 'It's interesting that you should *say* that,' in a way that suggested you'd inadvertently revealed a grimy corner of your soul by remarking that the weather had taken a turn for the worse.

'Mmm,' said Oliver again.

He glanced at his watch.

'Well, say something then. You must have heard about this, surely?'

'It's all happened very recently – there have been rumours, but his press office is keeping it very close to their chest. I knew a while ago something was going on. There were whisperings at the Department of Education – a contact let slip about the new faculty sponsorship and I imagined if something was being planned on that scale he'd be keen to have a finger in the pie, but the negotiations seem to have been very secretive. My colleague Chris Haughton is supposed to be looking into it for this Sunday, but it'll probably be out by then.'

'It's outrageous! It looks to me like all the negotiations have been done between Edward and George Fenton. I just can't believe the university would agree to a deal like this – can't they see it'll mean the end of everything we stand for?'

'Oh, you.' There was a pause. 'It's all consumer-driven these days, I'm afraid. And if they ran out of funding, they wouldn't have a choice.'

'I know.' I waved the familiar argument aside. 'It's inevitable, and it's happening everywhere, but still – it was the one place left where I thought people believed in something. You know, in the value of things that weren't necessarily directly related to profit. That's why I stayed there – but now even George – I can't believe he would sell out like this. But especially not to *Edward*.'

'Private finance.' Oliver carefully aligned his glass and his beer mat to produce a scale model. 'There's no stopping it. Here – Department of Education. University. Now' – he tipped a packet of peanuts on to the table – 'they can't get any more funding than this without raising taxes, so the little they've got now has to be shared among the new universities that don't have the luxury of private bequests and donations.' He duly swept the peanuts towards the ashtray. 'So you – the university – are in a vicious circle because you can't modernise without extra money, and until you modernise, the D of E is not going to give you any because you're embarrassing for its all-must-have-prizes image. Tradition and elitism are the last taboos, the only really filthy words now. Okay, so you know all that. But fortunately for the university, it's still got its name, it can still rely on the snobbery of people like Edward who want reputation by association and are prepared to offer a fat wad out of his own pocket' – Oliver patted the table, but had run out of peanuts so moved my pack of cigarettes over instead – 'and it's in no position to get precious about the source. It desperately wants – *needs* – to be associated with innovation, but at the same time it can't and won't throw out the traditions that keep it separate. But you know how it goes.' He rested his chin on his hands gloomily. 'It's the same with the *Enquirer*, we're all sliding towards a mulch of pop culture that has something for everyone. Anything too demanding is doomed.'

'But why do we keep accepting it? Why doesn't anyone have the balls to start a reactionary movement? Does no one at your place say anything?'

'Yes, but they only mutter it into their beer down here. It's all about money.' Oliver rubbed his thumb and forefinger together. 'More readers, more viewers, more students, same story everywhere you go – increase consumption, never mind what you're peddling, just bring them in, because punters mean money. And the governing assumption is that the punters don't want to be challenged any more. That's why none of my colleagues protest about the tat they're expected to write these days, because they'd be instantly replaced by clones who'd do it without complaining. They're turning us into a tabloid and hoping none of us will notice.' He shifted his weight and began idly pushing the peanuts with one finger. 'Look at me – I'm a trained political reporter and my big story this week is whether the mad editor of the *Daily Chronicle* is having a sperm donor pregnancy – which is perhaps of interest to my editor and about three of his friends in his Soho club and of no interest whatsoever to ninety-nine point nine per cent of our readers. But it's what I'm told to do. And that's the most insidious part, that's what really makes me cross – it's always dangerous when the press falls in love with power. But when the press falls in love with itself, we're really in trouble. As my colleague Wesley would say – the media class is up its arse.'

'It's not right.'

Oliver shrugged.

'That's the climate. Principles are very unfashionable. That's why the university won't stand up and say they don't want Renaissance Literature replaced by Television Studies, it's why no one bothered to tell the Prime Minister not to replace the Poet Laureate with a People's Poet – making qualitative judgements is considered potentially offensive. Any one thing is as valid as anything else. And then it's a downward spiral – if you feed on pap, you eventually lose your capacity for discernment or critical thinking.'

I smiled.

'All very well for you to say that, you're posh.'

'Well, exactly. That's the trouble – you can't defend elitism in its positive sense without sounding elitist in the wrong

54

way. Besides,' Oliver sipped his non-alcoholic lager and contemplated his very clean fingernails. 'I have to be extra careful what I say out loud – I've had to get past a lot of prejudice down in the Lobby. People tend to believe that extreme political beliefs must be hereditary somehow, and you can't speak up for tradition without being accused of conservative sympathies. Not round here, anyway, and not with *my* father.' He waved a hand towards the bar. 'They all expected me to change my politics when Dad died, as if I'd just been having a teenage rebellion. They sort of indulge me now, but I'm still not in a position to start suggesting that all our ancient institutions are throwing the baby out with the bathwater. You could say something, though.'

'Oh, what – protest against my uncle?'

'Why not? It would be great publicity, the two of you going head to head – you for tradition and high culture, him for modernising and populism. I bet you'd get on Radio Four.' Oliver looked quite excited at the prospect. 'Go on – rebel against him and start a protest movement – the last thing Edward wants is negative publicity before it's even on its feet.'

He smiled suddenly, a rare event that made him almost good-looking.

'Did I hear you say protest movement?' A balding man in a badly fitting synthetic suit and hiking boots shuffled across to our table, sloshing beer from the glass in his hand. He pulled the cigarette out of his mouth to allow greater freedom of speech. 'That's my kind of talk! I hope you're plotting the rise of the oppressed and suffering workers in that sweatshop up there against those star-fucking marmosets who pretend to be in charge of our paper but in fact couldn't edit their own bloody names? Peaceful strike or all-out throat slitting revolution? The latter, I think. Burn the newsroom! Let the truth run free! The readers deserve to hear the truth!' He flung his arms in the air dramatically, then straddled a stool and lurched closer to the table, eyeing me suspiciously. 'Are these your peanuts? All right if I eat them?'

Oliver coughed. 'Wesley, this is my friend Gaby. Gaby, Wesley Hemp, our outspoken political columnist.'

'Redundant political columnist unless I get a bit less outspoken, seems to be the received wisdom,' Wesley Hemp said gloomily. 'As you might imagine, the PM's not a huge fan of my work and our editor and guiding star is so eager to bask in the light that shines from the PM's arse that the last time they were together I was afraid Mike would start fellating him. Do you know what he said in conference yesterday? "I find understatement works better, Wesley." I said, "Mike, if you want understatement, why the fuck did you employ *me*? It's not even in my *vocabulary*!" Are you two shagging?'

Oliver turned a blooming shade of fuchsia.

'We're old friends,' I said, to help him out.

'Huh. Just thought I'd ask. Call a spade a spade, I say, except you can't any more because the political correctness gestapo have soiled that as well.'

'Talking of Mike, he was looking for you earlier,' Oliver said, collecting himself.

'Why d'you think I'm in here?' Wesley Hemp glanced around. 'I'm off message. Quiet, isn't it? Uncanny.'

'It's only four o'clock.'

'Never usually stops them. Are we the only Sunday broadsheet, do you think, whose investigative team investigates by looking up yesterday's papers on the Net?'

'I didn't think we could afford an investigative team. Do you mean Chris?'

'Chris *Haughton* –' Wesley spat the name across the table. The end of his tie was resting in a small pool of something but he appeared not to notice. 'Ha!' He turned to me. 'Our new so-called Chief Reporter is meant to be investigating that malignant old despot at Hamilton Harvey House and his latest privatisation antics – did you know this, Olly? – so his crack reporting technique is to have a three-hour lunch in the Wilsbury with some wonk from Hamilton-Harvey's Evil Empire and what does he come back with? The old bastard's squandering his pelf buying up one of our soi-disant venerable seats of learning. Which was as good as in the *Ledger* last week. No whys, no wherefores – no bloody *content*. The work experience slapper could have done a better job. Do you know how much he's *paid*? I don't know how that man sleeps at night.'

'Which one?'

'Either of them. Any of them. Whole country's run by cunts.' Wesley peered morosely into his empty glass. 'Let's get drunk. My round. Are you drinking poof's beer again?'

'Actually, Wes,' Oliver began tentatively, 'it's interesting you should *say* that –'

'No it's not, I say it all the time. I'm paid to say it. I'm a lone voice crying in a moral wilderness. I'm the boy with his finger stuck in a dyke. Now *there's* a thought.' Wesley's eyes goggled alarmingly.

'I mean, about the university, because we were just talking about that. Gaby is – uh – she's a graduate student there.'

'Really?' Wesley Hemp swivelled to look at me. 'You're buggered then.'

'You think it's that bad?'

'Oh, Christ, yeah – that bad and worse, even, than my poisoned imagination could conjure. Everything that man touches turns to shit. Look what he's done with the newspapers he's bought. And the publishers. I was a student there myself, God knows how many years ago. I used to be proud to say that. Now I'll have to hide it as a filthy embarrassing thing I did in my youth. Yet another one. Clive! Pint of the same, if you'd be so kind, and same again for my friends.'

Clive leaned over the bar. 'You've still got a forty quid tab from last Friday, Wes, just thought I'd mention it, mate.'

'Oh. Well, let's stick some more on and I'll sort it out later. What I can't comprehend,' Wesley Hemp continued, turning back to me, 'is that this buy-out, which will effectively be the end of our free education system as we know it, has managed to get past the Parliamentary Committee of

University Vice-Chancellors. Hamilton-Harvey's clearly got the Chief Exec in his pocket, if not the rest of them. It's not the university itself that bothers me – Olly, you know how I feel about these old establishments – that had to change sooner or later. What's evil about this deal is that students will have to pay extra tuition fees for that particular degree, it's a much more dangerous precedent than anyone seems to realise. Either you believe in free education for all, not just the few, or you don't, and if this goes ahead it will confirm everyone's suspicion that this lot don't. And even if that's the way they want to go, they, and the university, should have thought a bit more carefully about who they were jumping into bed with.'

'You can talk,' said Clive, setting down a murky pint in front of Wesley. 'When I think of some of the ones you've jumped into bed with.'

'Clive, don't join other people's conversations out of context. Go and polish your brasses. Have you got any gingernuts?'

'You know I don't do blooming gingernuts, mate. You always ask me that.'

'Call yourself a *pub*?'

'I don't actually call meself a pub, no. Forty-three pounds seventy, that makes it,' Clive reminded Wesley with a flick of his tea-towel. Wesley took a gurgling mouthful of beer and wiped the froth away with the back of his hand.

'As I was saying. Of all the fat cats in a position to invest that kind of capital, Hamilton-Harvey is about the most unscrupulous, untrustworthy, mendacious, unprincipled scheming weasel you could hope to find anywhere, and everyone knows it. They're just setting themselves up, because you can bet he's looking much further ahead than they are. He must have laid down at least fifteen million – you don't get an Ainsley Ryerson building for any less – and what's a professorship these days – two or three mill? Even Hamilton-Harvey wouldn't do that for a short-term gain. He means to take over the world, you mark my words. It'll end in tears. Back in a tick.'

He stood up and loped off in the direction of the Gents. A hot flush of embarrassment clawed at the back of my neck.

'Don't mind him.' Oliver rubbed my hand. 'He exaggerates for effect. I didn't tell him you're related, by the way, as you probably guessed.'

'He's right. It's just not nice to hear it. Silly really – it's not like it's my fault.'

'No, I know. People used to say worse things about Dad, and they were often right too. Still.' Oliver helped himself to one of my cigarettes. 'So – you seeing anyone?'

'Sort of. You know.'

Oliver's head tilted expectantly.

'Uh – he's called Paul. He's a biologist. He's quite nice.'

Oliver laughed. 'Quite nice? I guess that's more enthusiastic than you've been about most of your boyfriends.'

He lowered his eyes quickly; there was a slightly tricky pause.

'Well, you know me, always cautious. What about you?'

'Mmm – sort of. She's a human rights lawyer.' He hesitated. 'Pretty, but – dresses like a Christian.'

'Olly!'

We looked at each other for a moment and snorted into a giggle. Oliver choked slightly on his smoke and grinned, relieved.

'That's that out the way, then. Gab – I heard a rumour that they've already appointed the professor of the new faculty. Did Edward tell you anything?'

'Not really. Except that he's remarkable and apparently I'll really like him. But it looks like Edward's shoehorned him in – the other lecturers are seething. Why? What have you heard?'

Oliver studied the end of his cigarette for a moment, avoiding my eyes.

'Very little, in fact. I've spoken to one or two people but no one seems to know much about him. It seems he's some very plausible bright young thing who's been working in South America and no one quite knows what he does. It's intriguing – have you thought about it? – this is a fantastically important position and one could think of a long list of prominent people appropriate for it, yet this guy's coming out of nowhere and no one knows a thing about him. I just wondered if you'd heard a name?'

"Fraid not. George thinks he's meant to be the television face of the new faculty.'

'Oh, undoubtedly. You can bet he'll be everywhere in a few months. I'd be very interested to meet him. Presumably Edward will be giving some kind of party? He wouldn't let this go by without drawing every diary editor's attention to it.'

'He mentioned something. I think it's next month.'

'Are you going?'

I shrugged.

'I don't think so – it would look a bit hypocritical. This faculty's hardly something I want to celebrate. I hate those parties anyway.'

Oliver picked at a mole on his face and shifted in his seat, trying to look unconcerned.

'Uh – I wondered if you could use your influence to get me an invitation.'

'Your influence is greater than mine. You'll get one anyway, surely?'

He shook his head.

'Not to this. Edward doesn't much like me, I'm afraid.'

'That's not true. He's your godfather.'

'Only because he was friends with my father. I'm afraid I've turned out as something of a disappointment to both of them.'

I hesitated. 'But – he said a strange thing at lunchtime. He said you'd never dare to write a story about him under your own by-line.'

Oliver pressed his cigarette stub slowly into the heaped

ashtray, propped his elbows on the table and rested his chin on his hands again. He stared at me sadly for a moment.

'Yes. It's very difficult. I – well – we share a lot of history. He was very good to Dad – protected him, in some ways, from intrusive publicity, and they had –' He stopped, suddenly cautious. 'They'd been through a lot together. Edward knew Dad better than anyone, I think, and I suppose what he means is – I've inherited this kind of gentlemen's agreement he had with Dad to keep whatever confidences may exist.' He picked at the rough edge of the table. 'Since Dad isn't here to defend himself. So I have to be careful. That's all.'

'And do you? Know anything damaging about Edward?'

I leaned forward; Oliver smiled forlornly.

'Nothing that would be of interest to anyone else. But he bends the rules, so he's paranoid, naturally. About once a year, sometimes more often, Edward offers me a job on one of his papers.' He lowered his voice; two or three other early drinkers had trooped into the pub and were gathered at the bar, not far from our table. 'Chief Reporter, Political Editor, Deputy Editor – anything I want, I get to name it. He asks me how much I want to be paid – he's offered to triple my salary and more. And he gets incensed when I turn him down, because what he really wants is to bring me on side and keep me where he can see me, but I'm not having that. That's why he doesn't like me. The idea of me being on the loose, with my loyalties to another paper – it makes him nervous.'

Wesley Hemp slid back on to his stool.

'Hello children. Have I missed anything exciting?'

'It was ever so exciting. Wes – is Chris Haughton upstairs?'

'Can't say I noticed. Why?'

'Oh, I just –' Oliver turned vaguely to the window. 'There's something I have to talk to him about. Not to worry.' He stood up and brushed something invisible from his trousers. 'Excuse me, my turn.'

Wesley Hemp twisted to watch Oliver walk away, then turned his heavy-lidded stare back to me.

'That's a really good bloke there,' he said, nodding towards Oliver's receding figure. 'Much too nice to be a hack, you'd think, but actually he's a bloody good reporter. But I can't help feeling sorry for him. Poor Olly.'

Poor Oliver. That's what my father used to say.

I was first introduced to Oliver Dowland nine years previously by my Aunt Isabelle, at my uncle's fiftieth birthday party in a country house hotel somewhere in Warwickshire. I was sixteen, he was twenty. I thought he had nice eyes, he thought I had nice legs; under an hour later we had landed in a tipsy, giggling embrace half-hidden in the shrubbery of the hotel garden, his freezing, virginal fingers skirting nervously around my goose-pimpled and equally virginal nipples as the music and laughter drifted from the terrace above. A couple of shy letters were subsequently exchanged, followed by a weekend visit to his university college, during which intimacy had failed to progress much further, hampered by inexperience on both parts and an increasing uncertainty on mine.

I first took Oliver to my family home in north London after a visit to the cinema. As we came in we discovered, to my dismay, my father working late, seated at the dining-room table, grunting and shaking his head in mock despair over a fat manuscript. He looked up, pushed his glasses on to his forehead, studied Oliver for several excruciating seconds, tapped his pencil thoughtfully against his teeth and finally asked, in his most Dickensian voice:

'Tell me, Mr Dowland *Junior*, are you in favour of reducing state handouts to single mothers and the unemployed?'

'No, Mr Harvey, I'm not,' Oliver replied evenly.

'And are you a nationalist, a monarchist, a homophobe, an Anglican or a subscriber to any of the other pernicious ideologies your father seeks to encourage among the electorate?'

'No, but I am an active member of Amnesty International,' Olly said with a straight face.

62

'Very well then,' said my father, underlining something repeatedly and tucking away a smile. 'You may continue courting my daughter.'

'Come on,' I hissed, pained with teenage embarrassment, pulling Olly urgently towards the door while glaring at my father's bowed head.

'May I ask you one more thing?' my father said suddenly, in his own voice, as we were leaving. He paused. 'Do you admire your father?'

Oliver pulled himself up straight, looked my father firmly in the eye and replied:

'Not as a statesman.' He hesitated for a moment. 'But he's not been too bad as a father.'

Richard nodded slowly, as if impressed. Later, he said to me, 'You know, in spite of his gross misfortune both in provenance, and in having had my brother elected to oversee his moral development, your Oliver's turned out quite a decent chap. Must be made of stern stuff.'

The problem was that the more I grew to like and respect him, the less I wanted him to be identified as 'my Oliver'. Needless to say, I was never invited to his family home, and assumed that, in spite of his socialist bluster, this was because Oliver was in some respects a coward, hobbled by the Minister's forceful personality, whose approval I would not be sufficiently grand to merit. He never spoke at the time about his father's problems.

'That lad's quite in love with you,' my father observed a few weeks later, after Oliver had visited us for a family Sunday lunch where my coolness had been uncomfortably apparent to all. 'Make sure you let him down gently.' He grinned, and rubbed his hand boisterously over my hair, making it jump with static, which I hated. I wriggled away, tutting. 'He's a bit too earnest for you, Fluff, I'm afraid,' said my father, and laughed wickedly. 'Or perhaps you're a bit too frivolous. Poor old Oliver. On top of all his other trials.'

I did let Oliver down gently and, perhaps because he never

got around to relieving me of my virginity (that fell, two years later, to a boy called Patrice in Paris – he had a Vespa), we remained friends, and found particular comfort in the friendship after we both lost our fathers within eighteen months of one another. But the other tie that bound us, of which we hardly ever spoke before the Faculty of Cultural Studies came into our lives, and with it Piers Gaveston, was the history shared by Edward and Denham Dowland.

Chapter V

The gallery in St James's Park was a long, blue room sunk below ground level, with a mock-Georgian interior: high ceilings, beaded chandeliers and elaborate cornicing. On that damp March evening of my uncle's party, its walls sported a 'provocative' and 'fundamentally questioning' new exhibition entitled 'Unreal City: Chemical Visions of London': vast, acid-fuelled canvases of swirling, apocalyptic skylines, which *Out'n'About* magazine's Critic's Choice had deemed 'a mega leap forward in young English conceptual topographical art'.

I stood at the top of the stairs in the shadow of *Blackfriars Bridge, 3 a.m. (cocaine and pills): oil on canvas*, a dizzying work, and skimmed the brimming room, registering in the first glance three Cabinet Ministers, two broadsheet editors, several stalwarts of late-night arts review programmes, a handful of eminent novelists and a small huddle of nervously blinking academics. Roger materialised beside me, fist curled around a cigar that seemed comically too big for him.

'Didn't think you were coming,' he remarked, puffing out charcoal gusts like a squat industrial chimney.

'Neither did I.' I stuffed my hands into my pockets and nodded towards the central gallery. Solicitous waiters hovered at the elbows of each group, champagne bottles cocked. 'I changed my mind. Good crowd.'

'*Le tout Londres.*' Roger swept his arm in an arc that embraced the room, and ran his eye over my jeans, trainers and scuffed leather jacket. 'Nice of you to make an effort.'

As usual, I had misjudged the dress code. Everyone else was kitted out for a gala night at the opera. I wondered if Oliver would show up.

'Not to worry, I hear shabby chic is all the rage. Dressing down is the new dressing up.'

'That was last year.'

'Vol-au-vent?' Roger grabbed two from a passing tray and pushed them into his mouth.

'No thanks.' Rocking back and forth on my heels, I watched the crowd; as a precaution against getting drunk and making a fool of myself I had drunk too much coffee on the train and could feel my pulse racing so hard I felt almost capable of contributing to 'Unreal City'.

'Come,' said Roger, spraying pastry, 'Sir Edward wants to see you.'

I left my jacket on the coat rails and followed him down the stairs and through the braying, chattering guests. Women in garish tailored suits glanced with disapproval at my jeans. The gallery was stuffy and overheated. Roger ducked and wove through people, round pot plants, politicians and critics, under trays and between raised glasses with surprising deftness for one so portly; I was having trouble keeping up. At one point, losing sight of him altogether, I paused behind two men in grey suits earnestly contemplating a fifteen-foot high canvas that paid faint homage to Hieronymus Bosch, but without the imagination. *Houses of Parliament in the Rain (mushrooms and weed)*. Above it, a plaque boasted: 'Shortlisted for the Turner Prize'.

'If you ask me, that's the best argument I've seen yet against legalisation,' remarked the taller of the two, whom I recognised as the Secretary of State for Health.

Just then a tentacular arm reached out and hauled me into the midst of a group I recognised.

'My happiness is complete,' declared my uncle, beaming with public bonhomie and leaning on me heavily, cigar in one hand and champagne glass precariously balanced by the stem between two fingers of the other. 'My lovely niece comes to brighten up our little party with her beauty and wit.'

Gathered around him were George Fenton, who winked

broadly; Jake Lennox and Jonathan Pleasant, the newly appointed People's Poet. I didn't know him well, but knew that my father had turned down his first collection, many years ago, describing it as 'limp'. He looked me up and down dismissively and turned his acrylic smile back to my uncle.

'A-as you say, Sir Edward, it's an interesting question. I'd very m-much like to hear your opinion, as someone with such a very great influence over what we think of as English culture today. What exactly is the nature of p-patriotism at this stage in our history? What, indeed, is Englishness?'

'Mmm, what indeed,' said my uncle, nodding gravely, evidently hoping he was not expected to furnish an answer. Intellectuals rattled him.

'Jonathan has been commissioned to write a poem about England to infuse the nation with patriotic fervour,' George explained for my benefit, adding mischievously, 'for the World Cup.'

'B-but it's not just about football,' Jonathan Pleasant added hastily. 'It's more a question of how the people identify with their nation. It's about our hopes and dreams. It must be for everyone.'

'It's always so difficult to strike the right balance between elegy and jingoism,' said George, in a tone so innocent it could never have been construed as sarcastic – unless you knew firstly that George had once been mentioned as a possible successor to the late Poet Laureate, before the Laureateship was dissolved in favour of the more marketable office of People's Poet. Or, secondly, that Jonathan Pleasant had been appointed less on merit than through a keenly professed desire to work himself to a nervous breakdown writing government propaganda in verse form. 'Quite a challenge.'

'George wrote a brilliant sonnet sequence called *Shires of England* – you should look at that,' I suggested helpfully. 'It's about how landscape and history shape the people who live there, but with really beautiful –'

I stopped; Jonathan Pleasant seemed irked.

'Oh, now,' said George, tutting diffidently and waving my praise away, but smiling nonetheless. 'That's very old.'

'Well, of course, I've read *Shires of England*,' Jonathan Pleasant said irritably. 'I'm a great admirer of George's work, as he knows, but I can't help feeling that for a modern poem, it's a little – well – *rural*. You have to remember that an awful lot of schoolchildren in our inner-city comprehensives have never seen a valley, never mind a sheep or a fishing boat. That sort of poetry can be alienating, you see.'

'Well, I've never seen a great white whale, but I still enjoyed *Moby Dick*. Isn't that the point of literature?' Jonathan's smugness provoked me, and I sounded more aggressive than I had intended.

'More champagne, everybody?' asked my uncle cheerfully, still holding me in a headlock.

'The *point* of my commission,' said Jonathan Pleasant, glowering, 'is to impart a sense of national identity, pride, even, to a generation of kids – and adults – of all races and beliefs, who have no good reason whatsoever to feel it, in a language they recognise. It's a fundamental human need to belong, to identify with something larger than oneself, and in an age of fragmented families the nation becomes a substitute. But that definition needs to be w-wider than we have understood it up to this point. In the absence of war, the only spur to national cohesion is sp- sp- ' – he coughed – 'sport, and especially football. It unites us in patriotic feeling, pride in our country, and my task is to find a way of p-promoting that non-threatening sense of nationhood outside the stadium.'

'You don't really believe that?' I said. 'Have you ever been in a London pub when England are playing Scotland? I wouldn't call that non-threatening.'

Jonathan Pleasant's expression suggested that he hadn't. 'But the energy – that's precisely my argument. I'm not saying it's the only way. For myself, I've always believed a people's national identity to come from its art and literature, but that's a very middle-class view, isn't it? Art needs to make

68

itself relevant, all-embracing. You can't base a country's sense of self on traditions that are exclusive to the m-majority of its citizens.'

'Almost a republican sentiment, Jonathan,' George mused. 'Are you finally coming out?'

'Er –' Jonathan Pleasant looked nervous. 'I'm not implying all tradition is necessarily detrimental –'

'No, but you're suggesting it's unimportant to most people!' I said indignantly. 'And the next step is to advocate abolishing it altogether, and then you end up with something like this faculty –' The sentence tailed off; Edward's eyebrows implied rebuke. 'George?'

George was scratching his beard and grinning benignly. 'Well, Gaby, as you know, I'm a great defender of tradition in some respects, and I'm sure no one here would want to see it abolished entirely, but I rather suspect that, in speaking his mind, Jonathan is somewhat restricted by his briefs. Isn't that right, Jonathan?' Then he chuckled irreverently into his glass. Jonathan Pleasant almost smiled. After a small processing delay, my uncle gave a loud chuckle and sucked wetly on his cigar.

'Restricted by his briefs. That's very funny, Georgie, I must use that one myself. Dim sum, anyone?' He hailed an obliging waiter.

'Guys, guys, guys. Listen, right.' Jake Lennox jabbed his cigarette forcefully in the air and leaned forward, earrings a-jangle. 'What you've all totally failed to realise here is that the very idea of national identity is a construct, right? The nation state is only a manifestation of ideology, it's a hegemonic deception perpetrated by the ruling class in order to mask its own power. In effect, an exercise in class domination – nations are invented things, right? They have a point of origin and who decides what constitutes a nation? The Establishment, obviously, the dominant social group. I mean, look at *you* –' He waved his fag at Jonathan Pleasant, who stepped back, alarmed. 'You stand here, poncy middle-class liberal appointed by the Establishment, in a room stuffed to the gills with other poncy middle-class liberal representatives of that same Establishment, knocking back bubbly and truffles at a party celebrating the expansion of one of our oldest universities, itself a bastion of elitism, banging on about how you're going to reinvent national identity and impose it on the people, as if you have any fucking clue who the people are. If that's not class domination I don't know what is. I bet you've never even been to a football match.' He paused to inhale, and it seemed almost appropriate to applaud. Jonathan Pleasant was riled.

'I could point out that you yourself teach at the traditional, elitist university you so confidently dismiss. And I wasn't *banging on*.'

'Yeah, well,' Jake Lennox shuffled his feet and grinned. 'I'm working to subvert it from the inside. I still write for *Marxism Today*. And I went to a comprehensive.'

'Well done, you.'

'I think,' said George, gently intervening, 'it would be very interesting to hear Sir Edward's views on this subject, as an Englishman who has travelled widely and who might be said to operate a certain cultural hegemony in this country.' He raised a glass towards my uncle, who released his grip on my shoulder, freeing me to light a cigarette.

'Yes. Of course. Well.' A shadow of anxiety flickered briefly across my uncle's face, as it always did when he was called on to express an opinion that had not first been filtered through a team of advisers. 'Where's Rodge?' He looked around, to no avail. 'Hmm. England. As I see it –' he paused and drew thoughtfully on the stub of his cigar. 'As I see it, we live in global times. My business is communication, distribution first of information but also of art and entertainment, which are the same thing. Perhaps. Or, alternatively, perhaps not. But that's not the question. So – I like to think of England as one more dot on the great global Tube map. A significant one, to be sure,' he added quickly, 'with, you know, lots of lines intersecting and – ah – efficient escalators and so on, and perhaps a nice coffee bar, like Baker Street or something, but nevertheless, part of a great, indivisible, international network.' He glanced around for approbation. 'But don't actually, ah, quote me on that, anyone. It's just an image. I'm not making any comment about the state of public transport.'

'It was Rousseau who first equated the nation with the people,' said a new voice, smooth and confident, from immediately behind me. A distinct shiver passed through the group. Everyone fell silent and appeared to be staring above my head, but the speaker's closeness meant that I was unable to turn around. 'Instead of locating it in the person of the absolute monarch. But a nation has to be defined by two elements, politics and culture. Politics, needless to say, is imposed from above. So it's a nation's culture, its art, that comes from below, from the people, because it's considered to express the personality and psyche of the nation. And it's that shared history – myths and books and the language we speak – that determines our understanding of national identity. Obviously. That's why minority groups fight so hard to preserve their own languages and literatures. Englishness is all about words, and what we do with them. You can't deny literary tradition.'

No one looked as if they intended to deny the speaker anything; they all stood riveted, mouths slightly parted. I was intrigued – by his voice and his opinions – and managed to move aside slightly so that I could turn to examine him.

That was the first time I saw him.

It is almost impossible to describe the effect of looking unexpectedly at real beauty, except that it makes you gasp aloud, and catch your breath over again, and stare as if you could fasten the image on your retina in case it should disappear as surprisingly as it appeared. I nearly choked on my cigarette.

The man who had spoken was exceptionally beautiful. He was tall, taller even than my uncle, and lean; he stood confidently, legs slightly astride, hands tucked into the back pockets of his jeans. His hair was dark blond, and cut to fall loosely over his face. The lines of his sharp cheekbones and jaw formed a perfect parallelogram; his lips were straight and thin and his skin lightly tanned, with a faint spattering of freckles over his fine nose. It was a hard face, symmetrical, a touch haughty. He looked at me, twisting one corner of his mouth into a half-smile.

'Hello,' he said. 'Have we met?'

'Uh – hi, I don't think so,' I managed, barely audible. His eyes were the green of water, and his teeth astonishingly white. He continued to hold my stare; his gaze level, considering, and I found myself picturing his face above me, in bed.

I took a step back.

'Thank God, Piers, I was beginning to think you weren't coming.' My uncle grasped the tall young man firmly by the upper arm. 'I must introduce you – George you've met, of course, and this is ah – James –'

'Jake.'

'– Jake Lenin, who teaches at the university, and this' – he turned to me with a too-wide smile – 'is my own niece, Gabriele, who I've told you about. And *this*' – he reached up and clapped an arm around the broad shoulders, as if showing off a favourite son – 'this is Piers Gaveston.'

Piers Gaveston. I mouthed his name inside my head to see how the sound fitted. I liked it. Piers and Gaby. Gaby and Piers. Gabriele Gaveston. I stopped myself quickly, blushing. He was still studying me with that laconic smile.

Jonathan Pleasant cleared his throat and stepped forward.

'Jonathan Pleasant, People's Poet,' he said, offering a hand.

'I know. I'm familiar with your work.'

'Really?' Jonathan smoothed his hair. 'And what do you do?'

Piers Gaveston smiled, deliberately enigmatic. 'Oh, this and that.'

Roger gave an unmistakable snort; Piers shot him a look of undiluted scorn and turned back to my uncle.

'Can I get some water, Edward? Your service is shocking.'

'Of course, of course – ah –' My uncle cast around for a waiter.

Roger opened his mouth and then thought better of it, and turned quietly purple instead.

'Jonathan.' Piers Gaveston pulled a packet of cigarettes out of his back pocket and extracted one with his very white teeth, eyeing Jonathan Pleasant with something like amusement. From the breast pocket of his shirt he removed a slim gold monogrammed lighter, flipped it open, lit his cigarette and breathed in thoughtfully, aware that everyone was watching him. 'I wanted to say how much I enjoyed your poem commemorating the opening of the Metropolitan Line extension.'

Jonathan Pleasant bowed his head modestly. 'Oh – thank you very much.'

'Yes,' Piers Gaveston released a thin line of blue smoke. 'I was thinking that the faux-naif style was due for a revival.'

'Oh. Well, it wasn't really –'

'You know, that very simplistic, almost – what's the word?' – Piers Gaveston contemplated his smoke – '*banal* imagery, those very commonplace structures you use. It's impressive, the way you disguise the poetic process so convincingly.'

Confusion scudded across Jonathan Pleasant's eyes as his ego battled to interpret this double-edged compliment. It was obvious to everyone else that he was being mocked. Jonathan Pleasant appeared to realise this too.

'I always feel, reading your poetry,' Piers Gaveston went on, 'that it's rather like ordering pasta with pesto in a good restaurant. Very enjoyable, of course, but you can't escape the sense that you could have done it just as well yourself at home.'

I could see George chuckling amid his beard and struggling to hide it. I was impressed by this man's boldness; it spoke of a confidence in his own position. I wondered what that might be.

'It's – ah – not the m-most inspiring of subjects, you know,

73

a new Tube line.' Jonathan Pleasant lowered his head apologetically.

'Ah, but you can't get much more relevant to the people than that,' Piers Gaveston said, his face perfectly serious. 'Although some might argue it is by definition exclusive in being so – well, *metropolitan*. Perhaps you could do one about a rural bus-route somewhere in the Cotswolds, to redress the balance.' Then he defused the moment with a gleaming smile, looked at me and winked, and something snapped like an elastic band under my ribs. 'Although that's really your turf, eh, George? Are you well?'

'Tolerably.' George nodded. He was smiling too, though not necessarily at Piers. 'And yourself?'

'Very well, thanks. Yes. *Very* well.'

'And you're settled in now?'

'Well – settling. It's always strange to be back, you know?'

'Of course.'

Back from where? How did George know this man? How did my uncle know him? Why had I never met him before? I was consumed with questions, as well as by a frightening desire to reach out a hand and stroke the downy triangle of skin offered by the open neck of his white shirt. I stamped on my cigarette and rammed my hands purposefully into the pockets of my jeans.

'Here.' My uncle handed Piers Gaveston a glass of fizzing water, then looked up abruptly. His face stiffened. 'Bloody hell.' His eyes were fixed on the far end of the room. 'What in Christ's name are *they* doing here?'

I followed his gaze, and saw, standing at the top of the stairs leading into the gallery, Oliver Dowland and Wesley Hemp who, even at that distance, was clearly spectacularly drunk.

'Roger?' My uncle looked around wildly. Wesley Hemp had spotted us.

'Gaby! Lovely, lovely Gaby!' he bellowed across the room, flinging his arms open ecstatically, quite obliviously knocking the champagne glass from the hand of a Cabinet Minister's wife. The burble of conversation died away. '*La soirée peut commencer!*' Wesley yelled. 'We're here! Let's party like it's 1999! Let's do the hokey cokey and then turn around! *Come Comrades, come gather, and the last fight let us face!*'

'Gabriele.' My uncle loomed over me accusingly. 'What is Oliver Dowland doing here?'

'No idea.' I shrugged innocently. Oliver was scanning the room anxiously as if searching for someone.

Roger flustered up, puffing indignantly. 'I'm ever so sorry, Sir Edward, the staff did their best to stop them but I'm afraid they were rather insistent –'

'Sir *Edward*!' Wesley cried at the same volume, lurching through the crowd. 'Bring me some of your finest champagne! And those dainty little quails' eggs things that look like babies' eyeballs! I'll say this for you' – he paused, a glass in each hand, steadying himself. A low ripple of laughter spread around the room; the guests seemed to be enjoying the performance. 'You're a corrupt and evil man and the nation loathes you, but you throw a bloody good party, and don't let anyone say otherwise!'

'Get that madman out of here,' my uncle hissed through his teeth. Roger looked apprehensive.

'He's rather aggressive tonight. He won't stop singing the Internationale –'

'Get. Him. Out.'

'Right.' Roger scuttled sideways.

Oliver had pushed his way through to my uncle, folding his hands together with appropriate deference. 'I'm sorry about this, Sir Edward,' he said, 'it's just – a lot of my friends are here' – here he raised an eyebrow at me in an appeal for solidarity – 'and, well – I'm here as a friend, not as a journalist. I did think you wouldn't mind.'

'I *mind* Wesley Hemp,' said Sir Edward stiffly.

'Er – yes, sorry.' Oliver glanced apologetically over his shoulder. Wesley was moistly embracing the new Director

75

General of the BBC. 'It was sort of unavoidable. I wanted to make sure he got home safely – he's in a bit of a state. He tried to start a fight in the pub.'

'Marvellous. You might have phoned, Oliver. I could have arranged to send you an invitation. Alone.'

'*Roger!*' Wesley Hemp exclaimed happily, opening his arms wide. 'Roger *Mortimer*! My old mucker!' Roger blanched, approaching him hesitantly like a first-time toreador.

'Now, Wesley, you know you're really not welcome and you're very drunk, so perhaps –'

'Rubbish! I'm perfectly fine and all my loveliest friends are here, look.' He waved a hand imprecisely. 'Do you know, Roger' – he hooked an arm around Roger's shoulder and squinted at him through blotchy eyes – 'I'm always so pleased to see you. You're the one person I can rely on at any party to look even worse than me.'

Roger emitted a costive little squeak of protest, and clasped the knot of his Herbie Frogg tie.

'Come along, Wesley, please.' He tugged at Wesley's jacket. 'God, you stink of booze.'

'That's because I've been celebrating! Shall we dance?' Wesley hugged Roger and stared blearily around the circle. 'Oh, come on, you bunch of stiffs, loosen up, won't you? It's meant to be a party. You all look suicidal.' He clapped a hand to his mouth. 'Oops, sorry, Olly.'

Roger and my uncle attempted to lead Wesley away.

And in the confusion, this happened:

Oliver Dowland glanced sidelong at my uncle, then turned to Piers Gaveston, thrust out a hand forcefully and said, with something like triumph: 'Piers Gaveston? I'm Oliver Dowland. May I offer my congratulations?'

And, yet more surprisingly, this:

Piers Gaveston turned white. He stumbled a little, so slightly as to have passed almost unnoticed, except that a few drops of water spilled from his glass. His face froze, eyes wide, perfect teeth clenched tightly, and for several seconds he and Oliver stared at each other, unblinking, like opponents in a chess match. Oliver wore the same strange, forced smile that suggested he thought he was winning.

Finally Piers Gaveston took out another cigarette, almost composed again, propped it in his mouth without lighting it and replied coldly:

'So. Finally, the famous Oliver Dowland. It's a great pleasure to meet you. I hear you're with the *Sunday Enquirer*.'

'That's right.'

'Interesting.'

'Yes, isn't it?'

This wasn't Oliver, I thought; this was a false bravado. He spoke as if issuing a challenge. He was also at a disadvantage, being so much shorter. Piers Gaveston seemed to have regained his poise; his lip curled into a mocking smile.

'News?'

'Politics. But of course, I'm always interested in stories about people in the public eye.'

Piers arched an eyebrow.

'Of *course*. You seem very young to be so successful. You must have some valuable contacts.'

'Likewise.'

Piers lit his cigarette without taking his eyes off Oliver.

'A pity you were missed off the guest list. Still, that's the new meritocracy for you – family ties don't count for so much these days, I hear. But how nice of you to come anyway. I admire determination.'

Oliver's smile was thinning; he was in no position to compete with Piers Gaveston's hauteur. I could see him picking his nails with agitation.

'Oh, Christ Almighty,' said my uncle, arriving back on the scene and spotting this enigmatic exchange. He stepped over and grasped Oliver by the shoulders. 'Now then, Olly, since you're here we'd better get you a drink. You must know Charlie, do you? Here, come and meet Charlie, my Washington correspondent – he's only here for the week, you'll have lots to talk about.' And he wheeled Oliver tactfully away. I tried to catch Olly's eye, perplexed, but he was still staring over his shoulder at Piers Gaveston.

'What a very polite boy,' observed Piers to no one in particular, examining his long fingers. Who *are* you, I wondered, my gaze returning to his mouth.

On the other side of the room, a fresh commotion burst out.

'Yes, but you are a *bit* of a cunt, though, aren't you?' Wesley Hemp was saying loudly and cheerily to the Health Minister, poking him affectionately in the chest. 'I'm not wrong, I'm sure you'd be the first to admit it. I mean, who's going to pay for your short-termism in the long run? Eh? Eh? The working classes, go on, say it, the working classes, say it!'

Roger, who had let Wesley loose, turned crimson. I felt as though everyone was reading subtitles that I couldn't see. There was some shared knowledge here denied to me, and it centred on Piers Gaveston – who had been cornered by a sleek young woman I recognised from a society magazine. She was gazing up at him, nodding effusively, her body language unmistakable.

'Look at that.' I nudged Roger. 'She might as well just straddle him here and now.'

'What?' he snapped, still watching Wesley's anarchic progress.

'Oh, nothing.' I wandered away, feeling a tight pinch of jealousy.

Dabbing her face with powder from a slim black compact, Sara Croft, our eminent feminist critic, was leaning into the mirror under the mellow light of the ladies' room. We regarded each other's reflections for a moment. The glass was tinted, making us both unnaturally tanned.

'Got your eye on him, then?' she said, turning to face me. 'I saw you.'

'What?'

She laughed unpleasantly. 'You know exactly what I'm

78

talking about. Why don't you get your uncle to arrange it for you? After all, he buys you everything else you want.'

'Sorry –' I frowned, puzzled. 'I haven't got the slightest idea what you're talking about.'

'Your uncle.' She snapped her compact shut for emphasis. Powder sat in a dusty line across her nose. 'Has just bought this faculty. That's why we're here drinking his champagne. And all that time you sat like a little Pharisee in those meetings, with your oh-so-worthy arguments against private finance in the university, and the damage the new faculty would do to its academic reputation, when you must have known all along that you'd come out of it smelling of roses. You and George, thick as thieves, planning your little coup. I just can't bear that kind of hypocrisy.'

'I knew nothing about it. Honestly.'

'Do you think we were born yesterday? Well, anyway, there's your job for life up and running, while the rest of us are subject to his every whim. Nice work.'

I stared at her in disbelief as the full weight of her implication suddenly landed.

'Hold on – I had nothing to do with this! I certainly didn't put him up to it, if that's what you mean! I'm furious about it. I've got more reason than anyone here not to want him involved. It's not my fault he's my uncle!' I stopped, hearing the absurdity of my protest.

'Oh, you poor little princess.' She shrugged. 'Can't be helped. But the whole thing reeks of nepotism, quite literally – it's disgusting. There's no doubt who's running the show now – you and George, and the golden boy out there, while the people who've worked really hard to get where they are will just get sidelined. Same old bloody story.'

'What? I'm not running anything! I haven't even finished my thesis yet –'

'I hardly think that'll stand in the way of your irresistible rise now.'

'But I don't –'

I stared impotently at the door as it hissed slowly to a hydraulic close behind her.

For as long as I could remember, I had been trying to slough off the varnish of my uncle's name, to achieve something for myself. The university, with its ancient cloisters and chilly libraries, had seemed so remote from him that I had begun to believe I might escape his influence there. Now he had marched into my quiet life and stamped his logo all over it. I would have to leave the university. That was it. If I stayed, if I had anything to do with this new faculty, no one would ever believe I had done it through talent or hard work; he would own me and my reputation, my career, all my ambitions, and I would have to be grateful to him, always. Just as my father had.

I considered my reflection. The girl staring back from the mirror was tall and angular, with small breasts and bony hips, but long legs, and thick dark hair; a thin face, barely made up, flushed from champagne, with dark angry eyes and fierce brows in need of tidying. Not *classically* pretty, my mother used to tell me, but *striking*, which I always imagined was a nice way of saying not pretty at all – not compared with the magazine girl, anyway. Sighing, I rested both hands on the counter and leaned in towards the glass, so close that it fogged with my breath. 'You idiot,' I whispered to my reflection. I was ungroomed, scruffy, looking as if I'd come straight from the library. Which I had. Absurd to think that someone as beautiful as Piers Gaveston would look at me with anything other than contempt; I didn't belong in his glossy world. A tired sadness seeped over me; I belonged in the university, and now I didn't even have that. It was so unfair. I had been foolish to come to the party. Even Oliver was behaving strangely here. I decided to slip quietly away.

I was attempting to thread my way inconspicuously towards the stairs through the babble, when a firm hand clutched my shoulder. I braced myself for the affections of Wesley Hemp, but turned instead to find George chewing knowledgeably on the stem of his pipe and grinning as if caught in the middle of an enormous joke.

'Here.' He handed me another glass of champagne. I looked at it doubtfully, pushing my hair off my face. 'Drink and be merry. So, what do you think of him?'

'Who?'

'*Whom*,' George corrected automatically. 'The dashing Dr Gaveston.'

'Doctor Gaveston?' My eyes widened incredulously. 'What's he a doctor of?'

'Something frighteningly trendy, Aesthetics of Cinema or some such. We'd better find out, since we're all in thrall to him now.'

'In thrall – how?'

'He's an impressive talker, mind,' George continued, removing the pipe from his mouth. 'What do you think, honestly?'

'I think' – I hesitated – 'I think he seems very pleased with himself.'

'Yes, well.' George nodded significantly. 'Not without reason.'

'What reason?'

George squinted at me curiously over his half-moon glasses, as a Damascus Road expression spread slowly over his features.

'Oh my Great Good Lord in Heaven. No one's told you. I didn't realise.'

'Told me what?'

'I assumed Edward would have told you. I imagined it would be the first thing he would have –'

'*George!* Told me what?'

'That – Piers Gaveston is our new Professor of Cultural Studies.'

We swivelled in unison to sweep the room for the man in question, who was easy to locate, being a head taller than anyone else. Together we watched him tossing his hair like a racehorse and then checking to see who was looking at him.

'You're joking,' I said, without much conviction.

'Not a joking matter. Well – in fact, it might turn out to be, who knows. But let's give him the benefit of the doubt for now. Edward seems to think he's wonderful.'

'And what would Edward know?'

'He knows the value of a bright young thing for promotional purposes, that certainly. And this is a commercial venture, you must remember. No room for tweedy old goats like me on Channel Four.'

'He *can't* be the professor. He's barely older than I am.'

'He's older than he looks,' George said, with emphasis, taking out his worn leather pouch and restuffing his pipe with pungent woody tobacco. 'Lines around the eyes, always a give-away. But he's a handsome fellow, don't you think?' He fumbled with his lighter, trying not to smile.

'I suppose.'

George laughed knowingly. 'Why're you so glum, anyway? Edward?' He exhaled a cloud that smelled like a November bonfire.

'Because –' I sighed and slumped against the wall, then righted myself hastily, realising that I had knocked *Hackney Bus Depot (amphetamines): Watercolour* off kilter. 'How does anyone have the patience to do a watercolour on amphetamines?' I puzzled, straightening it.

'Gaby. Tell me why you're upset.'

'Oh, it's – this faculty takeover is absurd. I can't stay around now that Edward's all over the university, no one will take me seriously. I was stupid to think otherwise. Sara Croft thinks I engineered the whole thing.'

'Oh, Gaby. Come on, now. Sara Croft is just being unpleasant because she's probably had too much to drink. Don't even think of leaving the university. You're bigger than that.'

'It's not just her. They'll all think the same thing. How could I take his offer of a job in the new faculty and keep any kind of self-respect?'

'And how could you consider letting him drive you away

from everything you've worked for, and a place you've made your own, with any self-respect? Hmm? And think of me! You're my ally, my one kindred humanist spirit in a world of theory-touting philistines. Who else will answer my burning questions about the chronicle sources of the Arthurian myth, eh? Where will I find another protegee as good as you? *And*' – he wagged a finger in admonition – 'however would you find another mentor as brilliant and inspiring as me?'

I laughed reluctantly. 'That would be hard. But you don't understand, George, I can't be submissive to him. I don't want to owe him, it goes against everything.'

'Listen, Gaby.' George rested a hand on my shoulder and his face grew serious. 'You've been Edward's niece for twenty-five years and, short of one of you dying, that situation isn't going to change. You can't help it, and you can't pretend it doesn't exist. But don't let him start bullying you now. And if it's any consolation, you perhaps flatter yourself in imagining this is all about you. This is Edward proving a much bigger point to himself and to us.' He sucked on his pipe, then waved it in my uncle's direction. 'It's the Franco syndrome.'

'The what?'

'You know – most dictators were bullied at school. Or in the army, in Franco's case – but you see what I mean. Power brings the chance to compensate. Edward is not an intellectual, and highbrow universities make him feel inferior. Richard made him feel inferior, and so do I, and he hates to feel inferior more than anything. He's a smart businessman, but he doubts his own intellect, you know – that's why he affects this mixture of awe and sneering. So this is his way of showing us all that you don't need to go to a university when you can just buy one. That, and the fact that it is a splendid investment on his part. And it will be good for us too, I promise, or I wouldn't have encouraged him in the first place. But we should talk about this properly, when we're not drowned out by – all this. Oh my goodness, look.' He

83

pointed across the room. 'Wesley Hemp in dialogue with Jake Lennox. That's a Marxist too far, in anyone's book. I must go and eavesdrop, it'll be just like *Pravda*.' He ruffled my hair amiably. 'I mean it – pop in, we'll have a chat. But don't you dare think for a moment of abandoning us.'

I glanced at my watch: ten past nine. Heavily climbing the stairs to the coat racks, I paused, looking back over the room for one last glimpse of Piers Gaveston, but he seemed to have disappeared. Forget about it, I told myself, plunging into the swathes of expensive-smelling cashmere in search of my jacket.

'Leaving already?' said a voice behind me.

'Damn right,' I muttered, without turning round, wriggling one arm into a sleeve.

'Oh. Well, that's a shame, we didn't really get a chance to talk.'

Whipping round on my heels, I found myself staring into the startling green eyes of Piers Gaveston. He was standing between the two racks of coats, preventing me from leaving, his long hands resting on the metal rails either side. He didn't smile. Half in my jacket, I hesitated, wondering if I should stay. My right sleeve dangled empty behind my back. A curious silence grew. He watched me.

'Uh – I liked that thing you said before, you know, about language and literary tradition,' I offered eventually, feeling I ought to say something.

'Did you?' He raised an eyebrow and shrugged. 'Edward suggested I should talk to you.'

It was unclear whether he considered the suggestion appealing or otherwise.

'He says you're a literary historian.'

'Well – yes. In a limited field.'

'The thing is –' he slid his hand slowly along the rail until it was level with my shoulder, and continued to stare down at me intently. I had to look away quickly; my hands were growing sticky and hot. 'I need some help researching a project I'm working on. It's a television series, on the history of English culture.'

'Oh. Right. No small task.'

'Exactly.' He almost smiled. 'More precisely, it's looking at how national identity has been reflected or created through art and literature and film over the years. But the early part – it's not my period.'

'Every academic's excuse.' I looked up. This time one corner of his mouth curled gently.

'I know, I know. But the Arthur myth – I believe that's your territory. I wondered if I could persuade you to spend some time talking to me about this?'

'Er – it sounds interesting,' I said, as evenly as I could manage.

'Well, I would hope so, or there isn't much point in doing it.'

'Sure. I mean, I'd love to help, if I can. What's it called?'

'*Reflecting England*.' He held up a hand. 'I know, it's poor. We're working on it. The producer has a stunted imagination – he wants a big mirror on the opening credits. Imagine.'

I coughed out a nervous laugh that died away awkwardly to silence. I caught his eye for a difficult moment. He cleared his throat.

'Ed says you'll be joining the new faculty. So we'll be working together.'

'Well –' Well, I was thinking of leaving, I almost said, but caught in the fierce beam of his eyes I realised I didn't want to burn my bridges quite yet. 'Yes, I think so.'

'Good. I think you're just the person I need. Do you know something?' He tilted his head slightly and I felt his eyes skate over my face and down to my chest. My heart bounced up to my throat. 'You look very like Edward, it's uncanny. I guess that's why I thought I'd seen you before.'

I blushed. 'Is that good or bad?'

He watched me, unblinking, with the same half-smile. 'Well, Edward's a very good-looking man, for his age. Don't you think?'

'They were always mistaken for each other, when they were young, people often thought they were twins.'

'Who were?'

'Oh.' I looked down, flustered, as if I had assumed too much familiarity. 'My dad. His brother – Edward's.'

'The dead one?'

'Uh – yes.'

He nodded briskly, as if this were of minor interest. 'So – I'll be up and down to the university over the next few weeks. We'll grab a drink or something, if that suits you?'

'Sure.'

'Good. I'll look forward to it.' He walked backwards out of the coat racks. I pulled on my jacket. 'One other thing. That boy – Oliver Dowland – is he a friend of yours?'

'Olly? Yes, why?'

Piers Gaveston folded his arms across his chest and looked away, back towards the gallery. 'No particular reason. Just – he seems like an interesting guy. I met his father, once or twice. Maybe you'd mention that I'd like to talk to him some time? I'd appreciate it.'

'Okay.' I wondered why he wouldn't simply approach Oliver himself, but decided not to ask.

'*There* you are.' My uncle bounded up the stairs and stopped abruptly, eyeing us with a suspicion which shifted into a strained approval. 'Been looking everywhere. Now, where's that bloody woman? *Roger!*'

Roger followed him, panting, accompanied by a large, olive-skinned woman dressed in black who clutched a pendulous and professional-looking camera to her bosom.

'Quick photo-call, won't take a minute, chop-chop, over here.' My uncle clapped his hands.

Piers pushed his fringe out of his eyes. 'Must we? I'd really rather not do photos tonight, Ed, it's too soon and I'm tired,' he said, peevishly, as if he spent far too much of his time 'doing photos'. Which, with that face, he probably did.

'Yes, we must.' My uncle shot him a warning look. 'You

agreed. It won't take long. Gabriele, come here with me.'

'*Me?*'

'Yes, you – I want you in these pics, come here –'

'Why?'

He looked surprised. 'You're my niece, dammit – one for the family album.'

I shook my head.

'No, all right then. Because you're part of this university, and so am I now, and we might as well look like we're both pleased about it. It's good publicity. And Piers is the face of the faculty.'

'But I don't –'

'Gabriele, stop bleating, we haven't got long. We can argue about it afterwards, if you like. You, come *on*!' (This last to the photographer.)

Sir Edward spoke as if with a vested authority. The last thing I wanted was to be pictured smiling at his side as if complicit in his venture, but he was impossible to disobey.

He manoeuvred me in front of *Blackfriars Bridge, 3am*, and stood back, considering. 'Bloody hell. You look like a *student*. Don't you have a hairbrush?'

'Er – no,' I patted my pockets lamely.

'Here.' Piers pulled a tortoiseshell comb from his back pocket and held it out to me. Then he pushed his own hair from his face with both hands, dipping his head so that it swung back into place – a practised gesture.

'Right, right. Over here, that's it. Move in a bit, Piers.'

And so I found myself sandwiched between my uncle and Piers Gaveston in front of an altered-consciousness oil painting, my hip touching his, his arm around my shoulder, as the large woman ducked and twisted and clicked and snapped and stepped forward and stepped back, until finally my uncle said, nonchalantly, 'Now get these two,' and dived out of the frame, leaving me to be pictured with Piers Gaveston as if we'd just announced an engagement. My cheeks caught fire, as embarrassed as if I'd engineered it myself; his touch loosened on my back and I heard him draw a sharp breath, audibly irritated.

'What's this for?' I whispered.

He shrugged. 'Who cares, frankly?'

'Where are you from, again?' my uncle asked the photographer. She appeared surprised.

'Greece, originally.'

'Which *publication*?'

'Oh. Sorry. *UpTown*.'

'*UpTown* magazine, there you are,' said my uncle to me, overdoing the jocularity. 'That'll be nice – get your picture next to all those toothy debs. See – didn't hurt, did it? Now, Piers, you'd better come and meet the DG, he's got shocking breath so don't get too close, but you probably should get to know him . . .'

And with a hand on Piers's back, Sir Edward led him away down the stairs. I waited to see if he would turn round and look at me. He didn't.

Chapter VI

'I've never seen him before in my life, I promise.'

'Olly, I *know* you. There's something you're not telling me. He seemed to know about you, and I've never seen you act as strangely as you did that night.'

'Maybe I drank too much, I don't know.' Oliver picked at a loose thread on the tablecloth, his face tight, witholding.

'He said he knew your father,' I offered eventually, realising as I spoke the word that I had subtly altered it, unintentionally. Knew, met. Different altogether. Oliver looked predictably startled.

'He said *that*?'

'He also said he'd like to talk to you.'

'Did he? Shit.'

'Shit why? Are you going to tell me the truth?'

Oliver poked at his spaghetti and sucked in his cheeks. We were eating in the small, friendly Italian restaurant on Clerkenwell Green where we sometimes met for dinner; a Wednesday night at the beginning of April, two weeks after Edward's party. Oliver had asked me to meet him from the office but proved to be more unforthcoming than usual; he said work was complicated, but I suspected this was not the reason he was picking vaguely at his food and the wine lolled, untouched, in the ice-bucket at his elbow. I glanced around.

We were almost alone, tucked into a corner table as the air grew dusky outside. The restaurant was furnished like a Tuscan farmhouse kitchen; panels of smoky wood and dark terracotta tiles, tables with perky red and white chequered cloths. Bright enamelled plates and watercolours of Florentine vistas crowded the clean white walls. Cured hams

89

hung heavily on hooks above the latticed wine-racks stacked along the back counter, and from the tiny kitchen at the far end rose smells of basil and garlic sauces.

'The truth,' Oliver said wearily, as if this conversation were too much effort, 'is what I said – I've never seen him before.' He paused. 'But – all right, I had heard his name. He did know Dad, a bit, it was some time ago. They didn't like each other. I think he upset Dad – anyway, I suppose I just remembered that Dad disliked him. That's all. Maybe I was a bit rude.'

'How on earth did your dad know him?' This unexplained familiarity that everyone seemed to have with Piers Gaveston was beginning to make me feel resentfully shut out of some magnificent secret.

'Gaveston worked for Edward in New York, a few years ago. Dad met him out there, then I think he moved over here, he was making a film or something, I forget. Dad didn't like the way he manipulated Edward. Thought he was over-ambitious.' He bit his lip. 'I've probably said too much. Don't want to colour your judgement. Maybe he's changed.'

'Seems unlikely.'

Oliver shrugged, and fixed me with a very serious look.

'What did you think?'

My face coloured. 'I thought he was a bit – arrogant.'

'But you fancy him.' He lifted a coil of spaghetti to his mouth, still watching my face, spattering tiny drops of sauce over his shirt.

'What makes you say that?'

'Only the way you hung around him like a simpering poodle.'

'I did not!'

'Did. It was embarrassing.'

'I barely spoke to him!'

'He was looking at you a lot.'

'*Was* he? Really?' I leaned forward, knocking over my glass of water in my enthusiasm.

90

'Ha! Gotcha. No, not really.' Oliver gave a tired grin.

I scowled, then laughed.

'Oh, all right then – a bit. He is gorgeous.'

'Sure, and he knows it. But – well. Be careful.'

I laughed; it came out as an unconvincing bark. 'Careful? He's not going to look at me, is he?'

There was a small pause.

'I wouldn't have thought he was your type.'

'Oh?' I bristled. 'And what's my type?'

Oliver looked uncomfortable.

'Well – you know. He seems a bit – flamboyant. And he's so obviously sucking up to Edward – I thought you didn't go for that. And I'd guess you're not really his type.'

'Fuck you! I'm too unsophisticated, is that it?' I was half-teasing, but Oliver didn't smile back.

'Of course you're not, you daft bint. Just – you're not his type. Trust me.'

'Oh, like you'd know anything about it. Anyway, give me a break – I've only met him once, I haven't even thought about our compatibility.'

This was a lie, as Oliver knew very well. I had thought of little else since the night of Edward's party, and had spent considerable time dismantling all the objections Oliver had voiced and which had also immediately occurred to me. He was right; Piers Gaveston was unlike the men I usually met around the university – polished, successful, exotic – and had he not expressed an interest in seeing me again, I would have concluded at first sight that he was out of my reach and would never have dared imagine any further contact with him, too careful to protect myself from disappointment.

People talk of infatuation as though it were an irresistible force. I had always thought it to be more complicated than that; you made a decision to allow someone room in your imagination, I thought, you choose to linger on their image. On the train back home after the party, staring out at the strings of lights and empty parking lots blurring by, I had

91

decided that Piers Gaveston could be everything I'd been waiting for. I would make it my business to impress him, and then win him. This recognition meant I woke each morning with a jolt in my chest, and found myself smiling unexpectedly; it gave me the distraction I had badly needed.

Oliver was quiet, twisting spaghetti around his fork and watching it slide off again.

'He has asked me to do some work with him, though,' I said eventually, to fill the gap. 'Some television series he's doing. It sounds interesting.'

'I bet. Look, it's none of my business, but don't fall for him, for God's sake. He'll break your heart, honestly, Gab, and you're better than that.'

'No he won't. I'm not going to fall for him.' I heard the irritation in my voice. 'And in fact it *is* none of your business. But I'm not going to write someone off just because your dad didn't like him.'

'Fine, just offering advice. Don't get prickly.'

'I'm not.'

'Fine.'

'Good.'

We ate in silence, listening to the cadences of the waiters' quiet conversation drifting from the bar. Finally Oliver pushed his plate away emphatically and mouthed for coffee. The waiter sauntered over, gathered the plates in one hand and lifted the wine, dripping, out of its bucket, shaking his head in mock disapproval.

'You driving tonight, or what?' he asked, in a mixture of Firenze and Finsbury. 'You look like bloody misery, Olly, man, get you little something on the house, eh?'

'Just an espresso,' Oliver said gloomily.

'You want take him home and put a smile on his face, Princess,' the waiter nodded to me as he spun round, with a hideous wink.

Silence slumped over us again.

'Actually, I've got a problem,' Oliver said finally, without

92

looking up. 'Mike, the editor, wants me to write a profile of your friend Piers Gaveston for this Sunday, and I just thought – if there's anything you've heard around the university, you know, any background, maybe you'd pass it on.'

'I thought you were the one who knew all about him.'

'Bits and pieces. But I'd be very interested to know anything George Fenton has on him. His academic background, for example – or whether he even has one.'

I pretended to think about this.

'Say he's gorgeous, over-ambitious and manipulative.'

Oliver's lip twitched into a near-smile.

'Yes, all right. But seriously, though, any facts, credentials, history you might pick up. I mean, aren't you curious? He's effectively your boss now. And even if Edward masterminded his appointment, which he clearly did, someone at the university must have known something about him in order to condone it.'

'Why don't you phone George?'

'Well, I could, but I'm a journalist – you're his friend. George will talk to you. I'd just like to know if George has any doubts about him. And what kind of selection process they went through to choose him. If they did choose him.'

'But I just told you – Piers Gaveston said he'd like to talk to you, why don't you take him up on it?'

'I'd rather not.'

'Why?'

'It's a profile, not an interview,' he said impatiently. 'I'd be compromised.'

There is something else here, I thought, something bigger. Oliver looked away.

'Are you staying in London tonight?'

I nodded. 'I thought I'd go to the flat. I have to do some things in the British Library tomorrow.'

'Share a cab?'

'No, it's early. I'll get the Tube.' I noted the tiny flicker of disappointment across Oliver's mouth and felt a quick sting of guilt, as if I'd let him down; still, after so much time, I realised he occasionally harboured a mild hope. But walking with Oliver through the front door of the flat – my old family home – belonged to another life. We were different people.

'I'm seeing George on Friday,' I said, pushing back my chair. 'I'll call you if there's anything to tell.'

'Oh – and – if you should happen to see Piers Gaveston' – Oliver paused, as if unsure whether to continue – 'send him my best, and ask if he has any more news about Andy Epstein.'

'*Who*?'

Oliver shuffled slightly.

'Andy Epstein. It was – someone he and Dad used to know in New York. Just ask him – he'll know what I mean. See what he says.'

The flat was a mistake. Everyone had told my mother so at the time, and had later enjoyed the bitter triumph of being right. It was the basement of my family's old house on Highgate West Hill, which my mother had zealously knocked through, four years ago, into a two-room conversion so that she could rent out the rest of the house, the call of her new life not quite giving her the conviction to let go of the past entirely. Two rooms will do me fine, she had chided, waving aside protests from friends and family, refusing advice to move on, to rent somewhere new rather than sitting in the vaults of her previous life. She made it her project and clung to it, afraid that she would flounder.

In the weeks following my father's death, my mother had maintained the strange, protective lucidity of shock, and had bustled about with the lawyers, the estate agents and the bankers with alarming efficiency. She did not cry at the funeral. Afterwards, while I sunk into a pale, sullen grief, wrapped in a fug of cigarette smoke, she immersed herself in interior design magazines, kitchenette showrooms, letting agencies and the business of producing a constant supply of tea for chirpy Geordie builders. My contribution was sadly and carefully to put my father's books into crates, which took days; I kept pausing to read his inscriptions or marginal notes, to rub my thumb along the furred edges of his pages. These were mine, my lifeline to him, and I didn't want them staying in the house once it was rented, for some other family to maul; I wrapped them in paper and put them into storage. Even had the basement flat had room for them, my mother would not have wanted them. She had always felt excluded from my father's intellectual life: the world that sustained him, the world he shared with me, when we would snuggle in his study and read together. From the other room, over the television, she would hear snorts of laughter, private jokes spun out of puns, allusions, pastiches – games she could never play, or had no interest in playing. She is a kind and intelligent woman, my mother, who was once very beautiful, but she cradled an envy for that book-lined world that her husband and daughter owned, together, that she never quite forgot.

Friends watched anxiously for tell-tale cracks in her composure, but the weeks passed and still she wore the same serene smile, and when the builders had finished she moved her favourite pieces of furniture down to the basement, made new curtains and let the remaining floors to a very nice family who were something to do with the Swiss Consulate. But in the rare moments when I looked up briefly from my own self-absorption, I could see, as no one else did, that there was nothing behind her eyes. Perhaps if I had acted then, it might have turned out differently. But I failed. One evening, alone in the quiet half-light of a two-room basement flat, with her elbows resting on my father's old desk and the Swiss family clomping about on the other side of the ceiling, my mother had realised, with lacerating clarity, that nothing would be the same again. Softly, her world folded in on itself and she began to drown in the silence.

Highgate Hill was misted in drizzle as I emerged from the mouth of the escalator. A soiled pigeon chased a chip wrapper as the wind snatched it and scuffed it down the pavement. I began the climb up Southwood Lane. I was bothered by Oliver's behaviour, unused to him keeping things back; if I was honest, what worried me most was my awareness of Piers Gaveston's mysterious familiarity with Oliver, George, even Edward. It made his appearance at the university seem a sinister contrivance; perversely, it also made him more intriguing. Despite his casual invitation, he had not yet appeared at the university, and I had begun to feel foolish for believing his throw-away lines, for thinking he had sought me out. Perhaps he was just being polite to me for my uncle's sake. But the day after next, I remembered, I would see him and my scurrying pulse betrayed my hopes. I had marked the event reverently in my diary; an organised tour of the new faculty building by the celebrated architect himself, complete with press attendance and a buffet lunch. My inclusion in these invitations now appeared to be taken for granted, though whether this was due to my connections with my uncle or with George and the Faculty Committee was unclear. It seemed, with hindsight, that the two were interdependent. The crucial thing was that Piers Gaveston, I assumed, would be present at the lunch, and this was my chance to remind him of my existence. I would not have admitted it to anyone, but tucked into the back of a notebook by my bed was the page torn from the current issue of *UpTown* magazine; my uncle and I, side by side, could have been mistaken for father and daughter, glaring at the camera with the same dark brow and severe expression. On the left of the picture, Piers Gaveston seems not to belong to us, his face a perfect portrait pout, lips curled in a half-smile. I had already looked at it far too often.

After her nervous collapse, my mother was taken for a while to be treated for depression in a hospital in Hertfordshire. So, shortly after my release from the protracted vigil at my father's hospital bed, I had found myself pulled away from the university once more for days on end to sit with her as she lay, drawn and silent, wrapped in clinical whiteness, feeling that this time it was my fault, that I should have grieved with her instead of closing myself off. But words seemed useless by that stage, as they stuffed her full of drugs and tried to piece her back together. So I sat without speaking, holding her hand; only occasionally did she seem to notice I was there at all. When, after a few months' progress, the doctor suggested a long holiday, her friends Maggie and Don had taken her to their house in the south of France, assuring me that she would come back her old self. But it's never that simple.

Instead, at forty-nine, she discovered a new self, out there in Montpellier, a self I don't know very well, and she has been living there ever since. At first, keeping the Highgate flat, she promised, would ensure that she could 'pop back all the time', but she popped back less and less, as her new job – teaching English to French businessmen – took up more of her days. She rented a little apartment to the south of the city, on the coast. In time her telephone was answered by someone called Justin with a lustrous, golfer's voice, and I realised she was on another trajectory, distant from mine. I visit at Christmas, sometimes in the summer; she came to my graduation. There are occasional letters. Birthday cards still arrive faithfully, signed 'much love, Mum and Justin'. The flat remained empty, for the nights when I needed a place in London; the unexpectedly substantial amount my father left, and the rent from the house, keeps her comfortable and allows me to study. I never felt her absence as deeply as I felt my father's.

I put the heating on. As it cranked into life, I made myself some instant coffee and drank it black because there was no milk. On my father's old desk stood my favourite picture of him, in a dark wooden frame. It was taken eighteen years ago, when Stuart Graham, one of his authors, had won the Booker Prize for his epic historical novel *Iconoclasm* (now out of print). The picture showed my father and Stuart Graham, caught off-guard after the official photographs had been taken, looking ten years younger than they were and more like two mates who had just scored the winning goal for their Sunday League team than a distinguished publisher and prize-winning novelist. My father looks riotously and happily pissed, his head thrown back, bow tie undone and his dark eyes flashing in the middle of an open-mouthed laugh. Stuart Graham has his arm hooked around my father's neck and is leaning forward, grinning madly, his bald head gleaming under the lights. I wandered over to the desk, picked it up and wiped the dust from the glass with my sleeve. Stuart Graham now writes an occasional column for the book review pages of the *Sunday Enquirer* and hasn't published a novel in eight years; my father is buried in a churchyard in Marlow. *Sic transit*.

The desk is the only thing of his left in the flat, beside the photographs. When I was a child of five or six, my mother would put me to bed and I would lie, breathless, waiting for her downstairs footsteps and the click and chatter of the television, when it was safe to creep in my bare feet into my father's study and hide under the desk between his corduroy ankles.

Edward was right to say that his brother never quite lived in the real world. My father had an extraordinary generosity of mind, manifest in his inability to imagine anyone not sharing his own wide, surprising frame of reference. The upside of this was that he never patronised people. The downside was that half the time you had no idea what he was talking about. He always seemed impressed by my existence, pleased and amused by this little person he had conjured up out of nowhere in his own image, but he had no concept of childhood, its limitations, innocence and ignorance. He always spoke to me as to another adult.

He wanted me to delight in the stories that delighted him. So, from an early age, cross-legged under the battered antique desk where he edited his manuscripts, running my fingers over the chips in its legs or counting the checks on his slippers, I spent my evenings in the company of great stories. He read me *Beowulf*, *Gilgamesh* and the *Aeneid*; *Boccaccio* and *Chrétien de Troyes*; the adventures of Odysseus and Dante the pilgrim; Genesis, Exodus, Joshua, Judges and the gospels – all in the King James version and much of it unsuitable, to my mother's vexation ('Richard, did you teach her that kind of language?'). Most of it rolled over my head, but I used to love the dark boom of his reading voice wielding the baffling words.

I asked him one day about God. God, my father said, with the weary sigh of a humanist, is what we call a myth. Hauling me on to his lap, he told me that myths were stories people invented to make sense of the world, to explain the things that can't be explained. I knew that, I told him pompously, but were they true? Everybody has myths that are true for them, he explained, frowning with exaggerated seriousness. Grandad says God is true, I persisted. Yes, well, said my father, pursing his lips. Grandad's a vicar, so it's his job to bludgeon people with myth. Then his voice softened. The point is, Fluff, he said, Grandad found a myth that means something to him, that's what's important. You can choose to share it, if you like. But the best thing to do is to find your own story, the one that's true for you. But where did you go to find it, I insisted, squirming, and he said that often you didn't realise you'd found it until you were in the middle of it, which didn't really clear things up. Later, after he died and I settled into my Arthurian research, I used to wonder if he would have been proud of me. Like him, I had chosen to live off other people's stories.

But Piers Gaveston, I reflected, seemed like someone who determined his own story. I wanted to be part of it. I wanted his energy, his unassailable self-possession and certainty and boldness; his irreverence and refusal to tout for anyone's approval.

And I wanted him. Lying in bed, the night of Edward's party, trying to reconstruct his face in my mind, I imagined I might have found the drama that my life had been lacking.

This, of course, was not a coincidence.

Chapter VII

'"Above all, though, glass is the most effective conceivable material expression of the fundamental ambiguity of atmosphere: the fact that it is at once proximity and distance, intimacy and the refusal of intimacy, communication and non-communication. Glass is the basis of a transparency without transition; we see, but cannot touch. The message is universal and abstract."'

This was greeted by an uncomprehending but politely appreciative silence.

'I'm quoting Baudrillard, of course, uh – glass being, as you will have noticed, the prime component of Lord Ryerson's initial vision for this project. And architecture is a practice that locates itself through vision, both literally and metaphorically, if you'll pardon the pun.'

Saf Kapur coughed, twice, and staunchly continued, raising his voice a notch:

'When we were first approached with the germ of an idea for this faculty, Lord Ryerson immediately began work on designs that would reflect the fluidity of borders between heterogeneous disciplines, in the search for a building that would be representative of deconstructional theories but enabling us to find orientation without the fixity of place. Are you with me? And so the last eighteen months have been about the reifying of this concept, the result being this remarkable example of modern design in which we stand today' – here he gestured towards the domed glass roof – 'a structure that is, to all intents and purposes, a symbol rather than a building, nevertheless woven inextricably into the fabric of a consumer society, at once part and not part, reflecting the consumption, in this case, of nothing less than knowledge itself.'

Saf Kapur paused at last for breath, squinting and tugging again at the lock of hair curling over the collar of his neat shirt. He was a small, slight man, not much more than thirty, and given to flicking, lizard movements of his head. The strain of expounding Ainsley Ryerson's metaphysics – the latter having been regrettably called away to Reykjavik to deal with an emergency in the atrium of the new Opera House – was beginning to show in damp patches under his arms. He had also positioned himself unwisely, so that the glass shell of the building, as well as expressing the fundamental ambiguity of atmosphere, was concentrating the early April midday sun directly into his eyes. His audience, by this stage, was beginning to fidget.

We had reached the fourth and top floor of the new faculty building, freshly completed and already bearing over its portals, in gold Roman script, the legend 'Hamilton Harvey Faculty of Cultural Studies'. It was, in essence, a giant glass bubble, supported by a framework of chrome and white girders in tessellating triangular patterns, which gave it the look of a primitive deep-sea creature with a fragile skeleton visible through its outer membrane. The top floor offered a 360-degree view high over the Livingstone Site, the water meadows and the fields beyond to the east and, to the west, as far down as the trees, spires and courtyards of the colleges backing on to the river. The floors themselves seemed not to be attached to their overarching glass casing by any visible apparatus, appearing instead to suspend themselves miraculously, linked only by a series of escalators at each side. Between the floor surface and the convex glass walls was a gap of at least six feet on all sides, so that the ground beneath you simply stopped abruptly, giving way to a vertiginous drop like a medieval cartographer's impression of the Earth's edge. ('There's a lawsuit waiting to happen,' George had remarked pragmatically, peering over the sheer drop down four storeys on to solid marble.)

The tour had so far lasted almost fifty minutes. Saf Kapur's eagerness to discharge the responsibility that had fallen on him in his senior partner's absence had clearly overcome any awareness of his audience's patience; feet were beginning to shuffle, eyes to cast around at the impressive view. Here on the fourth floor, in the on-line archive where bank after bank of virginal computer terminals stretched the length of the room, their curved fat backs in gaudy colours like Christmas baubles, I hoped we might be nearing the end. But Saf Kapur had got his second wind. Sir Edward was also absent, having been called away on pressing business, and the might of Hamilton Harvey International was represented by the person of Roger Mortimer, standing near the front of the group with one hand in his waistcoat pocket like a figure from a costume drama.

'It's a question of form and content in a constant dialectic,' Saf Kapur was saying, squinting vigorously.

'Now I understand where I've been going wrong.' George leaned across to me, *sotto voce*, his breath tickling my ear. We were standing at the back of the small group of academics, university dignitaries and selected journalists; George was thoroughly enjoying himself. 'My horizons have never been sufficiently gyroscopic.'

'Hmm?'

I had not been paying attention, my eyes fixed on Piers Gaveston. He stood near the front, head and shoulders above the rest of the group. Sunlight sloped through the glass dome to dance off his hair, throwing a fuzzy aureole around him, against which his straight profile stood out in sharp relief. He looked like an icon. Noting the object of my gaze, George shook his head slowly and remarked, smiling, 'I thought you seemed surprisingly engrossed by this disquisition on architectural theory.'

'Oh, you know. Always keen –' I felt myself blushing slightly.

'Uh, as I was saying –' Saf Kapur coughed apologetically, squinted harder and craned his neck to see who was whispering at the back. 'Architecture can only be truly understood, as in the case of this building, when its idiomorphic aspects become readable and culturally relevant –'

At that moment, Piers Gaveston, perhaps feeling the weight of our stares, turned suddenly and his gaze caught fast on mine. To my surprise, he rolled his eyes in exaggerated boredom and curled his lip back in that curious half-smile, as if uniting us surreptitiously in ridicule. I smiled back rigidly, and might have remained frozen in that position, had George ('Oh blimey, it's me') not gently elbowed me aside as he strove to reach the front.

Saf Kapur appeared, most improbably, to have finished.

'Well, now. As Chair of the Faculty Planning Committee that brought this into being, and on behalf of Professor Gaveston, Chair of the new Faculty Board,' George began, also finding himself obliged to squint genially into the light, 'I'd like to thank Mr Kapur for a most enjoyable and, indeed, enlightening explanation of the design process. I'm sure those of us who've been involved with the project from the beginning, who've watched it gradually growing out of the muddy trough that used to be the car park – and especially those of us who have tried to continue teaching or studying over the noise of the diggers – well, we had no idea there was quite so much mystical philosophy involved.' A relaxing titter rippled round the crowd. 'But seriously – it's a great privilege to be able to work in a building so admirably suited to the innovative and radical nature of this new faculty project, even if we might need to run up some curtains for it in the summer.' Another collective chuckle. George glanced questioningly at Piers, who shook his head abruptly. 'Well,' George clapped his hands together, beaming, 'If no one has any more to say, I think that's enough talk for one morning – I for one would very much like to reify the concept of lunch. Oh, one moment – I'm sorry, Mr Mortimer – did you –?'

Roger was blustering his way to the front, wiping his hands nervously on his dog-tooth waistcoat. 'Just briefly, as the – ah

– representative of Hamilton Harvey International, first let me convey Sir Edward's sincere regret that he was, most unfortunately, obliged to travel to Beijing yesterday – but had he been here, he would have wanted, I know, to express his utmost admiration for Lord Ryerson's magnificent – indeed, we might say, unparalleled – project. This is, of course, not the first time that Sir Edward has – ah – collaborated with Lord Ryerson, but we at HHI feel sure that, given the – ah – *expansive* nature of this project – that's expansive with an a, of course, in case anyone misheard –' he permitted himself a small chuckle – 'and the amount of investment, it will become, in time, perhaps, the most celebrated instance of what is already an extremely valuable working relationship. And of course, Sir Edward is delighted that this splendid building can be his gift to this fine and revered university.' He paused expectantly. George was biting back a smile. 'So – ah – without further ado, thank you.'

There was a limp sprinkling of applause, as the group turned and moved as one towards the escalator. The grand tour of the new building was being marked with a buffet lunch and champagne in the ground-floor foyer. Piers Gaveston had disappeared, pursued by journalists. I jostled my way through to George on the escalator. He had been away for a fortnight, visiting his son in Canada, and I had not had a chance to speak to him alone since Edward's party.

'George, may I ask you something?'

'As long as it's not to explain the sectional flow of movement through the physical manifestations of open space. I'm afraid, alas, I'm utterly in the dark.'

'It's about Professor Gaveston.'

'Ye-e-s?' George pushed his half-glasses to the end of his nose and blinked owlishly at me over them. I could feel my neck getting hot again.

'It's just that – I was wondering. Remember at Edward's party last month, you said you didn't know much about him.'

'Well, he's a very enigmatic chap, that's part of his charm. Don't you agree?'

'George! I'm being serious.'

'I'm sorry – it's hard to tell.'

'Look – I know this is all a fit-up and he's been put in place by Hamilton Harvey Int –'

'Now, now. That could be construed as slander.'

'All the same – he's been made a professor here, out of nowhere, in one of the country's most prestigious universities – surely he must have some credentials? And don't we have a right to know what qualifies him to have this Chair? You must have had to check that before endorsing his appointment. I'm sorry to ask – I'm just curious,' I added, unconvincingly.

George sighed, and was quiet for a moment as we changed escalators, hesitating to allow others on first, so that we found ourselves at the back. Through the glass, clouds cast fugitive shadows on to the metal panels.

'Very well.' He tucked his hands into the pockets of his old jacket. 'I know this much of his CV – he has a doctorate from NYU in some obscure backwater of post-modern film theory and held a teaching post at a college in California for a few years. He was involved, in some unspecified way, in the film business in New York – I think direction and screenwriting – but also some acting, I believe. Some years ago, you probably don't remember, when Edward was expanding his American enterprises, he launched a cultural and current affairs magazine intended to rival the *New Yorker* which folded after a year or so. It was called *Forum,* if I remember rightly. Piers was its film critic – which is how Edward came across him, or at least I think that's right. And for the past couple of years, as far as I can gather, he's been engaged in research at the University of Buenos Aires. I'm afraid that all sounds very vague, but I can offer you no more.'

'It's a bit feeble. And how come no one's ever heard of him?'

George shrugged. 'The media is an ephemeral business, Gaby, as you know. You're only recognised for a moment. Besides, if he's spent most of his time living in the Americas, it's no surprise he's not a household name over here.'

'But odd that he should suddenly choose to come over here now, don't you think? I wonder why.'

George appeared impatient with the conversation. 'Well, you'd have to ask him that. Buenos Aires is not the sort of place one would want to stay too long, from my experience. Listen – I had the same concerns as you do at first, but I met with him several times before the appointment was sanctioned, and I was satisfied that he's an unusually talented young man. There's a very good mind there, even if –' His attention appeared to drift.

'Even if what?'

'What? Oh, doesn't matter. Nothing. Let's have some lunch, shall we? Keeping up with that young chap's theorising has given me a monster of an appetite. Ah, Miles! Did you enjoy the lecture as much as we did?'

Miles Park, apparently winding his watch at the bottom of the escalator, tugged his sleeve down as we approached, folded his arms and nodded affably at George's greeting.

'I couldn't help feeling its idiomorphic aspects weren't entirely readable.' He grinned. 'Mind you, I like all this business.' He gestured towards the small fountain that stood in the centre of the marble lobby, then looked up and around at the glass walls. 'Though it'll be like a bloody greenhouse in the summer – I don't think with all their symbolism and spatial awareness they've given much thought to the practicalities. Covered in pigeon shit before you know it, and imagine trying to get up there to clean it. Still – the equipment's *fantastic*, don't you think? I'm almost converted.' He nodded towards the refreshments. 'Here, let me get you both a drink.'

Miles wandered away to the long tables laid down the side of the lobby, decked with a selection of cold meats and dips. I had deliberately turned my back to the sliding glass doors of the entrance, where a distractingly life-like bust of Sir Edward stood atop a pink granite plinth, glowering imperiously across the marble with blank bronze eyes. I could feel its stare between my shoulder blades. The guests and faculty staff milled around the foyer, their chatter bouncing off the smooth surfaces.

'Very tempting to draw a large cock on its head, isn't it?' said Jake Lennox to someone behind me – evidently with reference to the bust – in one of those unfortunate moments when the white noise of conversation inexplicably dropped away, leaving his comment hanging loudly in the air. There was a sticky silence in which everyone turned to look at him, then the silence dissolved into embarrassed laughter.

Piers Gaveston, who had suddenly materialised beside me holding a small bottle of water, still wore that same curious smile that didn't show his teeth; a smile which suggested he was mildly amused at other people's expense.

'You must find this disconcerting.' He inclined his head slightly towards the bust, then ran a hand slowly over its moulded hair.

'It's a bit odd, yes.'

'Like looking at yourself.'

'Well – not exactly,' I said, mildly affronted. He watched me for a moment.

'I've told you before – you have the same mouth, look,' and he ran a finger over the bust's sculpted lips, while his eyes stayed fixed on my own mouth.

I wasn't sure how to respond.

'We were going to have a coffee,' he said after a while, stretching and looking past me, as if it were somehow my fault this had not yet happened.

'Oh – yes.' I couldn't look up at his face, so instead followed the direction of his gaze as it travelled calmly around the clusters of people chatting, and tried to ignore the pinch of disappointment that his original suggestion of a drink had now been scaled down to 'coffee'. Coffee was what you did in the afternoon, when you wanted to make it clear the meeting was not of a romantic nature.

'I'm away for the next couple of weeks. Week after suit you?'

'Uh – fine.'

'Wednesday? I'll be up here in the afternoon. Where's a good place to talk?'

I tried to think, my mind oddly empty, unsure whether 'up here' meant in town or in the faculty itself. I looked quickly up at his face. He was so – so perfect, too blond and sleek and Hollywood – he made this little market town seem somehow shabbier. I couldn't think of anywhere that might impress him.

'There's always the Brown Cow, I suppose.'

Predictably, his fine nose wrinkled slightly. 'Brown Cow's full of students.'

'Well – I'm a student.'

His half-smile widened briefly, offering a glimpse of white teeth. He touched me lightly on the arm.

'Yes, but you're a bit different, aren't you? You know the kind I mean, smoking their spitty roll-ups all afternoon and discussing the essence of being as if they have any idea what they're talking about.' He produced an affected shudder.

'If you don't like students, won't that be something of a handicap as a professor?'

'I'll do my best to stay away from them.' He twisted the corner of his mouth again. 'I remember the Brown Cow, it was exactly that crowd. Holding forth on the meaning of art, reading each other their tone-deaf poetry. Then they all go on to direct unwatchable plays at Edinburgh and none of them are heard of again. I don't imagine it's changed.'

'Do you know the town well, then?'

Piers smiled. 'I've visited. Listen – how about that new place down on the Quayside, with the palms in the window? That looks quiet.'

'Sam's? It is, usually, in the afternoons.'

'Good. Four o'clock, then – two weeks on Wednesday.'

Just at that moment, George wandered over clutching a samosa.

'Professor Gaveston, how nice to see you!' He wiped a hand on his jacket and extended it; Piers shook it briefly, with noticeable hesitation. 'Did you enjoy the talk?'

'Rarely have I enjoyed myself more,' replied Piers, unsmiling.

George twinkled. 'Perhaps we should ask that chap to lecture here. He seems admirably qualified.'

'Oh, he'd be ideal,' said Piers, this time breaking into a smile. 'Transparent as his building. Emperor's new clothes.'

'Pardon?' I asked, not wanting to be edged out of the conversation.

'Theories of theories. The *sine qua non* of academic success in our times – isn't that right, George?'

'Quite right.' George was smiling back at him, but analytically, as though enjoying a separate joke.

'The Russian novelist Dombrovsky,' Piers folded his arms across his chest and looked over our heads to the other side of the foyer, as if addressing someone else, 'wrote a book in 1978 entitled *The Faculty of Useless Knowledge*. Curiously, I find myself reminded of it more and more.'

George let out a barking laugh and clapped Piers heartily on the arm. 'I suspected you were on our side.'

A spindly woman from the University Press Office pinched nervously at George's sleeve.

'Dr Fenton, might I have a quick word?'

'Of course, of course.' He turned to go with her. 'Oh, and we must sort out this course content meeting, Piers, and go over the forms. Will you give me a call?'

'Certainly, George, let's keep our forms and content in constant dialectic.'

George was still shaking his head and laughing as he crossed the room.

'I must go too.' Piers finished the last of his water and made to move away. 'Oh yes' – he half-turned back, as if with an afterthought, his expression suddenly colder – 'and tell your friend Oliver Dowland that if he wants to write a profile of me, he'd be wise to check his facts with me first. I'm happy to talk to him if he wishes, but I get very unhappy if people print information that's conjectural or unsubstantiated. And Oliver should know better. Tell him to think very carefully before he writes a single word he and his sources wouldn't be willing to stand up and prove. You tell him.'

'Okay, but' – I was baffled – 'how did you know?'

'I'm very well informed. I mean it' – he pointed a finger close to my face, almost threatening, his smile displaced by a hard cast to his jaw – 'tell Oliver he's welcome to contact me before he publishes, but if he doesn't, he's got to be prepared for the consequences.'

He took a few steps backwards, still pointing meaningfully at me, then broke into an open laugh, as if this last exchange had been merely a joke, before spinning round, straight into the enthusiastic embrace of two female journalists and their attendant photographers, who had been lurking hopefully at his shoulder all morning and now greeted him with gratified smiles.

Buoyed with champagne and by the solid prospect of a meeting with Piers Gaveston in three weeks – and trying to quash my sense of his strangeness about Oliver – I walked home across the fields from the Livingstone Site in better spirits than I had been for some time. The paths were unusually quiet, but the sky seemed lighter and higher, somehow, rinsed and glassy from the recent rain, and there was a sweetness in the late-afternoon air that suggested spring might be about to settle properly at any moment. Around the fallen tree by the wooden bridge the red cows browsed moodily, churning up the grass; restless sounds disturbed the trees overhead. Along the river a row of poplars stood against the horizon like dark flames. I breathed deeply, unexpectedly optimistic, feeling the sudden thrill of possibility.

Tennyson Street, on the other side of the fields, was narrow and lined with tall, shabby terraced houses. Outside each house the railings were decked with rusting second-hand bicycles, some with a wheel or more missing, some just a wheel missing the bike. Cooking smells drifted up from the basement kitchens: frying onions, pasta sauces and cheap mince. We didn't mind it too much, Bobby and I; we had been living at number 42 for a year and a half and had grown to fit the house. I always felt the absence when he returned to the States for Christmas and the summer vacation; the house became colder, full of strange noises, the street dingier.

I hadn't expected to find anyone in, but as I pushed open the front door I caught a whiff of fresh marijuana and, from somewhere upstairs, faint strains of the Grateful Dead. A rack of Bobby's washing, all of it the uniform American grey of sweat pants, was drying in front of the radiator in the hall, blocking the stairs. For a moment, in my new-found state of optimism, I imagined bringing Piers Gaveston here – and almost laughed aloud.

I had meant, when I got home, to call Oliver at his office, to relay to him my curious conversation with Piers Gaveston and to quiz him again on the nature of their relationship, which was evidently more complicated than either of them was prepared to allow. But with Bobby in the house I felt inhibited, as if the matter were too private to risk being overheard. I unzipped my jacket and hooked it on the back of the door.

Bobby appeared at the top of the stairs in a pair of damp running shorts and a Harvard vest, a white towel draped over his head like a statue of the Virgin and a crooked joint in one corner of his mouth. I paused at the bottom, leaning on the bannister.

'What are you doing home so early?'

'Gave myself the afternoon off and went running, it was such a nice day. I just came back for a shower.'

'How far today?'

'Six, seven miles. Not bad.'

'You'd get further if you didn't light a reefer every time you stopped.'

Bobby pinched the thin roll-up between his thumb and forefinger, removed it from his lips and considered it for a moment.

'It's a Yin Yang thing,' he said, inhaling thoughtfully and allowing the smoke to saunter out through his nostrils. 'It's all about balance. Listen, I was going to cook some chilli, you want some?'

'Thanks.'

'Hey – and your friend Paul called. Again.'

'Oh. Today?'

I felt the familiar tug of guilt. I'd barely thought of Paul – nice, considerate, straightforward, unimaginative Paul, quietly excited only by his own researches into the aquatic development of polar bears – since the moment I was first caught in Piers Gaveston's lupine gaze.

'And yesterday. And the day before. Hey –' Bobby paused to exhale a gentle drift of smoke, 'it's none of my business, I don't care if you dump the guy or not, but it's getting a little embarrassing having to make excuses for you all the time. What do you want me to say when he asks why you're not returning his calls? I mean, I think he's a dick, but at least put him out of his misery – I can't do it for you. You breakin dat boy's heart, girlfriend, you a dog.' He made a peculiar hip-hop gesture with his right arm to accompany the accent.

'Don't be a git.'

Bobby grinned.

'Go call him now, or you don't get any supper.'

'All right, all right.' I pushed past the laundry rack to the basement stairs. 'Do you want me to do anything in the kitchen?'

'No, it's fine,' Bobby called back. 'Although maybe you could clear some of my shit off the table so we can eat on it.'

The basement sitting room was always dim and, because it opened on to the kitchen, stale cooking smells often hovered,

113

seeping into the soft furnishings. The top of the window was barely above street level, so that all you could see of the outside world from the sofa were scurrying feet and the lower halves of bicycle wheels. I switched on a table lamp, took out a cigarette and, fumbling irritably with a box of matches through two failed attempts, managed to get it alight. Breathing out slowly, I tried to will back my earlier, positive mood. I was bothered by Bobby's joking accusation that I was breaking Paul's heart.

It was a phrase that had always irked me. Romance, and the language of romance; the over-used tropes, the worn imagery – none of it was real to me. Nothing had occurred in the course of my brief history of relationships to convince me that such concepts bore any relation to what really went on between people. This history goes as follows:

First, Patrice, the laconic, Gauloise-chomping, scooter-riding Parisian barman and part-time philosophy student whom I have already mentioned. Not a great meeting of minds, perhaps, but he was good-looking in a Gallic, sallow way, and it was my first taste of sex, so I remember those nine months I spent studying in Paris, clinging to the back of his leather jacket as we tilted through the narrow streets of Saint-Germain, with some affection.

Later, in my first year at university, there was Ben – Classicist and county-level tennis player – a relationship that within months had slipped into a familiar and reassuring routine. Ben was a pragmatist; he avoided fulsome declarations, and I was glad, because they would have sounded false; though I have no doubt that we did love each other in our own way. We stayed together without probing very far beneath the surface because, all things considered, it was nicer than the alternative – but I was pestered by an anxiety that refused to disappear, a fear that I had missed something important. We finally ran aground the summer I graduated, when Ben proposed at the top of Mount Olympus and I realised, with an ache in my throat, that the stale conformity of a long marriage was already settling on us. We wore t-shirts in bed and had sex once a month if we were lucky. Nonetheless, I almost said yes; almost persuaded myself that it was time to stop looking – that this was all that could be expected. Not grand, operatic passion, but friendly compromise, unfolding into a comfortable family life; something you settled for. And yet, at the last minute I couldn't do it.

In three years we had acquired two items of property in common: a watercolour of the Norfolk Broads and a cafetière. I kept the painting, on the grounds that Ben had complained all the way through that boating holiday and had never even pretended to like the picture; the cafetière had been a present to both of us, so to save further argument and to satisfy a desire for symbolism, Ben threw it out of the window where it fell three storeys and shattered on the pavement. I watched it break, feeling sad and, at the same time, hugely relieved.

After Ben there was Declan O'Callaghan, a writer friend of Oliver's; short, witty, a committed drinker, good company – and, it turned out, keener to get to know my uncle than me. That lasted six months, on and off, until I learned about the other women – several – which hurt my dignity more than my heart. Since then there had been one or two brief encounters, hardly worth remembering, and, most recently, Paul. And still I had never felt the storms and the raging seas, never lost my appetite, never been driven to distraction and sleepless nights or sent tear-stained letters of anguished passion; never been in love. Almost as if I chose for safety each time. 'Do you good to get your heart broken, Fluff,' my father once said, thoughtfully but not unkindly. 'You'd see the world differently.' But I was not a cynic, I told him, just a realist. There was sex, and there was friendship, and if you were lucky, you sometimes got the two together. So I said, though secretly I still hoped the storms might come. My father smiled, in that infuriating way that fathers do when they know that they know better.

I crushed out my cigarette in a conch shell, once plucked from a golden shore in Costa Rica by Bobby's brother and now stuffed with cigarette ends and sweet wrappers, and turned my attention to the large dining table, lazily strewn with books, files, papers, newspaper cuttings, pencil sharpenings and, balanced on top of two uneven books, Bobby's laptop, whirring gently to itself as primary-coloured naked women swirled hypnotically over the screen. I shut the computer down and began to gather the papers together, trying to observe some semblance of order. Glancing casually at the titles on the spines, I arranged his books into a pile. I had never taken much interest in Bobby's work, though of course I knew, from his constant badgering about my uncle, his basic area of research. As I began to tidy, though, my eye was caught by various headlines, and I found myself pausing to read his notes, with the same guilty frisson you feel on stumbling across someone else's diary. Except that this wasn't particularly revealing; the papers consisted mainly of policy documents and lists of export transactions, together with back copies from the seventies of *Newsweek*, the *Middle East Journal* and the *New York Times* magazine. There were sheafs of photocopies from the U.S. Congress House Committee on Foreign Affairs, with titles like *Middle East, 1971: The Need To Strengthen the Peace* and *The Persian Gulf, 1973: The Continuing Debate on Arms Sales*, paperclipped to extensive ruled sheets torn from a spiral-bound notebook and covered with Bobby's fluid, strangely feminine script; dates were underscored heavily, some sentences highlighted in blue. Curious, I thought, how other people's research always looks more interesting than your own.

It was as I was sliding the photocopies into a file that I saw it. The topmost of a sheaf of similar articles, it was a brief news report from the *New York Times* dated October 1973, covering Egypt's attempted invasion of Israel. Why I paused especially to look at it, I don't know, but it was the by-line that caught my eye: 'ANDREW EPSTEIN Jerusalem, Oct. 7 –'.

Chapter VIII

He doesn't look like you would imagine a professor. It's not his movie-star looks – the bone structure to die for, the fierce eyes, green as a cat's, or his sensual mouth, with that strange smile that is somehow inviting and condescending at once, nor his long, languid limbs and the way he drapes himself over a chair, flicking his soft hair from his face. It's something more elemental, more physical. Piers Gaveston has an intense physical presence that you don't expect to get with intellectuals; there is a glint of danger about him, a sense that what he is is so much more than what he allows you to see. Just being near him is an adrenalin rush; he smiles, and I feel the neurocircuits in my brain exploding. He is wearing dark Mario Ricci jeans with an open-necked linen shirt, and smells of citrus.

We meet in the café of the newly completed Hamilton Harvey Faculty of Cultural Studies, already hailed as the most ambitious, progressive and costly development in higher education in the last twenty years. The glass-domed building itself, designed by Ainsley Ryerson and already shortlisted for the Hansen Prize, has cost over £21 million. Gaveston has just taken on the top job here, as Chair of a faculty that will have closer ties than any university previously had with commerce and the media, controversial not only because it's effectively the first English university funded by the private sector, but because it's set to modernise beyond recognition a university that prides itself on seven hundred years of unbroken and elitist tradition.

Gaveston takes this all in his stride. 'Of course I'm conscious of the need to recognise the value of tradition,' he says, thoughtfully. 'Not just in this university, but in the country's history as a whole. Language and literature, music and the visual arts – preserving this awareness of a shared cultural past is what gives us our sense of identity. Continuity is very important to me. The scaremongers try to suggest that modernising means indiscriminately sweeping aside the old values, but that kind of reactionary thinking is based on nostalgia, and nostalgia filters out a lot of the past, doesn't see it accurately. Progress and tradition are two halves of a whole. You can't build with no foundations, and that's not what this project is about.'

Gaveston's appointment surprised many in the academic community, who consider his qualifications as unorthodox as the faculty itself. But his novelty, his unusual history, are part of his powerful charisma. He has seen a lot of life in his 33 years. He has modelled for Van der Wald and Akemi Igawa. He has a doctorate from New York University, and taught Media at Carfield College, Sacramento, where he wrote a book on the history of English film. He ran his own film production company in New York, where he also did some acting, and has worked as a critic and journalist for various publications on both sides of the Atlantic. He is making a television series on the history of Englishness in art, to be shown here next Spring, and this week takes his place on the panel of BBC2's review and discussion programme In Camera. *So how does he feel about the criticism he will inevitably attract?*

'There will always be people who are bitter about someone else's success,' he says, with a frighteningly sexy smile. 'But boundaries are more fluid now – I think people have come to recognise that those who spend their lives cloistered in the academic world have very little of value to offer students. It's far more attractive if you can relate what you're teaching to a wider experience. That's why most of the teaching staff at the new faculty, with a few exceptions, will be people who've worked in related areas of the media, not solely in academia. A lot of academics, particularly at this unversity, have never stuck their heads over the parapet. I think it helps to have seen a different side of life.'

Mostly, he shies away from talking about his private life. He won't discuss whether he has a partner, and seems uncomfortable when I suggest that his appointment will inevitably attract hordes of young women to the university. 'I do resent this determination to intrude into people's private lives in order to categorise them. I fail to see why it should be of any interest. There's a media obsession at the moment with defining everyone always in relation to some 'other', which I consider entirely unnecessary. "I am myself alone", as Shakespeare's Richard the Third said.'

His eyes go right through you when he speaks, but you sense that there's a mistrust of intimacy. He pauses before answering questions, and you can almost feel the force of him thinking, weighing up his answer . . .

And so it went on, and on, for a further four glossy pages. Piers's flamboyant appearance in the magazine supplement of the *Sunday Ledger* ('Becki Burke Meets') was made yet more embarrassing by the editor's decision to revive his latent modelling talents and use the article to double as a fashion spread. Each page was illustrated with lustrous photographs of Piers in different costumes, draped evocatively over various architectural features of St Dunstan's College – lounging in the arch of a cloister gazing at the sky, one knee drawn up and an arm resting loosely on it, or leaning pensively over the balustrade of the old bridge, a breeze lifting his hair, or crouching on rickety steps, smiling seductively into the camera from under his long lashes – all framed with captions like: 'Piers Gaveston wears charcoal silk suit by Julio Moreno, £1,675, and ponyskin biker boots, to order, by Marietta Delaney, 147 Sloane Street. Hair by Shandi at Ponce's of Mayfair'. Even Piers's own words, some of which might have sounded reasonable in another context, appeared, against the backdrop of Becki Burke's whooshing prose, affected and ridiculous.

I might have missed it altogether, not being, on principle, a regular reader of my uncle's publications, had Oliver not called me on the morning of the Sunday after my meeting with Piers in the new faculty.

'Have you seen?' he squealed. 'Gaveston's done the Becki Burke interview! It's a huge spread too – I can't believe he's been so stupid!'

'I thought she was quite high profile?'

'Oh, God, she's hopeless, though!' Oliver crowed. 'You know – she usually does actors and pop groups, and she just gushes all over them and tries to bed them, but she's completely useless as an interviewer. She's only got that job because her mother used to sleep with – who was it? Some sixties rocker. Funny that Edward's decided to market Piers Gaveston through the frothy celeb corner – don't you agree? I thought they were bending over backwards to present him as an intellectual heavyweight.'

'What's the piece like?'

Oliver laughed. 'Terrible. It makes him sound quite in love with himself. Though why that should surprise me. But he's going to get some stick from his new colleagues – he says professional academics don't know anything.'

'Ouch.'

'I know – it's as if he wants to be lynched on his first day.'

'I can think of a few people who'll take serious umbrage at that. I suppose they must have rushed the interview through because he knew you were doing your profile?'

'No, that mag would go to press on the Monday, so they'll have done the interview at least two weeks ago. Sneaky. My piece got spiked in the end, anyway. Mike got wind of the interview.'

'So you didn't call him?'

Oliver paused.

'No – no, I didn't. Still' – his voice brightened – 'you have to admire what they're doing.'

'What are they doing?'

'Creating an image. Edward wants Piers Gaveston to be the next new new thing, so he's marketing him professionally – it's what Edward's best at. You'll see – he won't do any other interviews now. And hence the TV stuff – I bet there's HHI money behind that as well. And I'll tell you something else,' Oliver added, with a hint of gleeful malice, 'he's not thirty-three, that's for sure.'

'How do you know?'

'I just do. Now go and buy it, and call me back when you've read it.'

'Over to you.'

Piers Gaveston pulled his cigarette slowly away from his lips, paused for a beat, then breathed out silently, letting the smoke slide through his teeth. He was looking away from me, out through the plate-glass windows of Sam's Coffee Shoppe (you couldn't spell 'shoppe' any other way in this town, not if you wanted to bring in the dollar), out across the river. Sunlight skittered over the surface of the water, already crowded with punts; tourists stepped uncertainly on to slippery boards as the student tour guides cruised past them, tanned from the past week of good weather, flinging their poles in the air one-handed and catching them with a bored confidence, tossing out crumbs of cribbed history as they ducked under bridges. Against the bollards on the quayside, tangles of bicycles piled up and families with laughing children sat dangling their legs over the wall, dripping ice-cream. On the opposite bank, clumps of begonias bloomed crimson against the buttery stone of St Asaph's College.

Inside Sam's, the air was cooler, with piano jazz bleeding quietly from the overhead speakers. In the thick slats of light from the windows, motes of dust slowly spiralled.

I hesitated, watching his face. After three weeks of nervous anticipation I was here, opposite him, and he was expecting me to say something intelligent. A fine balance was needed between demonstrating my expert knowledge on the one hand, and avoiding the appearance of a bluestocking who didn't know how to have fun on the other. My heart was skidding just to look at him.

'I'm afraid the neurocircuits in my brain are exploding.'

His eyes narrowed, and for an awful moment he glared at me, unspeaking, and I feared I had overestimated his sense of humour. Then he covered his face with both hands in mock despair, and I heard low laughter trickling out from between his fingers.

'Oh, Jesus,' he said, eventually, pinching the bridge of his nose between his thumb and forefinger. 'It *was* that bad, wasn't it? Becki Burke, God save us. Edward told me she was their best interviewer.'

'She's, um – very well known.'

'Maybe so. She was the most vapid, talentless, giddy, irrelevant woman I've ever met.'

'She spoke very highly of you.'

'Hmm.' He pushed a hand through his hair. 'You wouldn't believe it – I couldn't get rid of her. And, for the record, at no time did she get close enough to smell me. That's entirely fictional.'

'So are you going to sue her?'

Piers looked briefly puzzled, then appeared to remember our last conversation. He sucked in his cheeks and his mouth curved into a slow smile.

'No. I'm going to have her fired.' He stretched his fingers and then cracked his knuckles, suddenly. 'Seriously – did you read it and think – "he sounds like an idiot"?'

'Not at all.' I paused, and couldn't stop a grin from twitching. 'I am myself alone . . .'

'Fuck. Off.' He flicked a sachet of sugar at my head. 'That's it, I'm not speaking to you again.'

'I did wonder why – you know – why you didn't do an interview with someone serious, like A. D. Lodge or one of those guys?'

He sighed and looped his hands behind his head.

'Oh, this is all Edward and George's project, I just do as I'm told. They're trying to strike a difficult balance. Difficult – impossible, in my opinion. I'm supposed to demonstrate how rock-and-roll this is, that's why Edward didn't want one of the old boys like Alex Lodge doing the first interview. But if I'd known – Becki Burke is beyond parody. Should've realised when she turned up in those unforgivable PVC trousers. Were the photos awful too?'

'Photos were the best bit.'

'Really? Better than my finely honed pronouncements on the future of art and scholarship?'

'I didn't know you were a model.'

'Listen' – he fixed me earnestly – 'I was very poor when I was younger. I didn't want to do those photos, but he told me it was artistic, he promised they'd never be published.'

He flicked his hair coquettishly and smiled his thin-lipped smile again, and I realised that he did know how to laugh at himself after all. Suddenly I liked him better.

'Don't you have a say in how you do your publicity? I mean, are you happy about it?'

'Am I *happy*?' He turned back to me briefly, surprised. He seemed about to say something, but paused on the edge of it, laughed harshly, and turned his gaze back to the window. 'God. Is anyone? Don't answer that – you're probably one of those annoying people who are, and then I'll despise you. Come on, tell me about Arthur.'

A waitress with improbably yellow hair and an apron smudged with ketchup arrived loudly beside me.

'Yes?' she asked, with menace, pencil poised.

'Uh – just a black coffee, thanks.'

She scribbled resentfully.

'Yes?' she demanded a second time, in the same tone, turning to Piers, then her jaw dropped.

He looked up and smiled. The girl straightened miraculously, breathing in her stomach.

'Um, how can I help you, please?'

'Thanks – decaf cappuccino, a bottle of still mineral water, and a croissant or something.'

'Or something – like what?' She looked anxious.

'Well – something like a croissant. What have you got?'

'What have we got that's *like* a croissant? What – but not *actually* a croissant? Um –' The girl was turning puce in her efforts to please. Piers looked wearily patient.

'Don't worry – a croissant's fine.'

'We might have a *chocolate* croissant,' she blurted triumphantly, dredging up this information from a recess.

'No, an ordinary croissant will be lovely, thank you.'

'Okay,' she said, breathing out with relief while folding her hands in front of her and making no move to go. She continued to stare at Piers as if paralysed.

He tapped his fingers on the wooden table top, lit another cigarette.

'And will it be long?' he asked eventually.

'Oh – no, sorry, sorry, sir –' And she flushed again and scuttled away.

I smiled. 'You must get that all the time.'

Piers shrugged, as if it didn't occur to him that I was half-teasing. 'You get used to it. But tell me about Arthur. That's why we're here.'

'Arthur. Okay. Where should I start? I mean, tell me what you need to know.'

'All right.' He swivelled his chair decisively to face me – he had been sitting side-on, so that he could look out of the window – and laid his palms down on the table, the smouldering cigarette poking straight up like a chimney between his second and third fingers. 'This series I'm doing – it's still called *Reflecting England*. Six fifty-minute programmes. Channel Four at nine o'clock on Sunday nights, starting next March if all goes well, to coincide with the opening of the English Parliament. High production values, big publicity, tie-in book, usual crap. In effect, it's a history of how art has been used to enforce or sell a sense of national identity. How art has defined the essence of Englishness, or been used as propaganda – but there's so much to get in, we're going to have to be very selective. At the moment, we're planning to divide it into three programmes on literature – to include drama – one on music, one on visual arts and one on film. And I want it to be quite an eclectic mix – the obvious, like Shakespeare,

Elgar, Constable, Hitchcock – but I want some quirky stuff in there too. Especially ideas of how English art has grown out of national crises of identity. That's why I'd like to start with Arthur.'

'How far back do you want to go?'

'How far do I need to go?'

'Ah. That's the tricky bit.'

That was the problem with Arthur. No one knew quite how far back you did have to go to find him – though everyone, from the New Age crystal-vendors in Glastonbury market to the most revered professors of Celtic and Anglo-Saxon in the land could, and did, argue about it until the cows came home and went back out again. How far back? As far back as Nennius, perhaps, the ninth-century Welsh chronicler whose *Historia Britonum* is the first to mention Arthur and his twelve triumphant battles against the Saxons? Or earlier, to the monk Gildas of Strathclyde in the sixth century, writing *De Excidio Britanniae*, his feverish jeremiad on the ruin of Britain, in which he gives an account of Arthur's battle of Badon Hill, the last (temporary) rout of the Saxons, though – significantly – failing to mention Arthur himself? Or a little later, to the anonymous tenth-century *Life of St Goeznovius*, the first document to call him King of the Britons and the first to suggest, enigmatically and by omission, that he didn't die like other men? Or perhaps we should leave these early Latin histories altogether; of doubtful provenance and untrustworthy, surviving only in damaged, later manuscript copies, vulnerable to all the errors and embellishments of transcription and dissemination – warped fairground mirrors of the past.

Piers became interested in a loose thread on his sleeve, and I thought for a moment I had lost him.

'This is good,' he said unexpectedly, looking up. 'Carry on.'

Pointing to where Arthur's enduring legend began is much simpler, I explained, now into my stride. In 1136 Geoffrey of Monmouth, that wily Welsh priest of Breton descent, conjured the patriotic Arthur who would stay with us all the way down to Tennyson and Hollywood. Adapted, ornamented, borrowed, bowdlerised, translated, twisted and reshaped, certainly, but the magical, mythical Arthur that furnished the romances of Chrétien and Marie de France and all the histories that followed is recognisably Geoffrey's. He also becomes Malory's *rex quondam, rexque futurus* – the Once and Future King, embodiment of that brave spirit of English resistance to would-be conquerors. Appropriated first by the British as their defender against the Saxons, later taken up by the Saxons when they were crushed by the Normans, and, later still, by the Normans who considered it might be prudent to find themselves a suitable national hero before Arthur provoked anything more serious than a few local uprisings – even going so far as to stage the exhumation of his tomb at Glastonbury to quell the rumours of his return – Arthur's political significance in the twelfth and thirteenth centuries almost overshadowed his marvellous sword, his Round Table, his Holy Grail and all the other stuff of fables.

I paused, flushed, waiting to see if I had acquitted myself. Piers uncrossed his legs, leaned back and linked his hands behind his neck again. He looked thoughtful.

'And nothing changes. Still the nation waits for a saviour. That's why England will never be a proper republic, and why the new parliament will be so popular – because the English are conditioned to look for a hero. They want someone stronger than themselves to look up to. Bring on any new political leader with an ounce of charisma, claiming to make the country great again, and they rush to believe in him, like children.' He tapped his lighter on the table for emphasis.

I frowned. It was hard to tell if he was being deliberately pompous.

'That's a bit of an arrogant generalisation. I don't think that's necessarily a national trait.'

'Oh, you don't? You think it's the human condition, I suppose? The void created by the death of God, perhaps?' He glanced up and caught my eye, briefly. 'Aren't you looking for a hero?' A corner of his mouth twisted in amusement. My face heated quickly. 'Although that would prove me right' – he went on – 'since I assume you're English.'

'Yes – aren't you?'

He looked out across the river again to the turrets of the college beyond.

'I was born here.'

'But you talk so derisively about the English, as though you're different.'

He shrugged, the merest twitch of one shoulder.

'My father was French. Apparently. And I've lived away from this country for a lot of my life. So – no, I suppose I don't really identify. I don't feel that I' – he tipped his head back, seeking the right word – '*belong*. But perhaps that's a good thing. It means you can observe from a distance.'

'Why are you so interested in English identity, then?'

He turned; a slant of sunlight caught his half-profile, casting the angles of his face into shadow. He glanced at me, quickly, with serious eyes, then turned back to the window. For a while he didn't answer.

'It's a way of looking for something you've been denied, I suppose. You always romanticise the things you've lost.'

I leaned forward, nodding, but just then the smitten waitress reappeared, sloshing coffee into saucers as she tried to lower her tray to the table without unfixing her eyes from Piers. The mood was broken.

'So Geoffrey made the whole thing up, did he, as Welsh nationalist propaganda?' Piers shook himself briefly, cracking the lid from his bottle of water.

'Well, opinion is divided, as usual. He wrote it at a time when there were some Welsh independence movements, but at the time a lot of people did accept it as true history, because he says at the beginning that he's taken it from a lost manuscript in the ancient British language. Although another chronicler – William of Newburgh – wrote a very damning criticism of Geoffrey's book right at the end of the twelfth century, saying he'd dreamed the whole thing, and that he'd invented the legend of Arthur for the Britons because he was afraid of them.'

'And William said that to keep the Normans happy?'

'Exactly. The Arthur cult was catching on by the twelfth century, becoming something of a banner for anyone opposed to Norman rule. Even a hundred years after the Conquest, there was still almost no mixing or interbreeding between the Norman aristocracy and the Saxons. In fact, there was an incident when some French monks visited Bodmin and caused a riot by suggesting to the locals that there was no truth in their belief that Arthur would come again. They were mobbed.'

'Hence the tomb, I suppose. How did that come about?'

'Oh, that was a very clever political move. Glastonbury was already the main English shrine by the time of the Conquest, and there was a great pride in its history, because it had been a great abbey before the Normans came. So the Normans quickly brought in their own abbots to run it, like they did with most of the English monasteries, and staging the discovery of Arthur's tomb allowed them very neatly to prove that Arthur was really dead, but also to reclaim Glastonbury from its pre-Norman myths. They claimed that the king had been told where to find Arthur's tomb in a kind of atavistic dream. At least, Gerald of Wales said so.'

'Did it stop the uprisings?'

'Not at first. The cult carried on, but by the end of the twelfth century Chrétien's Arthurian romances had taken off – not that they were widely known in England – but the legend gradually became more diffuse – it got jumbled up with fiction and lost some of its political edge. Even so –' I tore a strip from a sachet of sugar and dropped its contents into my coffee – 'in the middle of the fourteenth century, Ranulph Higden was still worrying about whether Geoffrey's Arthur had any basis in fact. But he acknowledged that every nation needs to build up their own folk hero so that he becomes a national symbol.'

'Good.' Piers sat up, tapping his lighter on the table, his face animated. 'This is exactly what we want. I wonder if you would write it with me, this part of the programme? You clearly know your stuff.'

'I'd love to – I mean, there's a lot of material to sift out, but –'

'Well, I'll leave that to you. Pick out the important bits – remember, it's for a television audience – upmarket, but not too much Latin, okay?' He drank quickly. 'Seems as though Glastonbury is the place to start. We should probably film some of it down there, do you think?'

'That would be great. Have you been?'

'Do I look like someone who goes to Glastonbury?'

'No, I don't mean the festival. The town – I know it's tacky as anything in parts, and full of mad people who are still waiting for Arthur to come back, or Jesus, but it's not all hippies and Druids. The Abbey ruins – they're beautiful – tragic, too, and you can walk up the Tor. You should go – it's a very romantic place.' Then I blushed. 'In the sense of – you know –'

'I know what romantic means.' He slipped into another sly smile. 'Good. So one day you can take me to Glastonbury and give me the tour.'

'Oh. Okay –' I stared, taken aback, unsure that he was serious.

'And tell me what *you* think.'

'About what?'

'Arthur. Was he real?'

I shrugged. 'No. I don't think so. Not in any way that we would recognise. But I always used to have this secret hope –' I hesitated, embarrassed.

'Go on.'

'Well – Geoffrey of Monmouth talks about this lost British book that he took his stories from. Most scholars agree that he just invented that to make it sound authentic, but there are those who think it could be true, because some of the same material appears in another saint's life that might pre-date Geoffrey. So they might have had the same source, you see, which just might have been the book Geoffrey mentions. And I always used to think – what if it *were* real? What if it was just lost when some great library was destroyed – the library of Glastonbury, for instance – and it could still be found? It would be amazing – imagine what would happen to English history!'

'I imagine the country would skid to a halt and fall to its knees and the BBC would suspend all scheduled programming.' He lit another cigarette. 'So that's your great quest in life? To find this book?'

'Oh, no – it was just a stupid thought I used to – I mean, I don't really think –'

He was smirking slightly, though not unkindly; nevertheless it irritated me. It wasn't the most glamorous of ambitions, I was prepared to admit, but he had no right to laugh at me when he had asked me for my opinion.

'There's no need to be snide. I thought you wanted me to tell you this stuff.'

'I'm sorry.' He leaned forward. 'I didn't mean to suggest it was stupid. I'm just surprised – impressed, I suppose. That this stuff should matter to you so much.'

'You couldn't live with it for three years if it didn't. Well – you've done research work, you know what I mean. You'd go mad.'

'Perhaps.'

A thin silence. The ceiling fan clacked round slowly above us, shredding his smoke in its draughts.

'But your research must matter very much to you as well,' I pressed. 'If you left your home to come here.'

'My what?'

'I thought – well, you came here from Buenos Aires.'

He made a small noise through his nose that sounded bitter.

'Buenos Aires is not somewhere I'd ever describe as *home*. Have you been? Insane place, worse than New York.'

'No. I've been to New York, though.'

'With Edward?' He raised an eyebrow.

'No.' I was puzzled. 'With my father. I don't have that sort of relationship with Edward. We never used to see much of him.'

'Oh. He thinks a lot of you, though.'

'I don't think that's true, I'm afraid. Edward despises everyone, except possibly people who are useful to him – and I'm not very much use.'

'You judge him very harshly. Besides, you never know what uses he may find for you.'

Smiling to himself, Piers poked a spoon into the froth of his coffee and turned back to contemplate the river, as if sealing the conversation. I had a sudden lurch of anxiety at the thought that he might leave.

'It seems a lot of work, this production. Will you write it all yourself?'

'What?' He half-turned back vaguely.

'The series. Are you writing it all?'

'Most of it. In fact' – he watched me for a moment – 'I was going to ask you another favour. You see, I can do the music and film programmes by myself – that's my subject – and with the film there's far less material to wade through, obviously. I've almost finished writing it. I've started with Hitchcock, pre-war, and actors like Naunton Wayne and Basil Radford, and followed the thread right through to the kind of post-industrial realism of directors like Nick Strachey. And I have a researcher for the art one, but the books –' He hesitated again. 'You obviously know a lot about the pre-Renaissance period, which isn't my –' he shrugged, holding out his palms to demonstrate their emptiness.

'Field. You said.'

'Yes. And I don't want to look for another researcher because they're usually so incompetent you end up doing their job for them anyway – so if you'd like to put together some ideas for the early programmes, that would be great. You seem to have a good idea of what I'm after.'

'Well – of course, I'd be happy to help. But you should talk

131

to some of the other dons here, you know – George is a genius on the fifteenth and sixteenth century, and Jake Lennox specialised in the Enlightenment before he moved into theory –'

Piers's lip curled into a sneer.

'Jake Lennox is a champagne militant who's learned how to talk the talk. I've not yet heard him say one interesting or intelligent thing. He has no personality – it's all manufactured.'

'Oh. Okay. But there's George –'

'Yes – George is brilliant, of course, but I'd rather not talk to him – thanks anyway.' He pushed his chair back and stretched out his legs, yawning. 'Look, if you're too busy, I can ask someone else –'

'No, no – it's not that. I'm not too busy –'

'Good. And I don't expect you to do this for nothing, I should have said. We can pay you the going rate for a researcher – there's plenty of money available.'

'From Channel Four?' A lump of disappointment wedged in my throat; was this only business? Was I just a hired researcher?

'It's being funded by an independent production company. Channel Four have bought it from them.'

I didn't ask, but I felt sure the production company in question would have something to do with Hamilton Harvey International.

'It's okay, I don't need their money –'

'Oh, that's right. You've got your big private income.' A sudden coldness in his voice; traces of the sneer still lingered around his mouth.

'How did you know about that?'

'Edward's told me a lot about you.'

I shifted awkwardly.

'It's not really a private income. Just some money my dad left.'

'Still – you'll never have to wait tables, will you? You should be grateful for that.'

Another short silence; embarrassed and slightly indignant

132

on my part, unreadable on his. I wondered what else my uncle had told him.

'Better get the bill, I suppose. And thanks,' he said, yawning again.

As he beckoned to his waitress with a brief inclination of his head, I considered whether this would be a good moment to put Oliver's question.

I had been sitting on the breakfast bar of our kitchen two weeks earlier, painting my toenails. Our Sunday mornings had worn over the months into a comfortable shape, like slippers; our version of family. Bobby, with surprised hair and a towel wrapped around his waist, padded effortfully around the kitchen making tea, fogged in a hangover and pausing occasionally to glance at the crossword; the girl – his latest – perched nervously on the sofa, hugging her knees, panda-eyed with last night's make-up and tented in Bobby's enormous Rangers hockey shirt.

'Bob,' I asked, curling up my left foot and biting my lip in concentration, 'have you ever heard of someone called Andrew Epstein?'

'Who?' Bobby turned, a mug in each hand, then stopped abruptly. His brow knotted quizzically. 'Why are you painting your feet purple?'

'It's Burnt Aubergine.'

'Whatever. You never do stuff like that – are you turning into a girl? I'll have to kick you out the gang.'

'I think it's nice,' piped the girl from the sofa.

'Why are you making yourself pretty?' Bobby asked, peering at the paper on the counter. 'New date?'

'No.'

'*Troglodyte!*' he exclaimed suddenly, and performed a little dance with the tea. 'Seven across – all *right*! Now we're cooking! And, by the way, I can tell you're lying. You have your eye on some guy, that's why you don't dig the poor science geek any more. Who is he?'

133

'No one. I mean, there isn't anyone.'

'Here.' He handed me a scalding mug. 'You don't mean Andrew Epstein the writer? Could you find me a pen?'

'Yes. No. I don't know. I saw his by-line on one of your cuttings the other day.'

'Yeah. So what do you want to know?'

'I don't know, really. Just – someone mentioned him the other day. So he's a journalist?'

'Was. He wrote thrillers too.' Bobby looked at me curiously. 'But he's dead.'

'Oh. Then I guess it can't be the same person.' There was in fact no good reason for me to assume that the name in the *New York Times* piece was anything to do with the name Oliver had asked me to throw at Piers Gaveston; the coincidence had just appeared neat. 'Forget it. I probably made a mistake.'

Bobby shrugged. 'Good Jewish name – there's probably more than one of them. Let me know if I can be of any more help.'

Piers reached inside his jacket, which was hanging on the back of his chair, and pulled out a collection of notes. He seemed impatient to leave. I needed to be decisive.

'Uh – do you mind if I ask you something?'

His eyes narrowed; he peeled off a note and laid it carefully in the saucer without looking at the bill.

'Depends what it is. I reserve the right not to answer.'

'Do you know someone called Andy Epstein?'

I had not anticipated his reaction: Piers jolted; his cup rattled sharply against its saucer, and his expression was the frozen one I'd seen when Oliver Dowland introduced himself at Edward's party, his face oddly pale. His lips pressed together into a white line and his eyes turned very hard. Barely a beat passed.

'Did Oliver Dowland tell you to ask that?'

'Well – I –'

'No – of course he did. What did he tell you?'

'Nothing. He just – wanted me to ask if you'd heard any news about him.'

Piers nodded very slowly. His voice was tight.

'That's all?'

'Yes. Well – he said you would know what it meant – someone his father knew?'

He sighed, though it was hard to tell what the sigh signified. Possibly relief. He laced his fingers together and rested his chin on them.

'Andy Epstein was a friend of mine when I lived in New York. He was a writer.' There was a silence; I waited. 'He died a few years ago. In an accident. So – no, I don't have any news of him.'

He lowered his eyes. I put a hand to my mouth, mortified.

'God – so it was – shit, I'm so sorry – I had no idea –'

'You weren't to know. Tell Oliver Dowland there's no more news, and I don't expect there will be, and be sure to thank him for his kind concern.'

'I don't know why he – perhaps he didn't realise –'

I twisted my hands together miserably; it was apparent that I had said something terribly wrong, though I couldn't fathom why Oliver would knowingly have played such a cruel trick. Piers reached over and laid one of his hands – cool and dry – gently over mine.

'Listen, Gabriele. This is in confidence.' He glanced up quickly from under his eyelashes and smiled; it was the same pose as in one of the magazine photos. I swallowed, with difficulty. 'Oliver Dowland's father didn't like me. In fact, I think he may have hated me. And Oliver has inherited that prejudice without questioning it – he doesn't know me at all. But he's a coward. And he's a fool, too, if he thinks he can –'

He looked away.

'What?'

'Nothing. I'll speak to him myself. But don't –'

He paused, his hand still on mine.

135

'What?'

'Don't believe everything Oliver tells you about me. If he should tell you anything else.'

Then he withdrew his hand quickly, as if scorched; as if he immediately regretted confiding in me. Reaching for his jacket, he stood up, his back to me. I had one more question.

'But why did Denham Dowland hate you?'

'How should I know? The man was a fruitcake.' He pushed a hand angrily through his hair. 'I don't want to talk about this again, all right? Forget it.'

A few steps ahead of me, he pushed forcefully through the revolving door and disappeared; I held back, confused and disappointed, thinking perhaps I should leave him to walk away. Outside, though, blinking into the sunlight, he stood waiting for me on the bridge. He leaned over its edge, watching the river traffic.

'One more thing.'

'Yes?'

'I meant to ask you. There's a dinner, next month. For the faculty – in the interest of good relations. I have to sell the idea of it to all the carping traditionalists who think film and advertising shouldn't be allowed to pollute the pure streams of knowledge. People like you.' He winked. 'It's in the Old Hall of St Dunstan's.'

I waited. Nothing happened.

'Well – I hope it goes well,' I said, lamely.

'It'll be terrible. But I have to do it. Also' – he scratched the back of his neck – 'I have to take someone. So – do you want to go, is really what I'm asking.'

'With you?'

'That's the gist of it, yes.'

'Okay.'

I was too surprised to offer any other expression of interest; this was remarkable. He wanted me to go with him, to a public university dinner. But – and this was the niggling anxiety, poking tiny holes in my puffed-up ego – there was also something strangely perfunctory about the way he dealt with me. As if it were somehow compulsory.

'Good. St Dunstan's, then – I'll see you there.' He gave me a sort of friendly tap on the shoulder, slid his hands into his pockets, and turned to go. Then he half-turned, walking backwards. 'Oh, and it's black tie. George Fenton can give you the details, he's organising it. And you'll put some stuff together for me on Arthur?'

'Of course.'

I blinked, stupidly; he nodded, once, and walked into the milling afternoon crowds. I watched his back for a moment, turned in the direction of the Old High Street, when I spotted, hovering in the gateway of St Asaph's College, astride a green bicycle and wearing a helmet that looked like surgical apparatus, George Fenton. How long he had been watching, I had no idea, but I detected from his broad grin and knowing nod that he had certainly seen me with Piers.

A rumour was born.

Chapter IX

St Dunstan was a character of eccentric sanctity. Born in Somerset in the early years of the tenth century, his devout nature, resourcefulness and wordly wisdom quickly saw him elected Abbot of Glastonbury – adviser to kings and nobles, and the brains that fashioned Glastonbury Abbey as a pre-Conquest tourist attraction and repository of English myth. But he was also given to prophetic and colourful dreams and visions, and dogged to an extraordinary degree by the Devil in various guises – usually a dog or a fox, which Dunstan would duly wrestle and defeat. Once the Devil unwisely approached him in the shape of a beautiful woman; Dunstan famously escaped by tweaking her on the nose with a pair of coal tongs, a scene captured comically in one of the surviving windows of the college's old chapel. A man who can tweak the Devil's nose is not to be cowed by morally flabby kings. When the young King Eadwig disappeared during his own coronation feast, it was Dunstan, in full Abbot's regalia, who located him in a side chamber in an interesting arrangement with his teenage queen and her mother, and who dragged him back to the banqueting hall, bristling with righteous anger, to give him a thorough dressing-down in front of his courtiers and royal guests. Eadwig, understandably annoyed, had him exiled to Flanders but Dunstan – not easily thwarted – waited cannily for the king's demise, returned post-haste and was promptly ordained Archbishop of Canterbury.

The college that bore his name had been founded in 1310 by Walter Pomfret, newly elected to the neighbouring bishopric. It was the university's first secular college, a sign of the Bishop's generosity of mind. Bishop Pomfret, like the saint he appointed patron of his new venture, was widely read in matter considered arcane and certainly unorthodox for a Catholic cleric – alchemy, mysticism, Ovid and other Latin poets, classical philosophy – and had amassed a substantial library of unusual and potentially heretical texts. He advocated a certain independence from ecclesiastical edicts in his new college, and watched carefully over the appointment of Masters and Fellows, keen to encourage an environment of free thought and scholarly speculation. But, like St Dunstan, Bishop Pomfret suffered because he would not turn a blind eye to royal corruption.

In 1312 the Order of the Templars was dissolved on the edict of Pope Clement V, amid accusations of witchcraft and unnatural acts. Templar property was supposed to be transferred to the Order of the Hospital, but in England it was seized by royal officials while charges were brought against the Templars; since these trials were long and tortuous and rarely had happy endings, such property was often silently appropriated by the Crown. This made the clergy nervous, and Bishop Pomfret – who was a wealthy man – spoke publicly against the precedent of secular authority simply grabbing unopposed the property of a religious order (even one that was officially defunct), gathering with him a weighty group of supporters from among the country's most influential churchmen. Unsurprisingly, it wasn't long before Bishop Pomfret was arrested and burned at the stake on charges of treason and heresy. Most of his library was confiscated and dispersed, though a handful of significant manuscripts were hidden by the scholars of St Dunstan's and can still be seen in the college library.

The fledgling college was closed down for want of a patron and its land handed over to the Crown, who used it for grazing cattle and allowed the buildings to crumble into disrepair for almost twenty years, until it was re-founded under the patronage of Edward III. The latter, preoccupied for most of his reign with the heavy financial burden of the French wars and the Black Death, gave the college his royal insignia and certain endowments but little of his attention, and St Dunstan's was left to its own devices. In 1354 the proto-humanist philosopher William Drayton was elected Master by the Congregation of Fellows; there he wrote his polemical treatise *Speculum Vitae*. Like-minded scholars flocked from all over Europe to study under him, and the college gained the reputation it still enjoys today for independent liberal thought. No coincidence, then, that three members of the present Cabinet were proud to call St Dunstan's their alma mater, nor that George Fenton had been the college's Senior Fellow for the past ten years.

It should be mentioned, however, that in English folklore St Dunstan is also the patron saint of tricksters.

The towers of the imposing fifteenth-century gatehouse cast long evening shadows across the Old High Street. It was May 19th, and the air was warm, carrying smells of summer: cigarette smoke and something sweet, like popcorn. Overhead, a light aircraft thrummed. Pools of shadow collected between the arches of the open gates and, inside the courtyard, low sunlight spilled across the lawns and soft snatches of Duke Ellington floated from an upstairs window. The streets seemed very still.

Piers Gaveston was late. I had tried to be late too, but, foolishly excited, had nonetheless found myself ready prematurely, obliged to perch, jigging nervously, on the edge of the sofa for half an hour, smoking a succession of cigarettes while Bobby mocked ruthlessly. Afraid of appearing rude, I had managed only a meagre five minutes of lateness; Piers, infuriatingly, had already achieved twenty and still showed no sign of arriving.

More minutes; another cigarette. Then, at the far end of the Old High Street, there appeared a mini-motorcade; two low, glossy cars with darkened windows and their own standards fluttering from the silver figurines on the radiator grilles. They advanced slowly over the cobbles, almost too wide for the thin medieval street with its steep camber, and drew up outside the gatehouse of St Dunstan's.

Edward emerged from the first car in a flawless tuxedo, followed by the long, sleek legs of Lady Isabelle, who levered herself with practised elegance out of the back seat in a gauze of perfume and silk, clutching a tiny, powder-blue suede bag. From the car behind clambered Roger Mortimer, red-faced and damp, his collar biting into the flesh of his neck, and two tall broad-shouldered men with identical suits, sunglasses and jutting chins, from whose left ears wires protruded uncannily. Flynn and Glyn – Edward's bodyguards (it was deliberate). Why Edward should have imagined he would need protection at a university formal dinner was beyond me; perhaps he perceived a hostility to the new faculty greater than any of us had imagined. Or perhaps it was simply that he still enjoyed the theatre of appearing in public with a full entourage, reminding himself – and the world at large – of his own potency.

'Gabriele!' said Edward, somewhat surprised, sticking out one elbow like a chicken for his wife to cling on to as she picked her way carefully over the flagstones. 'Have you been waiting for us? That's nice. Unnecessary – but nice, still. Where's this bloody thing happening, then?' He took a step forward, casting his head back for a desultory glance at the carvings over the gates. 'Good bit of stonework, that. Reminds me of – what was that place I liked, Roger, with the church?'

'Ah – Chartres?'

'Could've been, could've been. How old is this, then, Gabriele? Tudor?'

'These gates and the courtyard are mid-fifteenth century. The original buildings are in the courtyard behind, where the chapel is – they date from the early fourteenth –'

'Do they, now? Well, well. Makes you think, doesn't it, Roger? History. Look at it. Been here for centuries, this. And we're giving it a future – makes me feel rather good about myself, that. Right!' He clapped his hands. 'Come on, I could do with a drink.'

'It's nothing like Chartres, Edward, don't be ridiculous. You're thinking of St James's. Hullo, darling.' My aunt kissed me vaguely, brushing her soft, powdery cheek against mine. 'How's your poor mother?'

'I think she's fine –'

'Oh, I'm glad. She must be having lovely weather.'

'Yes, I expect so. Uh – how's Toby?'

She grimaced, elegantly. '*Don't*. That boy.'

Just then, the stillness was cracked by the virile growl of the motorbike that swerved around the corner and skidded to a dramatic, chrome-trimmed halt in front of us. Its dinner-suited rider pulled off his helmet and shook out his blond hair, grinning.

'Piers! Bloody hell – where did you get that thing?' Edward appeared horrified.

Piers laughed, his eyes shining.

'California. I've been waiting to get it delivered. 1957 Harley Sportster – first year they made this model. Isn't she beautiful? A bit extravagant, really – all the spare parts have to be flown over from Milwaukee. It'll cost a second fortune every time it breaks down. But I think it suits me, don't you?'

'You'll kill yourself on it!' protested my uncle, genuinely alarmed.

Piers smiled. 'I lead a charmed life, Edward – you know that. Good evening, Lady Isabelle.' He bowed his head deferentially, still smiling – though I noticed it came from the teeth only. My aunt pursed her lips slightly, her eyes stony, then returned an icy smile.

'Good evening, Mr Gaveston. What a long time it's been. How did you like Argentina?'

A muscle tensed, almost imperceptibly, in Piers's jaw.

'Not my sort of place. But you get used to it.'

'I'm sure you do. What a pity, I always found it very beautiful. You must have been so pleased to come home. I hear you've taken a lovely flat in Chelsea now.' Lady Isabelle turned away, pulling her frothy silk scarf around her throat. 'Shall we go in, everyone?'

Piers swung his leg over the bike, folded his helmet into the crook of one arm, and touched me lightly on the shoulder as he strode past.

'Sorry to be late,' he said, without looking at me, 'but I hate sherry.'

Edward laid a protective hand on Piers's back. 'So – you're going to give it the full PR whack tonight, then?' he could be heard saying, as they wandered ahead over the lawn, followed by the silent minders. Roger hovered uncertainly at my aunt's shoulder, sweating.

My aunt clutched her bag to her front with both hands and watched me curiously, tilting her head first to one side, then to the other, as if valuing a painting. A wisp of pale blonde hair came astray in the breeze; she tucked it behind her ear, tutted, shook her head as if mystified by me and asked, finally: 'What on *earth* are you doing waiting for Piers Gaveston?'

Lady Isabelle d'Aurignon Hamilton-Harvey, my father had told me, came from what they used to call 'a good family'. Unlike the man who became her husband, she was moneyed from birth; sole heiress of the d'Aurignon timber fortune, she grew up among the best families of Montreal before she was sent away, first to a prestigious day school in New York, where she lived on the Upper East Side with relatives of her mother, and later to finishing school in Switzerland. And finished she was; polished as a glass ornament, and just as brittle. There had followed residential art courses in Florence; instructive travels through Europe (the pretty bits); skiing in Whistler during the winter with her cousins. At twenty-one, newly returned to New York and living in a rented apartment with a girlfriend on Madison Avenue, she took a job as assistant to the Director of Exhibitions at the Metropolitan Museum of Art and contracted a semi-arranged engagement to the scion of a Manhattan banking family. Her course appeared set.

It was to a party hosted by her banking fiancé that Denham Dowland – who knew such people through his father's diplomatic contacts – took his friend Edward Harvey in the November of 1970. Edward had not long arrived in New York and, though already thirty, found himself intimidated in the company of these smart, opinionated, Ivy League Manhattanites; Denham Dowland had thought it his duty to augment his friend's social circle to the best of his ability. Edward Harvey became something of a curiosity. Arms trading was not, in 1970, the glamorous and lucrative business it was to become in America in the decade that followed. President Nixon's pivotal visit to the Shah of Iran, and the subsequent expansion of export policy, was still two years away. Vietnam was in full swing, and many of Denham Dowland's wealthy friends still remembered, with a guilty twinge, their student flirtation with the protests. Weapons, and those who dealt in them, were regarded as suspicious, if not downright immoral. Denham, who had grown up in Cairo, partially exonerated himself by insisting that he was not an arms dealer, merely a translator, involved in drafting the legal contracts; consequently Edward, lacking his friend's precocious political talent for strategically altering the truth, became the sole object of the Manhattan set's disapprobation.

Isabelle d'Aurignon thought him adventurous. She liked the Englishman's quiet hesitation, his way of listening instead of foisting his opinions on her; she liked his dark, nervous good looks and daydreamed naively of his dangerous expeditions to North Africa and the Middle East, lugging suitcases stuffed with guns. She was bothered, too, by the fact that he was the only man in her social set who seemed unaffected by her beauty – worse than that, almost uninterested. For the sake of her pride, and for the thrill of rebellion, she set out to win him.

144

Six months later she married him, in a registry office around the corner from the Gramercy Park Hotel; Denham Dowland was Edward's best man. Monsieur and Madame d'Aurignon were not present. Mortified by the dynastic rift caused by their daughter's broken engagement, they had disinherited her; Isabelle, needless to say, had the last laugh. After years without contact, during which her seemingly unpromising husband acquired a fortune that put her own lost one to shame, she sent her estranged parents a telegram, announcing her recent elevation to the lower ranks of the English aristocracy and signed with her new double-barrelled name (Edward had prefixed his mother's maiden name to his surname to render it more memorable). The ice melted; a decree of forgiveness was issued, the d'Aurignon deeds and testament were changed back, and the saw-mills of northern Quebec once more churned through maples and giant redwoods for the benefit of Isabelle and her heirs.

I had never felt comfortable with my aunt. My mother had always been overawed by her – her beautifully tailored clothes, her careful manicure, her poise and perfect manners, her easy use of the word 'winter' as a verb – and I absorbed her insecurity. Edward – in spite of his knighthood and palatial houses – was flesh of my flesh; we looked the same. Besides, he could often be reassuringly crass. Lady Isabelle, on the other hand, could persuade you to believe in a natural aristocracy. I always had an uneasy sense that she was waiting for me to make some unforgivable *faux pas*, just to confirm her opinion.

My aunt repeated her question, all the while pinning me sternly with her eyes. Her accent was still more French-Canadian than New York, soft at the edges, though overlaid with a thin veneer of received pronunciation. 'What are you doing with Piers Gaveston?' She sucked in her cheeks prettily.

'He asked me to come to this dinner with him,' I replied, feeling a little foolish, since Piers had barely spoken to me.

My aunt nodded, and her frown concentrated, as if she were engaged in difficult calculations.

'Did he. I see,' she said eventually, in a tone which suggested that what she saw was at once minatory and expected.

The pause became uncomfortable. We drifted towards the far side of the courtyard, Roger trailing in our wake.

'Do you know him well?'

She shook her head: a tiny, clipped movement.

'No, not well. Certainly as well as I would wish to. The question is, Gabriele, how well do you know him?'

'Oh – hardly at all – that is – I've met him a couple of times –'

'Has he done this before?'

'Done what?'

'Asked you to accompany him somewhere? Somewhere public?'

'No. This is the first time.'

'Although you had your picture taken with him at Edward's party in the Long Gallery. I noticed it in the society pages of *UpTown* magazine. I was rather surprised.'

'That was Edward's idea. We were just standing there –'

'Edward's idea.' She pressed her lips together, weighing this up. 'No doubt you find him very attractive.'

'Well, I –' Suddenly I felt guarded, resentful of her half-bored, knowing-better tone and the intrusiveness of her questions. 'Yes, I suppose he is, though I don't see why –'

'Gabriele.' She took my elbow gingerly between finger and thumb, the lightest touch, as though contact might soil her. 'Listen to me. Piers Gaveston is dangerous. He has a dangerous influence, and he is very ambitious. You may tell me not to interfere if you like, but I'm going to say it anyway. Whatever you do and whatever he says, don't ever be stupid enough to believe he has any feelings for you. He is in love with himself, and people who get involved with him tend to end up –' She hesitated. '*Damaged*.'

She fell suddenly silent, with a precise nod that sealed her sentence like a full stop. Piers and Edward were waiting for us outside the thick door to the Senior Combination Room, where a pre-dinner sherry reception was already underway. Piers smiled again at my aunt and I saw in his expression – or was it my imagination? – a hint of bravado, like a poker player who can't help revealing that his hand is unbeatable. All at once, it struck me: she was in love with Piers Gaveston! That must be it! Surely that would account for the bitterness of her tone; he had spurned her once, and now she was jealous that he had shown me some attention. This explanation – so fitting, the more I considered it – produced in me a strange sympathy for my aunt. But she was wrong about him, I thought. Or perhaps she was right, and it was the danger that drew me.

'Once more into the breach –' Piers looked expectantly around the group, gesturing towards the room, then – to my astonishment – he slid an arm firmly around my waist, steering me towards the door before pushing it open.

The Senior Combination Room of St Dunstan's is furnished as a gentlemen's club; long and low-ceilinged, with beams of dark oak; leaded windows which permit little light, and sombre portraits of long-dead patrons in Restoration perukes or Piccadilly weepers, all looking suitably Masonic. A cabinet of ancient books stands at each end of the room, and the air is steeped in the mingled scents of pipe-smoke and leather.

The room was milling with the university's most eminent men, in their full academic regalia; long, black gowns, white bow ties, the rich scarlet, gold or purple fur-trimmed hoods marking their rank and subject. Two of the older fellows wore full clerical dress, and one was in naval uniform, with a broad sash, and a ceremonial sword tapping gently against his thigh. Hearty guffaws punctuated the low noise of polite conversation. There were very few women. This, for all the bold talk of modernising, was the real university; these were men who could talk in metric Latin, to whom the minutiae of university tradition were the scaffolding that supported the world.

Piers glanced over the room and sniffed, shaking his head. 'Jesus. I'm in *Kind Hearts and Coronets*.'

I laughed. 'But it has a sort of charm, though, don't you think?'

'It's absurd.' But he was smiling.

'I thought you were in favour of maintaining tradition?'

'Well – in some ways. But how long can this pantomime last?'

The entrance of our party had caused a stir of interest among the gathered guests. On the far side of the room, by the fireplace, George was deep in a nodding conversation with the university's Vice-Chancellor when he noticed us and stopped short, a sherry glass halfway to his lips, switching his gaze from Piers to me and back again with metronomic rhythm and a baffled brow. When I smiled in greeting, he only frowned deeper, as if trying to decipher a coded message. The Vice-Chancellor patted George on the shoulder and excused himself, swishing his gown around him bat-like as he pressed through the crowd.

In an alcove near the door, to our left, Sara Croft stood with Jake Lennox, whispering suspiciously, her substantial bosom straining alarmingly the shiny green bodice of her evening dress. Lennox in his baggy dinner suit had the look of a truculent teenager; hands stuffed into his pockets, shoulders slumped. As Piers and I passed, Sara Croft elbowed Lennox sharply in the ribs and hissed, 'There's your answer'. I turned, catching her sneering expression, but before I could puzzle over her meaning, the Vice-Chancellor was before us.

'Professor Gaveston.' He extended a hand. 'What a pleasure to see you again. And Sir Edward and Lady Isabelle, of course – everyone is so much looking forward to your speech.'

Piers bowed slightly. 'Very kind of you to say so, Vice-Chancellor, but we both know that's not true. I'm here to be fed to the lions.'

'Ah, well. I'm sorry you should think so. *Fugit inrepirabile*

148

tempus, is it not so? We, the old guard, can't hide our heads in the sand, much as we might wish to. One either bends with the winds of change, or one is uprooted. It saddens me, of course – of course. It saddens many of us. But there – these old walls have seen so many changes' – he slapped the wall behind him – 'good and ill, and every one of them resisted at first. You just have to let *them*' – he gestured around the room – 'get used to the idea. And remember, it's nothing personal. A matter of pride – those of us who have spent our lives in this university' – here his good breeding did not quite disguise his pointed glance at Piers – 'well, we grow to love it, and we feel dreadfully ashamed and rather helpless that it can't muster its own resources without this kind of financial arrangement. Rather like having to sit by and watch while your elderly mother goes out begging on the streets. It hurts us, you see – but there's nothing we can do – the world moves on.' He sighed, smiling. 'Forgive me – foolish, fond old man, etcetera. And you are –?' He turned to me with a perplexed but kindly expression.

'Gabriele is Sir Edward's niece,' said Piers, his hand still resting on the dip of my back. 'She's a graduate student here.'

'Ah!' The Vice-Chancellor beamed and extended a hand to me. He was a short man, with springy white hair, a voice like a war-time broadcast and a genial face whose blotches of broken veins told of a long and happy association with the college port cellars. His girth was decorated with a cummerbund of episcopal purple. 'And which college are you at?'

'This one, sir.'

'At St *Dunstan's*? Really?' He shook his head. 'Yes, I suppose that's not impossible these days.' He chuckled fondly.

'Wasn't he nice?' I said, when the Vice-Chancellor had wandered away to fawn on my uncle. 'I've never spoken to him before.'

Piers gave a gentle snort and watched the room for a few moments before dropping his voice. 'Don't be fooled by all

149

that sentimental crap about elderly mothers. He's as corrupt as the rest of them.'

'What do you mean?'

'He put up a huge fight to stop this private finance deal going through – made all the right noises, stood up for tradition and independent scholarship and the university's values. Almost stopped the project going ahead at all. But –'

'But what?'

'The moment he could see some personal advantage, all his principles vanished like the morning mist.'

'What personal advantage?'

'This and that.'

My eyes skated over the room, as if everyone else must have heard too.

'You mean, he was *bribed*?'

Piers laughed. 'You are sweet. Don't look so shocked, it happens all the time.'

'By Edward?'

'Of course by Edward.'

'Oh.' I felt let down. 'I had no idea. Did George know?'

'George . . .' Piers watched me for a moment. 'Your childlike faith in George is very touching. Shall I tell you what I think of George?'

'Not if it's bad.' I was struck by a sudden fear that Piers would reveal a dark side to George that I would prefer not to uncover.

'No, no – I know you're very fond of him. George is one of the few men here I admire – though I don't know him all that well. He has integrity – which is not to say he's always blameless. But when George bends the rules, it's never for his own ends. It's always in pursuit of a higher ideal. He makes me think of Merlin.' He laid a finger on my arm. 'Unpredictable. But he's wise. I sometimes suspect he can see what I'm thinking.'

I nodded. Piers nodded slowly, too. Across the room, George – trapped against an antique dresser by Roger –

caught us looking at him and winked.

'All right? Smoke?' Jake Lennox appeared at Piers's elbow, shaking out a packet of cigarettes. Sara Croft lurked just behind him. Reluctantly, Piers took a cigarette, without smiling. He looked irritated.

'Thanks.'

'How's all the course preparation going?'

'Fine, I believe. Ask George. And your theory papers?'

'Oh, all right, you know.' Lennox shrugged. 'Lot of material to condense, you know? And – it's a bit tricky – there's a lot of overlap with some of the Philosophy stuff.'

'I should hope so. There ought to be overlap with everything – that's the point of an interdisciplinary course.'

There was a pause.

'Ironic, isn't it?' Jake Lennox said, lighting Piers's cigarette. Piers gave a barely disguised sigh.

'What is?'

'This. On the surface, this is a goal for democracy. Mass culture finally taken seriously by the high-culture elite. The gulf between high and low closing definitively. I always thought the day a faculty like this one was accepted into this university would be a triumphant day – like storming the Bastille.'

'How dramatic. And the irony is?'

Lennox blew out smoke. 'The irony is that mass culture is an illusion.'

'In what sense?' I asked, aware that Piers's attention had drifted.

'Well – it's obvious – mass culture is not autochthonous. It's created *for* the subordinate classes, not *by* them, by the producers of mass culture – who do it purely for profit. So it's comical that this faculty, which ought to be analysing questions like that, is being run by the biggest and least ethical dictator of mass culture in the country.' Lennox paused to swig sherry. 'So it's not a victory and there's nothing democratic about it at all. It's a huge, profit-driven, propaganda machine.'

'An even bigger irony,' said Piers coldly, looking past

Lennox's shoulder, 'is that you're happy to accept a salary from him.'

'Don't think I don't feel compromised. We all do – but – well, Hobson's Choice, wasn't it?'

'Good for you. Everyone admires a man of compromise.'

'Mm. Suppose it's difficult to compromise your principles if you don't have any in the first place.'

'Discuss.' Piers cast around for somewhere to put his cigarette. Sara Croft handed him an ashtray, smiling up at him with the same bovine expression. 'However – in spite of your amateur moral philosophising, your theories on the manufacture of mass culture sound interesting. You should write a book about it.'

'I have,' said Lennox, squaring his shoulders defensively. 'Two.'

'Oh, yes.' Piers stroked his chin. 'Wasn't it your first book that had that wonderful anecdote about Jung's seminal meeting with Orwell in Aberdeen?'

Lennox shuffled and looked down. 'Uh –'

'The one that unfortunately turned out to be apocryphal, which did rather undermine your nevertheless very original argument for a mutual influence. That's the trouble with these obscure little academic presses – they don't have the resources to employ fact-checkers.' He smiled disarmingly.

'Interestingly' – Lennox sucked fiercely on his cigarette, fighting to keep an even temper – 'I was looking for a copy of your book when I was down in London the other weekend, but nowhere seemed to stock it.'

'It was only published in the States,' Piers said, with a careless gesture. 'I'm updating it at the moment – then it'll be published in a revised edition in the autumn.'

'Oh? Who's publishing it this time?'

'Lexicon. Trade paperback, first print run of ten thousand.'

Lennox snorted. 'Lexicon? Which is now owned by HHI Media, isn't it? That's cosy.'

'Before you unleash your invective against Lexicon' – Piers

put a protective arm around my shoulder – 'please remember that Gabriele's *late* father was the publisher there for many years, and he made it the very fine list it is today.'

Lennox glared at me, opened his mouth as if to speak, then appeared to think better of it and shook his head with a look of disgust. I was too conscious of the weight of Piers's arm to contribute.

'Excuse me.' Lennox turned away.

'We have a meeting on Friday, Jake – don't forget.' Piers's tone was all friendliness.

Lennox turned back. 'Look – I don't know if I can make that. My old man's in hospital at the moment, so I'm up and down there a lot –'

'Oh, I am sorry. Nothing serious, I hope.'

Lennox shrugged. 'Difficult to know at the moment. Heart thing. They're doing tests.'

'That must be a terrible worry for you. After all' – Piers studied his fingernails with the most innocent of expressions – 'you'd be saddled with a hefty inheritance tax, from what I hear.'

Lennox stared, gaping in shock and fury.

'You bastard,' he coughed, eventually. 'You fucking bastard,' and pushed his way to the door.

'What was that about?' I whispered. Sara Croft was still beside us, wide-eyed as a child at the circus.

'That?' Piers curved his mouth into a private smile. 'Oh, nothing. Jake doesn't like to talk about his family.'

'Why?'

'His father's a property developer and his mother's some sort of Spanish countess, his full name is Jacques Oscar Augusto de Vega Lennox – and when his father dies, he's going to inherit half of the Home Counties. The cockney accent is entirely fake. But he keeps it quiet in case it makes his Marxism seem inauthentic.'

Sara Croft laughed abruptly in disbelief. 'You're not serious?'

'You can't say he's a fake just because he believes in left-wing politics,' I said, unsettled by Piers's thinly screened malice. 'Maybe he's embarrassed to have a privileged background.'

'Jesus – don't you *see* – the luxury of embarrassment is just another form of privilege? Anyway, how can you trust someone who lies about where they come from?' Piers fixed me with a suddenly earnest stare. It was the first time I had heard him speak about anything as if it mattered. 'He went to *Winchester*, for Christ's sake.' His chin jutted forward.

'It wasn't very kind, though,' I ventured. 'If his father's ill –'

'*Kind?*' Piers looked at me incredulously. 'What obligation do I have to be *kind* to Jake Lennox?' He laughed, not pleasantly. 'Come with me, there are some people you've got to meet.' With a guiding hand on my shoulder, he moved forward to find his way blocked by Sara Croft.

'Yes?'

'Dr Gaveston, hi –' she ran a hand through her hair.

'Hi.' There was a pause. She looked expectant. He sighed. 'Please – call me Piers.'

She simpered. '*Piers*. I just wanted to say – I thought *In Camera* was so great last week. You were really good.'

'Thanks.' Piers nodded graciously and attempted to move past her, but Sara Croft was tenacious.

'I just loved it when you totally contradicted Davina Withers about her take on the new Chekhov film – you know, you totally shot down her argument. She just had nothing else to say.'

Piers seemed unaffected. 'Well, she's not exactly Spinoza, is she?'

'Oh, I'm so glad you said that' – another flick of the hair – 'most feminists think she's really an embarrassment to women's writing, you know? – I mean, her last book is, like, she actually argues that women need marriage in order to fully develop aspects of their femininity, and I wrote this article last year saying –'

'Yes – sorry, but I've got to talk to someone quite urgently. Would you excuse us?' Piers shone his smile on her before impatiently moving on. 'Nice dress, by the way,' he said, over his shoulder, as he passed. Sara Croft's crestfallen expression brightened again to a smile.

'Grotesque woman,' he muttered, leading me to George, who was leaning against a book cabinet talking to three young men I had not seen before.

'Professor!' George called jovially, raising a glass of sherry (by a long way not his first of the evening). 'And Gaby! We must stop bumping into each other all the time. I'm beginning to think you're following me. I don't suppose you've met our new recruits yet, have you?' He gestured towards the three men, one of whom, on closer inspection, turned out to be a woman – wiry and aquiline, with artful hair and a man's dinner suit, tapered to fit. The second was a good-looking black man with a shaved head and fashionably thick-framed glasses, and the third was short and stocky, with a close-cropped goatee and heavy-lidded eyes. He was not wearing a tie.

'Hey, P.G., what's up, bonny lad!' exclaimed the goatee-wearer in a sturdy Sunderland accent, stepping forward to shake Piers's hand and slap him on the shoulder. 'Check this out, eh?' He jerked a thumb at the rest of the room. 'Worse than Cannes, and no tottie! Mind you – this is the real McCoy. My old mum'd be that proud!'

'Enjoy it while it lasts.' Piers returned the shoulder slap, then turned to the blonde woman. '*Candide*. Ça va?'

'*Magnifique*. Look at you, my pretty – all dressed up. I could almost eat you.' She ran a finger coquettishly the length of Piers's sleeve. I glared at her, my eyes boiling with jealousy, but she appeared not to notice.

'I think not. And Gil – good to see you!' Piers reached out with a wide smile, as the black man shook his hand warmly. 'Gaby – let me introduce you to some of the faculty's new teaching staff. This is Jerome Idle, executive producer at Prometheus Productions, who'll be lecturing on the practices of modern cinema –'

The goatee'd man nodded. 'Nice to meet you.'

'– and Candida Hampshire, former Head of Programming at Channel Four, who's running the course on television, advertising and design.'

The blonde woman reached out and gripped my hand with surprising force, skimming me with an approving glance as she did so. Belatedly, I realised I need not fear her with Piers.

'And Gilroy Achebe, former Director of the Chicago Center for African Arts.'

'Hi there,' said Gilroy Achebe, in a vibrating baritone.

'What's your speciality?' I asked.

'I teach Other Studies.'

I blinked like a sheep. '*Other* studies?' Had the world gone mad? Was every subject that couldn't be folded comfortably into the lap of Film and Television to be lumped together under the nebulous umbrella of Other Studies? 'Which other studies?'

Gilroy looked at me with infinite patience. 'Not other *studies. Other* studies. Studies of The Other.'

'The other what?'

'That which is considered Other by the traditional white hetero male middle-class Western European mainstream. So it covers gay studies, black studies, uh – other – *stuff*, you know, whatever falls outside the canon.'

'Right. Well, that sounds – varied.'

'You look confused. But then The Other is always partly threatening.'

'Is it?' I was beginning to feel as if I were at the wrong party.

Piers was smiling to himself. 'Gil and I worked on a film together in New York – must be, what, nearly ten years ago now?'

'At least.' Gilroy Achebe looked at his watch, as if this might confirm the lapse of time. 'Man, are we that old?'

'What was the film?' I asked.

Gilroy held up his hands in mock self-defence. 'Listen – it

was a terrible movie. I don't even want to *tell* you what it was called. It was about these two guys growing up in different neighbourhoods of the same city, and the black kid ends up going into politics and the white guy's a hood, but he saved the other guy's life when they were kids, so the first guy –' He stopped, and giggled through his nose. 'Man, there was some bad dialogue in that movie. Who in the fuck wrote that screenplay?'

'I did.' Piers pressed his lips together for a moment, then laughed, shaking his head. He looked more relaxed than I had seen him before.

'You were one know-it-all asshole. I said I'd never work with you again – what am I, some kind of fool?'

'You're working *for* me, boy.'

'Why, Lord-a-mercy, Mister Piers,' Gilroy bowed low, tugging an imaginary forelock, 'I's so sorry – I done almost forgot my place, sir.' He punched Piers affectionately on the arm. 'Still dance like you used to, white boy?'

'Not often.' Piers smiled to himself.

Gilroy leaned across to me. 'You want to see this boy move.'

'Uh – let's leave that.' Piers blushed slightly, still smiling, and turned to me. 'This is Gabriele Harvey – Sir Edward's niece.' The three of them gave a comprehending nod, as if my presence were now vindicated. Piers, I couldn't help thinking, still considered me an extension of Edward, and the thought disappointed me. 'She'll be working in the faculty too.'

'If she ever gets round to finishing her thesis,' said George, only half-joking.

'So – what persuaded you to leave such great jobs to come and teach here?' I asked the new lecturers, with a forced brightness.

· 'The money,' said Jerome Idle, then grinned. 'Nah, seriously – it's a kind of part-time arrangement. I'll still be down in the studios a couple of days a week – I could never give up making films completely. We've got Nick Strachey's new one in post-production at the moment, so I've got to see that through. But I liked the idea of putting a bit back – you know – for the kids. And it's much easier telling people about the theory of making films than actually getting down to it and making them. Truth is – I was flattered to be asked.'

'I been doing the same stuff in Chicago now for a few years,' said Gilroy, shrugging loosely.'Piers asked me if I'd come here and I liked the idea of doing something different, you know? I thought it might be fun to live here for a little bit, too.'

'I suppose. Have you done much teaching before?'

'Oh, bits and bobs, you know,' said Jerome, cheerfully. 'But it's not so much teaching, this, is it? It's more sort of sharing your thoughts about what makes a movie, int'it? Sharing your experience with the kids.'

With the kids? Behind his back, I spotted George making a face of exaggerated despair. I didn't respond; uncertain now of the extent of George's collusion in the web of bribery and corruption my uncle seemed to have spun around this faculty, I was less prepared to enjoy his jokes. If he didn't approve of people like these, why had he gone to such lengths to pave the way for them?

The hollow boom of the dinner gong prevented any further conversation. The guests emerged into the last receding sunlight of the courtyard and ambled cheerfully in the direction of the Old Hall. Piers walked on ahead with Gilroy Achebe, flanked by Jerome Idle and Candida Hampshire; George grasped my arm and drew me into step beside him.

'Gaby, I must ask you this. Are you – ah – *you know* – with the professor?' He was making a vague circling movement with his hand which seemed designed to imply intimate congress.

'No!' I swatted him with the back of my hand, embarrassed. 'He just asked me to the dinner, that's all.'

'I see,' said George, with much the same inflection as my aunt had used earlier.

'You don't like him, do you?'

'No, no – it's not that. In some ways he's extremely likeable. It's more a question of –' he paused on the lawn, looking up at the sundial as if for inspiration.

'What?'

'I don't entirely *trust* him. That's *entre nous*, of course, and it's none of my business but – well – if you were my daughter, I wouldn't be happy to see you stepping out with him.'

'I'm not.'

'No – no, of course, I'm sorry, Gaby – I didn't mean to presume –'

'I meant – I'm not stepping out with him. So you've no need to worry.'

George smiled, almost sadly, and I thought affectionately how like a father he had become. He watched Piers disappearing into the shadows of the passage outside the hall.

'The first time I met him –'

'When was that?'

'Oh, recently. That doesn't matter. I was going to say – it sounds ridiculous – but he put me in mind of Satan.'

'That's going a bit far.'

'Milton, Gaby, Milton:

He above the rest
In shape and gesture proudly eminent
Stood like a tower –'

George stretched out an arm to accompany his recitation. 'There's something about him – a sort of edge. It's like having a wild animal around that you think you've tamed, but you can never quite be sure. That bit about *considerate Pride waiting revenge* – I always thought of that when I saw him. *Cruel his eye –*' Abruptly he shook himself, as if from sleep. 'Oh, for goodness' sake. Listen to me, I'm talking nonsense. But I urge you to be careful. Keep your eyes open, Gaby, don't let his obvious charms blind you.'

I was ready to change the subject.

'George?'

'Hmm?'

'A different matter, but – there's been a bit of money changing hands in brown envelopes over this faculty, hasn't there?'

'Ah.' George rubbed his beard regretfully and glanced over his shoulder. 'Perhaps we should talk about this properly.'

'If you want to. But I'm right, aren't I?'

'Yes – yes, I do want to – I wouldn't want you to think – well. This is hardly the time nor the place, eh? But I will explain, don't worry. In time. Come along.'

He patted my back and ushered me into the hall.

Built in the late fifteenth century, the Old Hall has a high, vaulted roof; the ceiling patterned in red, green and gold like the upper parts of the walls, and decorated with carved painted angels on the hammer beams. At one end is a minstrels' gallery with a balcony of dark knotted oak, the same that panelled the lower part of the walls. Above the grand inglenook fireplace, enamelled tiles depict the months of the year; beneath these, a row of colourful heraldic devices honour the college's many benefactors over the centuries. Uneven stone flags pave the floor, chequered with diamonds of pastel light from the tall windows. The glass was replaced in the last century; Victorian figures of vivid colour now pose between the fan-tracery and crenellated transoms (the latter highlighted in the guide books as some of the finest surviving examples of the period anywhere in the country). That evening, simple chandeliers swung from the roof, giving out a blurred light, and down each side of the room a long table had been set, with tall candles in branched silver candlesticks whose flames fluttered and glinted back, multiplied as orange sparks in the curve of the crystal glasses. The air was warm and hushed, with an atmosphere of pleasing solemnity, and at the top end of the hall, facing the minstrels' gallery, was a raised dais where the High Table stood, presided over by two towering portraits: Bishop Pomfret and Edward III.

There was a great deal of shuffling and polite apology as the Fellows circled the long tables, debating the seating plan. George directed me towards the High Table, where the faculty's inner circle were gathering – 'Where else? After all, your family is almost royalty here.'

On the right-hand side of the dais, Professor Maurice Trott was being wheeled into place amid a confusion of instructions on how to operate the brakes on his chair ('Good Heavens, boy, put them both on at once or you shall have me going round in circles like a one-legged duck!'). Professor Trott was an astronomer, once a world authority; his age much disputed among his students and colleagues but generally reckoned at somewhere between ninety-three and ninety-seven, and he liked to boast that he had not missed a High Table since the end of the last war. He was a Renaissance man, one of the last – a great quoter of da Vinci, firm in his belief that science and the mysteries of the universe should not – indeed, cannot – be separated from art, music and philosophy – *there is mathematics in the sweetest music*, he used to say, *and poetry in the simplest equation*. He had been a friend of Eliot's. Almost completely bald now, and frail; his tissuey skin peppered with brown and purple spots and his pale eyes rimmed with liquid that constantly threatened to spill, he still delivered his lectures faithfully to packed halls, without notes or any aide-memoire, and could still hold an audience spellbound. His sense of humour, too, was undiminished. When Halley's Comet made its most recent appearance, an eager young fellow had asked the great man whether he would be going to view this unique cosmological phenomenon. Professor Trott considered for a moment and replied gravely, 'I don't think I shall bother, my boy – I saw it last time.'

Professor Trott took his place at the head of the table, where his wheelchair could be comfortably accommodated. The rest of us were ushered to our allocated seats. On the furthest side of the table, with the portraits behind him, the Vice-Chancellor sat by virtue of seniority in the centre, a vantage point that allowed him a commanding view over the entire hall; on his right hand sat Edward, on his left, Piers. Facing the Vice-Chancellor was George, with Lady Isabelle on his left, opposite her husband; I was to his right, facing Piers. To my dismay, Jake Lennox plumped himself down in the chair to my right; for a moment we stared at each other in embarrassment, before he nodded curtly ('All right, mate?') and flapped open his napkin with a flourish. Opposite him, next to Piers, was Sara Croft, and on her left, Miles Park. Roger, who was strangely muted that evening, as if quashed by Piers's presence, was seated to the right of Edward, near Jerome Idle, Gilroy Achebe and Candida Hampshire, who were already being harangued by Professor Trott. 'I'm an advocate of progress,' he was shouting, with the unwitting volume of the deaf, banging his spoon on the table for emphasis, 'naturally, but I'm profoundly at odds with your ethos. Mahler quite simply *is* better than the Rolling Stones, and Blake *is* better than tabloid newspapers – no offence to our benefactor over there – and there are some things, I think, that don't belong in this university and never will, and I'm afraid I won't be told otherwise by people who could be my grandchildren.'

Flynn and Glyn, seated either side of Professor Trott, laughed politely.

The usual sullen staff of the college kitchens had been taken out of circulation for the evening and replaced by brisk, efficient waiters in crisp livery, who circled the table, a bottle of wine in each hand, making sure the glasses were full as soon as the guests sat down.

'Red or white, sir?' the waiter began, standing behind Piers's chair; Piers clamped a hand over his glass.

'Not for me. Water will be fine.'

George watched him with a curious smile. 'You don't drink, Piers?'

Piers lifted his hand from his wine glass, picked it up by the stem and turned it thoughtfully.

'No. I think it's important to stay in control.'

'It's also important to relax sometimes.'

'True. But our grasp on reality is so precarious at the best of times – why take further risks with it? Why would you want to mess around with your own consciousness, when it's so fragile to begin with?'

George took a full, contented sip from his own glass of claret, holding it up to the candle flames so that it glowed a deep ruby, the colour of Bishop Pomfret's robes in the painting above us. 'Well, to each his own. You're something of a Puritan, then?'

Piers's eyes narrowed. 'If you'd seen –' he broke off, his voice taut. 'Judge not, George, lest ye be judged.' There was a strange pause and his stare seemed to grow hotter, then, unexpectedly, he laughed, and clinked his glass of water with George's wine. 'Cheers!'

George looked relieved. 'Cheers!' he responded, raising his voice. 'And – I'll tell you what – how about an informal toast to Edward, without whom we wouldn't be enjoying this fine wine and company?'

'Quite right, quite right,' cried the Vice-Chancellor, 'a little toast of thanks to Sir Edward, everyone!'

Reluctantly, I lifted my glass. But when I saw the expression of bashful pleasure on my uncle's face, I suddenly understood. For all his brashness, his belittling of the university and pretensions to despise all it stood for, he was awed by these people just as he was awed by artists and musicians, by all the things he couldn't comprehend. It was almost touching.

Piers leaned back in his chair and lit a cigarette, drawing a few disapproving glares. The Vice-Chancellor's face reddened, and he whispered discreetly, 'Forgive me, Professor Gaveston, but it is the tradition that smoking is not permitted until after the coffee has been served.'

Piers pondered this for a moment and then said, with impeccable politeness, 'Ah, but you see, Vice-Chancellor, in a sense this evening is all about unshackling ourselves from tradition. I believe in the importance of symbolism, don't you? Now – would you mind getting me an ashtray?'

The Vice-Chancellor opened and shut his mouth, twice, and after a brief internal struggle, beckoned a waiter and asked that an ashtray be brought. Beside me, Jake Lennox let out a short, unintentional laugh; Piers leaned across the table and offered him a cigarette. Lennox regarded him suspiciously for a moment, then slowly took one.

'Jay-*queese*,' Piers said, enunciating carefully, watching his own rising smoke. Lennox bristled. 'That inheritance tax. There are ways round it, you know.'

Lennox, betrayed by his own enthusiasm, leaned forward.

'If you can get on the right side of m'learned friends. Remind me – we'll talk about it another time.'

I don't entirely trust him, George had said.

The starters came and went, and conversation grew more animated with each finished bottle, rising above the clink of glasses and cutlery.

My attention drifted to the snatches of talk around me. On the other side of George, Lady Isabelle had the misfortune of being seated next to Dr Winthrop Wallis, eminent in the realm of Russian literature. A dismal man with waxy skin and a perpetually funereal expression, Winthrop Wallis had no aptitude for small-talk, and appeared to have launched into a homily on the inadequacies of contemporary translation.

'A language tells you a great deal about the character of its people,' he was saying, lugubriously. 'Significantly, there is no word in Russian for *détente*.'

'There's no word in English for *détente*, either,' my aunt pointed out sensibly.

To my right, Lennox, Sara Croft and Miles Park were arguing the merits of a recent newspaper article by a leading American psychologist on the links between creative genius and personality dysfunction.

'So apparently,' Sara Croft was saying excitedly, 'novelists and playwrights are seven times more likely than poets to be mad.'

'That's plainly not true – how do you account for Pound and Dylan Thomas?' Lennox challenged her. 'Mad as a basket, both of them.'

Lennox broke in: 'What did he say about academics?'

'Oh, academics are all bonkers – that hardly needs an in-depth study.'

'Not any more, sadly,' said Park, 'we're all far too self-conscious these days. Eccentricity is the luxury of those who don't have to fear for their jobs. The mad professor will soon be no more than a curiosity for antiquarians, displayed in museums and taxidermists' windows.'

Sara Croft smiled wickedly and leaned closer.

'Fortunately, there's always Winthrop,' she said, gesturing down the table. 'Did you hear the latest one?'

'No.' They both leaned in with relish; as, instinctively, though I was not included, did I.

'So he's trying to translate that early Bulgakov manuscript, right – the one they found last year – and he comes across a word he doesn't recognise. He can't find it in any of his dictionaries either, so he phones the World Service –' she paused to make sure her audience were still engaged.

'Go on,' said Park.

'So they're like, hold on, we'll give you the name of our resident Russian language expert, and so he diligently writes down the name and telephone number – and of course it's Dr Winthrop Wallis and the number's his rooms in Benedict College!'

She waited, mouth half-open in an expectant laugh. Park shook his head.

'You made that up.'

'Wait,' she went on, barely able to contain her delight, 'it gets better. He writes down the number without batting an eyelid, then he spends all of the next day trying to phone it, and the following day he rings the World Service back to complain that the number they gave him is permanently engaged!'

'Bollocks!' said Lennox emphatically.

'Here' – Sara Croft leaned as far as she could away from Piers and lowered her voice – 'what do you make of the new arrivals?'

I dropped my eyes to my plate and tried to pretend I wasn't listening.

Lennox snorted. 'The dyke's too smug, the Geordie's too gormless and the black guy's too damn cool. And not a higher degree between them. I mean, I'm sure they're good at their day jobs, but have you talked to them? They haven't got the first clue about university teaching.'

'I thought you were all for a more democratic approach, Jay?' Park whispered back. 'Seems rather elitist to insist that those who want to teach at university level should need academic qualifications.'

'Yeah – I'm also in favour of reviving English industry, Parky, but that doesn't qualify me to work in a shipyard. From each according to his ability – remember? And what I'm saying is – *their* abilities – impressive though they may be – are not in the sphere of university work. They're practical people. Artisans. You watch, it's all part of his takeover.' He nodded viciously towards Piers, lowering his voice yet further. 'He's got a lot more influence than we thought. One by one, his mates will come in and we'll be pushed out.'

'But that's his ethos: practical people over know-nothing academics. He said as much in that interview. Which – can I just say now – was one of the most excruciating things I've ever read. Or was that just me?' Park paused to empty his glass.

'He did look good in those leather trousers, though.' Sara Croft hissed back, grinning.

'You're disgusting, Crofty. Anyway, you've been beaten to it.' Suddenly Lennox stopped, appearing to remember my presence. He turned to me deliberately, his voice a notch louder. 'Uh – Gabriele Harvey –'

'Hum?' I looked up, hoping to appear sufficiently startled. 'Me?'

'Pardon me for asking' – he checked to see that Piers was still entrenched in his conversation with the Vice-Chancellor – 'but how long have you been – uh – seeing – you know? The gaffer.' He jerked his head again towards Piers.

I looked into Jake Lennox's brown eyes for a panic-stricken millisecond and, perhaps because I wanted to make myself seem more important, perhaps because I imagined that embellishing the facts might somehow give them more weight, I blurted, 'I'm not – that is – not long.'

Three faces stared at me with expressions I couldn't read.

'Nothing like keeping it in the family,' Lennox muttered.

I flushed, realising immediately that I had said the wrong thing, and started to say something else, I forget what, when all at once the sound of the gong resounded through the hall and silence gradually fell.

The Vice-Chancellor, looking amiably patrician, rose unsteadily to his feet and raised a glass. The shuffling of a hundred chairs echoed in the vaulting as the rest of the guests followed suit.

'Gentlemen,' he began.

Someone coughed sharply.

'*Ladies* and gentlemen' – he lifted his glass – 'the Queen!'

'The Queen!' murmured a hundred, faintly slurring voices, followed by the sound of much heavy sitting. Lennox made a big show of not raising his glass.

'Ladies and gentlemen,' continued the Vice-Chancellor, who remained standing, 'it gives me very great pleasure to welcome you here on this most special day, the feast-day of St Dunstan. It is also a special day because it marks for us the beginning of a new direction for the university. Ah – hardly something to celebrate, some of you may be thinking. But – just as Aeneas couldn't preserve Troy as it had been in its glory, though he always cherished its memory' – the Vice-Chancellor paused, and sneezed – 'excuse me – but went on to found another mighty empire from its very ashes, as it were, so we who might feel some misgivings at the intrusion of the business world with all its attendant – ah' – he rummaged briefly for a suitable word – '*business*, into our university, must remember that, as the old order comes to an end, so another, equally great, is being born. Our *raison d'être* is now, as it always has been, to further knowledge and understanding of ourselves and the universe around us.' He paused again, sipped his wine, cleared his throat and turned to Edward. 'And, of course, progress always comes at a price. We think of Lorenzo de Medici, do we not – or, in more recent times, Sergei Diaghilev – bold men who offered their own resources for the furtherance of art and scholarship – and this evening, I invite you to join me in thanking the university's most generous patron, the equal of those men – Sir Edward Hamilton-Harvey!'

The guests applauded with surprising enthusiasm. Sir Edward half-rose in acknowledgement, beaming delightedly. George leaned over and whispered, '*Etonne-moi*', before putting his head in his hands.

'And without further ado,' the Vice-Chancellor continued, 'I give you the university's newest professor – Piers Gaveston!' He sat down and arranged his robes, reaching at once for his wine glass.

There was a thin ripple of applause as Piers stood up slowly, folding his hands in front of him. Gilroy Achebe wolf-whistled. As the noise died away, a whisper dominoed around the long tables.

Piers watched his audience with narrowed eyes for a few moments. The expectant silence grew.

'There are three words that express my vision for this new faculty,' he began.

('Me, Me, Me,' whispered Jake Lennox, rather too loudly.

'Hamilton Harvey International,' Miles Park volleyed back.)

Piers gave no sign of having heard, though I noticed his eyes flick briefly to his right. 'Culture, Tradition and Progress.' He settled his shoulders back and breathed deeply.

'What is culture? English culture in particular? Many of you, I imagine, will have your own answers to that question – answers by which, I suspect, you would mean "high culture". Shakespeare is culture, you'll tell me, as is Elgar, as is Lincoln Cathedral. For culture, read "Art" – we can deem it Art because we've already valued it above what we choose to exclude from the canon. And is it only culture because it comes from the imagination of a high-minded individual, like *The Rime of the Ancient Mariner*, or *Dr Faustus* – because it's created to shed light on the human condition – because it's created for Art's sake – because it lifts us out of our miserable lives for a few minutes? And if something is produced commercially, for profit and for broad consumption – does it therefore have no artistic or human value? Who says so? The Sistine Chapel – do we deny that the name of Art because it was painted to commission? Or because it was painted to be seen and understood by anyone who cared to look up? Remember the outcry over the *Biblia Pauperum*?'

Around the long tables, white heads nodded thoughtfully.

'Put books into the hands of the masses – the monks and the university men protested – and what will happen to our position as the custodians of knowledge?' Piers paused, his hands spread wide. The hall was silent. 'What happened was that their position was irreparably weakened – from that day, knowledge – art – culture – could no longer be the exclusive province of the churchmen or the intellectuals. It became democratic. And when Gutenberg invented the printing press, Europe's culture industry was born.

'You ask me why we need this faculty. Why this university – this one, with all its pride and reputation – needs to approach men like Sir Edward to fund a place which teaches students that a car advert, an electronic operetta, a film about factory workers or a canvas daubed with excrement are all equally valid products of our national culture, just as deserving of our attention as the tragedies of Shakespeare. You don't agree with me, of course. You bemoan the passing of the intelligentsia, and you write stiff letters to the papers about the invasion of commerce into the public sector – worse, into the hallows of academe –'

This was not going down well. Around the hall, mutterings and stony glares multiplied.

'My answer is this – you're proud of this university – and with good reason. Its very name is synonymous with tradition and history. We are all proud to be associated with it.' He clasped his hands together behind his back, his profile silhouetted against the light. 'But you're living in a walled garden. You're besieged on all sides by a world that you don't belong to. And unless we can find a way to make this university belong more convincingly to that world, it will become a museum. It will be left behind and overtaken, and in years to come you'll be reduced to showing tourists around the few colleges that haven't been turned into conference centres in the hope of making ends meet –'

('Where's he been for the last few years?' hissed Sara Croft. 'Does he not know that happens all the time already?')

'This faculty is not about the destruction of tradition. It's about saving an institution that threatens to become mired in its own nostalgia –'

('So now he's our Saviour,' muttered Lennox.)

'It's a means of bringing practical knowledge of modern culture and its production to students, as well as theory. It is not' – he paused for emphasis – 'going to replace or in any way detract from the more conventional subjects, but it will offer students – and Fellows – the chance to operate within a wider sphere of opportunity.'

('I can't bear all this boardroom jargon,' said Park. 'If he starts talking about impacting the market or low-hanging fruit, I'll be forced to leave.'

But Sara Croft was no longer paying attention; gripping the stem of her wine glass tightly, she was gazing up at Piers, lips parted.

George folded his arms across his chest and murmured contentedly. 'Well, he's almost convinced me. About time they brought on the port, though, don't you think? Some traditions are too good to abolish.')

'And it will make money,' Piers continued. 'And – let's face it – money is the one thing this university – for all its architectural splendour and all the land it owns – is always desperately in need of. Profit that can then be channelled back into other areas of university life –'

(The Vice-Chancellor raised an eyebrow quizzically at George, who responded with an empty shrug.

'What's that about?' I whispered.

'It was another of these attempts to persuade the more trenchant opponents.'

'Another bribe, you mean?'

'Gaby, please.' George pressed a finger to his lips. 'Professor Gaveston is speaking.')

'I would like to leave you,' Piers continued, his gaze cruising slowly around the hall, establishing eye contact with his detractors, 'with a quote from T. S. Eliot –'

'Dear old Tom,' Professor Trott shouted to his neighbours, smiling merrily. 'Well, well.'

'"What is wanted is not to restore a vanished, or revive a vanishing culture under modern conditions which make it impossible, but to grow a contemporary culture from the old roots." And that, ladies and gentlemen, is the purpose of this faculty. Tradition and Progress. Thank you.'

Piers smoothed his jacket and sat down, to brief and listless applause. His face was remarkably calm. The murmur of heated opinion bloomed again around the tables, many eyes still on him.

'Platitudes,' Professor Trott noted, loudly, at the far end of the table. 'But superior platitudes.'

Gilroy Achebe leaned across Roger and Sir Edward to catch Piers's eye, laughing. 'You can still lay it on, man!'

Piers smiled tightly, and looked down. When he raised his head, he looked me straight in the eye. 'How was I?'

'Uh – great,' I said, caught off-guard.

'Thanks. Though I know you don't agree with any of it.'

The Vice-Chancellor interrupted to confront Piers with an irrelevant point about St Bernard of Clairvaux. Coffee was being served, and the guests were beginning to move around, swap seats, excuse themselves. I pushed my chair back and slipped out.

Outside the hall, the air was still warm, though the sun had set and the courtyard was sunk in blue shadow. Chirping laughter leaked through the slanted vents of the windows. The nearest toilets were in the old courtyard behind the hall, up two flights of stairs. The staircase light was out, and as I felt my way cautiously through the dark along the bannister, I caught the sound of voices drifting from the open door of the men's toilet on the first landing.

'He's a total fraud. I mean it – he doesn't fool me for a second,' said Jake Lennox. 'What do we really know about him? His whole history's dodgy – it's like he makes it all up to suit the occasion.'

'Come on, Jay, you're just narked – I don't blame you.' The second voice was Miles Park. I didn't recall having seen them leave the table; intrigued, I ducked into a shadowy corner of the stairwell. 'I mean – I don't like him any more than you do,' Park went on, 'but I think you're wrong. He's very astute. And his credentials must be kosher. You've got to trust old George – he couldn't just walk into a job like this if he was a nobody.'

'You can do it if you have the right friends, mate. Listen – I've been here for six years, and before that I was at Edinburgh, and was I even *considered* for this Chair? Were *you*? And where's *he* come from – have you ever fucking heard of Carfield Fucking College? Well, then. And I wouldn't trust *old George* an inch any more – he's up to his neck in this.'

'I don't know. George cares about the university.'

'Maybe – but he knows all sorts of things he's not telling. There's more to it than that. This faculty – all that money, the publicity – it's pure bribery. And *I* think it's all about him.'

'Gaveston?'

'Yes, *Gaveston*. Fucker. It's as if the whole thing has been created for him. He couldn't give a fuck about the university or the students – this is all about making him famous. I mean – why's *he* appearing every week on *In Camera* instead of you or me? Fuck – I'd *kill* to get that spot. *And* I'd be better.' The sounds of running water petered out. I climbed a few stairs higher, tucking myself where they wouldn't see me.

'Course you would. Why would Edward want to do him such a big favour, though?' Park mused, zipping up his trousers in the doorway.

'Can't tell you, mate. But I'll find out.'

'Oh dear. I think I smell burning bridges.'

'Don't worry, I'll be discreet. But I'll be keeping my eyes open.'

Their voices grew fainter as they descended. As they reached the bottom of the stairs, I could only just hear them.

'Jay? Can I ask you a question?' A pause. 'Is your mother really a Spanish countess?'

'*Et tu*, Parky? Fuck off!' There came the sound of the court-yard door moaning on its hinges. 'She's a marqesa, actually – it's completely different.'

The hall was slowly emptying. Flynn and Glyn were seated among a group of the older fellows, legs akimbo in appropri-ately virile attitude, smoking cigars and canvassing opinion as to the outcome of Saturday's big fight. Edward – amiably drunk by this stage – was keeping himself steady on the dais with an arm around George.

I met Lady Isabelle and Roger as they made their way through the abandoned chairs down the centre of the hall.

My aunt looked tired and oddly melancholy; she was holding Roger's arm, but released it to clasp me gently by the shoulders.

'Roger and I are going back to London now,' she said. 'We've space in the car – I wondered if you would like a lift back to your house. I wouldn't like to think of you walking back in the dark.'

'Uh – that's kind of you, but –' I strained to look past her. Piers was nowhere to be seen.

'Gabriele' – my aunt's tone was gently chiding – 'Piers Gaveston has gone with his friends. If you think you'll get another offer of a lift, you're mistaken, I'm afraid. I did warn you.'

My cheeks flushed furiously. 'I wasn't –' I have made a fool of myself, I thought. I didn't understand why Piers should have invited me to the dinner, but I was sharp enough to realise it was not because he wanted to get to know me better, and my fantasy of inviting him in for a drink when he dropped me home was exploded. Disappointment snagged in my throat. And it was worse that my silliness had been recognised by my aunt.

'Edward is staying to drink cognac with George and the Vice-Chancellor in that dreary room where we had the sherry. I can't wait to get away, frankly – I don't know how you can bear it here, Gabriele. Do come and keep me company in the car, would you?'

'Okay,' I said, resigned.

Roger, who was dutifully holding Lady Isabelle's blue clutch bag, now passed it back to her. 'Flynn! Glyn!' he called, with a spry clap of his hands, like a Victorian theatre manager. 'Come along – decide which of you is coming with us!'

Flynn and Glyn looked at each other, sighed, laid down their cigars; Glyn pulled a coin reluctantly from his trouser pocket and flicked it into the air.

'Gaby!' Edward bellowed as he and George came towards us. 'Where the hell is Piers?'

I shrugged, wishing everyone would stop drawing attention to his desertion.

Sir Edward gave a thick laugh. I had the feeling it was at my expense. 'Trouble with Piers' – he paused to swallow, then raised a forefinger in concentration – 'you never know where he is. You'll learn.'

'Edward!' Lady Isabelle looked peeved. 'I think you should come back with us – you're beginning to talk rubbish.' There was a warning in her voice.

'I'm bloody staying with Georgie,' said Sir Edward, drunkenly defiant. George made a face of helpless neutrality.

'Very well. I'll give Gabriele a lift home. And don't forget you have to be in Stockholm tomorrow night.'

'Stockholm – quite right. Goodnight, my darling. I shall give Piers both your regards.' He bowed ridiculously, puffed on his cigar, and swayed past us, still laughing.

'Never get married, Gabriele,' my aunt said darkly, as she led me away.

Chapter X

The summer yawned by, hot and slow.

An unusual humidity weighed down on the town; even in the shade of the towpath along the river, under the willows, your clothes stuck to your skin and your hair grew damp at the back of your neck. Heat wavered across the water by the weir. The students drifted away, leaving the college bars deserted, and the little streets clogged with busloads of tourists.

It was a summer marked by absences. Piers Gaveston disappeared altogether from the town and the late review programme *In Camera* – my guaranteed weekly glimpse of him – ended until the autumn. I heard nothing from him, and persuaded myself that I had not expected to. The *Sunday Enquirer*'s Washington correspondent broke both arms in a roller-blading accident and Oliver was sent over for two months to replace him. George left to teach a six-week summer school in Canada, gleefully celebrating in anticipation the inverse work/pay ratio and the prospect of visiting his grandchildren; Bobby shed his Balinese tie-die shirts, cut his hair and packed his neatly pressed khakis and tennis whites for the summer season at his parents' place in the Hamptons. The Hamilton Harvey Faculty of Cultural Studies lay fallow, its gleaming escalators stilled, waiting for the chill of October.

Meanwhile, I was rediscovering Arthur. The research I had promised Piers for his television programme began to take up most of my time, anxious as I was that I should justify his faith in me by making it faultless. I abandoned the numbing palaeography that had become the mainstay of my thesis work, and returned with relish to the stories, knitting together the crucial points of the main sources, imagining that I was introducing the history of Arthur as if it had never been told before. I started a draft script and realised, for the first time in over two years, that I was involved in my work again.

One afternoon late in June, as the temperature outside was climbing steadily, I was making my way down the corridor from the Manuscript Room of the university's central library when I stopped outside the steely doors of the newspaper archive.

I pressed my forehead to the wire-mesh glass and craned to see the room's extremities. It appeared to be deserted. I glanced up and down the corridor – empty – and tentatively pushed one of the doors. It wheezed open, more suddenly than I had anticipated, and I stumbled in too quickly; the librarian, looking up with shrewish eyes, registered immediately that I was not a regular and frowned. A man with a beard stared meaningfully from behind a computer screen. Academics, as well as being doggedly territorial about their fields of scholarship, are also absurdly protective of the physical space those fields occupy. It was like walking into a village pub in London shoes.

My probings into twelfth-century chronicle histories had not required much use of recent newspaper documentation; consequently I had not been through the steel doors for some time, but I recognised that the archive was in a parlous state. Along the back of the room were vast metal shelf units of the kind that you can roll along by turning a handle, capable of crushing unwitting browsers to death. These were crammed with tattered cardboard files, bulging with clippings, yellowing and torn at the edges; in them, if you only had the patience, you could find almost any news article from the Western world's major newspapers from the last thirty years. A plan to computerise the whole archive had been set in motion some years ago, but someone had to input them, billions and billions of words needing to be shunted from print to pixel, and the project had demanded levels of staff and finance that the university either didn't possess or saw fitter to distribute elsewhere. So the archive had been left, like the rest of the library, fraying at the edges; a stubborn ghetto of paper and microfiche in a world of bright, shiny, fingertip technology, all being transferred to the new faculty.

'Can I help at all?' The librarian was wearing glasses with flip-up sunglass lenses over prescription ones. They were flipped up and caught the light from the tall windows, making her look as if she had six eyes.

'Uh – yes.' I cleared my throat. 'I would like to look at some articles from the *New York Times*.'

She sighed, wearily patient. 'Perhaps if you could be a little more specific?'

'I'm looking for anything relating to a writer called Andrew Epstein.' I lowered my voice, checking over my shoulder. Stupidly, I felt almost guilty, as if I were spying on Piers. But since his reaction to my question, and the terrible embarrassment that Oliver had allowed me to stumble into, I had begun to wonder if there wasn't a mystery surrounding Andrew Epstein that might tell me something about Piers.

'I'm sorry?'

'He was a journalist.'

'When?'

'Early seventies, I think. In the Middle East.'

She sucked her pencil, assessing my competence. 'He might have a file. Try under "People", alphabetical, by sur-name. The far end is "People: Dead". Or you could try under "Subject", for Middle East, although I warn you, that'll be a lot of material – you'll want to narrow that down, unless you've got all day.' This was said as a kind of reproach. 'Or if you know the dates of the articles you could look on the microfiche. Do you know how to use that?'

'Yes,' I lied.

'Anything else?'

'No.'

'You can't take anything out of this room. And no gum.'

She clicked off on her neat heels into a cavernous shelf stack behind her counter. I had no intention of leaving the room; it was one of the few places in the building that was shady. Outside, a lawnmower hummed indolently.

I rolled back the first stack of 'People: Dead A–E', squeezed into the dark gap and began combing through the musty papers, standing on tiptoe to see the name felt-tipped in capitals at the top of each cardboard file. There he was, almost immediately, between *Epaulle, Jean-Yves Saint-Claude* – whose contribution to modern history had passed me by – and *Epstein, Brian*. Cautiously, I pulled out the one I had been searching for, taking care not to drop the bulging papers.

Epstein, Andrew. See also: Israel, 1970–76

I wriggled out from between the cabinets into the daylight and looked at my find. Someone had rubber-stamped 'DEAD' over the folder eight or nine times in red ink, as if to make sure. I laid it down on a table and began to peel back the cuttings.

The file, it seemed, had been taken out quite recently. The articles were not in strict date order, although some semblance of chronology had been observed; the papers at the front were yellower, thinner, and carried Epstein's by-line from the early seventies: reports of unrest on the Israeli borders; the Egyptian oilfields; presidential visits; wars and rumours of wars. All were much like the piece I had found among Bobby's papers. Behind these were cuttings dating from the mid-eighties; Epstein in another incarnation. BEST-SELLING AUTHOR WINS MAGELLAN PRIZE, announced a headline over an article by one Carrie McGrath:

Former journalist Andy Epstein has been awarded this year's prestigious Magellan Prize for American Fiction for his political thriller *Shifting Sands*, about the Arab–Israeli conflict. He fought off stiff competition from previous winner Hal Tucker and fellow bestseller Rainie MacPherson, author of last year's box-office hit

Wyoming Skies which starred Sean Gregory. Epstein was the *New York Times*'s Israel correspondent from 1970 to 1976 and spent some time with Mossad in . . .

There was a grainy photograph; a dark, curly-haired man with laughing eyes, cheerfully holding up a copy of a book; the flash bounced back from its shiny cover, obscuring the title.

I flicked again.

One or two book reviews. Andy Epstein's Christmas thriller round-up for a lifestyle magazine. Andy Epstein donates money to a school in the Bronx. Andy Epstein gives a guest lecture at MIT. More of the same.

At the back of the file was the freshest piece of paper of all; nearly ten years after the Magellan triumph, early in a new decade, the headline, in the familiar typography, read:

EPSTEIN WINS RECORD ADVANCE FOR EXPLOSIVE BOOK
Author and former journalist Andrew Epstein has signed the most expensive book deal ever paid by an American publisher for an unwritten non-fiction book (writes a staff writer). Sampson West Inc offered an advance of $400,000 for what promises to be a controversial history of US arms exports to the Middle East during the early 1970s. It is believed that Mr Epstein, who was the *NYT*'s correspondent in Israel during that time, may have unearthed evidence of illegal dealing by some top US arms manufacturers. Mr Epstein is still researching the book, which was bought on the basis of a 10-page proposal, and hopes to have it completed by next year. Sampson West would then publish in the fall. Sam Felberg, Publishing Director of Sampson West, would not comment on the book's content, admitting that he had not so far seen any material from the book but was adamant that he has made an unbeatable investment. 'Andy Epstein is not only a superb writer,' he said yesterday, 'but he is uniquely placed to have personal expe-

rience as well as a broad political and historical perspective that will impact the book very positively. We trust him to come up with something quite unique and expect to be looking at next year's giant bestseller.'

It was the last cutting in the file; fruitlessly, I turned it over as if something might materialise beneath it. I felt odd – slightly clammy, as if I might be being watched. There seemed to be a part of the story still missing.

All at once a pair of large hands clamped over my eyes.

Yelping, I peeled them away to see Bobby grinning cheerfully behind me.

'Hey, you.'

'You nearly gave me a heart attack. What are you doing here?'

'Oh, you know. Occasionally, I do some work. What are *you* doing here, though – there's technology in here.' He whispered, indicating two rolls of microfilm he had placed on the table.

'Hardly.' I laughed, self-consciously. 'I'm just, you know. Looking at stuff.'

He leaned over and turned the front of my file to read the name.

'Andy Epstein again, eh. What is your obsession with him?'

Taking the file from my hands, Bobby wandered over towards the windows to get a better light. He lifted one of the cuttings and fluttered it at me, eyes bright. The librarian narrowed her scowl and pinned us with a wintry glare.

'Jeez.' He shook his head. 'I remember reading all this stuff at the time. Why are you looking at it? Are you trying to solve the mystery or something?'

'What mystery?'

'Well – why he was killed.'

'What do you mean, why?'

'You know, like – was it over the book deal, like they thought? I'm sure it was.'

'I don't understand.'

'You know' – he scooted impatiently to the back of the file – 'it should be – wait – oh. Maybe there's another file.'

'I don't think so. But there's nothing in there about how he died, I've just read it.'

'He was shot.'

'When?'

'A few years ago – I forget – maybe six or so. I'd just gone to college and it was a big deal there, at Harvard, in the Institute for International Politics, because he was like the guy who knew everything in my field – he even came to give talks sometimes, you know? He wrote these thrillers, they were pretty good.'

'How was he shot?'

'What do you mean, *how*?' Bobby, wreathed in sunlight, looked baffled by the stupidity of the question. 'With a gun, you moron. But it was pretty obvious it was a hit-man, you know what I'm saying?'

'No.'

'Well – he'd just signed this book deal, right – did they have that in here?' He glanced at the file. 'Oh yeah. 'Kay, so you read that. So – he's investigating all this stuff which is pretty certain to implicate some of the big US arms traders.'

'Implicate them in what?'

'Selling arms illegally to Egypt during the arms embargo. We had this treaty not to arm Israel's enemies, right – but it was kind of suspected that some weapons were being sold to the Egyptians through Jordan. But if someone could prove it – actually name people – that would be a huge deal, especially for the pro-Israel lobby, and Andy Epstein was, like, fervently pro-Israel – he was way out there. You know – always on TV shows when they wanted an apologist for that side of it. I guess that's what the publisher hoped for when they gave him top dollar. But then – not long after that, I think – he was just shot and killed in the street.'

'And they think he was murdered?'

Bobby lifted the bottom of his shirt with one hand to flap air inside it.

'Well, I guess that's what everyone thought. I mean, it seems like a good reason, because of what he might have uncovered. If it was true, there must have been people who got nervous. But it was all speculation. I don't think the cops ever caught anyone. Also – he had this thing where he used to visit rent boys. I think I'm thinking of the same guy.' He looked out of the window at the bent figure of the man mowing the grass, as if this might provide confirmation. 'You know – so he used to go to parts of the city where you have to be pretty fucking dumb to go late at night wearing a hundred-dollar watch, you know what I'm saying? So it was maybe just a coincidence – or made to look like one.'

'But – no one looked into the background?' I was incredulous.

'I forget the details now – it was a while ago. Yeah, they investigated it for a year or more, but they didn't get anywhere. It's weird they don't have anything here.'

'They must have.' I glanced at the rolls of microfilm Bobby had left beside me on the table. 'What about if I check those?'

'Huh. Good luck. You need the exact date, else you'll be scrolling through green lights till your eyes pop.'

'Don't you remember the dates?'

'No. Well – wait. If it was my first year of college, it must have been – six years ago. Fall – late fall, maybe. Or maybe winter. Shit, I don't know. But six years ago – you'd have to get the microfilm for the whole year. That's a lot of reading. Why are you so interested, anyway?'

'Uh' – I picked at my thumbnail – 'I met someone who said he knew him. Epstein.'

'Could you please keep the noise down?' The man with the beard looked up peevishly from his screen.

'My apologies.' Bobby made an arc with his hand, as if to erase all his wrongs, then set the Epstein file down on the

183

table and seated himself at the far end of the room, slotting his reel into the squat microfiche reader.

'See you,' I mouthed, picking up the file.

'Later,' Bobby carolled across the desks. The bearded man humphed and tutted.

'Excuse me,' said the librarian as I made for the door. She made a pointed gesture to my arm, and I realised that the file was still jealously guarded under it.

'Oh – sorry. I was distracted.'

'Don't worry.' She gave a weighty sigh. 'I'll put it away.'

'Just – out of interest –'

'Yes?'

'Has anyone been using that file recently?'

She blinked over her flip-top glasses. 'You don't imagine I can keep track of every file that people take out, do you?'

'No. Sorry.'

'There's a notebook – there, on the table. If people have to take files down the hall for photocopying, that's where they sign them out. If they're just looking in here, there's no record, unless they're special ones that need to be ordered. But not if they just come out of the stacks.'

'It's just that – it doesn't seem quite up to date.'

'They're as up to date as they can be in the circumstances. I've only got one pair of hands. Well – there's Wendy, but she only comes on a Tuesday and even then she's next to useless. But she does type very fast.'

'Right. Sorry – I didn't mean to suggest . . . Never mind. Thanks.'

On the way out, I flicked – again, with the odd sensation of being furtive – through the photocopying book. No one except Bobby, as far as I could see, had taken the Epstein file for photocopying in the past six months. Trotting down the steps to the library's grand foyer, however, I began to feel distinctly uncomfortable. Six years ago in New York, it seemed, it was all happening. Piers Gaveston was meeting my uncle for the first time. Andy Epstein was researching a book about selling arms to the Middle East in the seventies. Andy Epstein – who was a friend of Piers's and, moreover, knew Oliver Dowland's father – was being shot and killed while out looking for rent boys, apparently.

Only connect. Perhaps I was inventing connections; seeing what wasn't there, looking for too much drama. But in the course of an afternoon, Andy Epstein had gone from being a name thrown idly into conversation to being a shadowy presence, lurking in the background of whatever relationship I imagined I might have with Piers Gaveston. Uncomfortably, the Middle East theme suggested only one possible link.

By the end of August, Edward was in trouble again. Electioneering had tentatively begun for the new English parliament, to be decided the following spring. The people's bright hopes in the present government were fading to disillusion, and the parliament was seen increasingly as the chance for a new start. A new England, itself alone, a clean slate. Swift to take advantage of this optimism was Lionel Phelps, the persuasive new Leader of the Opposition, an unabashed nationalist, staunch family man and moralist, whose popularity, the polls implied, waxed daily, and who was expected to carry his party if not to an outright victory, then at least to a coalition in the new assembly. Sir Edward, only just beginning to reap the fruits of his assiduous gestures of goodwill towards the incumbent government, was in no mood to start all over again with a new cadre. It could be no coincidence, then, that the *National Ledger*, Sir Edward's daily broadsheet, had revealed, in a week-long campaign of persecution, that Lionel Phelps was wont to walk his dog of an evening in a part of Hampstead Heath better known as a meeting place for certain gentlemen intent on less healthful pursuits. A member of the *Ledger*'s deft investigative team had accosted Lionel Phelps undercover and had been filmed conversing with him before departing in the direction of the public toilets.

No transaction had occurred, however, nor did the transcripts offer anything conclusive; Phelps had gone through the motions of initiating an expensive libel suit when, inexplicably, after a week of robust defiance, he suddenly crumpled, withdrew the legal action and promptly resigned as party leader. Sir Edward and his Editor-in-Chief, Mervyn Bland, were exultant. But elsewhere tempers were running high, since in the same week Francis Merry, a happily married junior minister in the Foreign Office, had been caught *in flagrante* in a lapdancing club being entertained by a fifteen-year-old performer, an episode to which Sir Edward's papers had scarcely alluded. Bland stood in the line of fire from politicians and rival newspapers alike, who bristled with indignation at his blatantly partisan coverage and accused Sir Edward of trading favours with the Prime Minister (who was tactfully off message in the Seychelles at the time).

Oliver had returned from Washington at the beginning of August, and it was shortly after the Lionel Phelps debacle that I went to meet him after work, in the hope of questioning him further on the subject of Andy Epstein. It was a Friday night, the Crown and Dragon's busiest time, and I found Oliver and some of his colleagues out at the back, clustered around a rickety table in what the Crown tried to pass off as a garden.

'So the next thing I know, she just *shoves* her breasts into my face!' Wesley Hemp almost jumped out of his seat, flapping his hands excitedly, 'and I'm thinking – bloody hell, woman – I know I'm irresistible, but at least wait until we're off air!'

'Wesley was on *HeadLines* last night to talk about the Lionel Phelps business,' Oliver explained, leaning across to me and flicking his eyes skywards.

Wesley lurched back, spilling everyone's pint. 'And she carries on asking me questions – as if I wasn't having enough trouble already – I mean, trying to follow the labyrinthine paths of Mervyn Bland's argument is like orienteering in the dark without a map at the best of times – how that man ever got to be an editor, I'll never comprehend. The concept of brevity doesn't even enter his consciousness and his tenses are leaping around all over the show like marmosets over the Cotswolds – so, as if that's not trouble enough, I have to contend with Sue Cousins's boobs in my face, and part of me's thinking, I might have a crack at this after the programme, and the other half's thinking, Oh my Christ on a bike, my wife will be watching – and Bland's carrying on unctuously about public interest, and I completely forget what I'm supposed to be saying – all I can see are these *tits*, and I'm thinking what is she *about*, and –'

'And?'

Wesley sipped his beer, looking deflated. 'Well – it turned out that in my excitement I'd knocked off my lapel mike at the beginning and nobody could hear a word I was saying. The producer told her to get close enough so that hers would pick up my voice. Yet another disappointment in my long catalogue. But that's enough about me – what did *you* think of my performance?'

'She's all right, Sue Cousins,' said a fattish man with glasses, thoughtfully. 'I'd do her. If it was a quiet week.'

'You were good, Wes,' said Oliver, raising his beer bottle. 'We approve of your calling Bland a pinguid stooge of government ideology. He was really stumped for a minute.'

'Well, he *is*!' Wesley slapped his hands down on the table indignantly, causing another spillage. 'I mean, I don't *like* Lionel Phelps, and if he will go a-cottaging with such devoted regularity just as his campaign's in full swing he should expect nothing less. But I do object to newspapers being used as bargaining tools for government and corporate interest. Whither free speech?' He threw his hands up dramatically again. 'But I'll tell you what – Hamilton-Harvey's set himself a trap with this – the faintest whiff of scandal from him and it'll all come crashing down on his head.'

'Hamilton-Harvey's clean as a whistle, unfortunately,' said the fat man.

'What are you *talking* about!' Wesley exploded. 'He wheels

and deals like it's going out of fashion! He's got more rackets going on than – than –'

'– than a tennis club,' said the fat man.

'Yeah, thanks, Vic – I was looking for something more creative.'

'You never hear about him having affairs, though, do you?' said Vic. 'Or going to dodgy clubs – the worst that's ever happened was his son got caught with the old Salvador. He must have *some* hidden vices.'

'He's too clever to let them show,' said Oliver, studiously peeling shreds of silver paper from the label of his bottle with a fingernail.

It was almost dark on the patio; gnats buzzed around a cracked lantern fixed to the garden wall. The pub's open door breathed out yeasty air and snatches of Edith Piaf. A short Scot in a lime-green corduroy suit came bounding down the steps, holding a pint in one hand and a whisky chaser in the other, an unlit cigarette propped behind his ear.

'Aye, aye, what's up, lads? Fuck me, thought I'd never get out tonight.' He set the glasses down on the table, squeezed on to the bench between Wesley and Oliver, plucked the cigarette out, flared a match and held it to the tip, then breathed in thankfully and grinned. 'Mike's in fine form tonight, Jesus H! Fucking nine-thirty and he suddenly wants to redo the whole front page – Gordon's about to lamp him.'

'He's been a bit upset since this morning,' said Wesley. 'I had to tell him that unfortunately that story I came up with in yesterday's conference was not quite as good as I made out.'

'In what sense?'

'In the sense that – it's not true.'

'Gaby – this is Duncan Doune, our Opinion editor,' Oliver offered. 'Duncan – my friend, Gabriele Harvey.'

'She's a princess of the Evil Empire,' Wesley added darkly.

'Is that so?' Duncan Doune sized me up. 'Of the International Media Harveys, are you? Oh – talking of which' – turning to his wider audience he prodded the cigarette in the air for emphasis, its glowing tip dancing in the gloom – 'guess who I saw Mike having lunch with today?'

He leaned forward expectantly, and was met with a universal shaking of heads.

'Becki Burke.' He paused to let this register. 'Aye. Hugging and back-slapping like they've just connived some deal. I wouldn't be surprised if we had a new addition to our happy family very soon.'

'Becki *Burke*?' Wesley groaned and grasped his head in his hands. 'Thus the charter flight of the *Sunday Enquirer* continues its irreversible plunge towards the dank polluted swamp of mediocrity. Tell me it's not true.'

'You know Mike – always keen to up the beaver count in the office,' said Vic. Then he looked at me. 'No offence, pet.'

'Mike prides himself on knowing how to separate the wheat from the chaff,' said Wesley, gloomily.

'And then he hires the chaff,' said Duncan.

'Do you think he's trying to shag her?' mused Vic.

'Of course – he's Mike. And he won't have to try very hard, by all accounts,' said Duncan Doune, pulling heavily on his cigarette. 'But if he thinks she's writing on my pages, he can fuck right off. Why did she get sacked from the Evil Empire, incidentally? Anyone know?'

'Bland's whim, I s'pose,' said Vic.

'Bland doesn't have whims,' said Wesley. 'He's a puppet. If there's any whims involved, they come straight from the Dark One. She must have upset one of his friends or something. Who cares? She's still a slapper.'

I remembered, suddenly, Piers Gaveston's throwaway joke about having Becki Burke fired after the interview, and glanced sideways at Oliver. He was still engrossed in tearing the label and didn't look up.

'Good arse, though,' said Vic, after a moment's reflection.

'Mate' – Duncan Doune shook his head – 'I'm all in favour of good arses, no one could be more so, but there's a time and a place, and it's not on my pages, right?'

He tore open a packet of peanuts, which the others fell upon like refugees.

In the kerfuffle I nudged closer to Oliver.

'So I asked Piers Gaveston your question about Andy Epstein.'

He looked almost guilty at being reminded. 'Oh? What did he say?'

'Well, not surprisingly, it didn't go down very well, since it turns out the bloke was a friend of his and he was shot dead.'

'I know.'

'You *know*?'

'Yes – I thought I told you that?'

'No, you bloody didn't.' I punched his leg under the table. 'Olly! Do you have any idea how embarrassing that was? You told me to ask him if he'd heard any news – I felt so stupid! Why didn't you tell me?'

'I told you to ask if there was any news about the case, I thought.'

'That's not what you said.'

Oliver was looking at his hands. 'Sorry. Did he look upset?'

'Well – yes, of course – wouldn't you be? What's all this about?' I pressed. 'How do you know Andy Epstein?'

'Did I hear you say Andy Epstein?' asked Duncan Doune, leaning round Oliver.

'No,' said Oliver.

'Yes,' I said, at the same time.

'That's the American hack who was killed over the arms dealing book, right?'

'God, you've got a good memory,' Oliver said, though he looked more annoyed than impressed.

Duncan grinned and took a gulp of his beer. 'I'd like to claim that's so, but it's pure coincidence. I was talking to Chris Haughton about it the other day. Did you know he worked on that story?'

'Is that right?' Oliver picked at the mole on his face.

'Inasmuch as Chris Haughton's ever really *worked* on anything,' Wesley chipped in.

Duncan ignored him. 'He was the *Herald*'s man in New York for a while, whenever it was – seven, eight years ago –'

'Six,' said Oliver automatically, then looked up, surprised. 'Something like that.'

'Okay, so he covered it for them. It's a great story – you should get him talking about it, he's still really obsessed. I was looking at his cuttings book the other day –'

'Christ, you must have been at a loose end.'

'Wes, would you shut the fuck up? Chris is all right – you never talk to him.'

'I have no desire to *talk* to him – I've read his copy. The man couldn't write "bum" on a wall even with a team of subs to rewrite it for him.'

Duncan sighed with excessive patience. 'Ignore this bag of shite, he's in a foul mood with Mike. But you know, they never caught the guy who killed him. Epstein. Or who paid the guy who killed him, I should say. Apparently he'd been investigating these illegal deals for years – it was all nicked, all his notes – but they reckoned he'd come up with something big. Poor bastard. You see?' He turned to me and thumped his chest. 'We are bold and fearless men, we journalists, facing death every minute of the day in our crusade to bring readers the truth about the evil and corruption that lurks beneath the veneer of civilisation –'

'Up the ante! *He*' – Wesley slapped an arm around Duncan's shoulders – 'spends his day on the phone to has-been economists and backbenchers and slappers begging them to write eight hundred words for about four pounds, then he comes in here at five o'clock, and the only danger he faces is lung and liver disease.'

'Whereas you sit on your arse and blow raspberries at the Government from behind your comfy desk, which is dead heroic.' Duncan beamed sweetly at his friend. 'I've been to the Balkans.'

'On holiday.'

'It's still further than the Party Conference cocktail lounge in Bournemouth.'

'Fuck you. I'm a revolutionary.'

'Fuck you back, with a ten-foot narwhal tusk. You're a fart in the wind.'

'D'you want to do the quiz machine?'

'Sure.'

Duncan sprang up the steps, clinking change, with Wesley shambling after him.

''Scuse me, just going for a slash,' said Vic, and followed them.

Oliver and I looked at each other for some moments in silence.

'So you're seeing a lot of Piers Gaveston, then?'

'Oh, you know. Not really. A bit.'

'But are you – *seeing* him?'

'Uh – I don't think so. I'm just writing some stuff with him.'

'Writing.'

'Yes. It's a thing about Arthur. A TV programme, I told you.'

'That's handy.'

'What's your problem, Olly?' Silence. I tried again. 'What did Duncan mean, about Andy Epstein's notes being stolen?'

'How should I know?' He looked away. There was a tight pause.

'Food?' Oliver said, eventually, with unconvincing brightness. It was apparent that the Epstein conversation would not be taken any further.

September brought the news that the Faculty of English Literature was to be closed down.

'It simply couldn't compete,' George said, without looking up from his desk, where he was hunched gnomically over a folder of typescript pages. 'They do proper cappuccini in the new building, you know.'

'This is exactly what I said would happen, and everybody promised it wouldn't. Everything's relegated to second best next to the new faculty – one by one all the old courses will go the same way, and everyone will forget. We'll forget our own history.' I slumped back on the battered leather sofa amid teetering stacks of books, resting my feet on the edge of the coffee table and poking the floating leaves on the surface of my tea with a pencil. George considered tea bags an unnecessary nod to the modern age.

'Quite right, Cassandra, quite right. But we didn't expect the numbers to drop quite so rapidly.'

George carried on reading, rattling a Werther's butterscotch around his mouth. Duruflé's *Requiem* floated comfortingly from the speakers either side of the fireplace. Through the windows, the last of the summer sunlight spilled in patterns, seeming already old and faded, and from the street below burbled up a gentle noise of traffic and children's voices. For six years now I had been coming here to seek sanctuary, cushioned in this sofa in this fusty, friendly, book-lined room where nothing could ever be found under the confusion of papers and poems and manuscripts and half-written things; where choral music always spilled, furious and otherworldly, from the speakers – Tallis, Ockeghem, Palestrina, Schütz – and where I would munch the familiar shortbread, pile sugar into the undrinkable tea and take courage from George's kindly smile, calm wisdom and certain advice. It seemed impossible to think of it coming to an end.

'George – sorry – but we're in danger of losing a great wodge of our culture here, and you don't seem all that concerned.'

'All shall be well, Gaby.' Finally he looked up, tucking his pen behind his ear and folding his hands. 'All manner of things shall be well. This isn't the end of the world – we'll just have to expand the Comparative Literature module in the new faculty. That's where they've all gone, of course, the new students.'

'That'll never work. You can't get the whole of English writing into a one-year course. And they don't do anything before 1830. What's going to happen to the rest of our literature? My stuff – *your* stuff? If this university of all places gives up on the beginnings, who else will bother? It will just wither and die.'

'You know – I've never like the word module,' George mused, his attention somewhere out of the window. He crunched slowly. 'It always makes me think of an unwelcome growth. You'd probably get it in an armpit – Doctor, I think I'm developing a nasty *module*. But it's unworthy of you Gaby, to assume that people will only read what's prescribed by a course structure. The curious ones – the good ones – will sniff out the interesting writers for themselves. You did.'

I smiled. 'I had you.'

'And the lucky, lucky young things on the Comparative Literature course shall have me also. We can move the goal posts once we're up and running. And I hope that, in time they'll have you too, to take up the baton when I'm old and frail.'

There was a sticky pause.

'Comparative Literature,' George repeated thoughtfully pausing to stuff his pipe with tobacco. 'As if there's any other kind. But it was inevitable, you're right. Who would willingly opt for the hard graft of learning medieval poetry when they could be over the road studying the latest Ismail Awena with the charming Professor Gaveston and a free job in a film studio thrown in?'

'*I* would.' I felt a blush spreading.

'Ah, well. They don't make many like you, Gaby However' – he held up the sheaf of papers before him and riffled it – 'this seems a little – *scant*, shall we say – for a whole summer's work from someone whose thesis is already late Am I being unfair?' He raised an eyebrow at me through a drift of oaky smoke.

'No, I –' I shifted slightly and a pile of books toppled off the arm of the sofa on to my lap. 'I know it's not – I've been doing some other things.'

'Such as writing Piers Gaveston's television series, for example?'

'Yes – how did you know?'

'He told me.' He laughed. 'I don't mind about that one bit – I'd have thought it was rather a good opportunity for you, in fact – going back to the basics might revive your flagging interest. And it'll be nice to use your talents a bit further afield. Make sure he gives you a credit.' He tapped the pipe on the side of his wide blue ashtray. The layered voices of the *Agnus Dei* hovered in the air like smoke. 'But you see – I know you don't like me mentioning this, but I'm going to – you have the luxury of funding yourself through this doctorate, which takes the sting of urgency out of finishing it somewhat. I don't want to see you lose heart and drift away without closing this chapter.'

'I wouldn't. I mean – I don't have anything else.'

'No – but I see you getting restless sometimes. You've been in this place a long time, and you're still young – it's only to be expected. You don't happen to know where Piers is at the moment, I suppose?'

I sat up, startled. 'No. I haven't seen him.'

George humphed quietly.

'Why?'

'Because I haven't seen him either. No one has. The last I heard, he was at the Toronto Film Festival, but that was two weeks ago. Honestly – in three weeks' time we've got to open the doors of this new faculty to its first ever intake of students, with all the media's thousand eyes upon us, and our professors is nowhere to be found. I've not heard from him all summer, and we've been breaking our backs to get the lecture courses and admissions up and running. I know he's only nominally in charge, but even so –' He reached for his tea, shaking his head. 'I'm sorry – I shouldn't be letting off steam like this to you. Entirely my own responsibility.'

'You appointed him.'

'Well – not exactly.'

'How, *not exactly*?'

'Oh dear. You know this already, Gaby – he came free with the faculty, if you like. It wasn't a question of my appointing him.'

'You mean, he was part of the sponsorship deal?'

'Exactly. He was the proviso. The reason Edward opened his purse so generously.'

'Why?'

George turned his chair round to face me and crossed his legs. 'You'd have to ask Edward. I suspect – though I didn't ask – that it's a matter of repaying a favour – you know how these things work in Edward's world.' He hesitated. 'I see the disapproval on your face. You think I've defected to Edward over this faculty, don't you?'

I picked at a threadbare patch on the arm of the sofa. 'I just don't understand why you've fought so hard for something that seems to be the epitome of everything we've always said we hated. *You* always said you hated.'

'Because –' George stood up slowly, stretching, and crossed the room to the tea-pot. 'More tea?'

I shook my head.

'What about a whisky?' He glanced at his watch. 'It's nearly six – will you have a whisky with me?'

'Okay. Thanks.'

'This is a good one.' He lifted a hefty decanter, half-full, and poured two large glasses. Handing one to me, he sat down, this time in the high-backed chair opposite me, where he used to sit for tutorials. 'Because sometimes you have to look ahead. And because I know Edward,' he said. 'I've known him for a lot longer than you have, in fact. He'd heard that the plans for the new faculty had run aground, but he knew the university authorities would be suspicious of him – some of his interests being rather less than liberal, shall we say. So he wanted me as a middle man. And the Vice-

196

Chancellor, whose word is law, may act the bumbling Luddite quite convincingly, but he's shrewd as a stoat and he knows an opportunity when he sees one. So I was made Chair of the Faculty Planning Committee so I could push Edward's money through and give it a gloss of credibility on the way. Because I could see he had decided he was going to have this, no matter what, and as you know, Gaby, Edward always gets his own way, in the end.'

'Only because people give in to him.'

'And if they don't, he simply bulldozes them out of the way and replaces them with people who will do his bidding. He wanted this feather in his cap. He wanted to buy into the university, in effect, to make it his, and the more it played hard to get, the more single-minded he would become in his pursuit. So –' he paused again to relight his pipe, 'I did think very carefully about this before I got involved. But I reasoned that I could do more good as Edward's ally than I ever could standing on the sidelines harrumphing. And – without blowing my own trumpet – he needed my name to dress up a corporate takeover as a respectable step forward for scholarship. But, you see, I do believe it can be.'

'With heavy casualties.'

'Ah, Gaby. There is a tendency in this university to fear change, and therefore to pretend it can't and won't happen. In fact, it's a tendency in this country. In recent years it began to worry me – I'm an Englishman to the core, but when England truly becomes 'England' again, I fear we will become a less tolerant nation, not more. And I see the same spirit of resistance at work here. Our friend Piers was right, you know – there is an enemy at the gate, and we can choose to let it in and befriend it, or wait for it to destroy us altogether. Culture doesn't stand still, Gaby, as you seem to wish it would. English culture, literature – it's not a rigid structure – there are other forces, other voices, other arts being woven in all the time. It's dynamic – it's a happy thing.' He smiled broadly. 'We gain more than we lose. And I think Piers Gaveston, for

all his easy words and his self-love, has a very good grasp o[f]
how to filter in the new influences without distorting wha[t]
already exists. At least' – he paused – 'he would if he coul[d]
direct his energies into it sufficiently.'

I swooshed the whisky around my glass, watching it slid[e]
smoothly down the sides. George sat sideways in his chair[,]
his elbow resting on the arm, watching me curiously.

'It's an odd thing, isn't it – beauty?' he said, after a while[,]
carefully avoiding my eye. 'Too much of it can be more of [a]
curse than a blessing. I mean real beauty – the rare, excep[-]
tional kind that Piers Gaveston has. *For such, being made beau[-]
tiful over-much, lose loving kindness . . .* '

A hot flush was spreading to the tips of my fingers. George
carried on, as if to himself: 'It fascinates me, you know, t[o]
watch how people respond to him. It's almost like sorcery[.]
Glamour – that's what it meant, originally, you know. To b[e]
beglamoured – to have a spell put over you. Even I – and [I]
assure you, I'm an old cynic with no interest in pretty boys [–]
I sometimes feel I would gladly agree with him on anything[,]
and I think, God help anyone who falls in love with him. H[e]
works a kind of magic. But I wonder what it must be like fro[m]
his side.'

'What do you mean?'

'Well – to have borne that all your life. To have learned that
your face outshines everything else about you – and that it has
this extraordinary power to persuade people to almost anything you want – it must be very dangerous. You'd take for
granted getting your own way, I imagine. And how you must
fear losing it!' George shook his head. 'Especially at his age.'

I sat up. 'Why – how old is he?'

'Piers? I think he's about thirty-eight, thirty-nine. Not far
off forty, anyway. He's damn well preserved. I think he's
happy to let people assume he's younger.'

I smiled to myself, hugging my knees to my chest like a
secret. So he thought he knew things about me? Well, I could
play that game too – now I had a nugget of information he

didn't know I had, and I would relish it until the time was right.

The record had come to an end and the turntable continued to turn with a slow, dusty click in the quiet.

'I'd better get home,' George said, scraping together some papers from the desk, 'or Mary will have a fit. Have you seen my glasses?' He lifted a couple of newspapers vaguely. 'Here –' he passed the folder with my work in back over his shoulder. 'Now then – have a read of my notes, and pop back in a couple of days and we'll talk about where you need to flesh this out. How do you feel about that?'

'I can do that,' I said, quite cheerful now. 'My television commission is almost finished.'

George chuckled. 'I knew you'd get the bug eventually. We'll make a telly-don of you yet. Now go and do some proper work. Oh, and Gaby –'

I paused at the door.

'Be wary of Piers Gaveston, eh? Keep your head screwed on.' He winked, and I rolled my eyes in return.

Leaving George's room, I crossed the old bridge over the river and saw, on the other side of the courtyard, Piers Gaveston walking towards me. At first I thought I must be imagining it. He wore a long, black leather coat over a high-collared suit, and a casual half-smile that gave no recognition of the fact that I hadn't seen him for three months.

'Hi.'

'Hi.' I blinked into the low sun, shading my eyes.

'Good summer?' He pushed his hair back, the fringe bleached almost white by the sun. His eyes seemed luminous against his summer skin; there was a small strip of fresh pink on his nose where he had burned and peeled, touchingly boyish.

'Oh – yes, not bad. You've been away?'

'Mmm. Here and there. California, mostly. I'm glad I ran into you, I was going to leave you a message.'

My brain jolted. 'Really?'

'I need you to come to a film premiere with me next week. Wednesday.' It was as matter-of-fact as his dinner invitation had been; he appeared to realise this, and back-tracked slightly. 'I meant to say – I would *like* you to come with me. Do you know Nick Strachey?'

I made an ambiguous gesture with my head, hoping not to reveal my ignorance.

'He's good. I think one of the best of the new English directors. But unusual. You might not like it – his techniques are quite – uh – innovative. Anyway. See what you think. Oh, and' – he turned as if to go – 'dress up nicely. There'll be TV. I'm interviewing him for *The Film Show*.'

'Okay,' I said, dumbly. I remembered what George had said, and almost laughed in recognition; the magnificent assumption, the fact that it had not once crossed his mind that I might be busy or say no.

'Do you know if George is in?' He jerked a thumb towards the opposite bank of the river, already edging away from me, walking backwards.

'You might catch him if you hurry.'

'Good. I'll see you next week. I'll get a car to pick you up from the station, about six. Don't be late – there'll be traffic. By the way' – he broke into a glinting, fluoride smile – 'you're looking very well.'

'Thanks.'

Very *well*? Did that mean I had always looked unwell before?

Leaving me frowning, he turned and strode away over the bridge, his coat flapping behind him like the wings of a great, leathery pterodactyl.

Chapter XI

'What's it *about*?' I whispered into the stuffy darkness.

Piers barely moved his head, his profile lit intermittently by the hard, purplish light blinking from the screen.

'I think that's rather a superficial question, don't you?'

I sighed, and rearranged myself in the cramped seat. Nick Strachey's plotless, jumbled feature was the cinematic equivalent of those unbound books that enjoyed a brief popularity in the early sixties, the ones whose pages you could rearrange in any order to reflect the essentially absurd, incoherent and meaningless nature of the human condition, or some such, provoking in me the ungenerous suspicion that the young auteur's reputation for innovation was perhaps not wholly deserved. Nevertheless, Piers Gaveston was beside me with his leg pressed against mine – though he seemed less overwhelmed than I by this progress – and for that alone I would cheerfully have sat through *World Without End* in all its baffling disjointed existentialism several dozen times over.

Unfolding on the screen before us was this:

A dystopian urban panorama; an empty lot strewn with burnt-out cars, disembowelled domestic appliances, patchy mattresses leaking wire and stuffing, and rusted oil-drums, on the horizon of which stand two buildings: a crumbling Victorian church and a twenty-storey concrete tower block. The church, blackened with neglect, has been converted into a warehouse, and is piled high with broken computers and televisions. In the foreground, an elderly man in a grimy waterproof coat painstakingly sets out a table of second-hand books, shabby and creased; the camera pans along them, showing the titles, all twentieth-century English novels. Here are Forster and Lawrence; there, beside them,

Woolf and Orwell piled high next to Waugh and Huxley; relics of a nation's imagination. From time to time, other characters – well dressed, like business people – cross the screen to the book-stall, engage in terse, cryptic dialogue with the old man, and purchase a book furtively, as if it were contraband. This scene cuts rapidly back and forth to another: a dingy room at the top of a tower block (the same tower block?) in which a crippled girl of about twelve or thirteen is supine on a bed among filthy sheets, watching television. People enter this room too, sporadically; men in suits, one at a time, or possibly the same man several times, led by a thin, androgynous youth who seems to be the girl's brother and who, it becomes apparent, is also her pimp. The girl lies, immobile, her head turned to the left, eyes fixed to the television, on which are rolling scenes from classic English films: *Brief Encounter*, *The Lady Vanishes*, *Tom Jones*, *This Sporting Life*, and others, all spliced together in a pointedly symbolic diorama; occasionally the lens switches, though the shot remains the same, to a grainy, quivering hand-held camera and it becomes clear that the boy is videoing each scene, compiling a library of hundreds of video tapes documenting the visit of each punter (or each visit of the same punter). It is hinted – though never made explicit – that the boy may be the same character as the old man, and that the entire scene might be purely the product of his imagination. Then again, it might not. Needless to say, it is almost always raining, and dark.

I eased my arm up against Piers's on the shared arm rest with a gentle, optimistic pressure, but he just muttered 'oh, sorry' without taking his eyes from the screen, and moved his own out of the way. I sighed again, crossed and uncrossed my legs, tried to stretch my back as unobtrusively as possible and glanced down at my watch, aware that an open display of boredom would not be the best way to impress Piers. I urgently wanted him to believe that my cultural interests reached further than medieval archives – had even looked up

reviews of Nick Strachey's earlier work in old film journals –
but I couldn't help wondering if anyone else in the cinema
was finding it as numbingly tedious as I was.

'Could you stop fidgeting?' Piers hissed, impatiently.

I froze. Are you actually enjoying this, I wanted to ask, but
didn't.

The thin-faced youth was delivering a sonorous soliloquy
in close-up in the style of Gerard Manley Hopkins over the
chorus of 'Carrie Anne' by the Hollies; Piers leaned forward
as if anticipating a climactic moment, so I followed his example. The screen went suddenly blue.

I had met Piers earlier that evening as promised, stretched
out in the back seat of the limousine that picked me up from
the station. He seemed relaxed – pleased to see me, even –
asking how my Glastonbury research was coming along,
chatting about his own work, with no trace of the brittle
reluctance he had displayed when inviting me. The car bore
us slowly through a snarl of traffic to the West End and up an
aisle of crash barriers through photographers and curious
passers-by, who were gathering around the cordoned-off
approach to the Arena cinema. Piers paused for a moment,
surveying the square with a hand slanted across his eyes, the
low sun clipping his face over the roof of the facing building.
He turned, slowly, to either side into a burst of flash-bulbs,
offering accommodating nods and half-smiles to the photographers – but the peering crowds looked nonplussed, as if
they'd been expecting a better-known face. The evening was
mild, edged with the sudden damp of autumn; Leicester
Square was bustling and lit-up and smelled of frying onions
and cigarette smoke. I fixed on an appropriate smile, took
Piers's arm and walked up to the entrance hoping to appear
as if I did this all the time.

Edward, tanned as varnish and bound tightly into a dinner
suit, was pacing the foyer, beset by photographers, with
Roger pacing watchfully at his heel. Flynn and Glyn lolled

either side of a pillar, looking like a pair of Mob enforcers.

'Piers!' Edward's face lit up as we entered. He clapped Piers on the shoulder; Roger skewered us with a particularly misanthropic glare. 'Is this thing going to take long? Because I quite wanted to get a bit of dinner afterwards – Roger's booked somewhere, where did you book, Rodge?'

'Apostolos,' said Roger, still scowling at Piers. Edward made a face.

'Huh. Well, better than a kick in the pants, I suppose. But we've got to show our faces at this bloody party, have we? What time did you book?'

'Nine.'

Piers shook his head, I thought with slight irritation. 'Not a chance. It's a long movie, and I've got to do this interview with Nick at the party – and there are people I want to see. You'll have to make it later – but don't count on me getting away even then. This is work for me, remember?'

'Yes – Roger, what were you thinking of – nine! Ridiculous. Make it later!' Edward turned back to Piers, wheedling. 'Not *too* much later, though, eh?'

Piers shrugged.

'Hey hey hey!' Jerome Idle descended on us in a carnival-esque shirt, arms wide as if finding us there had made this the happiest day of his life. 'My new boss, so to speak, and his lovely lady – how are we? Looking forward to the all-singing, all-dancing world premiere? Nick's that nervous, he could shit himself.'

Piers nodded curtly; I swallowed a squeak of disbelief. It was the first time I'd been acknowledged as Piers's lady – how did he feel about this? I looked up at him quizzically but he was staring absently across the room.

'Of course, he's late as per,' Jerome continued, oblivious, 'still takes the bus everywhere, bless him, can't get over the fact he's not on the dole any more – he just called but I couldn't make out a word he said – think he might be in Wandsworth, or possibly Woolworth's, so we might have to start without him. Hey – and you'll have to restrain me if he brings his bloody mother – I get this urge to kill her every time she opens her mouth. Mind you – if any judge ever clapped eyes on her, I'd get off with a caution, eh, know what I mean? Do you know Nick's stuff, ah – sorry, I've forgotten your name?'

'Gaby. Not – uh, not very well,' I faltered.

'Well, I think you'll be surprised – this is a bit of a departure, especially if you bear in mind *Who the Fuck Is Alice*? Of course, that was four years ago and he's trying to move right away from that sort of urbany angsty magicky realism thing – in fact, basically, it might be better if you don't compare it to *Alice* at all. Yes – try to forget *Alice* altogether while you're watching, won't you, basically, that's your best bet.'

'I'll – certainly try,' I said sincerely, without revealing just how easy this would be, then thought I should show a greater degree of interest. 'Is it a comedy?'

Jerome Idle threw his head back and guffawed; Piers smiled grimly.

'Depends on your sense of humour,' said Piers. 'And how you define "absurd"'.

Jerome slapped him on the back. 'Funnier than your bloody jokes anyway, mate. Oh yeah' – his face clouded – 'the word is, Neville Toynbee hates it. Not good news.'

Piers pressed his lips together tightly. 'So?'

'So – just saying.'

'What – you still yearn for his imprimatur?'

'Well – just that Neville's usually on the money, so to speak, with the box office. Just thought you should know – his review's coming out Sunday and people take notice. For God's sake don't tell Nick.'

Piers shrugged. 'Oh, screw the box office. Screw Neville Toynbee.'

Jerome grimaced. 'Don't let him hear you say that, mate. He'd love it.'

There was a crashing of doors, and in stumbled a tall young

man in some disarray, with a pocked face and a corduroy jacket rubbed thin with age.

'Nick!' Jerome flung his arms out again. ''Bout buggering time!'

'Sorry, folks.' Nick Strachey looked bewildered, like a small child who has been woken unexpectedly. He flapped a hand helplessly. 'Total nightmare getting here, you know – Mum hit a cyclist and we had to stop and make sure he was okay –'

He jabbed a thumb towards the sturdy, large-hipped woman behind him, who looked as if she ought to drive a Land Rover. She wore a long skirt and a burgundy sweatshirt that bore a white line-drawing of a mill and the proud slogan 'I've Been To Constable Country!'

'Oh, shit – loads of people,' said Nick Strachey in genuine alarm, pulling open the door to the cinema, as if he had not been expecting anyone to turn up and would have preferred it if they hadn't.

'Don't worry – they'll love it,' Piers said softly, and I noticed him rub Nick's arm in a friendly, comforting way. How nice of him to be so reassuring, I thought, warmed by the idea that he did have a good side.

For a dismal moment it appeared that Edward, who was trying to organise the seating, had condemned me to sit between Roger and Mrs Strachey, but with some judicious manoeuvring I contrived to get myself next to Piers, folded my legs into the narrow space and leaned as far as I could towards him without being too obvious. Jerome bounced into the seat on my other side.

'Here – have some popcorn,' he said, holding out a striped carton. 'I put sugar in it – I thought, most people like sugar, don't they? It's frigging disgusting with salt if you ask me.' I was about to take it when Piers leaned across me, looking exasperated.

'*Jesus*, Jerome – you're not at a Disney flick with your kids. I don't want to listen to you eating all the way through.'

'Uh – thanks, I won't,' I said to Jerome, regretfully.

Jerome nodded towards Piers and wiggled his shoulders in a mocking gesture, but he tucked the popcorn under his seat. From the row behind came Mrs Strachey's voice: 'Nick! How am I supposed to put my bag down if your feet are there? You'd think they could have forked out for a bigger auditorium, wouldn't you, still, that's the British film world for you – no vision . . .'

The lights went down. Elgar's *Enigma Variations* began to play, softly.

Prometheus Productions presents
WORLD WITHOUT END
a film by Nick Strachey
Producer Jerome Idle
with
Verlaine DuPrey   Lucy Vaughan   Anthony Gibbon

As the credits rolled and a damp sun rose over the tower block, I worked my shoulder close enough to Piers's to feel the rise and fall of his breathing in the inviting dark.

The blueness of the screen had apparently been a glitch in the reel. It allowed the audience a few moments for unrestrained coughing, and when it was repaired, the girl prostitute appeared to have died, though from what causes I could not entirely remember, if I had ever known in the first place. The final tableau – the young man kneeling by her bed, the camera moving slowly back from the window to a long shot of the landscape outside – heralded the credits and the house lights, and the cinema was filled with the rustling of trousers and people guiltily shaking themselves awake. The film had lasted nearly three hours.

'What did she die of?' I whispered to Jerome, perplexed.

'Aids,' said Piers, overhearing. 'She got ill while he was away in Ireland.'

'Who was in Ireland?' I turned back to him.

'The brother.'

'He was in *Ireland*?'

'Of course – when he was looking for his father. Were you asleep or something?'

'No,' I said hastily, 'I just wasn't sure if it was Ireland, or – uh – Scotland.'

Piers sucked in his cheeks. 'It was just before the helicopter crash.'

'Right,' I nodded, utterly lost. He shook his head.

'There wasn't a helicopter crash. So you *were* asleep.'

I blushed, but he was smiling.

'So – what did you think of the bits you did see?'

'I thought it was very – interesting,' I said carefully.

'That means you hated it.' He stood up to put on his jacket, stretching his arms.

'No – no, I just didn't quite –' I hesitated. 'It didn't have much of a story.'

'You are an incorrigible humanist.' He shook his head sadly, as if I were beyond help.

'What did you think, then?'

'I thought' – he rubbed his chin and looked up at the ceiling – 'I thought it was a deliberately self-parodying criticism of the creative process, in particular the cinematic process, highlighting the derivative nature of art while at the same time exposing the non-linear progress of history and the narratives we try to impose on it to limit our own sense of chaos.'

'Oh.'

He looked back at me and smiled, suddenly. 'I just made that up.'

'Not exactly *Lawrence of Arabia*, was it?' Roger said loudly, as we trooped down the stairs towards the foyer. Nick Strachey quivered.

Piers glanced at Roger, then leaned to Nick, with a whisper designed to carry: 'Ignore him – he's just the secretary.'

Roger bristled.

'And I suppose you'll be pronouncing the definitive critical verdict, will you, *Professor*?'

Piers smiled charmingly. 'That's right. And you'll be holding the coats, as usual?'

Roger's dyspeptic expression acidified further.

'Do be very careful your vowels don't slip on camera, Piers.'

'Roger, you are truly Wildean this evening.' Piers carried on smiling, though he was showing his teeth. Roger was saved by Edward's appearance at Piers's elbow, wearing a worried frown.

'Quick, Piers, you've got to give me a line,' he said, looking over his shoulder.

Piers arched an eyebrow, amused. 'Could you not wait until we get to the party?'

Edward's brow puckered briefly in confusion, then he shook his head impatiently. 'Not *that* – Christ – I mean, a line I can give that pack of reporters outside when they ask me what I thought of the film. Couldn't make head nor bloody tail of it, but I can hardly say that, can I? Piers? What do I tell them?'

Piers stroked his thumbnail along his lower lip, watching Edward thoughtfully.

'You tell them you thought it raised some provocative questions and the camerawork was some of the most impressive you've seen in recent years. That should do. Or you say "It's a film that has that rare ability to make you stop and think about your own life".'

'Makes you think your own life is too short to waste on films like that,' Roger remarked. '*World Without End*. Ha. *Boredom Without End*, more like.' No one took any notice.

'Provocative questions about what, though?' Edward looked concerned.

'About art and memory and the English class system, I don't know. Then you run for the car before they realise you're talking through your trousers.'

'Will it make money?' Edward asked, as if this had only just occurred to him.

Piers gave a derisive laugh; Roger smirked.

'No one in their right mind would pay five *pounds* to watch that in a cinema, let alone five million to make it in the first place.'

'Watch yourself, Rodge.' Edward pinned him with a warning glance.

'It was only two million,' said Nick Strachey, mildly aggrieved, 'and it's not about making money – I mean, you just don't make money with independent film. I'm not into that studio-driven, commercial mentality where film is made by committee – I mean, obviously it would be nice if it made a bit of money, but if that was all I cared about I could go to Hollywood.'

'Hollywood schmollywood,' said Mrs Strachey, bustling up with her handbag under her arm. 'You stick with your principles, Nicholas. Anyway – you know you can't be out in the sun. Is anyone else as famished as I am? They'd better have some decent nibbles at this do.'

'God help us if they don't,' Jerome whispered from behind me, giggling.

Piers had wandered a little way off and was deep in conversation with a man in a hooded fleece who wore a large pair of cushioned headphones round his neck. The fleece man was pointing to his watch and gesticulating.

'Who's that?' I asked Jerome.

'Him? Pete Lindsay, producer of *The Film Show* – you know P.G.'s doing this interview with Nick for them? Which reminds me – better gather the troops, we should get going.'

'Nick! Come on, we've got to get make-up.' Piers walked back to the group, hands in pockets.

'I'll come with you,' said Mrs Strachey, gathering her umbrella.

'No, you won't,' said Piers firmly. Mrs Strachey opened her mouth to protest, but Piers was staring her down, calmly, as

210

you would a fierce dog. 'Nick needs some time to concentrate. This is important.'

Mrs Strachey battled inwardly for a moment, then buckled into agreement.

Piers looked at me vaguely, as if only just remembering why I was there. 'I'll see you at the party,' he said. 'You know where it is, don't you? Edward's got a car going, he can give you a lift, I expect – it's just, I've got to do this thing.' He turned to go.

'Piers?' Edward called after him, stepping forward. 'I do want to get away from this party fairly early, you know.'

'Edward – no one will stop you,' Piers replied, with a defiance I had not heard anyone except his wife use to my uncle before. Evidently there was some understanding between them that either gave Piers licence to bypass the deference Sir Edward usually demanded, or which assumed the lack of respect was only in jest. I had not seen them together enough to determine which, but this antagonistic fencing hinted at a closeness I hadn't perceived before. How had Piers earned such familiarities, denied to my uncle's other courtiers?

A piano was being played, drunkenly, in another room, and the bar was a crush of hot, shouting people, swerving past one another, balancing too many drinks, spilling with each step. The air was thick with smoke, a layer visible under the lights.

'That's that bald chap from that detective series,' Roger observed, pointing with his cigar. We were trapped in a corner with an ebullient rubber plant; Sir Edward was circulating, in as far as circulation was possible in the narrow upper bar of the private members' club whose name was a shibboleth to those in the world of film and television. 'Isn't it?'

I shrugged. 'I don't know – I don't watch much television.'

'Of course – your interests are more rarified. Though I can't help noticing you've come out of your hermitage with surprising frequency since Piers Gaveston arrived on the scene. Quite the society girl.'

I ignored him.

'So? What's the story? Are you *together*?'

I shrugged. 'I don't know.'

'Well, let me fill you in. The only person who interests Piers Gaveston apart from himself is Edward.'

I turned to look at him, biting the inside of my cheek.

'If he pays you any attention at all,' Roger continued, 'it's only because you're the Crown Princess.'

'The *what*?'

'Oh, come now. You're being groomed as the smiling face of Hamilton-Harvey family values. Sir Edward needs to be seen to be investing in a continuum, it's good for his profile – don't tell me you haven't noticed how attentive he's become since Toby took off for California? Are you completely dim?' He tipped back his wine glass, loudly.

'I didn't even know Toby was *in* California.'

'Starting up a web magazine, which is to say he's there because the drugs are cheaper. Sir Edward's never really been terribly fond of Toby anyway – you're a much better investment, from his point of view. He'll be cannon-balling you into the Empire in some capacity in the very near future – trust me, I know these things. Think how benevolent he'll look, taking his brother's orphaned child under his wing, and he'll make you believe it was all on your own merit. And our Piers, I shouldn't wonder, no doubt also thinks you're good for his public image. It's his only chance to worm his way officially into the family. Rather like an arranged marriage. Oh – I'm sorry. Don't tell me that in the back of what I shudder to call your mind you didn't already know that?'

A sour smile leached across his face; riled, I felt my hands ball into fists at my side.

'Fuck off, Roger.'

'Tut, tut. What did you do with all that money, Gabriele?'

'*What* money?'

'The money your parents gave you for charm school.'

I decided this was too lame to deserve a response; at that

moment Edward pushed his way irritably through the fray with a large whisky in one hand and the Secretary of State for Culture and Heritage in the other.

'Oh – Gaby, Rodge. Where's Piers?'

I shook my head blankly; Roger said: 'Still entertaining the masses.'

'Huh. You know Raymond, I suppose. Raymond – my niece, Gabriele, and my – ah – my Roger.'

The Minister shook his right arm free of Sir Edward's anxious grip and held out his hand.

'Delighted to meet you, delighted – it's awfully hot in here, isn't it?'

'Did you enjoy the film, Minister?' Roger asked, all oily pleasantries once more.

'Well –' the Minister glanced at Edward, then leaned closer to us in mock confidentiality. 'Between you and me, it was a bit jolly depressing, don't you think? Makes you fear for the domestic film industry, really – all that grant money it's had –'

'You've been more than generous, Minister,' Roger agreed.

'And all we get are more and more films about people snorting crack cocaine and shooting one another. And saying the c-word all the time. We'll be lucky if people don't come out of the cinema feeling quite suicidal after this film.' He laughed, artificially.

'We'll be lucky if people go *into* the cinema in the first place,' said Roger, 'but don't say so in front of Sir Edward.' He tapped the side of his nose and gave a grotesque wink.

'Where *is* Piers?' Edward was still peering peevishly through the fug over the heads of the guests.

'I'll go and look for him,' I volunteered, wanting to escape from Roger.

Edward looked at me for a moment, seeming surprised, and I stared back, thinking of Roger's words. It had never occurred to me that my uncle gave me a moment's thought from one year to the next. Yet he had been unusually solicitous over his investment in the university, and had gone to some trouble to introduce me to Piers – could it be that my uncle was setting me up? But why? It made no sense to me; his relationship to Piers – that of a patron, as far as I could see – did not appear to require my intervention, and Piers was surely too assertive to allow Edward to manipulate him in such a way, and too shrewd to imagine that I might be a useful conduit. Roger's jibes, I decided, could stem from nothing more than envy.

Edward creased his furry brows together for a moment.

'Fair enough, you go and look for him. Tell him I want him to meet Raymond properly.'

Roger sniggered; I swallowed the last of my wine and pushed past him, standing heavily on his foot as I did so.

At the far end of the landing, in a small room separated from the main bar by a concertina sliding door, Piers was filming his interview with Nick Strachey. The door was open just a crack and a handful of interested guests was gathered around it, listening. I squeezed my way between them, and saw Piers, his tie loosened and his shirt collar undone, sitting in a high-backed armchair; Nick Strachey sat opposite him in another, and Pete Lindsay lurked behind the cameraman in a half-crouch, palms spread on his thighs.

'Nick – you have a very strong commitment to the present-ness of the image, and in this regard your work has some-times been compared to film-makers like Wolfgang Schloss, who have an almost phenomenological belief in the power of the held shot. Where does that come from?' Piers crossed one ankle over the other knee and sat back expectantly.

'I wouldn't compare myself to Schloss, no way – but, yeah, it is a conscious technique.' Nick Strachey scratched at his neck until a red patch spread to his collar. 'You have to sort of know when the life in the shot has died. It's easy to get that wrong. But I do like to make the audience think, I want them to be like, why are we looking at nothing? Sometimes they don't get it, but it's those extra few minutes that make the difference.' He thought for a moment. 'Most of the time they don't get it, actually, but I'm like, so what? It's about saying what I want to say through the shot. Yeah.' He nodded, biting his lip. 'And I've been really lucky having Willy Rollison as my DP – he gets it. He really has, like, a feel, instinctively, for the life of a shot.'

'This film is a very deliberate veering away from natural-ism –'

'Yeah.' Nick scratched his neck again. 'I've never had much patience with naturalism as a form, you know – I think you get more true to life the more extremely you get away from real life, paradoxically, and I've been, you know, really strongly influenced by, like, Theatre of the Absurd and cartoons and stuff.'

'Are these non-linear scenes a way of consciously resisting the audience's desire to impose narrative?'

'Pardon?'

Piers leaned forward, elbows on his knees, as if this might make it clearer.

'In the sense that you refuse to make meaning explicit, so that there's always a visual ambiguity which the audience has to interpret and which is often never resolved?'

'Yeah – I mean, people expect things handed to them on a plate, don't they, and that's not what my films are about – people have got to do some work. You know, with sub-text and meta-visuals, that's not always obvious. And they don't want to – that's why more people don't go to see them, I sup-pose.' He looked at once sad and defiant. 'What I really want-ed to do with *World Without End* was to make an experimental film that would, like, *say* something that everyone else is maybe too afraid to say, and also be commercially successful. Hopefully.'

From close behind me came a spill of gently mocking laughter.

'Dear, oh dear,' said a creamy voice. 'Nick Strachey cannot bear very much reality.'

I turned to see a short man in a plum velvet jacket, with a rococo waistcoat buttoned over an almost perfectly hemispherical stomach. He looked familiar. His greying hair was coiled in tight curls and he was smoking a slender brown cigarette with a gold band. He smiled plausibly, and gave a little bow.

'Post-modernism is *so* passé, don't you find?'

I smiled back.

'Judging by those eyebrows, I'd make an educated guess that you must be a Harvey. Would I be right?'

'Uh – yes.' I rubbed an eyebrow self-consciously, caught slightly off-guard.

'So, by careful process of elimination, you would be Richard's little girl.'

'Oh. Yes. Gaby.' I was at least five inches taller than him.

'Then we *have* met! Many years ago, at your house – *I* haven't changed a bit, of course' – he patted his hair – 'though *you* have – you must have been all of seven. Richard sat you on the kitchen counter and you recited *Ozymandias* to the *crème* of literary London, you little show-off. No, I'm only kidding – some party for I forget which of Richard's worthy poets. I was *royally* drunk, for which I belatedly apologise unreservedly. You probably don't remember. I barely remember myself.' He extended a hand. 'Neville Toynbee – *Sunday Enquirer*'s film critic, for my sins.'

'Of course!' I shook his hand warmly. 'I recognise you from your picture.'

'Don't tell a soul' – he leaned closer – 'that picture's fifteen years old, that's why I use it – not that you could tell.' He fingered his hair again. 'Mind you – I stopped dyeing it a few months ago. I said, Neville, you're fifty-three now and it's time to grow old *avec un peu de grace*. Cancelled my gym membership, too – there comes a day when one has to recognise that the qualities one now has to offer are not apparent on a chest press. I was a great admirer of your father. He was the sort of editor who knew that "simulacra" was not a sin-

216

gular, and you don't find many like that these days. Everybody misses him terribly, you know.'

'Thanks.' I judged that Neville Toynbee, despite his theatrical bluster, was sincere.

'Very handsome man – you don't mind me saying that, do you?' He touched my arm anxiously. 'But in a way that Edward never was, though they looked so alike – Richard was much more *refined*. Lovely bones. Like yourself. And Lexicon was a superb little house when he ran it – couldn't sell a book to its own grandmother, of course, but it knew what it stood for, and I think that mattered to a lot of people. Absolute crying shame what Edward turned it into – always amazed me that Richard didn't just walk out. Everyone expected him to – he was such a man of principle. What made him stay?'

'I don't know,' I said, honestly.

'No, quite – why should you tell me that, you don't know me from Adam. What brings you to this den of vice and depravity, anyway?'

'Oh – I came with Piers Gaveston.' I felt a burn of pride under my skin as I said it; I glanced at him through the door, running a hand through his hair and debating something with the producer.

'With *Piers Gaveston*, she says.' Neville Toynbee repeated it slowly, as if trying to decide whether this were at all possible. 'But – my dear –' he hesitated, on the cusp of adding something. He was looking at me oddly. Then he seemed to think better of it, and his eyes drifted to follow my gaze. 'Beautiful Piers. Never looks a day older, does he? Would you believe he once played Dorian Gray? Find me a better example of Life imitating Art, if you can.'

'Really? When?'

'Oh – fifteen years ago, at least. Execrable low-budget film made in Toronto – never found a distributor, needless to say. I dug it out because I was curious. He's not an actor, that's for sure, but my God, he was perfect for that part. I'd never seen anything so beautiful. And now look at him – he's barely changed. Really, it makes you shiver.' He shivered emphatically.

'Have you known him a long time?'

'Only since the last time he tried to take on London.'

'The last time?'

'Mm, it must have been – ooh, look, what's *she* doing here?'

He pointed to the door, clutching my arm excitedly. *She* was a tall, bearded man in a mink-trimmed coat. 'She'd go to the opening of a crisp packet. Tart.' He shook his head, disapprovingly. 'Let's get another drink, come on.'

He led me back towards the main bar; I cast an anxious glance back to the filming room but the interview showed no sign of finishing, and I was curious to hear what else Neville Toynbee could tell me about Piers.

'You were saying –'

'Oh, yes – Piers. Edward brought him over from New York – ooh, five or six years ago, must have been, and gave him God only knows how much money to make a film – an adaptation of the *Inferno*, if you please, which he was *apparently* writing himself – and he went about making a great noise about it for months, and then – phut!' He made a gesture with his fingers to imitate a bubble bursting.

'What?'

'Oh – usual story. Shot half of it, went cataclysmically over budget, never heard another word about it. Next thing you hear, he's left the country, under a bit of a cloud, is my guess. Then he's back and straight into a very nice job, thank you very much. Talk about falling on your feet. But he's much better off as a critic – he has a modicum of talent for that. He can talk well, but he doesn't know the first thing about making films. He must have spent at least ten million of Edward's money on that *Inferno* project, when anyone could have told him it was damned from the outset – pardon the dreadful pun. Now he does it vicariously.'

'Well – he says this film's very good.'

Neville Toynbee gave a fruity laugh, then stopped abruptly when he realised I wasn't laughing with him. 'My dear girl!' he squeezed my arm. 'Of *course* he does! Who's produced it?'

'Uh – Jerome?' I said, confused.

'Yes, but which production company?'

'Prometheus?'

'Getting warmer – which is part of which large transglobal media corporation?'

'Oh. Hamilton Harvey International,' I guessed, gloomily.

'Very good, she's catching on!'

'I didn't know.'

'Not many people do. It was bought out by HHI Media, oh, a couple of years ago, but Edward let them keep working under the Prometheus name because they had such a good reputation in the business – which, let me tell you, will get progressively worse if they keep knocking out the likes of this. *And* – where did Piers first write about how good this film was?'

I shook my head.

'In the *Sunday Ledger*, of course, which is owned by, need I go on? Do you see a theme emerging, hmm?'

Edward's presence suddenly made sense. I felt somehow heavier, as if I had been duped.

'So it's not independent at all?'

'Well – it is, in that it's not studio-funded – but it's been entirely financed by HHI Media and distributed by HHI Media, and now larded with praise from critics in HHI publications, which is no better in my book if you want to claim artistic integrity.'

'Why would Edward put money into a film like this?'

'Because he's a culturally illiterate man with a lot of it to spare. He thinks it's part of the current renaissance, if you can use that word, of English film, English art – of course he wants his name on it. Edward just does what he's told by people he believes to be informed. And this is all Piers Gaveston's doing, I suspect – he was always quite close to

Nick Strachey – an unfortunate influence, if you want my opinion, poor little Nick. His last film – *Who the Fuck Is Alice* – well, I thought that was really quite hilarious, very clever screenplay and some fine camerawork in spite of the low production values. But *this*! Urgh! It really was *egregiously* bad.' He flinched, largely. 'All that ghastly, ham-fisted symbolism – computers in the church – *please*! And Aids! Sweet Mother of God, you'd think he'd have had more sense than to tack that on the end. The poor boy needs to be careful – his career will be in serious trouble if he starts making the films Piers Gaveston wants him to make. Someone ought to tell him that is not the way to become the Antonioni *de nos jours*.'

'But it won't make any money, will it?'

'God, no. In spite of Piers's recommendation. Far too derivative and too slow and too existential. People don't want that any more, they want film to be ironic and knowing and self-deprecating and above all, funny. Ooh, you naughty girl, I shouldn't – go on then, one more.' (This last to a waitress who passed conveniently with a bottle of Chardonnay crooked.) 'And one for my friend – oh, now! Come with me – I'm going to introduce you to a movie star! Verlaine DuPrey – you'll enjoy this – he's so precious it beggars belief!'

His small hand still tight around my wrist, Neville navigated dextrously through the crowds to an alcove where a young man perched sullenly on a window sill crowded round by a twitter of PR girls. As we drew closer I realised that he was the androgynous youth from the film, even thinner and paler in the flesh – what there was of it – than on celluloid. His hair was dyed blue-black and he was almost certainly wearing eyeliner.

He looked up at Neville briefly with bleared eyes and then back to the window.

'Verlaine – I wanted to introduce you to a friend of mine, Gabriele Harvey. Gaby – this is Verlaine DuPrey, possibly the finest screen actor of his own or any other generation.' He winked at me.

Verlaine DuPrey flicked a hand loosely without looking up.

'Verlaine's tired,' confided one of the PR girls. 'He only got in from Vancouver yesterday and he's been doing nothing but interviews.'

'He gave an impressive performance,' said Neville, with a polished and splendidly insincere smile.

'They're saying it's possibly the best of his career,' nodded the PR girl, earnestly.

'Who's saying so, pray?'

'Well – critics.'

'Ah, *critics*.' Neville let the word slide through his teeth like used mouthwash. '"He whom nature has made weak, and idleness keeps ignorant, may yet support his vanity by the name of critic". Who said that?' He turned to me.

'Sounds like Dr Johnson.'

'Very good indeed, bonus points! And I should know, I've been at it for nearly twenty years.'

Verlaine DuPrey stirred unexpectedly; glancing briefly around, he examined his fingernails scrupulously for some moments and said idly, in a New York accent so stagily camp I felt sure he was sending himself up: 'I don't know if anyone cares, but the director's cut of *Victor/Victoria* starring Julie Andrews and James Garner is released on DVD tomorrow.'

Then he slumped back into silence and stared out of the window.

Neville Toynbee clapped his hands gleefully and giggled, as if this was just what he had hoped for.

'I told you so!' he whispered. 'Did you know – his real name's Mark Tilt and he comes from Medicine Hat. Well, you'd change it too, wouldn't you? You would. I'd better let you get back to Piers Gaveston.'

Midnight passed, and the fluted glasses collected in rows, lipstick-ringed, along wine-slick tables and window sills. The first animated sprint of drinking and conversation had subsided into a torpor that hung over the bar like the curtain of smoke; on sofas and armchairs artists, critics and cineastes sprawled, watching the room from beneath heavy lids, or entwined themselves in mis-timed clinches and approximate groping on the stairs.

Leaning against the bar, I breathed carefully, in and out, waiting for the room to stop pulsing, minutely expanding and contracting in time with the thudding in my blood. Piers had appeared and disappeared at intervals throughout the evening, always surrounded by questioning admirers and absorbed in energetic conversations, usually about the comparative merits of directors I had never heard of, or whether Super 16 was still a viable medium; he was fuelled by adrenalin and a kind of rhetorical urgency, barely pausing for breath, his eyes shining and his excitement contagious. I had tried to keep up at first, hanging self-consciously at his elbow as he greeted an endless stream of people he knew, or who knew people he knew and who brandished exclusive anecdotes full of names I had never heard and would never meet, until at one point he had leaned across and said, not cruelly but with a hint of warning, 'You don't have to follow me *all* the time, you know. You could go and talk to some people.'

Ashamed, I had drifted away, but not having that happy gift for easing into conversations with people I don't know, and my options therefore limited to Roger or my uncle, I had mooched from room to room, drinking steadily, holding out my glass willingly each time a flustered waiter managed to penetrate the crowds with a fresh bottle, colliding occasionally with people who seemed to think I was someone else, nodding vaguely and managing a clumsy exchange as we breathed wine and smoke in each other's faces. I had a long conversation with someone in glasses about the director Montoya, and heard myself at one point asserting his incomparable significance so confidently I almost convinced myself that I knew who he was. I moved on, keeping a hand on the wall for support as the wine took hold, catching glimpses of Piers across the room – a flash of his eyes or teeth, sometimes

222

a look – and stubbornly insisting on staying the distance because tonight, I had decided, I would be going home with him. I had come as his date, which must count for something, and I was determined that this time I would not let him evade me so casually.

But he was taking so long, and I was bored with this club and these people, and there was nothing to do but keep drinking, and now my vision was sliding and my face burning and I had lost him again. In hiccupping movements I found my way to the far end of the room, where Roger was roosting contentedly on a fat sofa, replete with canapes and picking bits of peanut from his teeth, a blonde PR girl on either side. He squinted like a rodent as I approached.

'Have you seen Piers?'

'Piers, Piers, Piers.' He waved a hand, smiling enigmatically. 'Everybody always looking for Piers. Why, I wonder. He's away with the fairies.' Then he broke into a cackling, snorting laugh which sent a glob of something gluey flying out of his nose on to his lapel. I turned away in disgust.

'Downstairs, playing the piano,' he called after me.

On the next landing, a crowd of people pressed against the doorway to a room as dim and smoky as the first. I couldn't see past them, but I heard it, unmistakably: a cascading swell of music, notes tumbling over one another quick as Piers's words, surging and falling. Squeezing under someone's arm, I half-fell through the door and there he was at the baby grand, the centre of the room; eyes blazing, hair damp, lips white in concentration as the muscles in his shoulders danced with the energy of his fingers on the keys. The lights melted in liquid reflections on the angled black lid of the piano.

'Astonishing.' Neville Toynbee came to stand beside me, folding his arms and shaking his head in admiration. 'Rachmaninov. I had no idea. Concerto Number Three in D minor, if I'm not mistaken. He really is extraordinary, is he not?'

I nodded, witlessly open-mouthed. Piers finished with a

crescendo and a flourish, looked up and caught my stare; he smiled suddenly, pushed his hair back, and a hot, sweet pain stabbed in my groin. I wandered closer to the piano. He winked, and dived straight into 'Ain't Misbehavin''.

Jerome Idle, leaning over the top of the piano and swaying slightly, took up the singing. Piers was laughing, breathing fast, his fingers faultless. They finished to a whoop of stamping and applause from their warmly drunken audience.

'Do "East St Louis Toodle-Oo", go on,' Jerome urged, batting at Pier's sleeve. 'Go on – he does it really well, that one,' he informed the crowd, slurring.

Piers reached for the cigarette burning down on top of the piano, his face serious. 'I haven't played that for years.'

'You remember it, though – you and Andy used to do it all the time. I'll never forget' – he turned to me, laying a hand heavily on my shoulder with the sincere emphasis of the profoundly drunk – 'never forget this one time. It was so funny – we were at Cappella – that's this really uptight restaurant in New York, see, in Tribeca, that's right up its own arse – and they had this pianist, he was total shite, all fucking "Strangers in the Night" and what have you – anyway, he gets up for his break and this one' – he jerked a thumb at Piers – 'he gets up to the piano and just starts playing, and then' – he folded up, laughing, clutching at Piers's shoulder – 'd'you remember – Andy just pulls out this harmonica and they do "East St Louis Toodle-Oo" and it's so fucking brilliant everyone stops eating to listen, and they get a standing ovation! Seriously – everyone in the fucking restaurant stands up cheering! Then the manager comes over and they think they're in the shit, right – but no – he basically asks them if they want a regular slot! It was so funny . . .' He paused, swayed, and sank a large gulp of wine. 'You sort of had to be there.'

Piers rubbed his upper gum with the side of his forefinger. He was no longer smiling. 'Well, I can't do it without the harmonica part,' he said, looking down at his long hands spread out, brown against the keys.

'Yeah,' Jerome gazed somewhere into the middle distance. 'We need Andy here, don't we?'

Piers pushed his stool back and stood up abruptly. 'I'm going to the bathroom.'

'Shit, sorry mate.' Jerome's cheery grin crumpled under his goatee. 'Sorry, I didn't mean – I'll join you.'

'Andy Epstein?' I asked, half to myself.

Piers's head snapped round. 'Yes?'

'Nothing.'

His eyes narrowed and he sniffed; there was a difficult silence.

Neville Toynbee sidled up.

'I'm most impressed, Mr Gaveston – not just a pretty face and a splendid figure, though I still can't fault you in those departments either. Tell me, have you been working out?' He held out a hand.

Piers accepted it, warily, almost rousing a smile. 'Neville Toynbee, doyen of the cultural elite. Congratulations on your Cannes Medaille.'

'Oh, shush. You know the Frenchies, big fuss about nothing. You *are* looking well.'

Piers bowed his head. 'So I hear you hate it.'

'*Hate* is not quite the right word. I was simply bored out of my tiny mind. *Piers*. Come on. It's shocking, You *know* it's shocking. And it should have been half the length.'

Piers drew himself up to full height. 'You don't think there's something of Antonioni about his work?'

'Only in the sense that they've both directed films, in the very loosest definition of either word.'

'You're a toxic snob, Toynbee.'

'Of course I wouldn't dream of challenging your critical judgement, but I wonder if you're perhaps a little too *close* to the material, shall we say –'

'Say what you mean, why don't you.'

'Now, now. Let's not bicker.' Neville held up a pacifying hand and glanced around. 'Charming party your *patron* has laid on. Where have you been since I last tried unsuccessfully to chase you into a darkened hallway?'

'Around.'

'So I've heard!' Neville Toynbee giggled wickedly into his hand and leaned over to me. 'Isn't he just *too* handsome to be alive?'

Piers rolled his eyes. 'Excuse me.'

'Ooh –' Neville waved his hand anxiously. 'Careful in the ladies' room, there, Piers – they had a police raid last week. Powder your nose with caution – believe me, you wouldn't enjoy it in prison! Then again – perhaps you would!' He dissolved into giggles once more. Piers blanched, scowled and turned his back emphatically.

I watched Piers and Jerome heading for the toilets and realised after a delay, kicking myself for my stupidity, what Neville meant – Piers was high, of course, which explained his distracted manner and manic eyes.

He seemed to be a long time in the bathroom. How much time, I could not be certain, long having lost the ability to judge time, space or distance with any accuracy, but it began to feel like an endless wait, and the walls were beginning to shift again, so after some effortful consideration, I settled on the idea of searching for him and attempting to edge him towards the door. Over three floors I searched fruitlessly, before rounding a corner on to a previously untried landing, to see Piers and my uncle apparently wrestling or embracing.

Edward had him by the shoulders; Piers was tossing his head back, jaw set defiantly, hands clamped to Edward's arms as if trying to push him away. I shrank back, alarmed.

'I am so *sick* of the way you do this! This is not some fucking *quid pro quo* contract, Edward!'

'I thought that's exactly what it was, for you –'

'I can't *breathe*! I've told you this – God *damn* it, we've had this all before – you don't own me, not then, and not now – *Fuck!* I have to leave –'

'You can't leave! Piers, you can't – you know –'

'*Now!* I mean, I have to leave this party, I need to be on my own, and you have to get' – he wrenched Edward's hands decisively from his shoulders – 'out. Of. My –' he spun round, caught sight of me and froze, momentarily, staring as if discovered in something prohibited. Then his green eyes flicked over me, up and down, once, and he let go of my uncle, strode across and grabbed my arm, so tightly it hurt.

'*There* you are. Come on, we're going.'

My uncle's face twisted into something unreadable, between confusion and disbelief.

'Piers! Come here, come back here now!'

Piers dragged me to the stairs; too surprised to argue, I glanced backwards. My uncle, more used to command than to entreat, seemed to be having trouble taking in the present situation. He raised a hand, helpless.

'Piers! *Please?*'

But Piers was racing down the stairs, two at a time, pulling me with him, his fury bristling around him. He paused at the front desk.

'Get me a taxi!'

'Certainly, sir,' said the girl behind the reception, with a painted smile and an absence of haste. 'Where would you like to go?'

Piers looked at me, frantic. 'Where are we going? Quick!'

'I don't know.'

'Where were you going to stay tonight?'

'At my flat, I suppose –'

'Which is where? Come *on!*'

'Highgate – but –'

'Good – Highgate,' he barked at the receptionist.

'Did you want that now, sir?'

'Of course I want it fucking now!'

'Where do you live?' I asked.

Piers looked at me as though I had gone mad. 'Not my flat – I'm not going there. Don't be stupid!'

I was out of my depth.

227

Sir Edward appeared at the top of the stairs. He seemed very far away. 'Piers!' His tie was awry; his voice less imperious than before. 'I'm asking one more time – I think it would be better for everyone if you –'

Piers turned desperately to the girl at the reception desk.

'That'll be about fifteen to twenty minutes, sir,' she intoned, replacing the phone.

He looked at me, looked at Edward, and back to me.

'Fuck it, we'll get one in the street.'

In the sodium light and shadows of Shaftesbury Avenue, still holding my arm, Piers flung himself into the path of an ambling cab, darting glances back at the street we had left as if Sir Edward might emerge at any moment in pursuit. Two thirty-seven: a few straggling partygoers stumbled belatedly towards Piccadilly through the quietening streets; clouds gathered, ultra-violet against the blue darkness. You never see stars in London, I thought, pausing unsteadily to stare up at the sky; except sometimes in Highgate, when I was little, on clear nights in winter you could see them over the Heath. My father used to stand at the upstairs study window with a small telescope and teach me the constellations.

'You never see stars in London, do you?'

'Will you *get in the fucking car?*' Piers banged his hand against the side of it for emphasis, holding the door open impatiently; jolted abruptly back to myself, I clambered inelegantly into the back and wondered how close I should sit.

Could I touch his leg? There it was, less than half a foot from my hand, jigging up and down in agitation, the ridge of his thigh outlined hard under the fabric of his suit. I edged my hand nearer, concentrating closely, holding tight to the edge of the seat with no idea where we were or how long we had been driving. What would he do if I touched his leg? Would he be angry? Pleased? Would he turn to me, relieved that I had broken the silence and reached for him first? Or would he – more probable, this – swat me away – then what would I do

228

or say? Pretend it was an accident? His body language was not encouraging. I looked up at his face, tight and inscrutable as he leaned out of the window into the close air, smoking, contorting his mouth into strange shapes by running his tongue obsessively round his gums between drags. His smoke blew back through the open window; I breathed it second hand as the lights slurred by like bright strings of beads.

'Whereabouts on Highgate West Hill, love?' The driver reached behind him to slide the glass panel back.

'Uh – can you stop a second –' I pressed my forehead to the cold window, fastening my gaze on a tree while I waited for the backdrop to solidify. 'We've gone past it. Sorry. Back up the hill a little way.'

'Does Edward know you've got this place?' Piers asked suddenly, as the driver swung round in the empty road.

'Yes. Probably. Well – we've always lived here. But he hasn't been for years – I don't know if he realises we still have the flat, if that's what you mean. I don't know. Shouldn't think he gives it much thought. Why – do you think he might come here?'

'Wouldn't put it past him.'

'Have you upset him?'

'Ha!' he said, meaningfully.

I told the driver to stop. Piers climbed out, paid the driver and stood in the road, head thrown back, staring up at the house.

'This is where you grew up?'

'Yes.'

'The whole house?'

'Yes.'

'Nice.' His mouth turned hard.

'My parents bought it when they first got married. Highgate was cheap then. Cheaper, anyway.' I was swaying, trying to locate the key in the depths of my bag. *How had I become this drunk? Could he tell?*

'Why were you arguing with Edward?' I negotiated the steps and tried to fit the key into the door. Piers leaned against the door frame, drumming his fingers impatiently against the jamb. Heavy clouds swarmed together, stifling the moon; the thickness of the air suggested a storm.

'Because. Because if Edward thinks he owns you, he gives you no room for manoeuvre. Free will is not a concept he can understand. I get tired of it.'

'I know.' I nodded, concentrating hard on the keyhole.

'I doubt it.'

'He seemed upset.' I tried a different key. In the basement porch it was pitch dark, and the lock kept moving about.

'Huh. He'll be furious that I left with you, it'll do him good. He's not used to being challenged. Though he should be, by now.'

'You've known him a long time?'

'Six years. Long enough.'

'Why will he be furious? About me?'

He hesitated. 'Because it's not what he expected.'

'What isn't?'

'That I would – he'll think – Jesus, give me that.' He snatched the key from my hand, glancing over his shoulder in case anyone might have been following us, then fitted it smoothly into the lock and, turning it, stopped suddenly and pointed a finger into my face.

'I need to stay here tonight.'

'Okay.' This was proving easier than I thought. I did my best to smile softly, but it was lost in the dark.

'Good.' He paused, as if about to add to this, but shook himself abruptly and opened the door.

I followed him in and switched on a table lamp as he threw his jacket over a chair and paced the small room like an animal, sniffing out his new surroundings. The flat was chilly and immaculate.

'Can you get me some water?'

In the little kitchenette I gripped the sink, watching the water twist and shiver in silver patterns against the stainless steel, waiting for it to run cold, wanting him, wanting him, but realising too that I was exhausted, the room still eliding, shifting, that most of all I wanted to lie down and close my eyes, but with his arms round me.

I found him seated at my father's desk, chopping out cocaine with surgical precision on a pocket mirror. For a moment I stood, a glass in each hand, surprised.

'Make yourself at home, then.'

He looked up. '*What?*'

'Nothing.' I placed a glass next to him. 'It's just – I thought you didn't –'

'Didn't what?' His attention returned to the materials before him.

'I don't know. Do stuff.'

'I said I don't drink. Allow me some recreation.'

'Isn't that a bit – hypocritical, though? I mean – why –?'

He snapped his head up, eyes bright and wolfish. 'What did you call me?'

'I didn't mean – just that it seems odd not to –' I faltered.

His jaw was tight. 'Look at you. So pissed you can barely stand straight, but that's all right, you think, that's *all right* because in your little world, drinking yourself fucking oblivious is something jolly and middle-class that you do at Christmas and publishing launches, and I imagine that when *your* father got drunk he was witty and entertaining and sang amusing songs, and everyone loved him, am I right?'

'Well – yes,' I said, blankly.

'And he didn't come home in a blinder and kick the living crap out of you, right?'

'No.'

'So. I don't need any more members of your family telling me what I can and can't do. If we're going to get along, and it seems we have to, two things you need to know about me – I need a lot of space. I can't cope with people making demands on me, expecting something. Promises. Expecting promises – I don't make any promises. So don't ask. Then you won't be disappointed.'

'I didn't.' I wasn't sure I knew what he was talking about. 'Did your father?'

'Did he what?'

'Hit you?'

'I've never met my father.'

He wrapped a note into a tight tube and leaned over the mirror, tucking his hair behind his ears to keep his loose fringe from brushing the carefully organised lines. I watched, fascinated, as the thread of white glided cleanly up his nose in one smooth, silent movement. He sniffed, discreetly.

'And the second thing?'

'The second thing.' He tapped the rolled-up note on the mirror, gently, and swallowed. 'I can't give you anything. So don't expect it.'

I leaned against the back of a chair, gulping my glass of water. The room was gradually righting itself; a tired headache began to sprawl behind my eyes.

'I never asked for anything. You're the one who invited me.'

'I *know*!' He was on his feet again, pacing distractedly. 'I'm not saying – Listen. You don't know me. I don't know you. It's best like that. If this is going to work. But you mustn't think we're – I can't be *involved* – I don't do that. It's no good expecting those things from me. I'm not –' he sighed, rubbing his eyes, as if this were too complicated to explain. 'I can't *belong* to anyone. Not in that way, it's not what I want. Which is not to say that I don't want to see you. Understand? If you can understand that, we'll be fine. I need a cigarette.'

I found a crumpled pack in my jacket and tossed it to him. *What? If what's going to work?*

'Why did you invite me?' I said, quietly.

He cupped his hands around the cigarette as he lit it, as if afraid of a sudden wind. He breathed out, then stopped abruptly, turned to face me, pointed the lighter emphatically.

'The fundamental difference between you and me is this – you're not a fighter.'

Stumped, I sat down heavily on the sofa.

'Fighter?'

'It's not your fault – why should you be?' He seemed to be thinking aloud. 'You've never needed to fight in your life, and you never will – how could you possibly understand what it means to have to fight?'

I stared up, uncomprehending.

'Fight what?'

'Anything!' He flung his arms out. 'Fucking adversity. Anything that gets in your way. Fight to get somewhere – because you've always had it all, haven't you, on a silver tray – there are things, sometimes, that you have to do – if you want something enough, and you know where you have to get to but you can't see how else to get there – but *you'll* never have to do those things, because you've never wanted anything you couldn't just *have*.' His brow creased and he stared at me for a moment, then pulled hard on the cigarette, moving back to the desk.

Why are you angry with me? I watched him hoover up another line, wishing I understood this veiled rage. *You are making no sense to me and I want to understand, I want to touch you –*

He was quieter now, paused in front of my father's old record player, eyes grazing the scuffed spines of the LPs stacked on the shelf behind it.

'Yours?'

'My dad's.'

He drew out a sleeve, bound with brittle yellowed tape, took the record from it and set it on the turntable.

'Vaughan Williams, *ha!* Welcome to England. Fuck, my head.' He pinched the bridge of his nose between his thumb and forefinger, rubbed his eyes.

'Piers –'

His head jerked, startled, and he caught my eye for a moment; I realised that it was the first time I had called him by name. Speaking it seemed to conjure an intimacy that hung awkwardly in the air and didn't belong to us, as if I had overstepped a boundary. I looked away.

'Why did you invite me tonight? And the other night?'

He was watching me. '*Why?*'

'I don't know what you want.'

His eyes narrowed, and a thin, secret smile slipped across his lips.

'Oh yes. Whereas I know exactly what *you* want.'

He crossed the room, crushing his cigarette in a plant pot as he did so, to kneel in front of me, one hand gripping the back of my neck, and pulled my face to his, unbuttoning his shirt with his free hand, his mouth hard on mine, his tongue invasive; instinctively my legs moved apart to bring him closer as he pushed me down, my hips lifting to meet him. There was no tenderness in this kiss, I knew without opening my eyes, no desire or affection, only mockery, but his force was exhilarating, and frightening. The music drifted on, absurdly pastoral.

And then it happens like this:

My hands are inside his shirt, spread on the warm skin of his back, feeling his weight on me, my blood rising –

'Do you want me to fuck you?' The words come as a hiss.

I am nodding, helpless.

He is breathing through his teeth, eyes glittering. 'Say it.'

'I want you.' Barely a whisper.

He snatches my wrist, presses my right hand to his cock.

'Want what? Say it again.'

'I want you to fuck me.'

But I'm nervous, already doubtful; unsure if this is a game he likes to play, or if he is serious – that smile is cruel; one hand eases under my skirt, probing deftly, without sentiment, almost medical – but I can feel as his finger slides in how much I want him, can feel my hips lifting again as if to encourage him.

'Turn over.'

And then he is inside, in quick, hard strokes, and my face is pressed into the cushions, eyes squeezed shut because if I lift my head and try to open them the walls are still liquid; I fight to swallow, tight gulps of salty saliva, carpet burning my knees – he pulls out abruptly and I feel him holding his breath.

Then I hear him spit on to his palm; the suction sound as he strokes himself with his wet hand, then the pressure of his thumb, and just as he raises himself on his knees to push, it occurs to me through the spinning in my head and the background sounds of the orchestra what he might be about to do, and I almost twist away but not in time, and that is when the pain comes – sharp and sudden – and he pushes harder, holding me by the hips so I can't move, and he keeps pushing though I'm begging him to stop, *Please!* I'm shouting, *don't!* and I can taste salt and realise it's tears as I brace myself against each thrust, and Jesus, fuck, it hurts, I want him to stop, *Get out, please*, hitting weakly at his hands on my hips – I have never done this, I'm embarrassed – *please stop, I didn't want this* – this is not how it should have been.

He moves faster. *Is this what you wanted*, he spits between breaths, through his teeth, *Is it? Do you like it like this, do you?* – and he's pushing harder while I grip the fabric of the sofa and squeeze my eyes shut and hope he finishes soon, wanting it to be over, and after a few more minutes he suddenly says, *No, no good, I've had too much coke*, and abruptly pulls out, zips himself up and lights a cigarette, leaving me exposed, and crushed by the absurd thought that I couldn't even make him come, as if this were somehow my deficiency as well. The smell slides into the air, sharp, unmistakable. I will have to wash the cushions, I think, stupidly, in case my mother sees them; hiding my face, not knowing yet if the humiliation is worse than the pain. And worrying about the fucking cushions, for goodness' sake.

'You're bleeding.' His voice is like glass. 'Was I the first? You should have said.' He gives a small, bitter laugh and leaves the room. I pull down the throw that covers the sofa and wrap myself in it, wiping my face with the back of my hand, quietly shaking. I am jabbed by a sudden, unexpected pang for Paul, with his anxious, predictable attentions and his slow, comforting breathing in sleep. I have been playing with fire. When I reach down, with a wince, and bring my hand back into the light, I see that Piers is right; I am bleeding.

When, after a few hours, I woke from a fretful half-sleep into a pale morning, my body was aching from my pelvis across my lower back, and a headache cleaved the space behind my eyes. Piers had gone.

Chapter XII

Picture this: driving into Glastonbury from the north east, the road crests a low rise, rounds a curve between hedges and furrowed fields and as it dips again you see, from a distance of perhaps five miles or more, the Tor, black against the sky, long before you see the roofs and lights of the town itself. Scarved in mists through every season, its skewed cone heaves up out of the Levels, topped with the ruined tower of St Michael's like a grave. This is the Isle of Avalon, the Celtic Isle of the Dead, which the Britons called *Ynis-witrin* – the Isle of Glass – in the days when it rose out of brackish marshes and wide lakes and could only be reached by boat or cause-way; Avalon, the realm where the English believe Arthur sleeps, waiting to be healed of his wounds before he returns.

As you approach through a succession of villages with Saxon names, the Tor ducks and hides itself between trees and church spires, until you are almost upon it. Fields spread out, flat as a dish, as far as the Mendip Hills to the north and the Quantocks to the west, patterned red-brown and green. Picture the Levels as they appear from the crown of the Tor, through the Gothic arch of the tower, laid out like a tapestried cloth with a scattering of farms and reservoirs. And picture the little town at the heart of it, the one called City of Glass by the Saxons, because this is the cradle of the English church, the chapel of St Joseph, resting-place of the Grail, Arthur's Tomb, guardian of stories, the meeting-place of myth and history. In its prime they called the Abbey *Roma Secunda*. This was, once, the heart of England. You either feel it or you don't.

I had sent Piers Gaveston my research notes on Glastonbury a week or so before the episode in the flat, and in the confusion of feelings that followed had forgotten all about them. So when he showed up on my doorstep at half-past eight on a Wednesday morning midway through October, four weeks to the day since the premiere of Nick Strachey's film and our subsequent grapple, I was wholly unprepared for seeing him at all – and particularly for offering honed advice on ecclesiastical history. I had not spoken to him in all that time, and as the silence stretched unbearably, I began to suspect that I would not see him again.

I was angry with him, of course; furious and hurt and above all, humiliated. In the immediate aftermath I decided that I never wanted to see him again anyway, while rehearsing each morning in the shower all the things I wanted to say the next time I saw him, just in case. For a while I tried to avoid the places I might bump into him, and then started to frequent them again, in the perverse hope of seeing him so as to deliver my fierce speech about never wanting to see him again. But he seemed to have retired to London almost permanently, while George tactfully shouldered his workload to save the faculty's face and patiently set about organising and administering the new courses, already over-subscribed by young people eager to touch the hem of media success in spite of the price. Piers's television appearances, demonstrably increasing in inverse proportion to his appearances in the faculty, stirred bitter mutterings among his faculty colleagues, Miles Park and Jake Lennox in particular. I was not the only one with reason to resent him, but my motives, I felt, were unique.

As the days slid by, I had to acknowledge that my resolute coldness towards him was being undermined by the fact that he was unaware of it. He had not sought me out since that night, nor did he appear to have any interest in doing so, and with this realisation came the shocking possibility that my anger might not be justified after all. Was I right to be angry? Had he taken advantage of me? I had to concede that, technically, he had not; in truth I remembered asking him repeatedly to fuck me and, it might be argued, I had not specified that I had meant more in the conventional fashion. Nor, technically, did I have a problem with anal sex *per se* – I hoped that I was not such a prude that I might not have been willing to give it a go, if he'd said that was what he liked, if he'd only asked – and this was where the lines became blurred. He hadn't asked, and I had seen his eyes that night, and knew that he had meant what he did to be an act of cruelty and a flexing of power. He had meant to humiliate me, to punish me – for what, I was not certain. Perhaps for daring to aspire to him, to put me in my place. Or perhaps the hatred was not meant for me at all; perhaps I had been unwittingly on the receiving end of some deeper rage. This was a useful thought; it allowed me to wonder how he had been damaged, and if I might be the one to help him get over it. And as soon as thoughts such as these crept in, I was ashamed of them, and the anger flared up again.

'You were right,' I conceded to Oliver two weeks after the fact, without revealing the circumstances. 'He is a bastard.'

'Why, what's he done?'

'Nothing. Doesn't matter. Just – he's a bastard.'

'Has he dumped you?'

'No! Nothing like that. I mean – he's just a nasty piece of work, you can tell.'

'Have you –?'

'What?'

'You know. Slept with him.'

'Oh. No – not exactly.'

'So you have.' He sighed, as if I had let him and myself down.

'Uh – kind of. But I won't be doing it again.'

'You say.'

'I won't! He's a bastard.'

'I thought women loved bastards. That's where I've been going wrong all these years – I'm too nice to you.'

'Bollocks.'

'Yeah, well. He's not good news, though, Gab – I've said it before. For your own sake – give him as wide a berth as possible.'

I had no intention of telling Oliver what had happened, sensing, rightly, that it would upset him, and not wanting to see Oliver's jealousy masked as friendly concern. But it seemed unlikely that I would ever have the chance to discuss the event with Piers. I tried to keep the anger boiling because as soon as I let it cool I had to admit that I missed him, that I still wanted him even after this; that I still lay in bed in the louvred light when sleep wouldn't come and allowed my mind to conjure happier versions of the night after the party, touching myself, almost guiltily, as my imagination floated.

The weeks passed, and my ruminations continued, veering one way and then the other, between anger, embarrassment and optimism. Unforgivably, I still jumped and quickened every time the phone rang. So when I opened the front door of number 42, Tennyson Street, that Wednesday morning, wearing only a t-shirt, with wet hair and clutching a piece of toast in one hand, I had genuinely forgotten whether I was still angry or not.

He stood there in motorbike leathers and carried a helmet under each arm, and he was heartbreakingly beautiful. Behind him the sky was grey and scratchy, dark with the threat of rain. When the wind lifted his hair away from his face, he was not quite smiling.

'Hello, Gaby.'

It took me some seconds to muster words. I became aware that my t-shirt was too short.

'What do you want?'

'I need your help. Hurry up and put some trousers on.' He glanced at my legs, and handed me a motorbike helmet, rather pointlessly.

'Look – I don't –' I handed it back, thinking as I did so that I really ought to hate him, and infuriated that I didn't, or couldn't. 'You can't just turn up after four weeks and –'

He stepped inside the house and shut the door carefully behind him. I took a step back, on to the first stair.

'I've been busy. I had to go to New York. Sorry. I got your research notes, thanks.'

'Oh. You're welcome.'

He was looking beyond me, at the wall.

'Bit purple, but still. You're no poet, are you?'

'At least I'm not a *shit*.'

I hadn't intended to say that aloud. We looked at each other, surprised. Piers laughed, unexpectedly.

'Well, since you're supposed to be my co-writer, I need your expert knowledge today. We've got work to do. Come on, get dressed.'

No mention of the sofa.

'I have a meeting with George this morning,' I said, tugging at the bottom of my t-shirt. It was difficult to evince hauteur in your underwear.

'So cancel it. We're going on a magical mystery tour. You have a leather jacket, don't you?'

I nodded.

'And you'll need a scarf – it's freezing on the bike.'

'Where are you going?'

He smiled then, almost a real smile, with a kind of warmth in it.

'*We*. Are going. To find England.'

Piers drew the bike to a standstill beside the market cross, where Glastonbury High Street curves steeply and begins its ascent towards the Tor. He took off his helmet and shook his hair out, still astride the seat in front of me; a group of boys wandered over, tentatively, to admire the bike from a respectful distance. My legs were so cold I could barely unbend them; for more than three hours I had sat behind Piers across the breadth of England, my arms around his waist. He rode fast, and I was nervous at first, unused to the rush of wind and the feeling of exposure, unsure of how to lean when he

241

took a tight corner, afraid to look down at the road blurring beneath us. But gradually, I began to relax and allow my body to soften into the motion of the bike; my thighs wrapped tightly around his, my groin pressed up against his back and, from time to time, if I leaned forward, I could catch a glimpse of his eyes in the mirror, bright with cold or excitement behind the visor. I learned the fraternal nod when we passed another motorcyclist, and watched the envious glances the bike drew from other drivers. Without gloves, my hands had quickly numbed, so I slipped them into the fleece-lined pockets of his jacket and leaned against him like that for the whole journey, feeling the warmth of his body through his pockets; he didn't appear to mind.

He swung one leg over the bike and let his eyes skate over the marketplace: a second-hand bookshop, a health food cavern, a tarot reader, two pubs and the Abbey walls, mossy and black, running the length of the street behind the car park.

'So this is it.'

I straightened up, feet tingling painfully as the blood slowly came back to them.

'Do you want to go to the Abbey?'

'I should think so. Didn't come here to get my runes read.' He lifted a bag from the hold-all of the bike. The boys edged a step closer. Piers fronted them with a fierce stare. 'Touch it and you're dead,' he said; the boys jostled, brashly, pushing out their chests, but they didn't come any closer.

Clouds banked up like cathedrals, towering shapes against a wash of paler grey, driven solemnly by the wind; they made the sky seem somehow higher. Inside the Abbey grounds, a middle-aged woman in a red waterproof sat patiently inside a glass-fronted wooden shed. 'Place to yourselves today,' she noted, in a Somerset burr.

'Not surprised, at four pounds fifty.' Piers fingered a note out of his pocket with bad grace. 'We're here on a pilgrimage, do we get a discount?'

'No.'

'Huh.' He turned to me. 'You're right – the modern world is corrupt in its soul.'

'The pilgrims used to get fleeced all the time. They'd sell you a chicken bone and claim it was the finger of Christ.'

He rolled his eyes in exaggeration. 'Is nothing sacred?'

'Everything's sacred in Glastonbury. Even the fish and chips have mystical properties.'

'Yes, I noticed. Quack City. Come on.'

All around the Abbey grounds, trees were turning the colours of metals and a dusting of red leaves covered the grass, still parched and patchy from the summer. The two towers of the transept stood sadly against the drifting sky, symmetrical in ruin, the stonework dull in the thin light. Scrubby grasses poked from the tabernacles whose statues had been beheaded centuries ago.

I wandered a little way from Piers and felt the familiar catch in my throat; a mixture of awe and anger. Concrete outlines laid into the grass showed the probable location of the remaining buildings, razed to the ground, but not the great library. Even its foundations were lost.

The air was silent; a disturbance of rooks took off suddenly from behind the trees at the far end of the grounds. I put out a hand and laid it against the stone, running my fingers over the texture, imagining I might absorb some of its echoes, and closed my eyes. This was a ritual I had learned from George, pure superstition, we knew, but I had come to believe in it; a means of bridging the past.

Piers was looking up at the towers, lips parted, nodding to himself.

'Do you feel that?' I said, in a near-whisper.

'What?'

'The *genius loci*.'

'Spirit of place. Hmm. Ghosts, you mean?'

'No, not in that sense. More like – lifting a veil.'

'Go on.'

'It's one of George's unscientific theories about history. He believes that time is not linear. Uh – you know – instead, it's made up of layers that co-exist to build up a picture, like transparencies overlaid on the one before. So there are places where history seems to be concentrated, so much has happened there, and in those places there are sometimes pockets where time slips, or you have a glimpse of the past.'

Piers was looking at me with amused scepticism, though not unkindly.

'Or a much stronger sense of it anyway. You feel it' – I thumped my sternum – 'here. If you didn't, you couldn't love the past, it would just be dates and papers. But when you stand somewhere like this, it's something living. There's a ruined abbey in Norfolk where George swears he's heard medieval monks singing mass.'

'George should see someone about that.' He bent down to delve in his bag, smiling.

'What are you laughing at?'

He looked up. 'I'm not laughing. I was just thinking – it's very attractive to watch someone doing what they're good at. Don't you think? You're impressing me.' He waved a hand at the ruins.

I blushed fiercely, and thought of how proud I had felt at the way he moved in the film world, watching his interview with Nick Strachey. All those words he had said on that last evening in Highgate; the cruelty in his face – where was that? It couldn't all have been the drugs, surely, and how could I still want him so much? I watched him, squatting on the grass, rummaging in his bag. I had not known it was possible to want someone in this way. I thought about reaching down to touch his hair, and the muscles in my groin tensed.

He looked up.

'Do you believe that? About time, and the spirit of the past?'

'Yes.' I hesitated. 'Well – I believe that there's more than we

244

see or understand – there has to be. Doesn't there?'

He frowned, and slowly stood up. 'Why? There's the imagination, which is extremely powerful – more than we know. Everything we can't see is explained by that. But beyond it, objectively, no. There are no gods, no chance, no Fate, no serendipity. You make your own luck, by force of will and your actions. Anything else is a lie.'

I turned my head to watch the clouds. 'But you can't control everything.'

'True. But you can try.' He smiled again. 'That's why I always wanted to make films. Because you get to be God, for however long that film lasts. It's a world you've made, all your own, and there isn't a shaft of light that falls or a footstep or the sound of a car passing that you haven't ordered. A whole world where every detail is there because you intended it. That's what I want life to be like.' It was hard to tell if he was being serious.

'Yes, but it isn't –'

'But it could be. You can always direct people, to an extent. Some people want to be directed – they wouldn't know how to live otherwise.'

'And what about illness, and accidents, and death?'

'Death.' He tilted his head. 'Well, that's the ultimate power, isn't it – to choose the ending. Not having that taken out of your hands. Don't you think? I don't find death frightening, but I'm terrified of the idea that it might happen before I'm ready. When I'm not expecting it. That's why I hate to fly, because I could die and it wouldn't be my own choice. As long as you have the choice of when and how, nothing can frighten you.'

'You mean suicide?' I was suddenly cold; his eyes were so bright. 'That's your answer to the fear of death?'

'If you like.' He offered a cryptic, one-sided smile. 'If there's one essential human right, it should be the right of every person to be in control of their own end. Choosing when to cut to fade.'

'But that's crazy. I mean, it's naive – life isn't –' I was struggling.

'Isn't what?'

'Like a film, or a book. You can't end it neatly and then stand back and have people admire it.'

'Why not? You should at least try to make it a work of art, otherwise –' he held his hands out, empty. 'Otherwise – what's the point?'

I studied him for a moment. 'Are you being serious?'

'Absolutely. I disapprove of humour.' Then he grinned, showing his teeth, and all at once I felt a quick fear, and wanted to grab hold of his arms with both hands, as if he might there and then start running and gloriously throw himself over a precipice just to prove the point.

'It's not heroic. Suicide, I mean. It's cowardly, and selfish. It doesn't take into account what everyone else has to live with, the people you leave behind – all the guilt. I know someone who lives with that –'

'Who?'

'Oliver. His father killed himself – Olly's never really got over it.'

Piers rubbed his cheek.

'Some people kill themselves because they feel it's the right time to go. And some people do it because they can't live with themselves any longer. You don't know what he might have had on his conscience.'

'What do you mean?'

'Nothing in particular. Just that – everyone has mistakes in their past. Maybe one day it just becomes too much effort to keep papering over them.'

'Surely no one thinks that until their mistakes threaten to catch up with them.'

'Ah.' He scratched his lower lip with his thumbnail. 'There you have it.'

He had taken from his bag a compact video camera, not much bigger than his hand, of the kind with a screen facing the operator to show what would appear through the lens; now he started walking backwards towards the Lady Chapel pointing it at me.

'This isn't much good, but it'll give us some idea of how shots will look before I get the camera crew down.'

'When will you start filming?'

'As soon as I finish turning your notes into a proper script. Probably next month.'

He turned and jogged a few paces, then turned back; I guessed he was trying to fit both towers into the screen.

'Can you move into the centre?' he called, motioning with his hand. 'Between the towers – that's it. You're me. Good.' He walked back a bit further, then took a few steps to right and left, squinting at me through the viewfinder.

After a few moments of angling and repositioning the camera, he gestured for me to join him in the shadows of the Lady Chapel, where the twin towers were framed by the proscenium of the empty doorway.

'Sometimes,' he leaned against the left-hand side of the arch, the camera dangling by its strap from one hand, 'a ruin is far more interesting than if the thing had been preserved intact.'

'I disagree. Think of what's been lost.'

'Is that really so bad, though? Nations are only like people – they can carry too much baggage from the past. Sometimes it's necessary to burn it down and start again.'

'No. Nations and people need to know the events that formed their character if they want to understand themselves properly. You have to face your own past and build it in. I mean, think how much richer we'd be if the library hadn't been destroyed.'

Piers shifted his weight against the doorway and was quiet for a moment. '*You* would. You would be richer.'

'Me? Why?'

'You and your band of heritage-seekers – you romanticise all this. This is only your version of England – don't misun-

247

derstand, it's not a bad thing that you care about it. But you only care because you can afford to.'

'What do you mean, afford?'

'Well – do you think it matters to most people? The people who live here, and in the villages around, and in the council estates on the edges of the cathedral cities – would it make the slightest difference to their lives if the library had never been destroyed, or if the Abbey was still intact? Even if it had survived, it would just be another part of the Gift-Shop-Tea-Room-Coach-Trail by now, and the manuscripts would all be in the university library or private collections for the benefit of you and your mates. And the ordinary people who live in the shadow of all that history – they don't come out of their houses every morning to go to their mundane jobs or hang out their washing and look up at some stained glass and Gothic tracery and suddenly feel that all is right with the world because they're in touch with what they came from. It's only people like you, cosseted away in your nice timber-framed university, that have the luxury of reflecting on history as an abstract concept, or a string of pretty artefacts.' He picked a clump of lichen from the wall and crumbled it. 'I don't mean that as a personal attack.'

'So – what are you saying – it's not democratic, so it's not worth anything? Or are you saying that if people haven't studied it they can't appreciate beauty? Now who's being a snob?' A tug of wind blew my hair into my mouth; I stopped to remove it, almost breathless. 'Do you think they'd be happier coming out of their houses and looking up at a sixties tower block? Would you want to live in a country where all the cathedrals and all the old churches had been destroyed? Imagine that – imagine a country without any sense of its history! I thought you were on the side of preserving the past.'

'Oh, I am. But not as a tourist attraction – it must inform what we go on to next, otherwise it just becomes a pastiche of itself. Preserving the past doesn't mean you have to live in it, like you'd like to.'

'I would not!'

'Come on – you'd have liked art and literature to have frozen somewhere around the end of the last war. I think you're somehow afraid that the new will displace the past, and you want to put your arms around it and protect and stop everything from changing around it. And "England" – your version of it – means nothing to most of the people who call themselves English, especially now – you can't just ignore that. This' – he slapped the wall beside him – 'is a pile of decaying masonry to most people. Only the elect have the privilege of imagining they feel your *genius loci*. People like you and George, and your father – you appoint yourselves custodians, and it's a closed order. It's not the only touch-stone, that's all I'm saying.'

'I didn't realise you were so political.' I thought you were only interested in yourself, I wanted to add.

'Everything's political in the end. It's just that you have a very fixed idea of how the world works that's based, from what I can see, on very little experience. Your humanist val-ues are the values of someone who's been blessed with a priv-ileged life.'

Dejected, I slumped against the other side of the arch, fist-ing my hands into my pockets. Sunlight began to press between the clouds. 'Then why are you bothering to make a programme about this, if it's meaningless to most people?' I kicked a loose stone down the steps.

'To remedy their ignorance. And because I'll make a pro-gramme about almost anything if it means I get my own tele-vision series – wouldn't you? As long as there's a no-nudity clause in my contract.' He smiled, and reached out a hand to touch my shoulder. I flinched, unintentionally. He drew his hand back slowly. 'Sorry. I –' He turned his face away from me, out towards the towers, as if he might have been about to say something. Perhaps he thought about apologising for the other night. But the moment passed, and he began to amble away from the buildings, nodding for me to follow. Never explain, never apologise – that was his method. I knew he wouldn't, not now, but I also sensed that for a minute he had been uncomfortable, which meant at least that he had not forgotten it altogether.

'And don't keep bringing my father into it. You don't know anything about him.'

'I'm sorry. Edward talks about him a lot. I've heard a lot of stories.'

'Huh. Well, please don't believe those. Edward hated him.'

Piers stopped still and regarded me with curiosity for a moment. He folded his arms across his chest. 'You know, you can be very stupid sometimes.'

'What?'

'He never hated Richard. Jealous of him, certainly – wanted to be better than him, worked hard to prove that he could be. But no one really hates their own brother – Edward's not as inhuman as you like to think.'

'He told you that?'

'Of course he didn't.' Piers looked impatient. 'But he didn't have to – it's obvious. I'm a bit better at reading people than you.'

'Oh.' I stared down at the crisp grass, trying to make this fit with my picture of my uncle. 'You must be very close, then. To Edward.'

He breathed out slowly and frowned, his breath clouding in the cold. Then he shrugged, as if this were not important. 'I'm sorry I never met Richard. He sounds like –'

'Like what?'

There was a pause. He started walking again.

'Like he would have been a good father to have had. The right kind. You're lucky.' His face was turned away as he said this, but there was a tightness in his jaw, and I looked at him and tried to imagine what it would be like to have the wrong kind of father.

All at once I realised I could be in love with him.

'I miss him,' I said, needlessly.

He nodded, once.

Patches of frost still crusted the grass where the trees cast shadows. A crow cawed intermittently, its call raking through the air. I walked beside him in silence through the dry leaves, out towards the wall at the far side of the grounds, unsure of what to say; he seemed awkward too, or as near awkwardness as his poise would allow, as if we had mistakenly got too close. Occasionally he paused to look back at the ruins, tilting his head this way and that as if sizing them up for the camera. The silence grew.

'Tell me again,' he said, eventually, 'but succinctly – why was the Abbey destroyed so brutally?'

'Well –' I pushed my hair back from my face, relieved that we were back to neutral ground and I could hide again. I put my hands in my pockets and became the historian. 'The destruction had to be in proportion, and Glastonbury was the most important monastic centre in England, so the Dissolution had to be really spectacular. They hanged the last Abbot too, up there on the Tor, on fabricated charges of treason. It was a warning, really. And money, too – it's always money. Henry wanted the Abbey's lands.'

'Why was it so rich, then? Because of Arthur?'

'Well, you have to go back to the twelfth century. The Normans had put a lot of effort into building up the Arthur connection, and the Abbey's reputation grew from there. Because it was always a crucible for different myths and religions –'

'I'm not saying "a crucible of myths" on national television. No Latin, no clichés. And I'm not saying "melting-pot" either.' He grinned, hitching the strap of his bag up on to his shoulder. 'Tell me about the Norman propaganda.'

'Well, it started really with William of Malmesbury. In the 1120s, he was invited to Glastonbury by the Abbot, Henry de Blois, to write a history of the Abbey. A Norman abbot, obviously – the Abbey was significant enough to have been put into Norman hands by then. Henry was the king's nephew, in fact. So he commissioned William to write this history that would make Glastonbury belong to the Norman ruling class. *De Antiquitate Glastoniensis Ecclesiae*. Or, *The History of Glastonbury Abbey*, for your viewers.' He nodded in acknowledgement, half-smiling. 'No one really knows what he wrote,' I went on, 'because none of the original manuscripts survived – all we have now are much later thirteenth-century copies full of additions – total fiction, trying to claim even greater authority and antiquity for the Abbey. The interpolations said that the church had been founded by Joseph of Arimathea with the blood of Christ, which William certainly never wrote, although he probably knew that myth.'

'But he did write about Arthur?'

'In another book – *Gesta Regum Anglorum* – he has a short paragraph about Arthur, where he mentions that the Britons invent fables about him. This is around 1125. And he says that Arthur's tomb had never been found.'

'But then the tomb appeared in the Abbey?'

'Two very important things happened in between. Geoffrey of Monmouth – remember him? – published his *History of the Kings of Britain*, which was the first widely read fictional treatment of the Arthur story. So it became quite fashionable, which suited Henry II. It was useful, from his point of view, because he had the material to create the kind of national myth that the Normans needed to rally England – you know, like a kind of English Charlemagne – and Arthur was already a folk-hero for the Britons. So they just appropriated him – a ready-made national icon. Henry's grandson was even called Arthur. But then they had this insurgence problem.'

'Arthur's return?'

'Yes. Geoffrey wrote that Arthur went to Avalon to be cured of his wounds after his last battle and the Celtic nationalists picked up on this idea that they would one day be delivered, which gave their cause quite a boost. So Henry had a stroke of genius. Because the other thing that happened was the great fire at the Abbey in 1184, when the old church was almost completely burned to the ground. So Henry put up some money for the rebuilding, and in all the chaos, they claimed the king had been told in a dream that the tomb of Arthur and Guinevere would be found beneath the two pyramids of the Abbey. So the monks started digging, and seven feet down they found a stone slab with a leaden cross set into the underside, with an inscription.'

'Saying?'

'*Hic Iacet Sepultus Inclytus Rex Arturus In Insula Avalonia.*' I grinned triumphantly.

He laughed. 'Give me a second – here lies – uh – King Arthur's tomb – and something about the Isle of Avalon.'

'That'll do. Then they found an oak coffin with the bones of a man and a woman.'

'But fake, of course?'

'Oh, yes. Well – the bones were real enough. But it was quite brilliant, don't you see? They killed two birds with one stone. The Abbey became an Arthurian shrine, which was very useful in attracting patrons and pilgrims to raise money for the rebuilding work. And in one blow they'd taken the sting out of this myth of the avenging *rex futurus.*'

'Henry must have been delighted.'

'Well, Henry died in 1189, just before the tomb was excavated. But it meant that Glastonbury was now equated with Avalon, not just in England but throughout Europe. Richard the Lionheart went off to the Crusades with a sword he claimed was Excalibur and came from the Abbey. And by the time we get to the Dissolution it's the most important shrine in the country.'

'Great.' He rubbed his hands together and blew on them against the cold. 'You're quite clever, you. There is some truth in the rumours.'

In spite of myself, I blushed, pleased.

'And of course Arthur, and Glastonbury, became staples of English romance and fiction for centuries.'

'Yes.' He looked up at the sky, seemingly distracted. 'I've seen enough of this for now. I need to eat.'

He took a last glance through the camera, turned a full circle to take in the compass of the Abbey grounds, then tucked the camera into his bag and zipped it decisively shut. 'Let's go somewhere else.'

We drove on to Wells, and found a pub which looked out over the green and the pompous façade of the cathedral. It began to rain.

Piers poked suspiciously at something posing as shepherd's pie.

'You're quite friendly with all those malcontents in the new faculty, aren't you?'

'No,' I said immediately. 'Which malcontents?'

'Lennox and his crowd.'

'Oh, no – not at all. I hardly know them. It's only George I'm close to, really.'

'Not George, the others. The once-were-radicals. Lennox doesn't like me.'

'Well, you haven't exactly gone out of your way to be nice to him.'

Piers seemed amused.

'I'm his boss, I'm under no obligation to be nice to him.' Then his eyes turned serious again, and he prodded his food some more, without eating it. 'But I hear he's going around checking up on me. Probing into my background, as if it might give him some leverage. That bothers me.'

'Why – because he might find something?'

'No,' he said, glaring emphatically. 'Because my past is none of his fucking business.'

I thought suddenly of my own trawl through the Andy Epstein file, and wondered if Piers had removed the cuttings himself. And if so, why?

'Well, I suppose – you did rather appear out of nowhere. And it's a small community, the university – people like to know your credentials. Where everyone's come from, and you're very quiet about that. And also, I mean, you've been very successful, and there's the TV and everything – and people like Jake Lennox naturally resent other people's success.'

He nodded. 'You're right.'

'And you can't win with people like that,' I went on, sensing I had his approval, 'because they always want to feel they're hard done by, you know, because they didn't have the right opportunities or something. So they probably resent you because they want to think you're only where you are because of – well. Because of Edward.'

'That's what you think, isn't it?'

'No, I – but isn't that part of it? You are quite close.'

Piers flicked his eyes over my face quickly, then gave up the pretence of eating and lit a cigarette.

'Edward's been very good to me, it's true. But only because he believed I had talent he could use.' He pointed a finger at me. 'You know Edward – he doesn't waste his time. And I've helped him out enough, he knows that. But I refuse to play that game of holding my life up for those bloody elitists to scrutinise. It shouldn't matter where I've come from – I've left it behind, and I'm not going to cash in on this "look at me dragging myself up by my bootstraps" vogue. It's nothing to do with that now. They should judge by what I am.'

And what exactly are you, I wondered.

'But people are always curious. Anyway, aren't you supposed to be proud of being a meritocrat these days?'

'Oh, meritocracy is another myth. It's still all about blood. Who your father is, or knows – that doesn't change.'

After a pause I said: 'Did you?'

'What?'

'Drag yourself up by your bootstraps?'

He laughed.

'I didn't have a rich influential uncle or a well-connected father and a four-storey town house in Highgate.' He leaned back, smiling – to himself, it seemed. 'I have to be careful with you – for some reason you make me want to confide all sorts of things that I'd later regret. It must be because you listen well.'

I smiled, shyly. *I wish you would, I wish I knew what goes on inside your head.*

'I will tell you about my tragic past one day, but then I'll have to kill you.'

'But – you've done all right, you don't need to be angry about it. Better than all right – I mean, I had a lot of advantages, as you never tire of pointing out, and you're doing better than me.'

'I'm considerably older than you. And I've made a lot more mistakes.'

'Forty's not old.'

'I am *not* forty!' he thumped his palm against the table, then looked up from under his eyebrows, half-smiling. 'Yet.'

We sat in silence for a few moments. The fruit machine blinked in the corner; at the next table a toddler started screaming. 'Shut it, Jarvis,' said the young father, turning round briefly from the satellite sports channel, and the child howled louder. I watched it absently, wondering what our child would look like, mine and Piers's, and then scuffed the thought abruptly to one side, embarrassed in case he'd seen it in my face.

'Why did you never use it?' Piers said, after a while.

'Use what?'

'Your father, Edward. All those opportunities.'

'Well.' I took a cigarette and frowned, considering. 'When I was young, it was just a part of life, you know? My dad always had – oh, all these people – film people and writers round the house. Stuart Graham, when he was really famous – Ismail Awenat, all these poets and journalists, whatever, and they were just – there. I didn't really think about it, they were just Dad's friends. And we used to go to Edward's parties too, when I was in my teens, and meet ministers and all the people Edward hangs out with, and it was nothing special. I just assumed I'd end up in the middle of it all.' I pushed my plate away. 'Then, when I was eighteen, my dad had this falling out with Edward. Because of him buying Lexicon, you know. Dad felt sort of cornered. So we didn't see him any more, not socially, and Dad never said it in so many words, but it became a kind of unspoken rule, that out of respect for Dad we would never take anything from Edward again. Because, like you said, Edward doesn't just give out of the kindness of his heart. It's always a way of buying you.'

Piers pressed his lips together and looked down.

'So you hide yourself away to spite Edward? Don't you think that's cutting off your nose in the end?'

'It's not –' I rubbed an eyebrow, groping for the right words. 'Everyone thought it was great for Dad, when Edward bought Lexicon and promoted him, and made it profitable, but really Dad was devastated. He was so proud of what the company was, because he'd built it up and he really had a lot of integrity about what he published. He believed in it. Then Edward just bulldozed in and turned it into total crap.'

'But it made money. Kept your father in work.'

'Dad didn't think in those terms. He didn't really care about money. I suppose I'm the same.'

'Because you don't have to worry about it. I see where you get it from. This high-mindedness.'

'It's not meant to appear like that. Preachy, I mean.'

'You're young. You'll learn.' He shrugged, and blew smoke. 'Or maybe you won't.'

'Don't patronise me.'

'Was I patronising you? How clever of you to notice.'

He smiled; I laughed back, but I was beginning to feel needled.

'But I like what I do,' I said, as if expected to defend myself. Then I realised this was not necessarily true.

'But you want things to stay as they are. You could be anything you wanted, you know – you're young, you're nice-looking, you're well connected. But you're afraid. They're all scared in that place, Gaby, you can see it in their eyes. Hiding in their turrets, stock-piling for the siege. And you want to be like them – shit, don't do it!' He seemed alarmingly earnest. 'You're still alive, at least. But all you want is to end up just like George.'

'That's not true. Anyway, there are worse ways to end up.' A blush of confusion travelled up my neck.

Piers laughed, without humour.

'Without a doubt.' There was a sharp pause. 'I should know.' He watched me, cigarette held thoughtfully in front of his face. 'You're very – untouched, you know. By life. It's quite refreshing. You have no idea.'

'Of what?'

'Oh, anything. God, Gaby, I've seen some of the worst ways people can end up – things you'll never have to see.' He shook himself and sat up, stabbing his cigarette stub suddenly out. 'One more coffee, then I have to go.' He glanced at the window. 'This rain is evil. I'm going back to London, does that suit you? Sorry, but I have to get back to see someone.'

Someone. One word, dropped in so casually, but enough to crumple my small illusion that we were achieving some kind of communication. Whoever this someone was, I hated them with a swift, smarting jealousy that was new to me. Piers stretched his legs, one after the other, then got up and walked to the bar. I watched his back and then looked down at my hands, ashamed of my lack of polish and the smallness of my ambitions. Perhaps he was right; perhaps I was afraid. But of what? Change. Risk. A world outside the one I knew, that might prove unpredictable. Looking at myself through his eyes, I realised I was not impressed. If I were Piers Gaveston I wouldn't be interested in me. So why did he give me these glimmers of possibility?

'I always start to get these near panic attacks when I visit the provinces, do you know what I mean?' he said, returning with two cups of thin coffee clotted with powdered milk.

'That sounds like unbearable metropolitan snobbery too, but it's true – these little towns feel so far away from anything that really matters, I'm always afraid I'm missing something important. That's when I start to feel like I can't breathe, and I have to get back for some smog and inane conversation.'

'Is that why you never show up at the university?'

I was partly teasing, but he didn't smile.

'In a sense. But I'm so dissatisfied, always – when I'm at home on my own I desperately want attention, and company, and then as soon as I get out to one of these pointless parties, I wish I'd just stayed in and watched a good film. You're going to wade in now with your amateur psychology and tell me that's because I'm not happy with myself, aren't you?'

'No. I was just going to say that – I'm the same.' Who is this someone you're seeing, I wanted to ask, and what am I to you, but didn't. He watched me curiously.

'In some strange ways, I think you are.'

We drank the rest of the coffee in silence, and afterwards Piers drove us back to London on the bike, unloaded me at the station, thanked me again and kissed me briefly goodbye on the cheek. There was no mention of when we might meet, no contact other than this kiss and my arms around him as we hurtled up the motorway, but I was left with a peculiar conviction, without anything having been said, that we had arrived at some kind of agreement. I had become, in some unspecified way, part of his life, and for the moment that was good enough.

Chapter XIII

And so, over the following months I became, at least as far as the rest of the world could see, Piers's – what? Girlfriend? Not really – that was a frivolous word suggesting something innocent and exploratory and above all, *friendly*, which was not how it felt from my end, though this was the word they chose to use most often in the picture-captions. *Partner?* Don't be ridiculous; the word by definition implies mutuality. *Lover?* Not that, certainly; excluding the night of Nick Strachey's film, which Piers never mentioned and which I knew better than to bring up, the peculiar relationship that had somehow become accepted without ever being discussed did not include physical intimacy, though not through lack of interest on my part. *Date*, perhaps, best defined it, with all the uncertainty and impermanence the word imparts in high-school movies. There were strict parameters. What we had was like the inversion of an adulterous affair; it existed only in the bracing light of the public eye, in front of the snappers and the diary hacks, at launches and screenings and gallery openings and all the whirligig of media social events that a handsome young cultural commentator credited with revolutionising a moribund academic institution might have been expected to attend.

The press seemed to approve of our association as it was presented to them, or at least to feel that it made *sense*. Like finds like; it was proper and only to be expected – and also, usefully, an easy target – that this ambitious new star should be stepping out with the niece of the man who had so evidently given him a significant push up the ladder. Sly theories of cause and effect were mooted whenever articles on Piers appeared, the word 'nepotism' never quite making so brash an appearance, but always hovering somewhere in the sub-text. And Piers, as far as I could see, was content with this arrangement; he wore me in public like an amulet, effectively warding off the attentions of other groupies, of which there were plenty, and reinforcing his now uncontested place in Sir Edward's entourage. Was I merely an accessory in his self-fashioning? It was a question I didn't like to ask, not even to myself.

I was frustrated, of course, by the absence of anything behind this public façade, and couldn't help feeling that this was not a relationship as I understood it, but Piers's unpredictability and aloofness, bordering often on indifference, meant that it kept the edge of an affair and kept my desire straining. There was no domesticity, no chance to relax – no evenings in watching videos, no late-night phone calls, no slow Sunday afternoons, no bickering over trivialities. No room for boredom to steal in. His absences were frequent and unexplained; often he would disappear without warning for three weeks at a time and returning would say only, 'I was in New York' or 'I had things to do', as if surprised that I had noticed at all. Perversely, this became exciting to me; that he placed himself constantly out of my reach, but only just, so that there was always the whisper of a chance, so that I had to work for him and often couldn't dislodge the niggling thought that I was merely tolerated in his life, never sought. But that was him, I was beginning to understand; this intractable solipsism and self-hunger. There was no *kindness* in Piers; there was a latent malice, certainly, but that was not so striking as this absence of kindness, this failure to take even a polite interest in the lives of those around him. But perhaps I was like that too, in my own way, both of us too concerned with ourselves, devouring our own tails. The difference was that I was in love with Piers, or believed I was, and Piers was also in love with Piers, or at least with the acceleration of his own life. I was smart enough to realise that the quickest way to drive him away would be to demand something he was incapable of offering.

But the sex thing continued to bother me. Though the opportunity to spend the night together rarely appeared, it was his indifference to me that began to eat at my confidence; he never suggested sex and after one or two rebuffs I became too nervous to initiate anything. Either he found me physically unappealing, or – my biggest fear – he was too busy getting it elsewhere; either way, I needed to find out.

'Why do you never invite me home?' I asked one night, after I'd sat patiently in his club until the early hours with a group of his television friends, doing my best to join in despite the fact that they were all flying at thirty thousand feet and I had no idea what or who they were discussing with such animation.

He looked impatient. 'What?'

'I mean – you never – we never. Sleep together.'

'Ah.' He glanced around to make sure his friends were out of earshot, then slipped an arm around my shoulder and moved closer on the sofa. 'It's difficult for me, Gaby – I'm –' He paused and looked down, suddenly vulnerable.

I put a hand on his leg. 'What is it?'

'I'm very sensitive to stress. When I'm tired, it becomes – you know. Difficult.'

He didn't look at me. Maybe you'd be less tired if you didn't stay up all night every night with your coke-snorting friends, I was tempted to say, and knew that I would sound like a nagging wife. Even if it were true, it was clear that Piers had his own priorities.

'I don't mind. But we don't even try –'

'Be patient with me,' he said, and smiled bravely.

It wasn't mentioned again.

'He's not the sort of chap who seems in a hurry to *settle* to anything,' George observed with well-meaning condescension on one occasion. 'So you've really got no idea where he is?'

'I haven't heard from him in a couple of weeks,' I admitted.

There was a film project in progress with Nick Strachey and Jerome Idle, a book he claimed to be writing, the television interviews and a new weekly column on the Arts in Edward's Sunday broadsheet; Piers was rarely seen in the town, and even less frequently in the faculty. George, as the increasingly irritated faculty staff knew, was effectively covering for him.

'He's not a *bad* fellow, but – I have grave doubts about his ability to stick at anything that requires a bit of commitment and hard graft,' George said. 'Not the sort of chap you'd want to have to rely on. Still – "Man's love is of man's life a thing apart". Remember that, Gaby – don't let it be your whole existence. As long as you're happy.'

Happy was not quite the right word. I was distracted, disorganised, excited, edgy, exhilarated, disappointed, often despairing; in a permanent state of thrill and fear of falling, as if I were all the time at the top of a ski run. But that was what I had wanted, wasn't it? At least I was living.

This – relationship, obsession, what-you-will – with Piers began to have side effects that I could not have predicted. Though I was not prepared to admit to it, I was moving gradually towards the life he applauded, the celebrity carousel, in the hope that in doing so his interest in me might increase exponentially. I submitted to a scissored haircut in a glaring London salon that resembled a laboratory. I had my eyebrows waxed, so that they no longer made me look mad. I ran every day, and lifted weights twice a week; I started, for the first time, spending money (my father's money, hitherto reserved through some lingering scruple of conscience for those things which would have won my father's approval – books, travel, theatre) on clothes that, if not exactly haute couteur, at least didn't look as if I'd found them in the cancer shop. 'Good dress,' Piers would sometimes say, with an approving nod, as I lunged into the waiting car en route to some event or another, but always with a tone that suggested

'Good dress' meant a dress in whose company he was not altogether ashamed to appear, and not necessarily one that made me look any better or more alluring or otherwise different in his eyes.

There were other adjustments too. At one of these parties, some star-freighted event at the South Bank Gallery, Neville Toynbee introduced me to Mike Gavill, the editor of the *Sunday Enquirer* and Oliver's boss. He was a tall, robust man with longish, twisting hair and restless shoulders, still dressing as if he were eighteen.

'Gabs, Gabs,' he said, grasping me in a bone-crunching handshake as if I were a long-absent friend, 'pleasure, finally. Hear you know Oliver. Says you're a dab hand with the old thingy.'

'Pardon?'

He took a huge, alarming drag of his cigarette which threatened to scorch his very bowel, and said, while exhaling: 'The old, y'know. Books.'

'Oh. I suppose,' I said, with a self-deprecating laugh.

'No, no – really. You should, uh – do some writing for us, some time.'

'What kind of writing?'

'Oh – y'know, whatever. Review some books or something for us – like books? Course you do. Do you know Magnus? Literary editor. I'll get you in touch with Magnus. You should do some writing. I hear good things. Good name for us, too.'

And so, without quite intending to, I found myself writing the occasional book review for the *Sunday Enquirer*, which over the months expanded into a fairly regular slot. My excitement was only partially quashed when, after speaking to Mike that first time, I ran to tell Piers with some elation of my potential foray into the world of print journalism and he replied, off-hand,

'Oh, yes – I told Mike to speak to you. I said he should get you before Edward snapped you up – that won him over. Now don't fuck it up.'

Little by little, usually indirectly and without offering anything in return, Piers was shaping me into someone befitting his persona, and I found myself increasingly anxious to please, to make myself worthy of his attention in the face of such determined competition.

A different party: dwarfed in yet another vast industrial space with lasers tracing fiery patterns over white walls and self-conscious air ducts, with flavoured vodka flowing through elaborate ice sculptures; Oliver was present. I had been talking to some people – a group of Oliver's friends – and afterwards, as we walked out into the street to find a taxi so that Piers could go on somewhere else and I could be bundled off home like a burdensome relative after Christmas, he suddenly pincered my arm and said, with alarming seriousness,

'Don't talk to the press.'

'I was only –'

'I don't care. That crowd from the *Enquirer* – stay away from them. I'm serious.'

'They're only Olly's friends.'

'I mean about me. *Us*. Don't ever discuss me with Oliver, or any journalists. I never talk about my private life in interviews, and neither should you.' He rested his hands on my shoulders and brought his face close to mine; gently, but his eyes were not to be argued with. 'Gaby. I have enemies.'

An involuntary snigger escaped me. Piers looked wearily patient.

'Yes, I know I sound melodramatic. But there are people who would love to take one careless remark out of context, one little aside you might let slip in the Crown and Dragon with your new mates at the *Enquirer* – don't give them any ground. Do you understand? *This*' – he made a sketchy gesture towards me and back to his own chest – 'this is private. And those people are not to be trusted, Gaby – no, not even Oliver.'

*

Oliver was already at a distance. I knew that he didn't approve of Piers, had some wrong-headed ancient grudge inherited from Denham Dowland, and he knew that I knew, and we were both aware of something else: the possibility that Oliver's disapproval could very easily look like jealousy.

Now, rather than risk his own dignity by repeating his dislike of Piers, Oliver simply withdrew. The phone calls became fewer, the visits rarer still. Sometimes I would arrive at a party with Piers and spot Oliver across the room with a catch of excitement, realising that it had been as much as six weeks since we had spoken, but there was always a distinct *froideur* in his bearing which was unfamiliar to me, and unsettling. Piers he seemed anxious to avoid altogether, and this was undoubtedly mutual. It seemed that winning Piers – if in any sense I could be said to have won him – entailed losing Oliver as its flip-side, and this saddened me, but the fault was clearly Oliver's and I was not prepared to give Piers up, nor to concede to Oliver that his prejudice might have any foundation. But at other times, when I was alone, or when I had to phone Magnus Strange, the Literary Editor of the *Sunday Enquirer*, and pictured Olly sitting perhaps only a few desks away in the same office, I realised that I was willingly letting a friendship wither, and wondered at my lack of depth. To lose Olly, who had always been there, for Piers, who I knew very well had no feelings for me? My father would not have been proud.

January: almost a year to the day since the meeting of the Faculty Planning Committee that had first announced Piers's entry into our lives. An epic wind was chafing at the river and St Dunstan's College was covered with a fine film of snow; I slid across the cobbled courtyard to George Fenton's staircase and took the stairs two at a time, in a hurry to show him the completed, almost-final draft of my thesis. Ducking under the wooden beams designed with five-foot fifteenth-century clerics in mind, I gave one, entirely desultory knock on the thick door while simultaneously crashing through it, and froze.

George had company.

He was sitting at his desk but with the chair half-turned to the room, canted over his knees with one hand propping up his forehead, doing his concerned face. In the centre of the room stood Jake Lennox, mid-rant: arms akimbo, veins straining in his neck, all his laconic demeanour exploded, and looking very much as if he might have been crying. They both snapped their heads round at the sound of the door, and the expression seized on their faces was not unlike the one I had seen on the faces of my parents when I stumbled in on them making love one morning when I was six.

'Gaby – oh dear – could you perhaps –?' George jerked his head towards the door with pantomimic exaggeration. 'Not a good –'

'YOU!' Lennox windmilled across the room, fixing me with a furiously trembling finger. 'I bet you knew all about this too, didn't you, you conniving bitch –?'

'Uh –' I took a step backwards; George quickly got to his feet.

'Now listen, Jake, that's unacceptable –'

'I'm afraid I don't –'

'No, *you* fucking listen,' Lennox said, the pointing finger whirring between me and George. '*This* is fucking unaccept-able. I will have the union on *you*' – (finger jabbing at George) – 'faster than you can blink, and I will see a lawyer and I will have that cunting *bastard*' – (finger jabbing now at me) – 'exposed as the fraudulent, lying, scheming little' – he wres-tled for the right word – '*catamite* that he is. You're all in this together, you lot, and you can all fucking go down together! And I'll make sure you do!'

He stood for a moment, breathing effortfully through flared nostrils, then swept past me out of the door and thun-dered down the stairs, the effect only slightly marred by the loud crack of his head on the timbers and the echoes of 'Shit, fuck, *fuck*!' coiling up the stairwell.

'What was that about?' I was still staring at the door.

George rubbed his hands over his face as if washing it. He allowed a long pause.

'Jake's been fired.'

'*How*? Who by? By whom?'

He looked up slowly, pushed his half-glasses to the end of his nose and raised one meaningful eyebrow.

'Piers?'

George nodded.

'Shit.' I sat down to absorb this.

'Shit exactly. As in, hitting the fan. As in, we're in the.'

'But he can't do that, can he? Legally, I mean?'

'Well. He can and he can't. They want to introduce performance-related tenure, bonus schemes, that sort of thing. This faculty is, after all, a private company, to all intents and purposes. So Piers is claiming that Jake's film theory lecture course has been poorly attended, *ergo* he's inefficient and no longer profitable. But poor Jake – honestly' – George reached up and smoothed his hair distractedly – 'his lectures are rather – difficult. They're all about post-modernist aesthetics, no wonder he couldn't compete with Jerome Idle and his so-called workshops. It's populism gone mad.'

'Will he get away with it?'

George shrugged, and his face was pained; it was the first time I had seen him looking as if things might have escaped his control. 'It happens in every other walk of life, doesn't it – if it doesn't sell, it doesn't make money, so scrap it. It's just that it's never happened like that here. In the university. And you and I know very well that it's nothing to do with attendance – your Piers has simply taken a dislike to Jake. Probably not without reason – Jake does have a talent for rubbing people up the wrong way – but as you can imagine, it's put the cat among the pigeons with the rest of the teaching staff. And if Jake challenges on grounds of unfair dismissal – which he certainly will – it will sully the faculty's reputation no end. Not to mention the university's. It'll be dragged through the courts and through the papers, and that's just the sort of scandal we could do without so early on.'

'Has Piers talked to you about it?'

'Oh yes. He's adamant he wants Jake out. Jake thinks the union will save him, but the union has no clout under the new faculty contracts. Did Piers mention it to you?'

'No.'

'No, I don't suppose you would talk about that sort of thing.' He shook his head. 'It's a very bad business altogether, Gaby. It isn't *right* – you know? I'm not Jake Lennox's greatest admirer, but still. Makes one very nervous about Piers's next target. Funny – he's very sharp but such a bad manager of people. I suppose we're fortunate he isn't here more often.'

Tell me about it, I thought. 'Jake's not a good enemy to have made, I imagine.'

'Oh no. Jake is very tenacious. And he will nurture a grudge and serve his revenge cold, I'm sure of it. Perhaps Piers thinks he's unassailable in his position – I don't know – but Jake is not the sort to slink away whimpering.'

No indeed, I thought. If Piers had concerns about Jake Lennox rummaging around in his personal history, surely publicly humiliating the man was not the best way to befriend him. But I was in no position to speculate on the workings of Piers's mind. He told me nothing.

'Did Piers make you tell Jake?'

'Well' – George scratched his beard – 'he didn't exactly *make* me. We decided it might be more prudent if I – yes, I suppose he did.'

I nodded, and stared at the numinous light behind the windows. It was snowing again.

'I do wish you hadn't had to witness this episode, Gaby. But then I suppose you would have found out sooner or later. Oh dear. There will be repercussions, you know.'

But mysteriously there weren't repercussions. At least, not immediately.

*

It was about the time that Piers's television series, *Reflecting England*, was broadcast that the paranoia set in. Eventually I became glad of the paranoia, since Piers's response to it was to draw me closer, to require my presence more often and more unexpectedly, but it took a while for me to realise that the two were linked.

Paranoia was a widespread condition in England by April. The elections for the English parliament had resulted in a tiny sliver of a majority for the incumbent government, but the rising Right were jubilant; there was a new surging of conservatism, a dusting-off of jingoism and national pride, even among the only-just-victorious Left. England had unshackled herself from the hampering extremities and was being reborn. On the south coast a mob vandalised an immigration centre; elsewhere there were pockets of protest generated by the new nationalism, directed against those whose Englishness might be considered doubtful. There would be casualties, later, although in the early spring the mood was still optimistic, despite the gloom of Wesley Hemp and other Leftish oracles, all prophesying a descent into ochlocracy. And in the midst of all this Piers's programme appeared, propelling him further into the public eye. 'The definitive history of English culture,' said the *National Ledger*, as generously as expected. 'His enthusiasm, wit and erudition make him quite possibly the most engaging presenter of serious programmes on English television,' gushed the reviewer in the *Daily Enquirer*. Viewing figures were surprisingly high for a serious cultural documentary; people stopped him in the street, and still he seemed restless, dissatisfied.

Piers's paranoia was of the most straightforward kind; he became convinced he was being watched. This began some time before I was aware of it, but even as early as April he started to display a distinct nervousness, a sleepless look around the eyes, a tendency to watch the door while he was talking to you. Raymond Mount, still Secretary of State for Culture and Heritage even after the seismic musical chairs of

the recent election, gave a reception in Bloomsbury for assort-
ed wonks, patrons and pundits; Piers and I were present, as
were Edward and Isabelle. Piers and Edward greeted one
another as we entered and drew together behind a marble pillar, muttering darkly, like dealers. Barely halfway through
the speeches, Piers hooked a finger into my collar and, leaning over, whispered, 'Let's go.'

'What, now?'

'Now.'

'Why?'

'Because.'

Outside, on the pavement, he tipped his face back into the
thin drizzle and glanced at the pigeon-streaked portico of the
museum we had just left.

'I want to get some dinner. I feel like I haven't eaten for
days.'

I suspected there might be some truth in this. Piers had lost
weight recently; the famous chiselled bones were close to
gauntness.

'You've lost weight, you know.'

He shrugged. 'It's all the work.'

All the charlie, I thought. These days he didn't seem much
concerned with trying to hide it.

We walked through the rain to Covent Garden, half-
heartedly lobbing out an occasional attempt at conversation
that would be batted limply back and forth a couple of times
and then allowed to drop. Settled in a new Thai restaurant,
a eco-sphere of intrusive verdure, running water and watch-
ful bronze elephants, Piers stared purposefully over his
menu at the entrance.

I tried again.

'Were you not enjoying the party?'

He raised an eyebrow. 'No. Vapid, self-obsessed spivs and
hucksters, all of them, with their intellectual wanking.' He
paused to gulp down mineral water as if he had a fever, and
ordered another bottle.

'They're the same people we see at every party.'

'Precisely. These are the people who run the country. If that's not demoralising . . . Sometimes I fantasise about planting a bomb in one of those rooms and ridding society of all its hideous movers and shakers and braying establishment cunts.'

'I thought you wanted to be part of that scene? It's what you've been working for.'

'What's the alternative? *Not* being part of it, because you're beneath its notice. Which is worse? And if you did plant the bomb you'd have to stay there and go with them, because there'd be no point in remaining, that's the ridiculous irony, if you want to call it that. No one would be left to recognise you.'

'Are you all right?' I feared I was losing the drift of this thesis.

'I'm tired. No – not tired. *Weary*. I am *weary*. I am going to give up smoking.'

He plunged again into silence, lighting a cigarette. I ordered a green curry; Piers looked up, distractedly, as if he had forgotten where he was, and asked for the same.

The food arrived. I ate mine, while Piers stabbed his morosely with a chopstick and drank water. After a few minutes he leaned across the table and said, 'Go to the loo.'

'Pardon?'

'I said, go to the loo. Go on.'

'But I don't need to.'

'For God's sake' – an infinitely patient pause – 'it's down the stairs. There's a man sitting at a table opposite the stairs – I want you to have a good look at him and tell me if you've seen him before. Reading a magazine. Be discreet.'

The man at the table by the stairs was reading the *New Yorker*. He glanced up briefly as I passed and, for an almost deniable moment, met my eye and quickly looked down. Thin-faced, he had dark, receding hair cut very short, rimless glasses and the stippled skin of a heavy smoker. Standing, he would be tall; he sat with the chair pushed some way back from the table to accommodate his legs, and wore an unobtrusive suit with no tie. There was a vaguely familiar look about him, but I wondered if that was only because Piers had put it into my head. On my way back up the stairs I had longer to contemplate him; he continued to read intently.

'Well?'

I slid back into my seat. 'Hard to tell. I mean, possibly. I don't know.'

Irritation twitched in Piers's eyelids. 'Not to worry.' The stress was on worry.

'Why? Who is he?'

Piers passed a hand over his forehead and pushed his hair back. Then he assumed a strange smile, reached out and took both my hands in his, forcing me to lean in towards him across the table.

'Doesn't matter. Just – I thought I saw him at the party tonight. Perhaps I've seen him somewhere else. Perhaps not. Forget it.' And he pressed one of my hands to his mouth, still caught in a slightly forced rictus.

I was taken aback; such a demonstration of affection was unprecedented, not to say suspicious.

'He's quite – normal-looking,' I said, trying to find some solid ground. 'I mean – a lot of blokes look like that.'

'Come home with me,' said Piers, out of nowhere.

'Tonight?'

'We don't –' he sighed, holding my hand against his cheek. His skin was cold. 'Spend enough time together.'

Not my fault, I wanted to say, but knew better than to threaten such an opportunity.

So it was that, on 19 April, for the first time, I accompanied Piers Gaveston back to his elegant but artful flat, in a square with a manicured garden and private tennis courts, just off the King's Road, where we had sex in his white room, across the acreage of his immaculate white bed; brief sex – perfunctory might be a better word – but I sensed no anger in him

273

this time. There was something else – resignation, perhaps – but I chose to ignore it. Having was better than not having. Afterwards he stood naked by the window for a long time, intent on the street, the blue-white of the lights slatting his body through the blinds. When he was satisfied that whatever he was looking for was not there, he folded his long limbs into the bed and lay without speaking in the half-dark. I touched his shoulder; he didn't move closer, but nor did he twist away. I don't think he slept.

In June, Sir Edward took off for a three-week business trip to Indonesia, where he hoped to persuade the fettered and disenfranchised proletariat – or at least, their overlords – to invest in digital television and a battery of hardware that would enable Hamilton Harvey International to fill their homes with Premier League football matches and Australian soap operas. This in itself ignited indignation among the chattering classes in London, as it did every time he tried to sell to a market whose humanitarian efforts were doubtful, and soon the Comment and Op-Ed pages of all the broadsheets except the *National* and *Sunday Ledger* were busy with disapproving treatises on the themes of conscience and responsibilities. This time, however, Edward took Piers with him. Mid-way through their stay, the *Daily Enquirer* – the *Ledger*'s chief combatant in the daily circulation wars – ran a frontpage piece under the headline 'Hamilton-Harvey's Golden Boy Charms The East'. There was a picture of Edward and Piers being fêted by Indonesian dignitaries; the jist was that Piers had insinuated his way into the fraught politics of international commerce by presenting himself as the smiling ambassador for Hamilton Harvey operations, and what a boon his blond beauty and splendid physique were for Edward's scheme. But the reporter, Kevin Lush, had managed to suggest, ever so subtly, and without infringing the libel laws, that there was a faint breath of something minutely beyond the ordinary in Piers's relationship with his patron.

A litany of Piers's recent accolades and successes, all achieved with Edward's name as a shibboleth. A catalogue of the other business trips – more than I had realised – on which Edward had preferred Piers's company to that of Isabelle. A sly allusion to their easiness in each other's company in the same sentence as a further emphasis on Piers's physical attractiveness. What Kevin Lush had left unsaid blared from the page in capital letters; the real article existed in the blanks left for the imagination to fill. Sir Edward Hamilton-Harvey, Lord Protector of Family Values, might just possibly have affections for his handsome protege that belonged more properly in the realm of the marital.

'That's ridiculous!' I said, smacking the newspaper down on the breakfast bar.

'What – that your man's a fag?' Bobby's voice floated up from under the coffee table in the sitting room.

'Yes! *No!* Or – my uncle, for goodness' sake! You only have to look at him. Incredible – these bloody journalists will try anything. *And* he's got a son!'

'That's no guarantee.' Bobby had crawled under there the night before, after taking bad acid and having to flee the flame-eyed wolves who were chasing him through the house but, as luck would have it, were too big to follow under the table. 'My buddy Zack's dad used to go to Mexico every month to hump his way round the boy-brothels and they never knew about it. For like twenty years or something. And he owned a software company.'

'These allegations are absolutely ridiculous,' said Roger, in the next day's papers, 'and furthermore, deeply offensive to Sir Edward and his wife and family. Sir Edward will not hesitate to personally take legal action over any defamatory allegations with regard to damaging his family and his good name.'

One tabloid had picked up on the story, but the others clammed up after that; Edward's litigious threats were buttressed, as everyone well knew, by the apparatus and all the necessaries to make libel writs a weekend hobby. Edward's history was strewn with the smouldering husks of those companies and individuals who had taken him on in the past, bearing pitiful testimony to the fact that he was always, without question, sure to win.

On his return, Edward – who had maintained a patriarchal silence, as if the whole business was beneath his notice – decided to throw a party. The late June days were growing warmer, the pollution in the London air was thickening with the promise of summer, and the party was held by the river, on the newly opened terrace of Wootton House. Along the railings, soft lanterns hung in garlands; the barges heaved past and the megalithic façade of the South Bank Gallery gleamed across the unctuous slick of brown water, which smelled brown.

Piers rested a hand on my back and engineered a passage through the sequinned crowds to the far end of the terrace. He leaned over the balustrade, staring into some place in the middle distance, and in profile his jaw was tight.

'Nice to have you back,' I said, after a while. Insects clouded up from the river and hissed around the lights.

'Yes,' he said slowly, and lit a cigarette. He turned to watch the guests clustering for a while, then looked back at me, his eyes vague. 'I had a chance to do some thinking while I was away.'

Another silence. I waited until it became unbearable; this sounded like the prologue to the end-of-the-road conversation.

'And?'

'And – well. I missed you.'

My heart started a discreet can-can under my ribs.

'So I thought –'

'What?'

'I thought' – he rubbed his lip with his thumbnail – 'we should get married.'

Granted, he was looking at the river when he said it, and he wasn't smiling, and it was not really a question; none the less, I was unable to speak.

'So?' He turned back from the river and graciously took the cigarette out of his mouth.

'Okay,' I said, eventually, too surprised for any cognitive processing. 'Yes.'

'Good.' Then he smiled suddenly, flicked the butt over the railings and kissed me, briefly, on the mouth. 'Excuse me for a second.'

I blinked into the chain of lights and abruptly felt the need to sit. Behind me was a stone bench; I took out a cigarette and saw my hands shivering. Piers returned after a few minutes with two glasses of champagne and the smile of a criminal who's just pulled off a risky heist.

'Cheers.'

'Cheers.' I couldn't think of anything appropriate to say. You still barely know him, said the small voice of reason, and you certainly don't trust him. I gulped the champagne back in one tilt, without quite meaning to, and the voice was momentarily quashed.

At the back of the terrace, a small podium had been erected and furnished with a microphone. Edward now climbed it, glass and cigar in hand, and the gathered crowd fell gradually silent like children at a school assembly.

'Welcome!' His voice ballooned back from the river with full reverb effect, giving the impression of a political rally. 'It gives me enormous pleasure to welcome you all here this evening to join me in celebrating eighteen years of Hamilton Harvey International in its present incarnation. Eighteen being the age of majority, I like to think that the company I began all those years ago has now reached maturity.' (A spattering of applause, led by Mervyn Bland and quickly taken up by others keen to show their appreciation.) 'I recall when my son reached his eighteenth birthday.' Sir Edward paused, and beamed. 'I told him, "Son, you are now an adult. And with freedom comes responsibility."' He paused again, perhaps realising that this was not a useful parallel to draw, his son and the concept of responsibility notoriously never having appeared together before in the same sentence. 'And I remain committed to ensuring that Hamilton Harvey International, as it continues to go from strength to strength, always remembers that responsibility is our watchword.' (More applause; Mervyn Bland's eyes were fairly bulging with admiration.) 'However!' Sir Edward raised his glass symbolically. 'I had no idea when I invited you all here that we would in fact be celebrating another wonderful event.' He allowed a dramatic silence. Piers laid his hand pontifically on the top of my head and nudged me towards the front. 'My beautiful niece, whom many of you will know as the daughter of my younger brother Richard, the esteemed publisher, who passed on so tragically five years ago this autumn, and my good friend, Professor Piers Gaveston, have this evening announced their engagement!'

A muted murmur went up from the guests; panic caught in my throat.

'Yes! So I'd like you all to join me in raising your glasses in a toast to these two lovely young people – where are you?' He shaded his eyes and scoured the audience. Piers shunted me on to the dais. My uncle kissed me stagily and shook Piers heartily by the hand before flinging his arm into the air – 'To Piers and Gabriele!'

'Piers and Gabriele!' brayed the crowd; flash-bulbs popcorned in the front row. Piers pushed his hair back, clamped an arm around me and assumed his photo-face; I stared foolishly over the heads of the snappers, thinking – absurdly – *well, he can't get out of it now, even if he changes his mind, it will be in all the papers*.

Over the heads of the crouching photographers I suddenly noticed, on the fringe of the circle, a tall man in glasses who caught my eye and half-raised a glass, with the smile of semi-recognition you use for people you think you probably know but can't remember how. I looked again. It was the man from the Thai restaurant.

I went home with Piers again that night, after the rush of congratulation and kisses from people I'd never seen before, or only on television, the hugs and handshakes and bleached women from *Happening!* magazine pleading to let them have the exclusive photoshoot. Piers smiled grandly and enigmatically at everyone, soaking up the attention, and I felt redder and increasingly flustered and convinced they must all be thinking how much better he could do and how he obviously wouldn't be marrying me if I weren't so usefully connected. Edward enjoyed the congratulations with avuncular pride, as if this were a dynastic match entirely of his fabrication, as if I were his property and he had just made a particularly well-advised investment.

We didn't sleep together in anything more than a purely literal sense. An awkwardness had crept in, which anyone else might have considered a bad omen; an inability to find a neutral subject. In the taxi, on the way back, Piers said casually, 'I think we should say we're not doing any interviews. Keep it private. Don't you think? If they bother you, just say we'll give interviews after the wedding.'

'When?' My throat was dry; I badly wanted another drink. I wanted to get drunk, to be beyond the reach of the real, which was shifting shape so violently this evening that only extreme and unbridled drunkenness could make any sense of it.

'Ah.' He leaned forward, hooked his hands together and stretched out his back. It cracked gently. 'That we have to talk about. Maybe not tonight, eh.'

I agreed; I didn't want to spoil this with detail, with logistics. I didn't want to ask questions in case the answers turned out not to be the ones I'd hoped for. Instead I lay awake long into the night in the crisp white bed, aching for him to touch me and prove that he had some involvement in this event, this momentous and hallucinatory thing that had happened to us. He fell asleep with a hand on my hair and I watched his face in sleep, tense and exquisite, lashes curled darkly on his cheek. Frequently he bit his lip. 'I love you,' I said, trying it out. It hung there, with nowhere to land, and the idea of saying it to his face, when he was conscious, filled me with sudden panic. So did the word 'husband'.

The following morning, when I woke, the bed was empty. Wrapping myself blearily in one of Piers's shirts, I shuffled into the bright front room, light drilling into my temples; he was not there either. I stood in the centre of the white room and looked around, guiltily, as if at any moment I might be accused of snooping.

Piers's flat was high-ceilinged and elegant, but, like its occupant, gave little away. The cavernous sitting room was lined with bookshelves along one wall, and at the far end, high French windows opened on to a plant-crowded balcony overlooking the square. On the wall above the fireplace hung a reproduction of a *Mappa Mundi* in a chunky oak frame, and on the wall opposite, a psychedelic canvas in muted colours, about six feet high, the oils glossy and clumped. Vaguely Art Deco, the furnishings gave the impression of having been professionally placed; it was a strangely impersonal place, immaculately tidy and lacking – strikingly so – any feeling of being a home. What was apparent here, however, I thought – my eyes floating over the bookshelves – was the money.

The books themselves were predictable; mostly hardbacks, beautifully published editions of Greek and Roman classics, European classics, philosophical classics, the pillars of contemporary English and American fiction, a few doorsteps on cinema history and theory. In the facing cabinet was a comprehensive video library, alphabetically arranged with careful labels, which I found oddly touching. And it struck me that everything about this flat – the wafer-thin wall-mounted television, the aerodynamic hi-fi, the post-code – was, subtly, very expensive. Piers's clothes, his Harley – all far more than anyone could afford on a professorial salary, even the swollen one Sir Edward's faculty must be offering, and surely more even than he would get from television work. There was another source of income involved here, and I wondered how it had never occurred to me to query this before. Where was his money coming from? Not family money, that was certain. I wondered if he might be dealing, and felt immediately shifty. If I was seriously going to marry him – the prospect seemed even more unreal by the morning – I should probably find out, though I was not entirely sure I would like the answer.

It was while I was tentatively stroking the laser-activated stereo, trying to figure out where the discs went amidst all the hydraulic smoky glass, and whether I dared touch Piers's music in his absence, that I noticed them, lined up precisely, with uniform bindings. Andy Epstein's novels in first editions: *Shifting Sands, Desert Tomb, Second Armageddon, The Beirut File*. Idly curious, I plucked *Shifting Sands* from the shelf. Winner of the Magellan Prize, it announced in raised gold letters. There, on the back of the jacket, was the photograph I recognised from the newspaper cuttings: Andy Epstein, smiling; a pleasant face, the forehead and eyes rutted by years under a Middle Eastern sun. I flicked to the first page, and as I did so, my eye fell on a hand-written inscription on the fly-leaf: *For Piers, who made sense of everything. Love always, AE.*

And the date: almost seven years ago.

'What are you doing?'

Piers stood in the doorway wearing sunglasses with a sheaf of newspapers under his arm.

'I was just – looking at your books.' I dropped *Shifting Sands* as if I'd been caught stealing CIA documents.

'Huh.' He glanced over my shoulder, then laid the papers on a mosaic table with lion's feet. 'I wouldn't trouble yourself with that if I were you, it's indescribable shite. Unpickupable.'

'He thinks very highly of you.'

Piers's eyes narrowed. 'Thought,' he said, emphatically, and I blushed. 'Yes – he did. Now. Come and look at this.'

On page 2 of the *Daily Enquirer* was a picture from the previous night under the headline PIERS GAVESTON TO MARRY INTO MEDIA DYNASTY. Piers's expression, slanted towards the camera, was one of professional knowingness, while I looked – yes, like a cartoon hedgehog crossing a motorway.

'God, I look really gormless,' I said, gormlessly.

He tilted his head to one side and considered the picture. 'Yes, you are without gorm entirely.'

'Oh well. I guess I should send a copy to my mum.'

Piers's face went into a peculiar kind of spasm.

'Your mum?'

'Yes. Well, she'll want to know.'

'I suppose she will. She's not – you're not close, though?'

'Not that close, not any more. But she'll want to be involved in the wedding.'

'The wedding.' He repeated it faintly, as if it hadn't registered that there might have to be a wedding. 'I see. I'll have to meet her, will I?'

I laughed, because I couldn't think how else to respond. 'Eventually. What about your family?'

'My *family*?' He looked somewhere between aghast and genuinely puzzled. 'Certainly not.'

'But won't your mother want –?'

'I don't have any family. I have no idea where my mother is, if she's still alive. I haven't seen her for twenty years. More.'

'Oh.' I placed a timid hand on his arm. 'That's sad.'

'Well, please don't shed any tears over it now.' He lifted my hand off. 'Hang on – I've got something for you.'

He left the room and returned a moment later with a small plum-coloured box with bevelled edges. 'Should have given it to you last night, sorry. Forgot in all the excitement.'

He handed it over without ceremony. I opened the box; inside was a silver ring with five substantial diamonds set into it. It was obviously expensive – almost gaudy. I looked up at him but he was looking for his keys and hadn't waited to watch me open it.

'Thank you, it's beautiful. I love silver.'

'It's platinum, you ingénue.' He smiled briefly. 'I've had it insured in case you lose it. Now, I've got to go out again in a minute, can you hurry up and get dressed? I can't leave you a set of keys because I don't have any spare, and I need to lock up.'

Outside the front door, in the peachy light of a June morning, Piers swung a leg over his motorbike and dipped his head so that he could put on his helmet without interrupting his hair. I set off towards the Tube, twisting the unfamiliar bulk on my finger, and he called out,

'Listen – don't give any interviews, remember? We have to protect our privacy. I'll give you a call tomorrow. No talking to journalists.'

When I arrived home that afternoon, there was one in my kitchen. Oliver was perched on a chair in the middle of the floor like an exhibit, smoking and reading *A Brief History of the Balkans* by Miles Park, with a mobile magnetically clamped to his ear; through the back door a spill of light was roasting the plastic tiles. Bobby sat cross-legged atop the breakfast bar playing his guitar with the string missing.

'Told you she'd be back soon!' Bobby cried cheerfully, as I dropped my keys on the counter.

Oliver swivelled abruptly; he looked younger than ever, and unusually pale.

'Olly! What are you doing here?'

'I couldn't get hold of you. I – we have to talk. Can we go for a drink?'

'Well, sure but – you came all the way up here to see me? Aren't you supposed to be at work?'

'You don't have a bloody mobile. I thought if I came here you'd turn up eventually.'

'D'you guys want to hear my song before you go? It's called Requiem for my Beaver.' Bobby picked up a plectrum hopefully.

'No thanks.'

'Seriously – it's about this little girl in Northern Ontario who has a pet – God damn it, where's your famous English humour?' Bobby threw a tea-towel at me on the way out.

I took Oliver, for the sake of expediency, to the pub across the road. The Tennyson Arms was a flat-faced rectangular building of brown brick on the corner of Tennyson Street which, despite its advantageous position with regard to our front door, remained almost entirely unvisited either by us or by any of the street's residents, on account of its being the worst pub in the northern hemisphere, and, more especially, on account of someone having been stabbed there only a couple of years before in the course of an argument over the jukebox. (It seemed a particular waste of life, since the juke-box only contained two discs, both of them by Led Zeppelin.) Once, boldly, we had ventured there shortly after we moved in, and had never gone back. Bobby had come out convinced that it was a front for a Cosa Nostra operation.

'But they're not Italian,' I pointed out.

'That is the kind of naive mistake you Limeys always make in your dealings with the Mob,' he had replied.

That evening it was empty, but for the usual straggle of gnarled old mutterers at the bar, and the usual troglodyte behind it, but it was warm enough to sit outside. I ordered a coke, though it mattered little; all the drinks in the Tennyson tasted slightly sulphurous anyway.

'Well – it's a pleasant surprise to have you drop in.'

'Look – Gab, I'll come to the point. I saw the papers.'

'Oh. So you came to congratulate me?' I grinned; Oliver didn't.

'No – I came to say you can't possibly marry that man.'

'Pardon?'

Oliver sighed. 'Gaby – you'll think I'm mad, but you seriously can't marry him. Really. It would be –'

'Be what?'

'Fatal.' He brought his glass down on the table like a full stop.

'Olly – firstly, this is none of your business, but mostly –

what the fuck are you talking about? What are you trying to say?'

'I can't really –' Oliver removed his glasses, squinted at me, rubbed them on his sleeve and put them on again. 'You have to trust me – I'm saying this as a friend, because it'll end in tears and I don't want them to be yours. Maybe it's too late, but – he's dangerous. He'll hurt you.'

'And where do you get this wisdom from?' I pulled myself up. 'Is there something specific you want to tell me about, or are you just being an arse?'

'He doesn't love you.'

'Fuck off, Oliver.' I screwed up my face and concentrated on lighting a cigarette, because I suspected this was probably true. 'Like you know anything about it.'

'Gab –' Oliver lifted his hands in exasperation. 'Haven't you even noticed the timing? Did he ever speak to you about marriage – did he ever let you take him seriously – before he came back from Indonesia?'

I thought about it. 'Not really.'

'Well then! Can't you see – it's just face-saving? He's done this to scotch the rumours about him and Edward – didn't that occur to you? It's a publicity gig. If you think I'm wrong, challenge him about it yourself. But it's obvious to anyone with any nous about how the media works.' He paused. 'Guess that's why you're so easily fooled.'

I swirled the coke around in my glass for a moment, watching it eddy stickily, then got up.

'I'm afraid you've had a wasted trip. I've got no interest in your stupid' – I hesitated, put the glass down – 'jealousy.'

'*Jealousy?*' Now Oliver looked surprised.

'Yes.' I looked at him, and realised I wasn't sure how to back up this accusation.

He shook his head. 'No, Gaby. I'm not jealous of him, he's – well, you'll learn. But I do care about you, and I hoped to keep you out of it.'

'Out of what?'

'Everything to do with him. I wanted to warn you. But I can't say any more than that. You have to open your eyes. I'm sorry you've taken it the wrong way – if I could tell you more, I would. Anyway – you know where I am if you want to talk.'

'You love to make yourself so important, don't you? You love pretending you know more than everyone else. Well, I don't think I've got much else to say to you.' I took my keys out of my pocket. 'I thought you'd be pleased for me – for once something remarkable is happening to me, and you just want to bring everything down.'

'Gab! I *would* be pleased for you if –' Oliver stood up. 'If it wasn't him. But I had to say something. There's no need to get nasty.'

'Well, you've said it. Now shouldn't you be getting back to London?' At that moment I glanced back to my house, opportunely, and spotted the familiar navy-clad figure hunched over a notebook. 'Oh, and' – I gestured across the street, barely concealing my delight – 'I think your car's just got a ticket. It's all residents' parking here. Sorry.'

'*Shit!*'

Grinning, I skipped up the steps to my front door with a gleeful sense of poetic justice. What kind of friend would behave like that anyway, I reasoned?

If I'd stopped hugging my pride and my doubts to me and allowed myself to dwell on that question, I might have understood; the kind of friend who is trying to save you from yourself. Perhaps even the kind of friend who loves you.

PART TWO

Chapter XIV

If knowledge is power, as Francis Bacon wrote in 1597, then foreknowledge would be absolute power. This is what separates the gods from the rest of us. And because foreknowledge is impossible, hindsight loves to speculate on it – especially now, with all our helpful technologies. Perhaps this is why, in the aftermath of a tragedy, so much time is devoted to contemplating those few, still innocent, hours and minutes that preceded it, with all the rapt horror and morbid prurience of hindsight. Here's President Kennedy, smiling and waving in his open-top car. Here's the CCTV footage of the crowded shopping centre, just before the bomb went off. Here are the blurry backs of two young boys, the toddler trustingly stretched between them as they walk away. Here's the pilot's cheery hello to his two hundred passengers, minutes before they all fire-balled into the Atlantic . . . We watch the pictures, riveted, and we can replay them as many times as we like, but we can't change the outcome. We know, and they don't; we see the catastrophe spiralling towards them and we have no way to warn them, because it's already over.

And the fascination is spurred by our own fear, our own lack of prescience; we dwell on the innocent ignorance about to be shattered, because we are just like those people, because we have no way of knowing what's waiting for us around the next corner. Because we live – we have to live – as if we are untouchable; the alternative would be impossible. It won't be your train that crashes, your child that is snatched from the playground, your father who dies of lung cancer at 53, though he's never smoked in his life. Think of all those sweethearts bicycling down leafy lanes in August, 1914, a gentle English summer. Never such innocence again.

August again. The night before it happened – a Saturday night – I had spent not with my fiancé, who was engaged elsewhere in the schmoozing salons of the film world, but in the gloaming of our sitting room in Tennyson Street with Bobby and a cluster of his stranger friends, who sat on the floor playing guitars and patiently rolling joints of industrial-strength grass they had acquired from some guy with a PhD in anthropology who lived on a houseboat at the edge of town. Smoke billowed pungently through the windows to the street above as if from an East Berlin bar.

The following morning, for obvious reasons, I woke late with an operatic headache. Outside, the sky was bland and damp. Sunday morning television floated up the stairs; I swallowed vitamin C and stood for a long time under a thudding shower, the bathroom still faintly yawing, feeling odd. A slight depression, an increased anxiety – chemical guilt, Bobby always called it.

As I came into the kitchen, Bobby switched the television off deliberately and placed himself behind the breakfast bar, hands flat on the heft of the Sunday paper. He stared at me in difficult silence.

'What is it?'

He opened his mouth slightly, and then closed it, as if the words weren't quite ready. Suddenly I was afraid.

'What's the matter? Has something happened?'

'Gab –' He leaned forward slightly. 'Did you – were you listening to the radio this morning?'

'The radio? No – okay, wait, I know what you're getting at. Yes, I was playing your Lou Reed CD, no, I didn't ask, sorry, I'll put it back –'

'Oh, fuck, no!' Bobby's voice was an octave higher than normal. 'No, it's – shit. Come sit down over here.' He pulled out a stool. 'Listen – there's some bad news.'

'What?' A slow-burning panic began to rasp at the back of my throat.

'Uh – you'd better read it yourself.'

Bobby handed me the news section of the *Sunday Enquirer*.

What I saw on the front page, under the masthead, was this: HAMILTON-HARVEY'S GAY AFFAIR SHOCKS MEDIA WORLD.

Beneath it, a photograph that appeared to be a still from a home video: two men, embracing, one blond, one greying, their faces webbed with static and partially obscured by their kiss. The taller of the two was shirtless.

Then the standfirst: 'Media baron's affair with his protégé Piers Gaveston: Exclusive investigation by the *Sunday Enquirer*'s Chief Reporter, Chris Haughton.'

It is 12.17 a.m. The television premiere party is drawing to a close; handsome writer and broadcaster Piers Gaveston, Professor at the Hamilton Harvey Faculty of Cultural Studies, takes a taxi back to his £800,000 flat in south-west London.

At 12.31 a.m. Sir Edward Hamilton-Harvey leaves the same party, but instead of taking a taxi back home to his wife, he follows Gaveston back to his flat – the flat Sir Edward bankrolls. They share some wine. There they spend the night together – for this is no ordinary friendship. It is a pattern repeated often since Gaveston first returned to London fifteen months ago from Buenos Aires. Sources close to Sir Edward suggest that on this occasion, Lady Isabelle had forced her husband to send Gaveston abroad, and that Sir Edward, who pays him a monthly allowance of £50,000 plus additional expenses, had been looking for a means to bring his lover of some six years back into the country.

I tried to stand and experienced a sudden torsion of the stomach, a rising wave of nausea. The room felt very cold and far away; I wanted to scream but all that came out was a squawking laugh and –

'Wesley was right, then.'

Bobby screwed up his face anxiously, as if waiting for the hysteria to kick in.

'Who's Wesley? You mean you *knew*?'

'No – I mean – right that Chris Haughton can't write. That's not how you start a news story, is it – fuck's sake –' I sat down again, heavily.

'Gab' – Bobby laid a tentative hand on my arm – 'you do realise what it's saying, don't you? Did you never – notice?'

'It's a set-up. It must be – it's lies.' I was floundering. Bobby reached under the toaster and slipped out a packet of cigarettes.

'Emergency rations. I think this may accurately be described as an emergency.' He lit one for me and stuck it between my lips.

'Listen – I've read it. The whole thing – and the stuff inside. They have photos, leaked e-mails, letters – there's a lot of evidence. They've been watching him for a while. I think they'd make pretty damn sure before they put out a story like this. So – shit, I don't know what to say.'

'But it can't be true.' I was barely whispering. 'I've slept with him. I'm supposed to marry him – I –'

'Lucky you found out now. Sorry – guess that's not helpful.' He slipped an arm around my shoulders. 'Gab – do you want to read this now? Because – well, I guess it'll be all over the news by lunchtime, you should probably –'

'I can't believe it.'

'I know – it's a real bummer, eh, but –'

'I really can't.'

'Hey, come on. People cheat, it's not the end of the world. Damn it, my brother Hal slept with my first-ever girlfriend when I was like sixteen. She wouldn't sleep with me because she said she was saving herself, and it turned out she'd saved it for my god-damn brother. So –' Bobby realised I was looking up at him incredulously. 'Okay, I know it's not quite the same thing, but it makes it worse when it's your family, doesn't it?'

'I have to call him. Piers. I have to speak to him.'

'Gab – seriously.' Bobby put his face very close to mine, his freckles magnified. I could see the scar on his eyebrow where he singed it trying to light a joint from the gas ring. 'I would read it carefully before you talk to him. Anyhow – I think he may be out of radio contact for today.'

So he sat me on the sofa with a large cup of tea, an ashtray and the *Sunday Enquirer* in all its majestic bulk.

As instructed on the front, I turned to page two for the full story and recognised, with an absence of surprise, Chris Haughton's picture: the thin-faced man in glasses we had seen that night in the Thai restaurant, the man who had raised his glass to me the night Edward announced my engagement to Piers at the riverside party. My *engagement*. And he had been thorough, Chris Haughton – oh, how he had been thorough! He had unearthed intricate data on Sir Edward's private accounts; he had even corralled one or two people who had been associates of Piers's from New York, from the days before *Forum*, who were only too happy to denounce him as a self-promoting flirt whose one talent was to use his charms to secure the interest of wealthy and influential men. Chris Haughton had dragged up a character by the name of Warwick Trent who had collaborated on Piers's abortive Dante film, four years ago, who bore witness to the money Sir Edward had pumped in without question while asserting plangently that he had done all the writing, all the work, that Piers couldn't direct the proverbial piss-up but still wanted all the credit.

There was even a short comment piece by Jake Lennox – 'My personal experience of the nepotism and corruption of Sir Edward's dealings with the university', a robust venting of spleen over Piers's monomania and indolence.

'It doesn't make sense,' I repeated, though the more I read, the closer I looked at the pictures, the more I realised that in fact it made perfect sense. Piers's sudden appearance at the university, his smooth progress along the celebrity conveyor belt, my aunt's dislike of him, his money, his privileges, his clothes, Edward's strange and awkward jealousies, Oliver's warnings.

Oliver's warnings.

Oliver knew – and must have known, all along, but he didn't tell me.

He didn't tell me.

Or was it that I didn't listen.

There was a picture of Piers and me, not the night of our engagement but some previous occasion, arms around one another. We looked happy.

Sir Edward and Gaveston cleverly used Gaveston's sham relationship with Sir Edward's niece, Gabriele Harvey, a doctoral student at the university, as a cover for their own affair, to deflect attention . . .

Sham relationship.

Except that it wasn't, not for me and sometimes, I had felt, not for Piers. Not always.

'What am I going to do?' I wailed, suddenly. 'I can never go out again!'

'Well, listen. It's going to be tough, but it'll blow over. For you. They're more interested in your uncle.'

'But, God, how can I show my face anywhere? How could he – how *could* he? Set me up like this –'

'Still – I guess the papers will come looking for you while it's still hot.' Bobby jumped up. 'You know what – we should call the college and tell them not to give out your address.'

I sat, mute and inert, smoking and watching. He picked up the phone.

'Hi – could you give me the number for St Dunstan's College? Thanks.' A pause. 'Hello, yes. This is Robert Mailer from Tennyson Street, I'm a graduate student on the Middleton Programme. Yeah. Mailer. Listen – I need to ask a favour. Do you generally give out student's addresses if people enquire? Well – uh – my house mate is Gabriele Harvey – yes – and if anyone should call asking for her address could you please not –' Bobby stopped pacing and frowned. 'When? Shit. Okay, but no one else. It's extremely important. Yes, I understand. Stalkers, you know. Sure. Thanks.'

He clicked the phone dead and looked up. 'Some guy called this morning. I suggest you lie low if anyone comes to the door. I don't think my friends would say anything.'

'Which friends?'

'The hippy guys that were here last night when we heard.'

'You heard last *night*?'

'We were – uh – sitting up pretty late and that show came on, you know, where they go through what's in the next day's papers. And it was on that.'

'Why didn't you tell me?'

'Uh –' Bobby scratched his eyebrow. 'I figured you needed one last untroubled night of sleep.'

The sky was growing dark with the threat of rain. I stayed on the sofa all morning until my face felt kippered with smoke, images of Piers and my uncle revolving persistently. I tried not to picture it. Piers and Edward. Edward and Piers. Piers fucking Edward – or would it be the other way around? It couldn't be true. It could easily be true. It explained everything. Piers and Edward. I ran to the toilet and was violently sick. Bobby held my hair.

At one o'clock he switched on the lunchtime news and we hunched together in awkward solidarity. A feral pack of reporters bayed and jostled outside the stuccoed columns of Sir Edward and Lady Isabelle's bright white five-storey town house. *Fucking Queer* had been eloquently spray-painted in purple across the white wall – unfortunately, of the house next door – like a gash. There had been no sign of Sir Edward, the reporter earnestly informed us as he tried to withstand the knocks and buffets of his co-professionals, and Lady Isabelle was apparently in St Lucia. And cut to the outside of Piers's house, the square dismal under the rain, where the same scene was being played out. Piers's windows were all shuttered.

Bobby stood up on the sofa to peer through the basement window into the unnervingly empty street.

'Gab, don't take this the wrong way, I mean I'm happy to fight them off when they come here, but do you think maybe you should go into hiding?'

'Hiding?'

'Yeah – go to your place in London for a few days, because it's not going to take them long to find you and you really don't want to walk out into that shit every morning, those guys are monsters.' Bobby gestured towards the television.

'You're probably right, but –' I felt too heavy to make it up the stairs, let alone all the way to Highgate. 'How will I get there?'

'I could drive you down tonight, when it's dark. Then when they come we could tell them you've gone to your mom's in France or something. If the Shaggin Wagon will make it to London.' He began pacing the room again, as if trying to shoulder some of my burden himself.

The Shaggin Wagon was a battle-weary estate that Bobby had purchased for £350 when he first arrived at the university in a fit of enthusiasm for touring England's extremities. So far, he had not managed any shagging in it, nor indeed any touring, thanks to its tendency to wheeze bronchially for about five miles and then sputter to a standstill and require several hundred pounds' worth of new parts before it could be coaxed back into life.

'I think – you're right.' I stretched my legs and bunched them underneath me again.

Piers's mobile was switched off. His home number gave off a screeching, disconnected tone. I wanted to hear his voice. If he would just tell me it would all be all right, I could believe him. I wanted to believe him.

Piers and Edward.

I felt too tired to cry, or even to move.

The reporter arrived at half-past two. The sound of the doorbell arrested us; Bobby motioned to me to be quiet, as if I might have been tempted to rush up to the front door and announce myself.

'I'll go.'

I listened to the creak of its opening.

'Can I help you?'

'Afternoon mate. Sorry to disturb you – Martin Keen, from the *Daily Chronicle*.'

'Bob Mailer, from the Manhattan District Boy Scouts' Association.'

'Uh – hi. So – tell me. I'm looking for Gabriele Harvey. I understand she lives here. She in?'

'Well –' Bobby seemed to give this some consideration. 'She lives here some of the time. But she's presently away.'

'Away?'

'Yeah. She left this morning.'

'Are you expecting her back?'

'Nope.'

'Can I come in?'

'Um – no, you can't. I have some friends here, for lunch.'

'It won't take a minute.'

'I don't think so.'

There was a pause.

'How about' – I waited for the seductive riffling of a cheque book – 'you and me pop over to the pub and have a little chat? About Gabriele. You must know her well?'

'Not really. She's very enigmatic.'

'Did you ever meet her fiancé?'

'I told you, we're not close. Listen, Mr – uh –'

'Keen.'

'That's funny. Listen – like I say, I have guests. I really should get back.'

'Come on. I'm serious, there's money in this. You students can always use a bit of extra cash, eh?'

Bobby pretended to deliberate. 'Well, you know – not really.'

'Come on, son – I'm not messing. Serious money. Let's just pop over for a quick drink, eh?'

'Mr Keen, I'm not interested in your money. My father owns most of Long Island. Was there anything else?'

'I'll tell you what. I'm going to go and sit in the pub across the road, and see if Miss Harvey comes back at some point. If she's really gone away.'

'Are you calling me a liar?'

'Not at all, mate. If you should change your mind and want to tell me something – or if you speak to her – this is a big story, you know that. So does she, and she'll have to talk to someone sooner or later. Might as well be me.'

'Oh. Why?'

'Because I'm – sympathetic.'

'Well, your sympathy will be appreciated,' Bobby said solemnly. 'If she calls, I'll pass it on. Now, goodbye.'

'I'll just be across the road –'

'Okay. If you want to make friends with the locals, ask if you can put some Simon and Garfunkel on the jukebox. They love it.'

'Right. Cheers, mate.'

The afternoon slouched on, endlessly, as Sunday afternoons will. This one seemed longer than any Sunday afternoon had the right to be. I lay in bed and didn't sleep. Dimly, I heard the phone ringing.

'Gab! It's George.' Bobby called up the stairs. 'George Fenton! Do you want to talk to him?'

'I don't want to talk to anyone.'

'But it's George!'

'I don't want to talk to anyone.'

There are times when kindness can be painfully intrusive; George's infallible, fatherly kindness would split me open, I knew, bursting out all the rage and hurt in uncontrollable tears and sobbing, and I wanted to hold it together, keep it inside. I couldn't bear the weight of it. Folded on the bed, I stared at the square of sky through the window. Autumn was early; the clouds were blank and cold. Bobby brought me another cup of tea.

298

'Do you want something stronger?'

'I don't know. Maybe later.'

'That asshole is still there. Outside the pub. I was hoping he'd have been glassed by now. Did you throw some stuff in a bag? We'll leave when the pub shuts. If he goes.'

If I closed my eyes, I could see Piers's smile. I could remember the smell of his hair. I turned my face to the pillow and cried from pure self-indulgence. I hadn't lost him. He wasn't mine.

Martin Keen sat doggedly at the bench outside the Tennyson Arms, sipping hopeful pints and watching as the wind scuffed stray pages of newspapers past his feet. When it began to rain, he went inside and we lost sight of him behind the smeary dark windows. Bobby kept up a vigil for his departure, but he stayed until closing time, when he tucked his magazine under his arm and set off with a final, forlorn glance at our house.

'He'll be back tomorrow,' Bobby said ominously. 'We should get going.'

Half an hour later, at midnight, I checked the street.

'Okay, all clear.'

The Shaggin Wagon hiccupped into life, and Bobby drove out through the quiet streets to the edge of town and on to the motorway.

'Pray this baby stays alive.'

I peered out into the rain. The initial panic and disbelief had been displaced by another, bleaker emotion: guilt. The tightness in my stomach was the old, residual childhood fear of punishment, of retribution; the feeling of coming dread that follows a summons to the headmaster. Why I needed to feel guilty wasn't clear, the trouble I feared was unspecified. I only knew that a process had been set in motion that would get worse before it got better. And how could it get better? I would be remembered for this event alone, for the pictures in today's paper. When people heard my name they would think, ah, yes, that poor girl. Or 'that stupid girl. How could she not have seen?' But I didn't see. I didn't – it isn't so hard to believe, is it? People marry wife-beaters. They marry killers or rapists or sado-masochists or drunks or serial adulterers or depressives or homosexuals, and they don't see it until it's too late. Because – oh dear, a truism, but a watertight one – because love is selectively blind.

The traffic was sparse on the motorway at half-past midnight. Bobby persuaded the car up to sixty.

'This too shall pass,' he said, without turning, after a while.

I considered. 'He never lied to me, you know. Piers. Not really. He didn't tell the whole truth, but he never pretended –' I turned to the window.

'What?'

'That he was in love with me or anything.'

'Were you in love with him?'

We were hurtling down an avenue of impossibly tall motorway lamp-posts, two lines of perfectly symmetrical orange streaks converging at a centre point in the distance, like a Kubrick shot. I wished we could just keep driving through the dark, and never have to arrive.

'Yes.'

'Really in love? Or just infatuated?'

'What's the difference?'

'Fucked if I know.'

Muffled in our own thoughts, we passed the rest of the journey in silence.

Betray. First used in English in the thirteenth century, from the Latin *tradere*, meaning to hand over or deliver. From which we also derive tradition, that which is handed down. But Piers had not betrayed me, I reflected, as I sat the following morning in the front room of the basement flat on Highgate West Hill with all the curtains drawn. Bobby had stayed the night and driven away early, after stopping at the garage at the bottom of the hill to buy me food and papers.

'You're famous, Gab,' he said, breathlessly, handing me a tissuey blue-and-white striped plastic bag full of packet pasta and canned soup. 'I suggest you don't go out too much. On the bright side, looks like your neighbours are away.'

The upper stories of the house were quiet, the curtains drawn.

'I should get back. Listen – you need anything, just call. And don't worry, I will guard your secret. I'll say you've gone to France.'

'God. My mother. I'll have to warn her.'

'It'll take them a while to get there.' He grinned, and offered an awkward embrace. 'Look after yourself, little sister. I got you a bottle of wine and three packs of cigarettes, don't drink it all at once. Everything's going to be okay. Here –' he passed me an envelope that crunched when I pressed it. 'Best quality weed. Use it sparingly. You might want something to make you laugh. And if you get lonely, call, okay?'

'Thanks, Bob. I – I am grateful, you know.'

'Whatever. You can do the same for me when my child prostitution racket is exposed by the tabloids. God damn, I've said too much. Bye bye, now.'

So Piers had not betrayed me in the literal sense, I reasoned, scrutinising the newspapers with a paleographer's eye; he had always made it clear that I was not to consider him exclusively mine. But someone had betrayed Piers. There were details here beyond the legal reach of the most assiduous investigative reporter, details – Edward's accounts, private e-mails – that could only have come from a party intimately involved in Piers's life, or in Edward's. Someone who hated both of them enough to hand these over. Roger, perhaps? Or my Aunt Isabelle? Or someone else, someone I didn't yet know about? I ran through Piers's acquaintances in my head and ruled them out. Of one thing I was certain – Chris Haughton had not uncovered this all by himself.

Bobby was right; the story was on the front page of every daily paper, except the *Ledger*, which stoically ignored its proprietor's shame and contented itself instead with an ano-dyne piece about wrangling in the new parliament. Since no one had managed – yet – to gain access to any of the main players in this drama, the articles for the most part regurgi-tated the *Sunday Enquirer*'s facts, inviting high-profile com-mentators to flaunt their casuistry in showy thousand-word opinion pieces. Agreeing with the unanimous contempt for my uncle came easily, but, though I trawled deeply for it, I failed to find in myself a genuine hatred for Piers. Because I had this thought, you see: that, if Piers had never said he loved me, I was at least certain that he didn't love Edward. Piers had been ambitious; Edward was a meal-ticket, that was not so unusual. And if I could just see Piers, if I could show him that I understood, in part, why he had done what he had done – I believed that the tiny flicker of interest that he had shown in me, though slight and under duress, might kindle something else. I thought, absurdly, that if we could get through this, there might still be a chance. Perhaps we could still get married, and defy the rumours.

After a while I couldn't read any more and, contrary to Bobby's advice, I wrapped an old scarf of my mother's around my head and went out for a walk on the Heath. As I was leaving the flat I lifted my hand to lock the door and noticed my engagement ring. I'd been so afraid of losing it, knowing that he expected no better of me, and now it struck me as a meaningless trinket, paid for by my uncle as part of his pantomime. I felt suddenly absurd, a child dressing up in someone else's jewels and pretending to be a princess. Twisting it off my finger, I threw it inside the door before slamming it symbolically. But there was no one there to wit-ness.

Under the sagging clouds, the Heath was almost deserted, but for the usual straggle of tramps loitering near the toilet block. Climbing the hill between the stooping trees, oily London rain streaking a film on my face, it was easier to feel distant from the Pandora's box opened, down there in the city, by Chris Haughton. Strange, I thought, how newspaper stories always appear so far removed from your own world, even when they're about you. No one would have guessed, watching me trudge through the wet gravel and mud with unsuitable shoes, my shirt soaked to my back, that I was the person on the front of today's papers. I started to run, without quite knowing why, and as I ran, I realised I was crying, and choking out between creaking lungfuls of air, 'I never wanted this, Edward, I never – wanted to be this person, you did this to me, you – fucking *fuck*, you did this' – (and coughing, and crying) – 'I didn't ask to be your puppet, you bloody – bloody – BASTARD!', until an old lady walking what appeared to be a fat hamster stopped in alarm and shrank back from the path toward the shrubbery, concluding (quite reasonably) that I was clearly a fearful maniac. On a bench at the top of the hill, I cried until I was leached, sodden and exhausted, and then I walked home.

And Monday dragged itself by, as bleak and soulless as the day before. I couldn't remember ever having felt so alone and fragile and hopeless. I wanted to phone someone, just to have some contact, but no one came to mind. I opened the wine, drank most of it, and fidgeted around the flat. In the afternoon I fell asleep, fitfully, for a while. When I got up it was already growing dark. I heated some soup, let it go cold and then threw it away.

Roger was on *HeadLines*, the late-night news and current affairs show, his skin looking more glutinous than ever, his wattles compressed by an ill-judged tie.

'This is, as you may imagine, an extremely difficult time for Sir Edward and his family,' he was saying, preachily, 'and he has asked for some privacy while he and his family come to terms with these allegations and determine the most appropriate response.'

'But surely,' the presenter said, in his customary accusatory tone, 'Sir Edward is not intending to deny that there is any truth in these revelations? Surely the evidence is unquestionable? Isn't there a telling irony in the fact that Sir Edward has made his fortune from exactly this kind of intrusive, under-handed journalism with regard to the private lives of public figures, and is now being made to swallow a taste of his own medicine?'

'Sir Edward,' Roger said, gravely, 'has only ever allowed his newspapers to publish stories that he considered to be in the public interest. And I don't think anyone could claim that this vicious tittle-tattle is in the public interest in any sense of the word. Words.'

'Surely it would be better for Sir Edward in the long run if he were to start telling the truth?'

'What is truth?' said Roger, sonorously, and the presenter grimaced and turned instead to his left.

'Mervyn Bland – how do you justify the inherent hypocrisy in the editorial stance Hamilton Harvey International news-papers have always taken over matters of legislation regard-ing homosexuality in the light of these revelations about your proprietor's private life?'

Mervyn Bland, Editor-in-Chief of the two Hamilton Harvey International broadsheet newspapers, fingered his moustache with some disquiet.

'Well, Evelyn – as I'm sure you don't need me to tell you, Sir Edward has never attempted to impose editorial policy on his papers –'

'Except for the time when David Wigmore was fired for refusing to pull his story about human rights abuses in Indonesia?'

Bland allowed a superior laugh. 'Now, Evelyn, you should know better. Wigmore had many faults as an editor and he was fired for entirely different reasons, that was purely leftist tabloid gossip. If we could return to your question? – I have always taken a broadly – not tub-thumping, you understand – but a broadly – how shall we say – middle-ground moral stance in the matter of sexual ethics, not because I have any personal prejudice, but because I think this is the prevalent mood of the English people at this point in our history. The liberals would have you think differently, but I believe – and I think I'm right in believing – that most parents would prefer their children to grow up in a society which reinforced what have always been considered traditional family values. And this is in no wise a viewpoint that has been imposed on me or on the paper from above.'

'And has it affected your respect for your proprietor, now that he's been exposed as actively homosexual?'

'Ah, now, we must be very careful here, Evelyn. I think there are various ways of defining that term, hmm?'

'Well – not really, no.'

'But I would say that people's private lives and morals are entirely their own business. I don't feel it's my place to comment.'

'I see. So if someone is the owner of a multi-billion pound media empire and your employer, it's a matter of private morals and individual choice. But if they're a gay schoolteacher or a member of the armed forces, or a gay couple who want to get married or adopt a child, or – for the sake of argument – a Member of Parliament whose private life happens to diverge from his public position, then it *is* your editorial duty to pass judgment? How do you justify that?'

As Mervyn Bland was attempting to dig himself out, I heard a noise outside the window on the basement steps. I turned the small television off and sat up rigidly in the dark, waiting.

For a moment, there was nothing. Then I heard it, unmistakably, again; feet scratching on the wet steps. I crawled over to the window on my hands and knees; behind the curtains was the silhouette of a figure, hands pressed to the glass either side of his face, trying to peer in. My heart was kicking; I pulled myself up to the window sill and, in doing so, inadvertently brushed the curtain. I froze. So did the figure outside.

'Gaby?' A whisper, hissed through teeth. 'Are you in there?'

305

I didn't move.

'Gab! It's me, Oliver. I know you're there. Gaby, let me in, come on.'

I sighed, and twitched the curtain back half an inch.

'What are you doing here?'

'Looking for you. Now let me in before somebody thinks I'm a prowler and calls the police.'

Half-reluctant, half-relieved, I unbolted the front door and Oliver stepped inside.

He coughed. 'God, you've been having a smokathon. How long have you been here?'

'Since last night. How did you know I was here?'

Oliver took off his coat. 'Because I know you. I called your house and Bobby said you'd gone to stay with your mum. Which I knew couldn't possibly be true. So I guessed you'd be here, even though you weren't answering your phone.'

'I unplugged it.' I tried to walk backwards and tripped over a small table.

'Are you pissed as well?'

'No. A bit.'

Oliver looked at me in the orange light that spilled through the top of the window. 'Jesus, Gab, I'm so sorry.'

'You knew, didn't you?'

'Yes. I did try – '

'Did you always know?'

'No. Not right at the beginning – I mean, I suspected a while ago. From what Dad had said about Piers, you know. He never came out and said it, but he hinted. He said Piers and Edward were too close. But I only really knew when Chris's investigation was quite far along.'

'Olly' – I clutched a handful of his jumper and shook him – 'why didn't you – why didn't you tell me?'

'I tried to warn you, Gab, but you didn't want to hear it –'

'No, you didn't! You could have just *said* it, you could have spelled it out! How could you let me make such a fool of myself?'

'Listen.' Oliver placed his hands gently on my shoulders and fixed his eyes on mine. 'I said as much as I could. I was obliged to – it was all in the strictest confidence, you must understand – it was the biggest scoop the paper's had in years. Only a few of us knew, and we had to sign confidentiality agreements. And I don't think it's fair to blame me for your – making a fool of yourself.'

'So your loyalty to the *Enquirer* was more important than your friendship to me?' Tears of anger burned behind my eyes. I swallowed.

'That's not fair either. Don't you think that over the last year your friendship with me has been much less important to you than – than your infatuation with Piers Gaveston?'

I slumped on to the sofa – the sofa where Piers had first taken me all those months ago. If that hadn't been a warning . . .

'Why are you here, anyway?'

'To take you away. You can't stay here – sooner or later the neighbours are going to notice that the flat's occupied. You need looking after – look at the state of you.'

'I'm all right.'

'You're not. I bet you haven't eaten. You can't deal with this by yourself, Gab, even if you think you can. They'll find you here eventually, the mob, and you're not Edward – you don't have a private army of bodyguards and spokespeople.'

'Where am I going to go?'

'I want you to come and stay with me. It's the last place they'd think of looking for you. I've asked Mike for the rest of the week off – you can lie low, I'll take care of you and then when the excitement dies down a bit, maybe we could get you off to your mum's, or at least somewhere out of the way. Give it a week or so. But you're going to go out of your mind here on your own. Come on, get your stuff, my car's on a meter.'

'Olly –' I stood up and walked over to him, feeling suddenly weak and childish. 'Thanks.'

'Come here.' Oliver put his arms around me and rubbed

my back; I snuffled my face into his warm jumper. He smelled clean, of fabric conditioner and fresh towels. 'It'll be all right, I promise.'

Oliver's flat in Barnsbury was everything my house wasn't. It was clean and uncluttered and smelled of Forest Fresh cleaning products, and a Colombian woman came once a week to keep the bathroom and kitchen show-home impeccable. Oliver's uncontroversial, mid-range music collection was arrayed neatly in a teak display case fixed to the wall. I had to smoke with my head out of the window.

Together we watched the story unfurl as the week passed. My attempts to phone Piers had all been fruitless; all his numbers appeared to be disconnected.

'There's something I don't understand,' I said to Oliver on Tuesday, as approved stills from the incriminating video were broadcast yet again on the evening news.

'What's that?'

'Well – I don't know that much about journalistic practice, but – that film, and the e-mails – surely it's illegal for a journalist to do that? I mean – to bug someone's house with secret cameras? Couldn't Piers take Chris Haughton or the *Enquirer* to court for breach of privacy or something?'

Oliver frowned, and looked at me for a moment as if I were a child. 'Chris didn't set up that video, Gab.'

'I don't understand.'

Oliver sighed patiently. 'It was Edward's video. He used to – film them together. You know, for – I don't know. Some people like that.'

'*Edward*'s video?'

'Of course. There was no breach of privacy.'

'But how did Chris –?'

'Someone gave it to him. And the e-mails, everything.'

'Who?'

'I don't know! He wouldn't say.'

'But then someone else was in on this! They must have

been – someone who knew Edward really well! Do you think it was Roger?'

'I have no idea. I would have thought Roger's loyalty was beyond question.'

'He hates Piers.'

'Gaby, most people hate Piers, if the truth be told. He goes out of his way to make enemies.'

'What about Isabelle?'

Oliver frowned. 'She's known about this for years and tolerated it – why would she knowingly expose herself and her family to public scandal?'

'How do you know she knew? Did she talk to you about it?'

'Of course not. I'm assuming.'

There was a pause.

'You hate him.'

'I have no great affection for him. That's slightly different.'

'Did you ever talk to Chris Haughton about him? About what your dad used to say? Did you put Chris on to this story?'

Oliver folded his arms and walked to the window.

'For God's sake. I hardly ever talk to Chris. I'm at Westminster most of the time, I barely see the guys on the newsdesk. Don't look at me like that, Gab – I had nothing to do with this. Do you think I'd deliberately try to screw someone as powerful as Edward?' He stopped abruptly and rubbed the back of his neck, embarrassed. 'Sorry. Never mind. But don't start suspecting me. I only ever tried to help you.'

The clichés continued to roll off the presses. Flew too close to the sun. He who lives by the press must die by the press. And so on. By Wednesday some of the broadsheets had moved on to the university's guilt by association; both George and the Vice-Chancellor had been accosted and had asserted with scholarly affront that they had certainly had no notion that they were party to bribery and moral lassitude. The *Herald* presented a two-thousand-word piece by Lionel Phelps, disgraced former Leader of the Opposition who had been brutally outed by the *Ledger* some months earlier, gloating delightedly and scattering the word 'Pharisaical' throughout his copy far more often than any sub-editor should have allowed.

On Thursday, the other residents of Piers's building, inconvenienced by the fray of journalists besieging their porch, had appealed to the Metropolitan Police to clear them a safe corridor to their front door. The journalists raged behind their enforced cordon and, for the first time since the story appeared, Piers stepped outside, accompanied by two bullish bodyguards – Flynn and Glyn? – who smuggled him into a car and took him to his private members' club in Soho. The reporters gave chase but were barred at the door; happily for the press, an anonymous member happened to have about his person a disposable Kodak, with which he snatched a few shots of Piers having dinner with Jerome Idle and Nick Strachey before he was discovered and his camera confiscated.

None the less, the amateur snaps decorated the front of Friday's papers. Piers looked etiolated; hollow-cheeked, wild-eyed and unshaven, skittish and paranoid, one hand shielding his face, a cigarette hanging from his lower lip.

'Jesus,' said Oliver, 'he looks like a junkie.'

On Friday evening it was the BBC's turn for a *coup de théâtre*. My cousin Toby, Edward's prodigal son, had flown back from Los Angeles especially to give an exclusive interview to *HeadLines*. Toby, by contrast, with his Venice Beach tan, looked remarkably unlike a junkie, in spite of the fact that he was one.

'We've always been a strong family,' he told Evelyn Harpur, the interviewer, in his hybrid West-Coast public-school drawl, wearing an expression tinged with sorrow and a hint of conflicting loyalties, 'and we have weathered some storms, but my mother and I feel that this is one shock that's going to be too difficult to overcome. I've spoken to my mother from her house in St Lucia, and she has asked me to make public the announcement that she will be filing for a divorce.'

She's understandably really like upset and not ready to talk about it publicly yet.'

'Did you ever suspect your father of having homosexual relationships?' asked Evelyn Harpur, leaning across the desk while affecting concern and sincerity.

'Well.' Toby glanced up and fiddled with his hair. 'You know, ever since I was a kid, I was aware that my parents lived very – separate lives, you know? But I didn't think that was so abnormal – I think a lot of wealthy people do live like that and whatever. So no. No, I didn't. He never – well, he hid it very carefully.'

'And how do you feel about your father now?'

'I'm totally fucking disgusted, to be quite honest with you.' Toby folded his hands together decisively. They bleeped out 'fucking', of course.

Oliver turned off the television. 'Good to see Toby's still as much of a prick as he was at school. He's the last person to ask, anyway – he's oblivious to anything outside himself. Toby wouldn't notice if a bomb went off on the next table.'

'I never liked Toby,' I mused. 'Everyone always thought he was my brother when we were kids. He used to call me Skinny Minnie.'

'What did you call him?'

'Pig-brain.'

'A hair-trigger wit, even back then.'

'Shut up.'

'Hey.' Oliver handed me a glass of wine. 'We should think about what you're going to do. It's been nearly a week now and, while it's a pleasure having you here, it's making it very difficult for me to bring girls home.' He looked down and smiled. I knew he had never been in the habit of bringing girls home just like that; even the lawyer who dressed like a Christian seemed to have faded out of the picture some months earlier – 'We weren't really suited,' he had said, vaguely – and I had not heard him mention anyone else since then.

'Sorry for cramping your style.'

'I'm not trying to push you, but you're going to have to make some kind of decision. Are you going to try and go away somewhere, or are you going to bite the bullet, put your head over the parapet and give your side to a newspaper – a serious newspaper, where you get to use your own words?'

I eyed him suspiciously. 'Like the *Sunday Enquirer*, for example? Are you trying to pimp me as well?'

Oliver shrugged. 'Not because I want credit, just – we broke the original story, our coverage was very anti-Edward – we'd be sympathetic to you. And you have written for us. Then at least you'd have got it over with and you could try to move on – you might find it cathartic.'

I snorted. 'And what would you get – a bonus?'

He ran a hand through his hair impatiently. 'God, you're impossible, Gaby. I'm trying to *help* you. What are your alternatives? Stay here and never go out for the rest of your life?'

'How am I going to – what do you suggest, go back to the university and pretend nothing's happened?' I held up a hand to stem some imagined objection. 'Okay, maybe you're right. It's just – I don't want to talk to the press before I've had a chance to speak to Piers. Because I don't understand any of this, Olly, and I just want to hear his side of it, I want to hear him defend himself.'

'You won't *get* a chance to speak to Piers, don't you realise that? He doesn't have to justify himself to you. He's only concerned with himself now.'

'But – why would he risk being chased and photographed to go and see Nick and Jerome and not try to get in touch with me?'

'Because –' Oliver shook his head. 'Because you – how can I explain this when you won't see it? You're persisting in this delusion that you still play a part in his life. You don't. You were a useful smokescreen for a while, and now you're irrelevant to him. He's forgotten you. You force me to be this blunt because you're behaving like a teenager.'

312

'Fuck you!' I lit a cigarette and stomped off to the bathroom. 'You don't know anything!'

Five minutes later I came out again.

'Sorry.'

Oliver was talking on his mobile. He held a finger to his lips.

'Sure. Okay. Yep, will do. Appreciate it. Cheers, then.' He flipped it shut and smiled too brightly.

'Who was that?'

He sighed again. 'Sit down.'

I sat.

'That was Roger Mortimer. It occurred to me that – well, Piers might want to get in touch with you and not know how. I've asked Roger to pass on my number, so I guess he'll either call or he won't. And if he doesn't bother – well, at least you'll know.'

'*Roger*? Why would he –'

'You can guarantee he'll be communicating between Piers and Edward. So he'll know how to get hold of Piers.'

'But how could they trust him, when it might have been him that –'

'Because they don't have anyone else. They need him, and that will make Roger feel powerful which is what he loves best, so in this instance he'll rise to the challenge and make himself trustworthy.'

'Hmm. I didn't realise you were so friendly with Roger that you'd have him on your speed dial.'

'*Friendly* is not the first word I'd reach for. He can sometimes be a useful contact. We respect each other's confidences. We exchange small favours – information. That's how it works in our game.'

'You've got all the answers, haven't you.'

'I'm doing my best, Gab. You want to find Piers – Roger's your only hope.'

'There's a sentence I never thought I'd hear.'

So we waited.

*

313

By Saturday we were developing cabin fever. Oliver fetched sandwiches and coffee from the deli for lunch, and midway through the babble of day-time television his mobile bleeped.

'Oliver Dowland.' He glanced at me nervously as he flipped it open.

'Oh. Hello.' A pause. He looked at me again and frowned through the other party's speech. 'That's not how it – it was never a question of winning.' He pressed his finger against his ear and walked to the window. I turned the television off and watched him. 'I'm just helping out a friend. Well, it may seem like that to you – No. I've said nothing. *I* didn't begin this, remember –'

Oliver's face pinched with quiet anger. 'Certainly.' He crossed the room, extending the phone to me. 'Piers Gaveston.'

I barely had time to register shock; Oliver picked up his coffee, lit a cigarette and left.

'Hi?'

'Gaby. Piers. Listen – I'm going to be away for a while. I wondered if you wanted to meet before I go – I feel that perhaps we should talk. Though I understand if you don't want to. How are you, by the way?'

He sounded strained, as if only thinly tethered to reality. As if he might burst into hysterical laughter at any moment, all his smooth composure gone. I felt a pang of anxiety for him, in spite of everything.

'I've been better. How are you?'

'Oh, on top of the world. Though I don't have the excellent Oliver Dowland tending to my every need.'

'Olly's been very kind.' I checked over my shoulder.

Piers coughed out a strange laugh. 'I'm sure. Come to my club this afternoon. Get a cab or something, ask for Marcel at the door. That way we shouldn't be bothered. Four-thirty, before it gets busy.'

'Okay.'

'I thought we should probably talk, that's all. Don't –'

'What?'

'Oh, nothing.' He sounded suddenly weary. 'I'll see you later.'

The man called Marcel wore a white jacket and showed me up the twisting stairs to the third floor with expressionless politeness. I was still wearing sunglasses, but there had been no sign of the anticipated hordes of snappers outside the club's front door; only a solid American couple wrestling with a street-map, who asked me the best way to Buckingham Palace and thanked me without a moment's recognition imprinting on their faces.

The top-floor bar was a jumble of eccentric, homely furniture, dusty in the streams of crooked afternoon sun; melancholy in the way that bars often seem in daylight. Piers stood facing the window at the far end of the room, outlined against the light, smoke skeining slowly towards the ceiling. My heart gave a small kick at the familiar shape of his back.

For a while he didn't turn around and I stood there awkwardly, not wanting to break the silence.

'Before I met you,' he said, eventually, pressing his cigarette into the ashtray on the window sill, 'I was quite convinced that I would despise you.'

I didn't know how to reply.

Finally he faced me and buckled his legs so that he was half-sitting against the window. He pulled out another cigarette and lit it, watching me with his still, green eyes. He seemed stripped, somehow; not weaker, but more human, lacking the carapace that always held people at a distance. The hard glitter in his eyes was not there; I felt, for the first time, as if I could go to him now, cross the small space between us and touch him, and he wouldn't push me away, might even welcome it. And at the same time I felt a tightening of my own defences, a certainty that I didn't want to touch him now. Still, when I looked at him, there was a small spasm of something that might have been love, but it was

315

coloured with sadness now, and pity. He could say what he liked now, and it wouldn't hurt me.

He breathed smoke and his skin looked stretched and matt, as if he had been smoking at this pace for some days.

'I thought it was a bad idea of Edward's,' he continued, 'and I told him that. When he wanted me to come back from Argentina – I said it was ridiculous to expect someone to play a part convincingly when they don't know what's going on. And he said, don't worry – she's bound to be smitten with you, it'll be quite authentic.'

He gave a small, bitter laugh and looked down; my teeth clenched slightly.

'But you have to understand – the *idea* of you. You were everything I resented – over-privileged, well-connected, good liberal middle-class family, could just hold your hand out for anything you wanted without even breaking a sweat. Over-indulged rich kid. Provokes all my worst prejudices.'

I opened my mouth vaguely to protest but he held up a hand.

'I wanted to hate you. I didn't *want* you to have to be part of my life, but Edward insisted and I was in no position to argue until I got back to London. So I was disconcerted to find that I didn't hate you.'

'Oh.'

'I started to like you. Not –' he saw my eyebrow lift in question, and his mouth seemed to dry. 'I'm not about to start explaining myself to you – not in that way. That's not what I wanted to talk about. But I thought you were – a *good* person. I found I – respected you.'

'Not noticeably,' I managed, with careful self-control, thinking of that first night on the sofa.

He appeared to remember too; rubbed the back of his hand across his eyes and looked suddenly tired.

'Good people frighten me. And they make me angry, because I'm not one. I've done some evil things, Gaby, things you couldn't even –' He looked down. 'But this is one I'm especially ashamed of, because you didn't deserve to be dragged into this. Any of it.'

I swallowed, confusion quickening up my spine, and thinking suddenly that I very much wished I had a cigarette to stop me looking quite so awkward. I patted my pockets limply and realised I had none. Piers held out his packet and, before I could cross the room, with his own half-smoked in his left hand, he took out another, propped it between his lips and lit it, then held it out to me, his eyes still on mine, unreadable. It was perhaps the most intimate moment that had ever occurred between us.

'If this hadn't' – I swallowed again, trying to make it sound right – 'if the papers hadn't – would you have gone through with getting married?'

'I don't know. I thought at the time it was one of Edward's stupider ideas. But I don't know. I don't know.'

He pushed his hair back with one hand, and the light caught it, spiralling golden patterns.

'Did you love Edward?'

His mouth tensed; there was a pause.

'No. But I needed him.'

'Did you love me?'

He shifted against the window sill and looked away.

'Don't ask me that. There were times when I felt close to you, when I wanted to tell you things. But –'

'Do you think you've ever loved anyone?'

He lifted his head suddenly and fixed me with something like his old stare.

'Have you?'

I let my eyes stay pinned to his for a long while, unblinking, hoping he might read something there.

You. I loved you. 'Yes. Once.'

'I'm not convinced that I have.' He made a brisk movement with his head, as if brushing away cobwebs. The air in the room was very still. Not me, then, I thought, stupidly. Not me.

A single knock at the door, and Marcel discreetly leaned round it. His hair had a blue-black sheen, like the wet head of a mallard.

'Photographers outside, Mr Gaveston. If you want to leave now through the back it might be wise –'

'Thank you.' Piers nodded him away and stood up, stretching his back. He came to stand in front of me, and I couldn't look up at him, not so close.

'I told you I was going away?'

I nodded. 'Where?'

He didn't answer. 'I think it's time I – got out. I don't think I can carry on here – in London, the university. *England*.'

A small catch of panic in my throat. 'Are you leaving the country?'

He took my face in his hands and lifted it towards him, suddenly serious.

'We won't see each other again. That's why I wanted to say – for whatever it's worth – that I am sorry.'

I twisted my head away and walked to the window so he wouldn't see the beginnings of tears and the give-away torsion of my mouth.

The door clicked softly behind him.

In the ashtray, his cigarette end still gently plumed smoke into the stale air. I put it between my lips and pressed my forehead against the cold glass, the noises of Soho muffled and grey. The tears came silently.

We are not blessed with foreknowledge.

I hadn't slept well for a week, and Saturday night was no better. I tangled myself in the sheets in Oliver's spare room, sighing and fractious, wishing it had not been so hopelessly inconclusive with Piers, wondering where he was and worrying what fresh horror the Sunday papers would offer.

When Oliver's mobile started to parp its insistent and irritating tune in the front room, I sat up and glanced at the clock.

2.17 a.m., I thought, and then: maybe it's Piers. *It was 2.17 a.m. Oliver's phone rang unanswered in his spacious north London flat. Gabriele Harvey lay awake, wondering if it might be her former lover –*

The phone continued to ring; then it stopped. Oliver appeared not to have heard. It rang again, plaintively, and then again, until finally a door opened at the other end of the flat and Oliver emerged muttering, 'Bloody hell,' as he tripped over furniture. I eased the bedroom door ajar and listened.

'Frank, hi. No, I was just – well, yes, I was asleep. *What*? When? Is it serious?' There was an agitated silence. 'Oh, *Christ*. Christ Almighty. You've got Chris there? Have you heard anything else? No, no – I'll be in shortly. Jesus. Okay. No, no problem. Okay, cheers.'

I stood blearily in the doorway of Oliver's sitting room in the half-light. He turned slowly and didn't register surprise. He was shaking.

'Gaby. Sit down.'

'What's happened?'

'Just sit down.' Oliver lit a cigarette with panicked hands and without opening the window, a sure sign that something was gravely wrong.

'What?'

'That was the night News Editor. There's been – an accident. Piers.'

I stared. My throat clamped shut.

'On his motorbike. Somewhere off the North Circular, he's – they've taken him to hospital –'

'Is it bad?' I whispered.

'Uh – I think it is. I think it is. Oh, *Christ*.' Oliver looked suddenly as if he might break down.

'Which hospital?'

He stared, uncomprehending, then numbly registered.

'I have to go into the office. They need all hands on deck – we might get it into the final edition –'

319

'Forget the paper! Olly – *please* – I have to see him, what if something happens and I don't speak to him – you have to take me, please –'

'Gab – it'll be crawling with press, you'd be walking into – he might be okay, they haven't really heard. Chris Haughton's on his way to the hospital now.'

'*Chris Haughton* gets to see him and I can't? I *have* to see him, Olly, I don't care, I'll get a cab – tell me which hospital?'

Oliver gripped me firmly by the shoulders.

'I can't let you do this – you don't understand. The state of you – and there'll be photographers, you'll just humiliate yourself. And if he's in Casualty you won't get to see him anyway. You mustn't go. Please trust me, Gab –' Then he seemed to crumple. 'Oh, God, I never expected he would do this –'

'Olly, you can't leave me – how will I know what's happened?' I was nearly shrieking.

'I'll leave you my mobile and call from the office as soon as I hear anything. I'll try not to be long. Put the satellite on – the twenty-four hour news channel – they'll probably be there soon.'

'I'm his fiancée and I have to find out if he's alive on the fucking *news channel*?' My voice sounded like someone else. I remembered that I was not his fiancée any more.

'Trust me – you must not go to the hospital. Oh, Christ –' Oliver was already out of the room, dragging on trousers and shoes. On his way back, reaching for his coat, he suddenly looked up and caught my eye; I had never seen him look so afraid. His usual pallor had sunk to a kind of translucent blueish hue; his eyes were bulging.

'I promise I'll keep you up to date,' he called. It was only as I heard his footsteps on the stairs that I realised he had locked me in.

Shivering, I flicked on the news channel. In a chilly hospital car park, a man in an overcoat with clouded breath shouted into a microphone, his faced sluiced intermittently with blue lights from the convoys of ambulances. I couldn't focus on what he was saying, but it didn't matter anyway; I knew already. I felt it in the pit of my stomach, in the friction of my chest.

I would not see Piers again.

Chapter XV

He died as he had lived, surrounded by people and still alone. There was no family, no next of kin, and the two people who loved him stayed away from the hospital to protect themselves. In fact, the only ones who rushed to be with him in the Emergency Room were the reporters and photographers. But it was too late by then, anyway.

'Imagine having to die alone,' I said, pulling at Oliver's jumper, when he returned from the office in the early hours of Sunday morning. I was drunk and numb, my voice thick and clogged with whisky.

Oliver picked up the bottle and stared at its label for some moments before tipping back a heavy slug. He was visibly shaken. 'My father died alone,' he said, almost defensively, as if the two things were in some way linked.

I pictured Denham Dowland, slumped over the wheel of his car, Oliver's mother finding him in the morning. My father had died in a halogen-bleached hospital room, with me holding his hand on one side, my mother and his mother on the other. When he died, a doctor with brown suede shoes put his hand briefly on my shoulder, then slipped the drip gently from his arm. At least my father had known he was loved.

'But you can't kill yourself with an audience.'

Oliver sat up sharply. 'You think Piers killed himself?'

I stared at him dimly, trying to focus. In truth, the idea that Piers was dead seemed so remote, I hadn't stopped to wonder about his motives. I was still at the stage of hoping that if I fell asleep, I might wake in the sober light of morning to find it wasn't true.

'I just assumed – why, do you think he didn't?'

'It looks like an accident, Gaby. He lost control of his bike on the motorway – he was speeding. I don't know much else, but it sounds like an accident. They have to do an autopsy – you know he took a lot of drugs, so maybe he was – Why would you think it wasn't an accident?' Oliver's voice was rising. He took another, almost desperate, gulp of whisky.

I'm going away, he had said. *We won't see each other again.* Cut to fade.

'Nothing Piers did was ever an accident. He never left things to chance, he was too – determined.'

'He just didn't seem like a potential suicide. I can't believe it.'

'And how do you spot a potential suicide?'

'Oh.' Oliver sighed, and passed the back of his hand across his forehead. His eyes were tired and strained. 'Some people, you see it in them. They carry the possibility of it around with them like a coin in their pocket, waiting for the right time to spend it.' He paused. 'I read that somewhere, I always thought it was a very accurate description. Other people were surprised about Dad, but I'd always known, somehow, that he would. But then, he was a clinical depressive, and Piers always seemed so –'

'What?'

'I don't know. Calculating. Too much interested in self-preservation. I could well have believed he'd be capable of killing someone else, but not himself. He was a narcissist – loved himself to the point of obsession.'

'You didn't know him, Oliver.'

'*Neither did you*, remember?' Oliver looked at me pointedly; I stared back for a moment, then hiccuped into an unintentional sob.

'Oh, Jesus, I'm sorry, Gab, I'm so sorry. Come here.' He put his arms around me and stroked my hair while I choked and dribbled into his jumper.

'I loved him.'

'I know you did. I saw it. I'm so, so sorry.'

323

We fell asleep like this, rocking gently, wrapped up in each other on the sofa.

Barely a mile away, in St Pancras, a pathologist was taking Piers apart and a toxicologist was mapping his blood, boring into the depths of him for an explanation. I tried not to think about it. The pathologist could tell the world to the micro gram the precise chemical make-up of his last meal, but he could never dissect Piers's last thoughts. Would it be a good or a bad thing, I wondered, staring blankly at the trees in Barnsbury Road, their leaves already curling, if the brain were a screen, if you could open it up and find someone's last thoughts stamped across it? Probably bad; it would rob the loved ones left behind of the comforting delusion that the departed had died happy, or peacefully, replete with warm affirmations of affection. Piers, now. As he rode his bike out through the suburbs of north London, out to the motorway, was he clear-headed and resolute, or was he afraid? Did he know the exact spot where he wanted to die? Perhaps he had been there before and planned it – he was capable of that. Or perhaps he was just driving, running away, with no knowledge of where he was going except that he wouldn't be coming back.

I was certain that, whatever conclusion the coroner drew, Piers had chosen the time and manner, as he had confidently claimed that he would one cold day in Glastonbury. He had made his own fate. Oliver was right about suicides, but wrong about Piers; his trajectory had always been taking him towards this. Piers was not prepared – no, he was unable – to be a failure. Whether this was heroism or cowardice, I didn't know.

'I brought you this,' said Oliver on the Wednesday, placing a jaundiced takeaway beside my bed. 'Come on, Gab – get up, eat something, take a shower. You're making yourself ill. You look terrible.'

'So do you.'

Oliver was white and dishevelled, and looked as if he had not been sleeping or eating either. This I couldn't fathom; surely he couldn't be grieving for Piers? His face wore the lines of anxiety and distress.

'I spoke to Roger Mortimer today. He's organising the funeral.'

Roger organising Piers's funeral. What better act of final triumph? I pictured Roger's small pig eyes glittering with glee.

'It's on Friday. They're trying to keep it pretty quiet. I told him you might want to go.'

'Yes. I suppose Edward will be there?'

'Don't know. I should think so. It might make you feel –'

'Feel what?'

'I don't know. Better. If you go. At least you could feel you'd said goodbye.'

'Too late for that.'

'Well.' Oliver got up from my bed and stretched half-heartedly. 'I'll drive you if you want. I think you'd regret it if you didn't go. Think about it.'

It was a fitting irony, I thought, staring at the coffin displayed on the bier like an inappropriate piece of furniture, that the reporters and camera crews outside the crematorium chapel should have outnumbered the mourners inside by at least two to one. Piers might have found it funny, that this should be his media apotheosis. I glanced around the chapel. Nick Strachey was there, with Jerome, who was accompanied by a statuesque woman in a long black skirt, and led a small, bewildered boy by the hand. Oliver and I sat close to the back, at the edge of a pew, ready to make a hasty exit. To my surprise, Neville Toynbee shuffled in beside me and squeezed my arm wordlessly. His eyes were rheumy.

The service managed to be simultaneously agnostic and blandly ecumenical. My uncle stood hunched in the first row to the left of the aisle in dark glasses, head bowed, and next to him, Roger, in a long dark overcoat, one comforting hand on Edward's arm, his face impassive.

> *I mourn you, and you heed not how;*
> *Unsaid the word must stay –*

Nick Strachey, chaotic in a funereal suit, had shambled to the front and, in a halting voice, announced that Piers had been a good friend and a great influence and this was a poem by Housman which said it better than he ever could. He coughed.

> *Oh, many a month before I learn*
> *Will find me starting still*
> *And listening, as the days return*
> *For him that never will.*

> *Strange, strange to think his blood is cold*
> *And mine flows easy on;*
> *And that straight look, that heart of gold,*
> *That grace, that manhood gone.*

My uncle turned at that moment and lifted his glasses; his eyes, red-rimmed and parched, snagged on mine and held them taut, and we stared at each other for a flicker of a second. His face seemed to offer something – perhaps an acknowledgement that we were the only ones here who could properly understand the depth of this loss. But I might have imagined that. Then my uncle registered Oliver, and his mouth tightened. He dropped the glasses back into place and fixed his gaze again on his shoes.

> *The word unsaid will stay unsaid*
> *Though there was much to say;*
> *Last month was time enough: he's dead*
> *The news must keep for aye.*

No, I thought, as Nick's voice crumbled and he clamped his hands over his face, that's not enough. There is still too much to say, there's too much in this that I don't understand. And Edward knows. Edward stood with his arms folded and his face grimly set as the sepulchral organ lurched into 'Amazing Grace'. A ghost of stubble troubled his jaw. I tried to summon hatred for him, but he looked too much like my father, standing there wearing his dignity like a disguise that no longer fits, that isn't fooling anyone. *You think I don't matter*, I said inside my head, hurling my thoughts down the aisle towards him. *You don't know that I loved him, or you don't care, and we are no longer family, you and I. But if I never see you or speak to you again after this, I will do this one thing: I will make you understand what you have done to me. And I will make you tell me why.*

'So now everyone will know where to find you,' Oliver observed as we drove back to London in the rain. 'Mike will go nuts when he hears I've been harbouring you like an illegal immigrant. Not that it matters what Mike thinks,' he added, quickly.

I said nothing.

'I'm serious, though – you should think carefully about what you want to do. Why not give a short interview, then head out to France and stay with your mum for a while until it's over?'

'What makes you think it's not over now?'

'I just –' he scratched his eyebrow. 'Everyone will be looking to dig up more dirt. The news is still quiet at the moment, it's the only story with legs. It might be easier for you to come to terms with everything if you're – out of the eye of the storm.'

'Maybe. But first I want to find Edward.'

'What good will that do?'

'He owes me an explanation. I want to know about Piers – and he's the only one who has any idea of how I feel. Which is nicely ironic, I admit.'

'What –' Oliver had his worried face on again. 'What do you think Edward might be able to tell you?'

'I don't know. Anything would help.'

'You're really set on this?'

'Yes. I have to do it, Olly – for myself. So I can start to – oh, I don't know, make some sense of it. Then I want Edward out of my life for good. But I want to tell him to his face. I want to make him feel guilty.'

'What makes you sure he doesn't already?'

'Edward? Don't be stupid.' After a pause, I said, 'Will you give me Roger's number?'

He sighed. 'Okay. On one condition.'

'What?'

'If you carry on staying at mine, you'll have to agree to talk to the *Enquirer*. Otherwise I can't – it's too much of a conflict for me, do you understand that? If I'm giving you refuge and you go off and talk to another paper – I'm sorry to ask this, but it's very tricky. I don't know where I am with this.'

'I'm not talking to anyone until I've seen Edward.'

'But if I could just tell Mike you've promised to give us a nice big exclusive?'

'Yes, okay. Whatever. It's not really my first concern at the moment.'

'Sure. I understand. Do you think Edward will be prepared to see you?'

I shrugged. 'If I could second-guess Edward I wouldn't be here, would I?'

The plan was scuppered by the news in the following day's papers that Sir Edward had staged a flamboyant disappearance. Reporters had been swiftly despatched to each of the country's international airports in case he was trying to flee abroad, but so far there had been no sightings.

Oliver sat silently while I digested this news.

'Fuck,' I said, eventually, putting the paper down. 'He can't just vanish. It's impossible.'

'Not impossible if you're well connected. Look at Lord Lucan.'

'But that means someone must know where he is! Roger must know.'

'Are you still so determined to find him?'

'He can't just run away. He's a coward.'

'He's grieving too, though. I know he's a hypocrite, but he needs privacy just like anyone else.'

'Where would he go? Do you think he'd . . . do anything stupid?'

'Top himself? No. Not Edward.'

Oliver went to the kitchen to make tea and toast. When he came back, he stood over me, something complicated wrestling in his face.

'Look –' he began, with difficulty. He folded his arms, and then unfolded them, shifting his weight from one leg to the other. 'Gab – I might know where Edward is.'

I jerked up and spat my tea. 'What?'

'Not for certain. But I can guess. I'll tell you this if – if you swear not to tell anyone.'

'I'm not in regular contact with the press, as you might have noticed.'

'If you decide to look for him – he might not be there, but – if you just want to go there to resolve something between the two of you, I'll tell you.'

'How do you know so much about all this, Olly? You seem to have a handle on every side of the story, why aren't you just printing it?'

Oliver ignored the question.

'When I was a kid, my dad used to take me every autumn up to Argyllshire, with Edward and Toby, for a shooting party. They had a friend, Rory Campbell, who's part of the Scottish barony and he has an estate up near Loch Awe, on the west coast. It's in the middle of nowhere. We stopped going when I was in my teens – Dad's depression was quite severe by then and he used to get hysterical at the idea of killing things.'

'What things?'

'Game, all sorts. But it upset him. Then I went through my Young Communist phase and got very anti-hunting. I think Edward kept on going, though. It's very – wild. And peaceful. And I don't know for sure, but it's the safest bet. Of course, if he is there, the press will catch up pretty soon, but I don't think it would be their first guess. You could look for him there, if you're prepared to take the chance of a wasted journey.'

I stood up, and the room flashed and spun. I sat down again.

'You're light-headed. You haven't eaten properly for ages – make yourself some food. I have to get into the office. If you still want to go later, you can have my car. Leave when it's dark. It's a long drive.'

I levered myself up cautiously. 'Olly – thanks. You've been so kind – I won't forget this. I really owe you.'

'No, you don't,' he said, and then, emphatically: 'You really don't.'

I drove out of Glasgow along the Firth of Clyde, a salt breeze spiking my face through the open window. As the city's fringes faded at my back, low mountains bubbled out of the ground, violet ridges against a limpid September sky. I lit a cigarette and breathed it out into the cold, clean air. The radio was playing 'Me and Julio Down By The Schoolyard', and I was feeling nothing.

The car crested the brow of a hill between trees and Loch Awe was laid out silver below me, inverted trees shivering in its stippled surface. Slowing, I strained to pick out the road along the opposite shore, beyond the ruins of a thirteenth-century castle that jutted from a small island joined to the bank by a stone causeway. There was a time when I would have yanked the car to an immediate standstill and pounced on a piece of history like this, brown and craggy above the water, begging to be explored. Seagulls chivvied one another overhead. The road was empty.

Innischonnell Hall. I missed the entrance three times before I finally uncovered it, carefully tucked away behind shaggy foliage. My eyes were tight and dry from the long drive, my head aching. I had suspected once or twice, leaving London, that I was being followed, but I put it down to nerves and paranoia; the cars always turned off just as my neck began to trickle with sweat.

Crawling along the western shore of Loch Awe after looping back for the third time, I suddenly spotted a gap in the trees and swerved in a skidding scattering of gravel, between crumbling stone pillars and wrought-iron gates to a narrow drive, hardly more than a dirt track, curving between lines of dark firs and trailing overgrown rhododendrons. As the trees thinned, the drive opened out and forked around a circular lawn with a fountain, and I caught my first view of the house.

Vast and imperious, Innischonnell Hall was a once-grand ancestral seat now in advanced stages of neglect, its architecture the height of Scots Baronial, with castellated parapets and perpendicular mullioned windows. The frontage was stifled under Virginia creeper, bright ruby seeping into the greenery from the edges; an absurd turret protruded from one end of the house like a folly. The masonry of the western wing was badly decaying and many of the windows had been boarded up; beneath the guttering on one side ran a dark smear where the stone had been scorched by an abortive fire and not repaired. The gardens were overrun with dry brown stalks and tall weeds. In front of the colonnaded porch sat a squat, mud-encrusted jeep. I drew up to one side of the fountain and stepped out of the car, stretching my legs, and wandered across to examine it, glancing furtively up at the house. I had a prickling suspicion that someone was watching me.

The fountain itself had long run dry, its grimy stone patched with white and orange lichen, and the sculpted creature in the centre – a gryphon with scaly wings – who had once belched forth a cascade now dribbled a line of phosphorescent green algae down its front where the water had dwindled to a trickle. Dark sticky moss lined the basin. At dusk, the house might have been eerie. Now, in the smoky sheen of mid-morning autumn sunlight, it looked merely apologetic and sad.

I scrunched across the gravel and under the heavy Doric columns of the porch to heave on the bell-rope.

There was no answer. I tugged again, certain I had seen a curtain twitch.

After a very long pause the door opened with a groan of complaint, and a wary eye appeared in the crack.

'Yes?'

'Uh – I'm here to see Sir Edward?'

'Who?'

The door eased open a fraction further to reveal a small, bird-like woman with a scowl grooved into her leathery face.

'Sir Edward Hamilton-Harvey.'

'There's no one here. Sir Rory is away from home at the present.'

'But – I've come from London,' I protested. This cut no ice.

'I dinnae care if ye've come from Africa. There's no one here.'

My legs buckled lightly and I stumbled backwards, supporting myself against a pillar. I should have known. The weight of exhaustion, held at bay by nervous energy for the last few days, began to settle behind my eyes and I turned away, fearing that I would cry from sheer frustration. He wasn't here. Or, if he was, he had no intention of seeing me.

The old woman didn't close the door, as if to do so would be ill-mannered while I was still there; instead she lurked in the gap, waiting for me to have the decency to take myself off. I was about to walk back to the car when heavy footsteps echoed on a tiled floor and my uncle loomed on the threshold, one arm in the sleeve of a green waxed jacket. We stared at each other.

He had aged. He looked like an old man, the skin under his eyes sagging and creased, his chin a mass of silvery bristles. He had lost weight too, but it was not that – something in his eyes had aged him. His expression bore the bruises of grief and defeat.

'So,' he said, eventually. 'It's you.'

'It's me,' I said, stupidly. I was surprised by his lack of surprise.

'Thought you might show up. It's all right, Moira, this is my niece. I've been expecting her. Nice to have family around you at a time like this, eh?' He produced an arctic sneer.

The old woman nodded suspiciously, but made no move.

'Oliver's remorse got the better of him, then?'

'Oliver?'

'I'm assuming Olly told you how to get here. You weren't just – passing by.' He waved a hand towards the road.

'No – Olly did, but –'

'Course. Over-active conscience, his father was the same. Can't carry guilt for very long. This is Oliver's way of apologising, to you and me. I don't hold it against him, you know. He's a good kid, really. Had his reasons.'

I was baffled. 'For what?'

'Oh, bloody hell, girl.' He glanced over me at the sky and his eyes flitted back to my face. 'What are your shoes like? Can you walk in those?'

I was wearing trainers. 'Yes.'

'Fine. Let's go for a walk then. You should see the local scenery, it's beautiful. We're lucky – you managed to choose the one day of the year when it's not pissing down like a drain.' He brushed past me and down the steps. 'Don't wait for us, Moira. We might be a while.'

He strode over to the jeep, gravel rattling under his boots. 'I don't want her hanging around listening, either. We'll go and walk by the lake. You picked a good time of year.'

'I didn't exactly plan it –'

'I've seen a golden eagle up here before. Don't know if you particularly – no. Perhaps not. Is that Oliver's car?'

'Yes.'

'Hah. Good old Oliver. Can't be helpful enough, can he.'

At that moment the shrubbery rustled and shook vigorously; a straggly red setter lolloped out and wiped its nose along

333

the back of Edward's trouser leg, leaving a silver streak. Its tongue dangled, giving it a demented air. Edward looked down at it dispassionately.

'I have to take you as well, do I? Bloody hell.'

The dog tilted its head and looked up, panting, a beseeching wrinkle in its brow. 'Rory's dog,' said my uncle, opening the rear door for the dog to bound in. It sniffed around fastidiously before flopping athwart a coil of rope. 'Friendly old thing but a bit dim. Like Rory. It's called Heathcliff – imagine me running round Scottish moors yelling *Heathcliff* at the top of my voice.'

'Who's Rory?'

My uncle climbed into the jeep and wrenched the ignition. I wound down the window to vent the conjoining smells of jacket wax and old dog.

'Sir Rory Campbell, sixth Earl of Orchy. Old friend. He's been kind enough to give me shelter from the storm.'

We drove down to the gates in silence, the dog panting breathily in the back. I glanced at my uncle; his skin was sallow in the pale light.

'So what do you want from me – an apology?' he said, eventually.

I shrugged. The journey here had been more promising than the arrival; now that we were together, I was less sure of what I had imagined this confrontation might achieve.

'I knew you'd show up at some point,' he said again, without emotion.

'How did you know?'

'Because you were always an inquisitive little thing. Always had to know *why*. Why things happen the way they do. So now you want to know why I am the way I am. And why I did what I did. Am I right?'

I shrugged again and made an imprecise noise.

'And if you know why – then what? You think you can rebuild, do you?' He didn't wait for an answer. 'My life is a wreck, Gabriele. I had to get away – poetic justice, isn't it?

334

Bloody newspapers. But I can't believe he's gone.'

'Did you think –' I stopped, and cleared my throat. 'Did you think I wouldn't find out, in the end?'

He gave a bitter laugh. 'I didn't plan that far ahead. He wanted to get out of it. Piers. The thing with you. After a while, because – because he liked you. He said he didn't think it was right. Only time I ever saw him show a glimmer of conscience.'

In a clearing off the thin road on the slope above Loch Awe, Edward pulled the jeep to a halt; the dog, released like a greyhound from a stall, yapped and belted over the heather in wide circles, chasing back to buffet our legs before disappearing again. I raised a hand against the glare and looked over the open stretch of water to the forest on the opposite bank.

Edward clutched his jacket tighter against the wind. 'That mountain across there is Ben Cruachan.'

I nodded.

'Home of a goddess called Bheithir who guarded the well of eternal youth. She forgot to replace the stone one night and the well overflowed down the mountain and formed the loch. So the gods were furious and cursed her, and she became a witch. On winter nights you can hear her howling on the mountainside.'

'Really.'

'I don't charge extra for the guided tour.'

'What did you mean about Oliver?'

My uncle blinked, and stared at me. 'Oliver?'

'You said – Oliver was feeling guilty.'

He stared at me again, his brow rutted quizzically. 'Good God, are you completely stupid? You know this was all Oliver's doing?'

'What – which part?'

He shook his head in mock despair. 'Oliver set that lizard Chris Haughton on to me. Told him what he'd find and where to find it. And Roger was only too glad to be of assistance, poisonous little gimp, just waiting for his chance. But Oliver set it all in motion.'

'Oliver?' I took a step back. 'But how did he – *why*?'

Edward gave a dry, rattling laugh.

'Revenge. He hated Piers, and he hates me. He wanted to see Piers humiliated, that was it. But of course Oliver had no way of knowing it would end like this. He didn't know Piers well enough. I knew this would happen, though. I had to try and protect Piers. It must have become very complicated for Oliver when you got involved.'

'I don't understand. Revenge – how? Why should Oliver hate Piers?'

My uncle stuffed his hands into his pockets and began to walk. A sandy track, pocked with hoof-prints and split by a narrow ridge of yellow sandy grasses, led down through the bracken to the shore of the loch. Gulls swooped in wide trajectories, keening. I trailed him to the edge of the sand where the water sloshed gently, rinsing the pebbles.

'Oliver thinks Piers killed his father.'

'What? But that's –'

'Absurd. I know.'

'He gassed himself.'

'Of course he did. He'd even tried it a couple of times before, long before Piers, before they put him on the lithium or whatever it was at the end. He wasn't long for this world. But Oliver thinks Piers pushed him over the edge.'

'Why would Oliver think that?'

Edward peered across to the far side of the loch, and sighed. 'It's a long story.'

'I've got all day,' I said, defiantly.

'Let's walk.'

We set off along the sand, my thoughts whirling. Finally my uncle said:

'It'll all come out eventually, I suppose. Or perhaps it won't. I don't really care any more. But the least I can do is tell you the whole story. Then you can know exactly what I am, and what Piers was, and you can do what you like with it.'

I scuffed sand with my toe and waited.

'Denham and I went back a long way, as you know. And Piers' – he sighed again, a great weary breath heaved up from his chest – 'Piers was part of our lives – we couldn't get rid of him. Not that I wanted to – but the three of us had an odd kind of – Piers controlled us. Den and me. Because of something that happened, years ago – and finally Denham couldn't stand the fear. Piers threatened him. If you didn't know Piers well, it's hard to tell how serious he was. So perhaps he did push Denham too far. Oliver thought so, anyway. And this – secret – this thing that bound us together – no one knew about until Denham killed himself, when he told Oliver. Wrote him a letter.'

'What secret?'

'Piers was . . . ruthless. You saw that side of him. He – it used to shock me. I thought I was ambitious, but he was entirely without conscience. Entirely. He wanted to be successful. He thought he had a right to *be* someone, you know? To be more than he was born to, but he didn't much like having to work for it. And he wanted to put me in his debt so far that I couldn't leave him.'

'How do you mean?'

'He killed a man.'

The loch was silent.

'To save me, and he never let me forget it.'

I glanced at him, uncertain; his eyes were frosted and fixed on the water. He took a couple of paces backwards and sat heavily on an outcrop of rock.

'Come and sit here by your old uncle, and I'll tell you a story.'

PART THREE

Chapter XVI

Six years ago, on a mild September evening, Edward was standing on the shore of Liberty Island, looking out over the black water. Across the Hudson River, Manhattan spangled back at him, its billion eyes all winking approval. Edward lit a cigar and allowed himself a contented smile. New York had always been good to him, he thought; in a sense New York had made him, and now it wanted him back, one of its favourite adopted sons. New York would be generous to him again, he knew it.

At his back, around the plinth of the statue, at the very gateway to the free world, opulent marquees had been erected and were now replete with Manhattan's most desirable guests. Beads of lights had been draped between the trees at the edge of the lawns and a jazz band played discreetly under a fringed canopy. Nobody was dancing, but then it was still early; in the warm air, insects chugged and whistled towards the lights, no doubt bringing dengue fever, Edward reflected. Still, he had to admit that Joey had done a fine job. They would remember this launch party, these vain primping media tarts; they would talk about it for years to come. Let it never be said of him that he was afraid to paint on a broad canvas. Was that the phrase he was after?

Edward had arrived in New York two days earlier to prepare for the launch of *Forum*, the current affairs and culture magazine that would bring the *The New Yorker* whimpering to its knees. He had already managed to poach three of the latter's respected writers – one novelist, one art critic and a political analyst – and had invited the rest to this evening's lavish spectacle in the hope of seducing them too; if not now, then later. They would be imploring him. Edward smiled again. His affairs in New York were going really rather well, in his opinion; this magazine was an important investment but one which would consolidate his gradual but purposeful insinuation into the American publishing market.

He turned to gaze upriver as far as he could, and then rotated slowly back to look east, out towards Brooklyn. There, a few yards away, also apparently gazing at the judder of lights on the water, was the tall young man he had noticed earlier. Edward found something disconcerting about him; he had no idea who he was, of course, but then he had no idea who most of his guests were – Joey had simply assured him that 'everyone you need, Edward, believe me' had been included on the guest list. No, it was more to do with, not so much the fact that the blond young man was extraordinarily beautiful, though that was not a word Edward would have liked to use, but something about the intensity of his eyes. He looked right at you as if – and this was what made Edward uncomfortable – as if he was quite well aware of the thoughts that were passing through your mind as you looked at him.

Perhaps sensing Edward staring at him, the tall young man turned his head, tossed his hair back and nailed him with that green stare again, curving his lips into a knowing, cryptic smile. He flicked his cigarette end over the parapet without allowing his gaze or his smile to swerve. Edward pulled at his collar with a forefinger, nodded with what he hoped was polite acknowledgement and walked briskly off in search of Joey Kempinski.

Joey Kempinski was Edward's transatlantic Roger, though with entirely antithetical attributes, ones evolved to deal with life in New York City. Where Roger was pompous and uptight, Joey was louche and expansive; where Roger was snobbish and condescending, Joey relished the underbelly of the city: the gambling dens, the strip-bars, the run-down movie theatres and other clubs he would only hint at, where he spent at least as much time as he did at Manhattan's glitziest film and music and literary parties. He had been – among other things – a professional card sharp and a casino owner before he became an agent; battle-hardened gamblers thought twice before sitting down at the poker table with Joey. Sir Edward found him refreshing, and immensely useful, though he sometimes had the impression that he was working for Joey, and not the other way around.

Edward found him holding forth to a crowd of bug-eyed young women with some brutal anecdote or other that in anyone else's mouth would have been dismissed as implausible.

'I need a word, Joey,' he said, gently steering his arm.

'What can I do for you, boss?' Joey asked genially, rocking on his heels and folding his hands together. Joey Kempinski was a tall, stocky man whose head was almost entirely smooth, though he couldn't have been more than forty-five. His impacted features and small eyes set slightly too close together gave him an expression not unlike a bald eagle. Whenever he called Sir Edward 'boss' it always sounded as though he was making a deliberate joke.

'That boy –' Edward cast around and noticed, as he had anticipated, the tall blond young man standing at the entrance to a nearby marquee, still watching him.

'Him?'

'Yes. Don't stare. Who is he?'

'Who is he?'

'Yes.'

'Why you asking me?' Joey shrugged theatrically.

'Because you were in charge of the bloody guest list – you must have invited him. I've never seen him before and I think there's something suspicious about him. I don't like him. I think he's following me.'

Joey laughed indulgently.

'Edward, Edward. *Eddie*. I've got you here just about everyone who matters in New York City which excuse me that's not as simple as it sounds. You don't know who the half of them are – *I* don't know who the half of them are, but you can bet your ass they might come in handy somewhere down the line. And you always get the liggers who of course are going to follow you around because excuse me they are only here because they want you or somebody to give them a job or publish their fucking novel or I don't know what else. Maybe he wants to assassinate you.'

Sir Edward twitched slightly and scratched his ear.

'Not funny.'

'I apologise.'

'Joey – don't give me this horseshit. You know everyone. Find out who he is.'

Joey executed a mock bow and flamboyantly disappeared.

The young man had also moved off. Edward caught sight of his wife flirting egregiously with a late-night comedy talk-show presenter and wished, not for the first time, that she wouldn't insist on accompanying him to these things as if she never got out of the house. At least she was leaving the following night.

A few minutes later, Joey resurfaced with two fresh glasses of champagne and handed one to his boss.

'His name's Piers Gaveston. He wasn't invited but somehow he got in. He knows Casey, I forget how. One of these singer-dancer-actor-model-screenwriters, all of the above who excuse me actually waits tables in SoHo – introduce them to a producer and oh they just happen to have made a short movie, introduce them to a publisher and oh they just happen to have written this book, maybe you'd like to see it. You know the type.'

Edward knew the type.

'Actually he's English. Writes some film stuff for the *Village Voice*. Used to teach film at some college in Sacramento. Likes to hang out with writers – puts himself out there, you know?'

Edward nodded. All at once Casey rounded the corner of a pavilion with the tall young man whose name was Piers Gaveston.

Casey Michelangelo De Witt (the Third) was a formidable polymath whose passion for indie-car racing had confined

344

him to a wheelchair four years previously. He was also the new editor of *Forum* and was, somewhere in his complex genealogical tracery, related to the Kennedys. Edward always found him a little intimidating – not solely because his mind scampered over the entirety of Western culture with the agility of a mountain goat, often leaving Edward stranded, but more importantly because Edward was always conscious of trying too hard not to talk to Casey as if he were a cripple.

'Hullo, Sir Edward, are you enjoying the party?' said Casey with his Boston vowels.

The tall young man had fixed Edward with his unsettling stare again; Sir Edward pretended not to notice.

'Very much so.'

'Good, good. Allow me to introduce to you Piers Gaveston, who writes for the *Village Voice* and also plays jazz piano at Café Arete.'

'Where?'

'Café Arete. It's on Bleecker Street,' said Piers Gaveston, extending a hand.

Edward felt oddly reluctant to take it.

'I play on Thursdays,' Piers Gaveston added, with a silky smile.

'Joey' – Casey curved his wheelchair dextrously round the back of Sir Edward's legs and laid a hand on Joey's arm – 'I wonder if you'd mind coming with me to find Santiago, he's desperate to introduce you to his new wife – she's some kind of choreographer.'

And suddenly Edward found himself standing alone with Piers Gaveston.

'So' – he said, to break the silence which was clogging his throat uncomfortably – 'you live in New York, then?'

Piers Gaveston smiled again, cryptically. 'I don't think we need to bother about all that, do you? I've been waiting to speak to you.'

'Well' – Sir Edward held out his hands, palms upward, in an accommodating gesture – 'what can I do for you?'

345

Piers gestured to the terrace where the strings of lights danced like static off the river. 'Perhaps we might walk over here? It's quieter.'

Edward glanced nervously over his shoulder, but his guests appeared not to be taking much notice of him. He followed Piers Gaveston away from the music. A breeze lifted off the river and Piers leaned over the parapet into it, gratefully. Then he turned, abruptly, to face Edward and leaned back against the stone balustrade, studying the older man's face with a kind of amused curiosity, the smile still sliding about his lips.

Edward was beginning to feel irritated.

'What is it?'

'Well, you see, Sir Edward, it's like this. Do you smoke?' He held out his pack of cigarettes with exaggerated politeness.

'Only cigars.'

'I have a business proposition.'

Edward sighed. If he had a pound for every time he'd heard that . . .

'I don't believe you were invited to this party, were you?'

'Not technically, no. Do you mind if I smoke?'

'No. Look – I've got a lot of people to –'

'Okay, I'll come to the point. I need your help.'

Sir Edward laughed, almost with relief. 'If I had a pound –'

'Yes, but this is slightly different.'

'Why's that?' Edward narrowed his eyes; the anxiety was creeping back.

'Because, although you don't know it yet, you need my help too. More than I need yours.'

'Why would I need your help?'

'Because you're in some significant danger.' Piers drew elegantly on his cigarette and watched Edward's face.

'Of what? What kind of danger?' Edward's mind was groping wildly through images of masked assassins and bomb plots.

'I don't think this is the time or the place to discuss it, do you?' Piers smiled pleasantly. 'Let's just say – as we both know – you have one or two skeletons in your closet that just might be hauled out in the near future. You've done one or two things in your life that might be considered – well' – he paused and looked upwards at the rising tendrils of smoke, running his tongue around his lips as if searching for a suitably delicate term – '*illegal*, for want of a better word.'

'I don't know what you think you're talking about,' said Edward, stiffly, through closed teeth.

'I think you do. What if I were to say to you – oh, I don't know. Jordan? Ibrahim Said?' He paused, almost genuinely, for a moment. 'VX?'

Edward, predictably, turned pale and leaned heavily against the stone wall. He twitched slightly and gripped the young man's arm.

'Ah, I see that's touched a nerve. No pun intended.'

'Tell me what you mean.'

'Not here, I don't think. I want to have a drink with you tomorrow evening. In your hotel.'

'In my hotel?'

'Yes. At ten o'clock.'

Edward was jolted, certainly, but a significant element of his discomposure was caused by the ferocity of Piers Gaveston's eyes. There was something in those green shallows that reflected the thoughts he would rather suppress.

'I don't know if I can –'

'VX nerve gas. Nasty business.'

Just then, Isabelle appeared in search of her husband.

'There you are! I've been looking for you – Marlon and Judy are dying to see you. Did I tell you Marlon's just been made Head of Development at Universal?' She took Edward's arm in both hands as if to make certain it came with her, shot Piers Gaveston a brief look of distaste, and marched her husband away. Edward glanced over his shoulder; Gaveston raised an eyebrow questioningly and Edward nodded, once. A sweat had broken out under his jacket.

*

The following evening, having seen Isabelle safely into a taxi to JFK, Edward sat in the bar of the Four Seasons Hotel nursing a large scotch and feeling nettled. It occurred to him that he had not told Piers Gaveston where he was staying; it also occurred to him that, given Piers Gaveston's inexplicable possession of facts that Edward had believed safely out of the public domain, he would almost certainly find his way here without too much difficulty. These stories were twenty years old, he thought; why should someone begin digging this up now? What does he want from me?

Piers Gaveston arrived punctually at ten o'clock, wearing a loose white linen shirt and dark jeans and slid into the seat opposite Edward without the formality of a handshake.

'Drink?'

'No thanks. Let's go to your room.'

Edward blinked. 'I beg your pardon?'

'I assume you have a suite where we could talk in private. I'm anxious not to be overheard.'

'There's hardly anyone here.' Edward gestured around the bar optimistically; he didn't like the idea of this handsome young man coming up to his room. Or rather, he did like it, which was why he was concerned it shouldn't happen.

'Nevertheless . . . Do you want to hear what I have to say?'

'Of course.'

'Then let's go.'

Edward felt himself fettered. He led the way to the elevator.

The windows of his suite afforded a magnificent view of the Manhattan skyline. Piers Gaveston admired it, nodding, while Edward poured himself another, larger, scotch.

'Drink?' he asked again.

'Water. Thanks.'

Edward felt slightly rebuffed. 'Nothing stronger?'

'No. Never touch it.'

'Any reason?'

Piers Gaveston turned back to the room with a look of slight surprise, as if he had forgotten Edward was there. 'My stepfather was an alcoholic. Put me off.'

'Oh. I'm sorry.'

'No need, it wasn't your fault.'

'So. What's all this about Jordan and VX?' Edward decided it was time to remind this over-confident young thorough-bred who was in charge.

Piers Gaveston half-sat against the wide window sill, and took out his cigarettes. He lit one, slowly, keeping his eyes on Edward, the amused half-smile returning.

'Well. I presume you've heard of the novelist Andy Epstein?'

Edward nodded.

'You may remember, a couple of months ago he was signed up by Sam Felberg at Sampson West for this history of the golden age of US arms trading, $400,000 advance, big head-lines, etcetera?'

'I remember.'

Piers Gaveston scratched his upper lip thoughtfully with his thumbnail. 'I wonder if you'd be kind enough to get me an ashtray?'

You are a cocky little sod, thought Edward, but he was worried, so he did as he was told.

'You were a sales consultant to Jordan for Lockhardt and North around that time, weren't you, Edward? May I call you Edward?'

'We sold to various places,' Edward said, as evenly as he could. 'Jordan, Iran, Saudi.'

'Yes. It's Jordan that we're interested in here, though, isn't it, because you had a special responsibility there, I think I'm right in saying. You had an end-user certificate from Jordan, didn't you, which gave you almost carte blanche with regard to the trades you made? You and – what's his name now?' Piers looked up and pretended to consider. 'Denham Dowland. That's right. Secretary of State for Defence now, back home, unless I'm mistaken? Which seems neat for a man with such – wide experience in the traffic of weaponry.'

349

'What's your point?'

Piers crushed out his cigarette and looked Edward straight in the eye.

'My point is this – that you were a bit naughty out there in Jordan, weren't you, and you thought no one would find out about it. And you've managed for over twenty years and so far no one has, but I'm afraid that Andy has been digging around asking too many questions, doing some over-zealous research in the Jordanian ministries, and he's got your number. I'm advising you of this because it will be extremely *embarrassing* for you and for your friend Mr Dowland when Andy's book is published. And quite apart from the embarrassment, the underground trade of VX nerve gas is a criminal offence, as I'm sure you know. And there are all kinds of wider implications – who was producing it out there, how you got hold of them.'

He folded his arms.

Edward picked up his scotch glass; its rapid clinking betrayed his unsteadiness of hand.

'First of all – why should I believe you? No one knows the contents of Epstein's book, not even his agent's seen it. I know, because I –'

'Because you what?'

'I have a mole in there.'

'Oh yes. He thought someone might. All right, how can I convince you?' He unfolded his arms and floated his gaze to the middle distance as if in earnest contemplation. Sir Edward was becoming impatient. This was all a carefully rehearsed act, and Piers Gaveston was enjoying it enormously.

'Andy Epstein and I are' – he hesitated – 'close friends.' He waited to see if this drew a reaction, but Sir Edward looked away. 'And I'm' – here he leant forward and rested his palms flat on the front of his thighs, looking at Edward from under his long lashes – 'very good at persuading people to tell me their secrets. People trust me.'

'I don't trust you an inch.'

'Shall I go on? Andy's told me, in confidence, that this would be the meat of his book – this exposé of some top American arms manufacturers, Lockhardt being the biggest, who got around the embargo on selling weapons to Egypt during the early seventies by trading illegally via Jordan, particularly by selling nerve gas which was being manufactured in the Middle East. So I put it to you, Sir Edward,' (he stood up and began pacing in front of the window) 'that on your several visits to Jordan, you were very well aware that a percentage of the deal you were brokering was going to be passed on through Cyprus to the Egyptians with a tidy commission for Lockhardt, and for yourselves, and that those weapons would almost certainly be used in attacks on Israel, the ally of the country you were representing. Am I getting warm?'

Edward sighed and passed a hand through his hair. 'Look, this was all a long time ago. We were the middle men – the people who brokered those deals are dead. We had no idea really what was going on.'

'Just following orders, eh?' Piers Gaveston smiled, not kindly. 'Please, Sir Edward, you can do better than that. I hear VX is tricky to transport, quite dangerous. I hope they paid you well for your trouble?'

'VX was never used by the Egyptians against Israel. There was a secret agreement.'

'That doesn't alter the fact that you sold it to them. Do you really want that to get out, Sir Edward? Could I have some more water?'

Sir Edward obliged. Then he felt the need to sit.

'So – Mr Gaveston.'

'Please. Call me Piers.'

'*Piers*. How do you propose to help me? You want money, I suppose?'

'I have a proposition, as I said.' Piers Gaveston was still pacing thoughtfully by the window. 'I realise that in telling you this, you might decide just to take matters into your own hands, but of course you're smart enough to realise that it would be very difficult for you to do so without incriminating yourself.'

'You'd be surprised. I have a lot of friends in this city.'

'Oh, I have no doubt. But the fact remains, Edward, that I could solve this little . . . problem for you much more easily than you could yourself.'

'Are you trying to blackmail me?' Edward finished his scotch rather too quickly, and rose to pour himself another. Piers Gaveston watched him with something approaching amusement.

'Not at all. I'm proposing an *arrangement*.' He paused to let the word hang in the air with the threads of smoke. 'Whereby we help each other.'

He waited until Edward, who by now was feeling slightly drunk and more than slightly apprehensive, had reseated himself.

'I have an idea which would ensure that Andy's book is never published, and which would appear to have nothing whatsoever to do with you.'

'Go on.'

Piers walked around the front of the sofa to stand directly before Edward, and looked him right in the eye.

'Andy has' – he hesitated, as if trying to find an appropriate euphemism – 'a bit of a bad habit. He likes boys.'

Edward concerned himself with the contents of his glass and did not look up.

'To be more specific,' Piers went on, 'he likes rough trade, if you see what I mean. He visits rent boys quite regularly in Alphabet City – not a nice part of town.'

Edward mumbled agreement.

'Like you, Edward, I have some – useful contacts in this city. Alphabet City is a dangerous place to walk around at night, you know. It's quite likely that Andy might be caught off-guard one evening – mugged, perhaps.'

He lit another cigarette, green eyes glinting. Edward looked at him warily.

'And?'

'Well – let's imagine that this unfortunate attack were to take place – it's quite possible that he might be mildly roughed up, and that his wallet and keys might be, well – stolen.'

'*Mildly* roughed up?'

'Enough to make him nervous, nothing serious. But it's plausible, don't you think, that an intelligent attacker might find some document on him that gives his address, and might then have the nerve to visit his apartment and – remove some items?'

'I suppose that would be possible. If highly suspicious.'

Piers took another sip of water. 'If his computer were stolen, for example, he would lose what he has of his book to date. And if someone knew where his back-up discs and notes were kept, in the general disarray of a burglary, those files might just go missing and since no one else knows about these files, they wouldn't be missed by anyone.'

'Except Andy Epstein.'

'Yes, but I suspect they're irreplaceable. And he might just be nervous enough to give up the chase.'

Edward shook his head. 'The man's a veteran war reporter. I read somewhere that he had his legs broken twice in Baghdad. I doubt he's going to be scared off by a mild beating. And how do you know his publisher doesn't have copies of these files?'

'Because he doesn't trust his publisher, or his agent. All the information that's going in that book – all the information that could put you away – is there in Andy's apartment. I *know* this. And a mild beating can be interpreted in various ways depending on who you employ.'

'I thought you said this Epstein was a friend of yours?'

Piers Gaveston sighed, somewhat affectedly, Edward thought.

'Edward – are you telling me you've never screwed a

friend to get what you wanted? I think you and I have more in common than you'd like to admit.'

'And what is it that you want exactly?'

Piers Gaveston smiled slowly; then, advancing towards Edward, he began to unbutton his white shirt. The room suddenly seemed very still; Edward could feel his back and armpits grow damp. He watched, horrified and fascinated.

Piers opened his shirt to reveal a streamlined, effortlessly honed torso, tanned the colour of honey.

'Look at me,' he said. 'Look at this. I've been a model, an actor, a pianist, a writer, and I'm bloody good at all of them. Bloody good. And I've got this face and this body – and I haven't made it.' A bitterness, verging on suppressed fury, had crept into his voice. 'I haven't made it. Not because I'm not good enough, but because I was born in the wrong place. I didn't have the connections, and that's the way it works, isn't it – it's all about your family and who you know. And I've worked hard, but I just haven't been lucky enough to know the right people. I'm thirty-three – I haven't got that long any more. I'll tell you what I want, Edward – I want to be famous. Does that sound childish? Only as childish as wanting to be rich. That's why I need you. I need your contacts, your friends. I need a patron – this is the deal.'

Edward levelled his stare at Piers Gaveston's chest, finding it hard to meet his eye.

'And how do you propose this will work?'

'I want to make a film. I'll sort out your little – predicament – and then I want to come back to London. New York tires me now. I want to come back to London and make a film – there's a guy I know, an independent producer, who's interested. You find me a place to live and give me the money to make this film, introduce me to the right people. That's it.'

Edward emitted a nervous, cynical laugh. 'That's it, is it? And how much will this film cost?'

'Let's start with five million. I'm not entirely sure – won't be until we start planning it properly.'

'Five *million*? You want me to give you five million – are you out of your mind?'

'Edward, Edward. You wouldn't notice that missing if you dropped it in the street. And I could go to the papers tomorrow with your story. What price do you put on keeping that out of the public domain for good? I've got the ability to destroy you, just as you've got the ability to make me. It's rather a nice symbiosis, don't you think?'

'You can put your shirt on now,' said Sir Edward, who was feeling very hot and quite drunk. 'Please.'

Piers Gaveston placed his hands wilfully on his hips. 'Would that make you more comfortable?' He made no move to button his shirt. 'Illegal arms trading is not your only embarrassing little secret, is it, Edward?'

Edward stood, in a shaky attempt at decisiveness.

'I think you should leave now.'

'Do we have a deal?'

'I need to – think. And I must speak to Denham, you understand.'

Piers Gaveston's gloating expression was briefly eclipsed; he began doing up his shirt sulkily. 'I wouldn't do that, if I were you.'

'Why not? He's involved.'

'The fewer people that know about this, the better.'

'I have to talk to Denham. He – he needs to know.'

Piers shrugged. 'Call me in two days. Or I might get bored with the idea of helping you.'

Piers Gaveston turned at the door, and suddenly produced a smile of such energy that Edward felt considerably weakened. Then he winked and left.

'*Without a minder*?' Joey Kempinski was staring at Edward as if he'd just announced a desire to walk through Harlem naked wearing a Ku Klux Klan hood. 'What, are you fucking nuts? At least let me go with you.'

Edward sighed. It was Thursday. He had not slept the

night before, his thoughts interrupted continually by images of Andy Epstein, Richard Nixon, Ibrahim Said and Piers Gaveston's naked chest. His stomach was playing up again; he had spent most of the morning on the toilet.

'I'm fed up with being surrounded by bloody people all the time, Joey. I just want to walk down to the Village and have a quiet drink on my own – nothing will happen to me, for God's sake. I'm six foot two.'

'You're a fucking maniac is what you are. I'm supposed to take care of you.'

'You're supposed to take care of my *business*,' said Edward, irritably. He glanced at his watch. In four hours' time, Denham would be catching the first flight from Heathrow and would arrive at JFK the following morning. Then perhaps he could settle; Denham would know what to do.

'Edward, you are really starting to fry my ass. Casey's expecting you for dinner.'

'Well, tell him something's come up.'

Edward took a cab down Sixth Avenue and got out at West Washington Place. The little streets were charged with young people, self-consciously casual in their dress, laughing and milling in the shadows of the trees and high-rises with their painted, asymmetric fire escapes. A busker standing below a striped canopy strummed almost tunefully through a Dylanesque lament about a railroad. Edward stopped to listen for a moment, breathing deeply; the city air reassured him. He walked east along Bleecker Street, mingling with the crowds, then doubled back and walked back west along the facing pavement.

Café Arete was in a basement on the corner of Bleecker and West 10th, hot and smoky with red velvet on the walls. Edward paid his fifteen dollars, folded his jacket over his arm and edged along sideways to a table in the shadows, near the back, as far as possible from the stage. He ordered a whisky and soda.

Piers Gaveston sat there under the spotlights behind the

baby grand, frowning in concentration, biting his lip as his hands slithered over the keyboard. A flamboyant bearded man accompanied him on the double bass, as did a quiet guitarist; Edward was no expert on jazz, but he knew enough to recognise that this ensemble was competent, if unspectacular. But he watched Piers Gaveston's face; the way the lights flicked shadows on the hollows of his cheeks, the geometric lines of his jaw and cheekbone, the ferocity of expression that suggested everything depended on his playing, the way he was feeling the music. And Edward knew, as he ordered another drink without taking his eyes from the band, that whatever Denham said, this mysterious and troublesome young man would not easily be removed from their lives. For the first time, Edward almost believed in Fate.

'Not a single shred of evidence does he have to offer,' Denham Dowland said contemptuously, reaching again for the decanter. 'Not one. Just a scheming little opportunist hoping to extort some money through bluff and half-baked research. Even if what you're accusing us of happened to be true – and it's a very serious allegation – what possible evidence could exist that would incriminate us? I can't believe you've been so gullible, Edward.'

Edward looked at Denham under the tangerine light of the restaurant and wondered how he could have aged so much in the last year. He was enormous, his face puffy and red – though, granted, that might be the medication – with creases of skin under his eyes that looked as if they had been pumped up and left to deflate slowly. Edward was surprised, given the circumstances, that his first thought was a kind of swaggering gratitude that he himself looked at least ten years younger than his old friend. He had even been for a jog in Central Park that morning with two of Joey's boys, and they hadn't had to slow down all that much for him. If Piers Gaveston were to compare the two of them, he, Edward, would certainly come off favourably.

Piers Gaveston smiled evenly at Denham Dowland, and lit another cigarette without taking his eyes off the Minister.

'Anyone with a bit of nous can root around and dig up some names,' Denham blustered, 'but I don't see you producing any of these so-called documents or photographs, and I'll tell you why – because they don't exist. And Edward and I have very powerful legal representation between us, young man, don't be mistaken. Very powerful. We could take you out like that.' He snapped his plump fingers.

Piers Gaveston rearranged the cruet in front of him without putting his cigarette down.

'Minister. You'll appreciate that it would be very difficult for me to remove documentary or photographic evidence from Andy at this stage. And don't you think the fact that you've dropped everything and jumped on a plane to New York suggests that you're slightly nervous?' His eyes narrowed. 'You seem to forget, I'm doing you a favour. I could sit back and wait for this book to be published – it makes no difference to me.'

'You don't expect me to sit idly by while I'm being threatened by some jumped-up little grasper?'

'Do you know how many innocent people died in the seventy-three invasion of Israel, Minister?' Piers asked casually. 'Do you know what VX gas does to the human body? Do you ever think of them as you lie down to sleep?'

'This is absolutely bloody preposterous!' Denham spluttered port in a neat arc around his plate. 'It's a shameful confidence trick, in fact, it's downright blackmail – I should just call my lawyer right now. And even if we did at one point sell VX – which I'm not saying we did – it was certainly never used during the seventy-three invasion and if you had any idea what you were talking about you'd know that. Edward?'

Edward sighed. 'Den – I don't think – oh, I don't know. This is a pointless argument – I for one don't want to see this book completed, and serialised in papers both sides of the Atlantic – imagine the London press! Think how they'd love to bring us both down with this – it won't matter how much we protest then, we'd still have to go through a libel case and even if we won, it would stick, and it might prompt more investigation. And, frankly, Den – let's not beat about the bush here – we wouldn't win, would we? You know that as well as I do.'

'And what,' Denham poured himself another glass without offering the others, 'makes you think we can trust this boy afterwards? If he's prepared to go this far, what makes you think he won't go straight to the papers with his story of what we were ready to do to protect ourselves?'

Edward looked appealingly at Piers, who was watching, quietly, with a smirk hovering at the corners of his mouth.

'Because I will give you my word,' Piers said, as if it were obvious. 'I'm not helping you for nothing. We're making a deal here. I'm getting something back, something that matters to me more than a quick buck from the press. If I wanted that, I could go to them now. This is a gentlemen's agreement.' He smiled winningly.

'You are a poisonous little snake,' said Denham decisively.

'I'm not asking you to fall in love with me, Minister,' Piers said smoothly. Edward interested himself in the tablecloth.

Denham Dowland glowered like an enraged hippo, then flicked a hand in the air and summoned a bottle of brandy. When the waiter had gone, he said, 'Let's suppose, then, for a minute, that we go along with this. How exactly will it work? I want to be certain there will be nothing whatsoever to relate it to me.'

Piers sat back in his chair and breathed out smoke, slowly. 'Andy sets off one night to go about his business in Alphabet City. As he's walking down a dark street, he's set upon and given a bit of a kicking, and his assailants relieve him of his valuables, including his wallet and keys. Andy carries business cards in his wallet with his home address – careless, I know, but he's strangely ingenuous about certain things, Andy. He thinks he's invulnerable. Then, we assume that his attackers, being particularly sharp, jump in a cab straight over to Hell's Kitchen, on the other side of town, and give his apartment a good going over. Lift the obvious stuff – computer, stereo, whatever. But in the process they turn the place over – wreck it. And by the time he's put it all back together, he'll realise that there's a few files missing.'

'Well, quite. And when he realises which ones, he'll see it's all been a set-up and trot along to the police, or the press.'

'With what? An unsubstantiated story about how some people he's been investigating might have had him beaten up? I've told you – those files are irreplaceable. And what matters to Andy more than anything as far as this book is concerned is being the first to break the story. So if he's lost his evidence, he'll have to retrace his steps, and the last thing he'll want to do is put the story out in the public arena where anyone else with an eye on a news story could go and dig it up for themselves. Particularly because if he's beaten to it, he'll have to pay back the advance, which he's already spent. Andy's been in this game a long time – he knows that the last thing you do with volatile information is hand it to the police.'

'Well, how much evidence is there? Do you know exactly?'

'I have no idea, Minister, how well did you cover your tracks?'

Denham Dowland sucked in his cheeks – no small effort – but said nothing.

'What I do know,' Piers went on, 'is that Andy has been researching this for nearly ten years. He's collated all kinds of documents from Egyptian government archives, first-hand interviews – he's not going to be able to put it all back together in a couple of months. Once it's gone, you're safe for some time to come. And there's another thing – he's not out.'

'Not out where?'

Piers looked impatient. '*Out*. He's a big tough manly war reporter, it's not widely known that he likes to pay to fuck teenage boys, Minister, is that clear enough for you?' Denham lowered his eyes. 'If he has to start explaining why he was wandering round the East Side with a wallet full of used notes in the small hours, it'll soon come out, and he won't want that. He'll take a hint – believe me, I know him.'

'And there would be nothing to link us to this – you're certain?' Denham looked dubious. He toyed nervously with the napkin spread over his paunch.

'Nothing except me.' Piers offered a confidential smile. 'And I'm on your side.'

'And the people who would administer this so-called gentle kicking, where do you plan to find them? And how do you know you can trust them?'

'I have a wide variety of acquaintances, Minister. Some you would get on with, others not. These people don't talk.'

'But you said Epstein was your friend.' Edward roused himself to speak; he felt himself unusually lessened in Piers's presence, and the thought made him anxious.

Piers turned the full beam of his eyes on him. 'That's such a nebulous term, don't you find, Sir Edward? Friend can have so many nuances. I like to think that *we're* becoming friends.'

Denham snorted theatrically, and fastened on the brandy.

'But I'll need some money up front,' said Piers, suddenly businesslike, folding his hands together.

'How much?' asked Edward, nervously.

'Absolutely not,' said Denham Dowland.

'I'm afraid you don't get something for nothing.' Piers smiled again. 'Think of it as a small advance. Two thousand.'

'Dollars?' Edward could hear his voice squeaking.

'Of course dollars.'

Edward exchanged a quick glance with his friend, but Denham's expression now was veiled with alcohol. He nodded vaguely.

'And you'll wait for us to leave the country?' Sir Edward was finding it hard to swallow; he tried to clip his cigar and found his fingers trembling.

'Sir Edward' – Piers leaned close and offered a lighter –

'don't underestimate me. I'm not stupid. In fact I have a doctorate, did I mention that? I will manage this for you much better than you ever could yourself.' He snapped the flame into life, and Sir Edward bent his head towards it. Their eyes locked, and Piers Gaveston smiled.

Two weeks later, Edward was sitting behind the broad desk in his executive suite on the seventh floor of Hamilton Harvey House in the City of London, reading the morning papers. It was Edward's custom, before his morning meetings, to read through his rivals' work and assess his own, so that he would be fully appraised of the day's events and the media's varying interpretations of them before he was obliged to answer any tricky questions. He also liked to find a reason to telephone Mervyn Bland at least once a day to complain about something his papers had missed.

But since his return from New York, he was not sleeping well, and had taken to reading the American papers before anything else. He had heard nothing from Piers Gaveston and had begun to wonder if the whole business had been an elaborate joke; still, he scanned the news pages of the *New York Times* as if his life depended on it, fearful of some headline revealing that Piers Gaveston had bungled the thing and that he himself might be implicated. So far, he had read nothing relating to Andy Epstein.

'I'm only agreeing to this, Edward,' Denham Dowland had said, shortly after their arrival back in London, 'because you seem to think it's the right thing to do, and after all, it seems to be you he's targetted. If you want to be blackmailed, it's up to you. But I don't like it one bit. You're handing him a noose to hang you whenever he chooses. Both of us.'

'I don't see that there's any choice, Den. Do you want to see this book published? Well, then.'

'Edward. Don't think I don't know what's under all this. I can see the way you look at him. You are heading for an almighty fall, my friend. He's got you under his thumb already. Well, that's your funeral. But from now on, I am nothing to do with this. None of it. I don't care what you do with him, but I never want to hear his name or see him ever again. I want to go on as if this never happened. Take that how you will – it's a friendly warning. You can be so bloody pig-headed.'

Pig-headed. Edward folded his hands behind his back and stood by the plate-glass window, looking out over the roofscape of EC4. Denham was right, of course. But he wanted to see the boy again. He had made a promise.

The telephone on his desk bleeped, once.

'A Mr Gaveston for you from New York,' said Lucy, his PA, in her bleaty voice.

'Good, put him through,' said Edward, his hands growing clammy.

There was a soft pause and a crackle.

'Good morning, Sir Edward, I hope you're well.'

Edward glanced at his watch; nine o'clock. It would be four in the morning in New York, no one would call at that hour, unless . . . His pulse was banging uncomfortably.

'Well?'

'Oh, I've got them. The files. They're all here in front of me as we speak.'

The tone of Piers's voice struck him as odd.

'Uh – good, good. Did it – all go smoothly?'

'Well –' a hesitation. 'Not *exactly*. There's been a slight' – Piers Gaveston paused as if to select an appropriate phrase – 'complication.'

'What?'

'I'm afraid they – used a firearm.'

'They *shot* him?' Edward struggled suddenly for breath; he also glanced up to see Roger peering around the door holding a leather attaché case and wearing his politely intrigued face. Frantically he waved Roger away.

'He put up more of a fight than they anticipated, and they're not all that bright. But he'll be all right. And it gives us more time.'

'I can't have this conversation on this phone line,' Edward whispered hoarsely. 'I'll have to call you back. Are you sure he's all right?'

'He's in hospital,' Piers Gaveston said, smoothly. 'And it doesn't much matter which phone line you use, from my point of view – I'm recording this conversation. Now listen. I've got a flight back to London in two days. I'm going to come and see you at your office –'

'Don't be ridiculous!'

'Calm down, Edward. It's far less suspicious than sneaking around. I'll come to your office, and we can discuss your side of the bargain.'

'And I can have them?'

'Have what?'

'The files.'

Another pause, and then a faint laugh, mocking. 'Do you think I'm an idiot? Of course you can't have them.'

'But we agreed –'

'I want to see your money where your mouth is. I've done my bit. Perhaps we'll have dinner and talk about it. I'd like that.'

'Dinner,' said Edward weakly. In two days' time, Piers Gaveston would be in London. He was beginning to feel afraid. 'Fine. Dinner it is.'

'I'll look forward to it,' said Piers, and put the phone down.

The following morning, Edward picked up his *New York Times*, and in the bottom left corner of the front page he read the following headline: 'AWARD-WINNING NOVELIST DIES AFTER GUN ATTACK'.

Chapter XVII

'So Piers came back to London, and that's where things really started to go badly.' My uncle looked up at the sky, where the clouds had ebbed away, leaving only the soft wake of an aeroplane etched against the watery blue.

He stood, kicked the sand uncertainly and began to walk off westward along the shore of the loch. I stretched my legs and hurried to catch up with him.

'But didn't they investigate the shooting?'

'Oh yes. It went on for a long time – it didn't take the NYPD long to guess that it might have something to do with Epstein's book. I was bloody terrified – imagine, I'd gone to New York to launch a magazine and come back having paid to have a man killed. Not intentionally, but still . . . I went through months of reading the New York papers every day with my heart in my mouth. And Denham was a million times worse – Denham could panic for England even when he didn't have blood on his hands. But somehow they never put two and two together. It was still a long time before we could relax. But they closed the case, finally, after a year or so.'

'Was Piers afraid?'

My uncle leaned forward and began tracing patterns in the sand with a birch twig. 'If he was, he would never have let it show. Piers wouldn't speak about it. Not to me. I didn't know – still don't – whether he'd meant to have Epstein killed all along. Den thought he had, that it was part of his trap. But somehow I didn't believe it. They had been lovers, you know. I never had any idea what Piers felt about Epstein's death. It was as if he just erased it when he came back to London. Like it never happened.' He almost laughed.

'Did he give you the documents?'

'No. Never saw them. He said he was holding on to them until he was established, for insurance. I used to wonder whether they really existed. But it didn't matter by then, because we became –' He stopped, and shaded his eyes.

'Lovers,' I said, heavily.

Edward sighed. 'Not really, Gaby. Not in the way you'd understand. I – God, it's absurd to be talking about this to you.' He rubbed his hands over his face. 'I was in love with him, yes. Obsessed might be a better word. And he was always so elusive – I lived in fear of one day finding he'd just disappeared. Fifty-three, Gaby, and I'd fallen in love for the first time in my life. I didn't know what I was doing. But sex –'

I turned my face to the loch, biting the inside of my mouth, partly fascinated and partly wanting to slam my hands over my ears before I heard the end of this thought.

'Well – you slept with him. I know, because he told me. So you'll understand. Piers wasn't interested in sex, not really, not for its own sake. But it was his currency, I suppose, and its value increased the more he withheld it. It was his way of reminding you that he was the one in control.'

In spite of myself, I was nodding. A breeze scuffed the water. My uncle continued: 'So I bought him a flat, gave him money, paid for him to travel, paid for his drugs, funded his bloody pointless Dante film that seemed to go on and on for years with no discernible progress, losing hundreds of thousands, all for a few hours of his company a week. And I suppose in a way I was happy. I mean, I knew I was being exploited, but I thought I could justify it.'

'Did anyone know?'

'About Piers?'

'Well –' I turned to face him, caught his eye briefly and then looked down, hands deep in my pockets. 'About Piers, or just that you were –'

'A homosexual? Is that the word you're looking for?'

'Uh – I suppose.'

366

Edward tore a stick from an overhanging branch and paused, poking it into the sand.

'Oh, yes. The obvious people. Isabelle, Denham, Roger, Richard. That's all. Toby didn't know, poor kid. I feel a bit bad about that now. Must have come as a terrible shock.'

'Dad knew?'

'Of course he knew. He was my brother.'

'Is that why you –' I paused again; he was looking at me quite openly, as if he were almost pleased to be unburdening himself. 'Why you wanted Dad working for you, so he wouldn't say anything?'

Edward gave a tired laugh. 'Don't be stupid. You know so little about my relationship with Richard, and you think you understand so much – you're so quick to judge, aren't you? I always trusted Richard. Mind you, he could be very judgemental too – you're very like him, I've said it before. You know – he was a very *upright* man, Richard, so bloody principled. He didn't care what leanings I had, he just wanted me to be honest – couldn't bear hypocrisy, that's what he objected to. And in the end, that's the backbone of all front-page scandals, mine and everyone else's – the relish of discovering that someone's public claims and their private life don't match. Watching someone fall – that – what do you call it –' He looked at me hopefully.

'*Schadenfreude*.'

'That's the one.'

'But – so Isabelle knew about Piers too?'

Edward glanced up from his absent scrawlings in the sand and a sad smile touched the corner of his mouth.

'Isabelle is a stronger woman than you'd think. We had what you might call an amicable arrangement. We were always quite fond of each other, you know – probably more so than most normal marriages.' He tweaked his fingers in the air to suggest ironic inverted commas around 'normal'. 'She had her affairs, I had mine – though not many, granted – and the deal was that we did everything possible to protect each other's dignity in public. In other words, we didn't get caught. We kept up the charade of the happy marriage and actually we were pretty happy, most of the time, because we got on with our own lives. But Piers was –'

His mouth tightened again, and he stood up, his knees cracking, stretched his arm behind his back and lobbed the stick into the air where it traced an arc, spinning, and landed in the water; Heathcliff loped out of the bracken, burrs clinging to his fur, and charged into the loch, swimming clumsily with the stick between his teeth.

'Piers was different,' said Edward, striding off again. 'He became the most important thing in my life. I'd have given him anything, and the people close to me could see that. And it upset them – they worried that I was being used and manipulated, and I suppose it made them jealous, too. Isabelle was afraid I was getting reckless. She said: "If this ever gets out, Edward, I'm divorcing you quicker than you can blink." She meant it.' He frowned. 'But Denham was the worst. That's where things started to go wrong.'

'How?' I was fighting to keep up; the path was single file here between the birches, the sand scattered with yellow leaves like confetti. Wet branches brushed my face.

'Den was serious when he said he wanted Piers out of his life after the Epstein business. I think he really believed it would be that simple, you know – that we'd pay Piers off and the whole thing would be forgotten about. But when he realised how – *involved* I was becoming –' Edward passed a hand through his hair and shook his head. 'I suppose as my oldest friend he felt it was his responsibility to protect me. And his own interests. So he warned me, many times, and then when he realised I wasn't listening, he made the mistake of telling Piers to back off. He hated Piers being around, it fed his paranoia – so he told him to get back to New York. But he didn't know Piers very well. No one did, really. But it was a red rag to a bull – Piers hated being told what to do. Got his hackles up. So he thought he'd have some fun with Denham.'

'In what way?'

'Frighten him a bit. There was the business of these documents, witness statements, or photographs – the ones he did or didn't have from Epstein. But he was threatening Denham – I didn't know about this until afterwards. And my guess is that –' He hesitated, stooping to duck under an overhanging branch and holding it back for me to pass through behind him.

'What?'

'There was another side to it. This is only my guess, but – Denham had been to a boarding school, you know, with all the usual boyish horseplay. And his university college, at the time he was there, was a real conservative forcing house, and I think there was a lot of *stuff* going on there, not serious, just experimentation. But Denham was always so emphatically homophobic – not to me, that was different – but so bigoted sometimes that I wondered if he wasn't afraid of his own thoughts.'

'You mean Denham was gay?'

'No, Gaby.' He sounded irritated. 'It's not as black and white as that. But I think Piers bothered him, because he did find Piers attractive – well, everyone did. And I think Piers played on that, and made suggestions, and it was only Piers exercising his influence, you know, reminding us all that we had a weakness. But he didn't know –'

'What?'

We had emerged from the trees to another patch of open shore. The water caught the autumn colours in the afternoon light and I felt, for the first time in days, oddly peaceful. The dog snuffled optimistically at Edward's pockets.

'The trouble with people, Gaby, I've often thought,' he said, walking to the edge of the water,' is that we build these pretences and then we don't really know anything about each other. That's why people get hurt.'

'You'd know. You're the master of lying.'

He turned to face me, his expression curious and half-

369

sorrowful. 'You've got every reason to hate me, I know that,' he said. 'But try not to hate me too much. Hear me out – I'm trying to explain to you the best I can. Piers had no idea when he started his persecution of Denham quite how bad his condition was.'

'The depression?'

'Depression, paranoia, near-breakdown – he was living on a cocktail of anti-depressants and working himself into the ground, and this went on for nearly three years, with Denham getting worse, and I had no idea that all this was going on with Piers – the threats, the blackmail, all so Piers could amuse himself by proving something. And I could have told Piers that if he carried on, Den would lose his grip, but Piers didn't know him well enough to see that coming. And finally he did.'

'So it *was* Piers's fault?'

'Not entirely, no. I didn't mean that. I think Den had got to the point where he couldn't see a life without the medication, and when he hit that point he wasn't long for this world really – he lost his spirit. But I think Piers fed his fears – it's funny, they were quite similar in some ways. Neither of them could live with public humiliation.'

'Oliver believed it was Piers's fault, then.'

'Oliver believed it because it suited him. There was all sorts of – well, I'm hardly in a position to criticise, I haven't won any prizes for being a good father, but Oliver and Denham – very messed-up family. And I think it suited Oliver to have someone to blame, because it meant he didn't have to feel so guilty himself. Den was a very meticulous man. Before he killed himself, he wrote Oliver a long letter, all the things he felt he should have told his son and never did. And of course it was all in there, Piers and me, the business in Jordan – and my first thought was to get Piers out of the country as soon as possible. I didn't know what Oliver might be capable of. Well – I found out, eventually.' He passed a hand across his forehead and sighed. 'I don't blame Oliver, you know. Almost came as a relief to find the boy's not so ridiculously nice after all.' He curled his lip into a near-smile and glanced at me briefly. 'He just wanted revenge, I suppose that's a primitive instinct. Get even, get the fuckers. He wanted Piers to pay, and he didn't care if I had to pay too, because in his mind it was my fault, I'd brought Piers into our lives.'

'I had no idea. Jesus, how could you – how could you bring me into the middle of all this, knowing that – how *could* you?'

I grabbed his jacket and shook him; he seized my arm.

'Do you want to hit me? You can, I deserve it –'

'I hate you!' I shouted, wind stinging my eyes to tears, 'I really fucking hate you, how could you do this to me?'

'Gaby, I'm sorry, I'm so sorry. I just wanted him back, I never thought you –' Edward covered his face with his hands. Perhaps he was crying.

'I fell in love with him!'

'I know you did, I know – I'm so sorry –' He took his hands away. 'You know what's so bloody stupid and ironic,' he gave a kind of choking laugh, 'you've made a virtue out of hating me all these years, with no good reason, and now I've given you more reason to hate me than anyone and I'm asking you to try and forgive me.'

'With no reason? You destroyed my dad's life, you took away everything he had and then you never even went to see him once when he was dying! Your own brother – that's good enough reason, isn't it?'

'You know nothing about it!' He turned on me, and his eyes were like dark metal. 'You have no interest in knowing the truth because you wanted to hate me, just like Oliver, you want someone to blame. Do you really want to know the truth?'

'You don't know what that means! You just lie to everyone, that's what you do, you –'

'Listen to me!' He clamped my arm, held his face a few inches from mine. 'When Richard told me he was dying, I went to see him. He told me before he told you or Helen, you didn't know that, did you? He was terrified, do you know why? Because he had nothing. I've said it before – Richard didn't live in the real world. He had his house, but he had debts and no savings, no life insurance, no pension – and he was terrified because he didn't know how his family was going to survive. And he never asked me for anything, and I had a hell of a job persuading him to take it, but he did, in the end.'

'Take what?'

'Money, Gaby, for Christ's sake! The money you live on, the money that pays for you to fuck about with ancient history instead of getting a real job, the money your mother lives on, all the money that paid for Richard's medical treatment – I gave it to him, *I* did. He didn't have a penny. And he didn't want you or Helen to know, so I never told anyone. Only Roger knew, because Roger knows all my business. And I'm not telling you this now so you'll be grateful, or because it might make you hate me any less, but if you're going to hate me, do it for the right reasons, not for Richard. I did everything I could for him, and I miss him more than you'd believe. But don't accuse me of mistreating Richard, I don't deserve that.'

He let my arm go, and we stood silently for some moments, staring out across the water. A great choking sob was brimming up from somewhere deep in my chest.

'I had no idea.'

'I know. It doesn't matter.' He tugged at his hair and kicked at the sand, his face difficult. 'But – uh, look – now that you do, don't feel – I mean, that money's indefinite, you know. Unless you decide you don't want to take it any more. But your mother needs it, I think, and it might be a good thing if you didn't tell her where it's coming from.'

'No, I wouldn't.'

'Fine. Then let's not mention it again. One day you might even get yourself a proper job, then it won't be necessary.' He gave an effortful laugh. 'But I won't have it said that I don't look after my own.'

A thin film of cloud, the colour of heather, had drifted across the sun, casting a stain of shadow on the bright water of the loch. Edward looked at the sky.

'We should get back,' he said. 'Are you hungry?'

'Not really.'

'No, neither am I. I've hardly eaten since I got here, Moira's been trying to force all sorts of bloody stews down me like I'm an invalid. It's getting cold.'

We turned to retrace our footsteps along the path, Heathcliff padding alongside us, exhausted from his scamperings.

'I still can't believe he's gone,' said Edward, after a while.

'Nor can I.'

'He was always away so often that – you got used to him not being there, and then just suddenly turning up with no explanation. It's hard to believe that he won't –'

'I miss him,' I said, quietly.

'He was – unique, I think. I don't expect to find anyone like him.'

I didn't reply.

Edward put a hand on my back to guide me through some undergrowth, and kept it there for a moment. 'He did care for you, you know.'

'I don't think so.'

'No, he did. As much as Piers ever cared for anyone. He told me – when he started getting to know you, that he thought it was unfair. He didn't want you to get hurt.'

'Bit late by then.'

'I know. I fucked up. I didn't care about the mess that was made.'

'Haven't you built a career on that?'

'That's different. I loved – well, I loved my brother, I love my family, perhaps not in the right way, but I did, I loved Denham, you know – but I'd never loved anyone like Piers. I thought I was going mad. For as long as he was around, nothing else mattered.'

I nodded. My uncle retreated inside his own thoughts and we trudged on through the trees, time curling silently around us.

'Does anyone else know about – about the stuff in Jordan?'

'Only Oliver. And now you.'

'Do you think Oliver would say anything?'

'No. I don't think so – Oliver's had his revenge now. But he's not a bad boy – he had no idea what he was getting into. And we'll all have to get on with our lives, somehow.'

'That's easy for you to say.'

'No, Gaby, it's not. It's not easy, believe me.'

'Aren't you afraid someone will dig it up one day?'

'It would be impossible to prove, now. Unless someone was very determined, but I don't think it could happen. It's history.'

I stopped walking. 'How can you dismiss something so – you had a man killed! And you sold illegal nerve gas – is that something you can just forget about?'

Edward turned round.

'Jesus, Gaby – you have no idea what it was like out there. We were being manipulated by the men at the top on both sides. They're all dead now, of course.' He paused. 'It all gets a bit murky when you're involved in these kinds of deals, we just did as we were told. We barely even knew what it was, we were green boys –'

'You were thirty-something! And I don't believe you didn't know what you were doing. God, I knew you were without conscience, but –'

'We were selling weapons anyway, that was our job. Guns and missiles, it's not as if they don't kill people somewhere along the line. Seemed a bit late to start getting humanitarian scruples at that stage. And of course I've regretted it, but sometimes you have to put things behind you.'

'Why did you tell me all this anyway?'

'I thought you wanted to understand. Talking about him's the next best thing to talking to him. It's not as if your opinion of me could be much lower. And you should know what Piers was capable of, if you didn't already. God, I never wanted to have a man killed, Gaby, I've explained that. If you think it doesn't weigh on my conscience – and I do have one . . .'

'Why would you trust me?'

'Because what are you going to do – go to the press?' He looked defiant, then sighed again. 'And because you're all the family I've got left, really. And vice versa. Blood's thicker than water, they say. Maybe I hoped you'd feel you could forgive me.'

'I don't know what I feel.'

There was a long silence. A haze of cloud now partially covered the sun, thin strips of light seeping over the edges, wreathing itself around the distant cap of Ben Cruachan. The forest shuddered under the wind; gulls screamed and dived to the water.

My uncle was looking at me.

'You look just like Richard,' he said, eventually.

'So do you.'

He almost smiled.

'Huh. Look – buzzard,' he remarked, pointing vaguely at a dark shape sweeping over the trees.

Later in the evening, we sat at either end of a long table in a dining room of faded splendour, my uncle and I, all the preceding Earls of Orchy glowering down at us in oils with their bristling whiskers and tartans. We ate in silence in the quivering light of a branched candelabrum as cold air whistled under the door. At least, we made the pretence of eating, to Moira's disapproving clicks and tuts, shovelling food around our plates with evident lack of interest. It was not a hostile silence, but a kind of shared exhaustion and, if not forgiveness, then perhaps the beginnings of acceptance. We ate alone, the knitting-needle click of cutlery on plates the only sound echoing into the high ceiling, like the last two survivors of a once-proud dynasty.

Finally, my uncle laid down his knife and fork and looked up at me. For a long time he didn't speak; Moira cleared the plates, muttering, and returned with a steaming silver pot of coffee.

'I won't be staying much longer,' he said, when she had closed the door. 'Have a smoke if you want to.' He reached into his jacket for a cigar and clippers. 'Press'll be all over the show in a matter of days if I don't resurface.'

'What will you do?'

'Go back and face the music. Can't hide for ever. I've got to do something about it.'

'Like what?'

'Oh – I've decided to grant an interview. On telly – one of those special one-hour jobs – Alex Lodge or one of the heavy hitters. You know the thing – all trembly lips and apology. I bloody hate that stuff, as you know, but it's a sure way back into the public's hearts.'

'Not necessarily.'

Edward flared his match with a sizzle and shook his wrist vigorously. 'I know more about this than you, Gaby. The public just want to be taken into your confidence. They think they own a part of you if you're in the public eye – that's the democracy of the media. So what they won't put up with is being lied to – hypocrisy is the heart of every tabloid scandal. Now I do the interview, I do the old mea culpa, here I am on a plate, sorry everyone, look at me suffering, and there we are – no longer public enemy number one.'

'Oliver thought I should do an interview for the *Enquirer*.'

'I bet he did.' He looked at me, suddenly wary. 'Well, it's up to you. I don't feel I have a choice, but you do. And believe me – it might make you feel better for a while, but privacy is one of the most valuable possessions you can have. You won't realise that until you lose it. No need to share your pain with the world all the time, whatever the papers say.'

I nodded. 'And what about you?'

'Well, once I don't have to hide, I can get on with all the

ther stuff. Someone's got to clear Piers's flat, and I don't
want Roger doing it. Actually' – he watched the smoke curling in thick cables from his cigar with sudden interest, as if an
answer had mystically appeared there – 'I wonder if I could
get that into the programme. That would be a tear-jerker, eh,
a bit of footage of me packing away his letters. I wonder.'

I bit my lip. He was sounding more like himself again.

'Didn't he have any family?'

'Mother in a dismal fen village somewhere, married to a
man dying of alcoholism – not his father. I wrote to her when
he died, told her when the funeral was, but never got any
response. He left home when he was seventeen or eighteen
and didn't seen her again. I think they'd tried to forget each
other.' He looked up, as if seeing me for the first time. 'We're
the only ones who'll remember him, Gaby. You and me.
Remember him properly. I'm not asking you to – I know how
you feel about me. But that's our responsibility – not to forget
him. He wasn't a good man, Piers, but he was – oh, I don't
know. We won't find another one like him. He deserves
something better than a few tabloid headlines as a memorial.'

'I thought about writing it down. About the time I knew
him.'

'Maybe you should. I suppose you'll go back to the university now, will you?'

I lit a cigarette and thought about it. 'I don't know. I haven't
got anywhere else to go. What will happen to the faculty?'

Edward waved a hand dismissively. 'I'm going to sell it
back to the university. I don't think they really want my name
associated with it after this.'

'The university can't afford to buy it back.'

'Oh, I'll sell it at a loss – I'm not really all that bothered. I'd
lost interest in it anyway. Poor old George has been left with
egg on his face, but he can turn it around once they make him
professor. The D of E will put the money in this time, and I
don't mind keeping up a bit of investment in the short term,
as a silent partner. It'll sort itself out.'

'Edward?' I watched the end of my cigarette, the tip quickly eating the paper.

'What?'

'Don't say what.' He laughed, abruptly. 'Did George know?'

'God.' He rubbed a hand across his eyebrows. 'Know about which bit?'

'About you and Piers?'

Edward laughed again and leaned back in his chair, eyeing me across the length of the table with genuine surprise.

'Yes. At least, I imagine he guessed. George and I –' he paused to suck thoughtfully on his cigar. 'George never mentioned this?'

'Mentioned what?'

Edward was still smiling, as if something in the conversation were amusing him.

'You know we went to the same school. Typical boys' grammar in the fifties, I must have been levered in somehow because I had this problem with the dyslexia and no one bothered with special help in those days, so they all thought I was stupid, and I wasn't very good at sport, and I used to get the shit kicked out of me all the bloody time. I mean *all* the time. They called me a faggot, you see. You'd come in for games and some little shit would have written "Nigel Harvey is a faggot" across the changing room walls. Little fuckers.'

Though his voice was light-hearted, his teeth were pressed tightly together.

'There was one incident – behind the cricket pavilion where a crowd of the older boys held me down, got my shorts down and threatened to push the handle of a cricket bat up my arse, because they said that's what faggots liked. And I had absolutely no idea what they were talking about, of course – I must have been about eleven – anyhow, someone stopped them and I got told to go and see the Head Boy.

'Now, the Head Boy was your ideal English schoolboy – he was going to a good university, he was a star cricketer and

ll-round decent chap, and they used to leave him to deal
with these kind of problems, things the teachers didn't want
to get involved in. And I'll never forget standing in front of
him in this empty classroom, and this Head Boy – who you
know better as Dr George Fenton – saying, "Now, Harvey, I
hear the chaps are calling you a faggot. I'm sure you're not
one, and there's no excuse for what they've done, but my
advice would be to show a bit more interest in sport. You'll
find in life it's very hard to get on if people think you're a faggot. You'd have to go into the theatre."' Edward threw his
head back and laughed, without humour, at the memory. 'So
that was old George's advice. Stood me in good stead, as you
can see.'

'I can't believe George said that.'

'He was sixteen, and it was fifty-two. I expect he's acquired
some slightly more progressive notions in the intervening
years.'

'So he guessed about Piers?'

'Oh, I don't know.' He tapped his cigar carefully into the
ashtray and spread his hands on the table, regarding them as
if they belonged to someone else. 'I expect he did. George has
a knack of seeing the things you do your best to hide.'

'He tried to warn me. Not to get too close to Piers.'

'I'm sure he did. He's very fond of you.'

'He didn't dislike Piers, you know.'

'George sees the best in people, always. It's a talent. Not in
a naive way, but – really. He gives you a chance. He's one of
the few men I've ever genuinely respected.'

'Piers said that too.'

'Yes. Yes, I imagine he did. George was probably the father
he wished he'd had, though he'd never have admitted it. He
was never happy, Piers, even when he got what he thought
he wanted. He always wanted so much, but he never really
knew –'

'What?'

'How to let anyone love him.' My uncle shook his head and

looked down as he stirred his coffee. 'But maybe none of us learns that properly.'

'Maybe.'

'I wanted to ask you a favour.'

'A favour?' I sat up, suddenly suspicious.

'Not a big thing. Just – when I get back to London, when all this mess is sorted out – I wanted to give Piers a proper grave. You know, like a plaque or something, in a Garden of Remembrance somewhere – somewhere decent, not that depressing crematorium at the airport. And I wanted to put some poetry on it.'

'And?'

'And – well, you know about that side of things. I wondered if you could think of something appropriate. Not now, just, if you get a chance. Then at least – it would be some sort of way of saying goodbye.'

I nodded, remembering.

'He above the rest
In shape and gesture proudly eminent
Stood like a tower –'

'What's that?'

'Milton.'

'Huh. Something along those lines.'

I sat back in my chair. It was not yet nine, but the blue darkness outside made it feel like midnight. A moth thudded against the window. Edward drew his chair back and stood.

'I knew you'd come to find me, you know.' He paused; I didn't reply. 'I was dreading it. But now' – he ran a hand through his hair with some embarrassment – 'it's probably a good thing you did.'

I nodded again.

'Stay here as long as you need, eh.'

His eyes met mine briefly and we looked at each other. Edward gave a curt nod and turned to go.

'Uncle Edward?'

He jerked back with an expression of quiet surprise.

'Uh – I just –' I shrugged. 'Thanks.'

He smiled, and closed the door. I had never called him that before.

Edward made his arrangements and left two days later. We didn't speak much in that time, though we ate together; I walked in the grounds of the Hall and by the loch, and he kept to the silent parts of the house. On his last night we played billiards together, mostly without speaking; once he let me win. Occasionally we laughed. Something indefinable had been settled.

Until the rains came back, I spent the days out walking with the dog, thinking of Piers, and of Edward, and of how I could try to rebuild my life. When the weather made it impossible to go out, I shut myself in the dim library with the furniture all swaddled in dust sheets, and tried to write about Piers. At night I dreamed about him, and sometimes he spoke; when I woke in the cold light it was almost possible to believe none of this had happened, until it came rolling back, like a punch in the gut.

After a few days, the skies cleared and I took Heathcliff out again down to the shore. When we returned to the house, there was an unfamiliar car in the drive, parked next to Oliver's and bearing a sticker that identified it as a rental car from Glasgow airport. My first thought was that Sir Rory had come home, and I would have to explain myself, and probably leave. But when I opened the door to the kitchen, I found Oliver sitting at the table, with Moira beaming as if she'd found a long-lost son.

'It's wee Olly come to visit!' she exclaimed with evident delight.

'So I see.'

Oliver and I stared at each other, his eyes somewhere between pleading and apology.

Moira was clearly ecstatic about Oliver's arrival, flitting here and there around the kitchen with the kettle as if suddenly needed again. I was less so.

'I was worried about you,' he said, producing a helpless shrug.

'Your concern for my welfare is very touching,' I said tightly. 'It's a shame you didn't think a bit more about it before you and Chris Haughton broke your big scoop.'

There was a startled clatter as Moira dropped a saucer and pretended not to listen.

Olly sighed. 'Can we go for a walk?'

'I've just been for a walk.'

'Gaby – please? We have to talk.'

'I'm sick of walking round this fucking loch talking about stuff that can't be changed. We could talk all day and all night and it won't bring him back. It's all too late – and it's too late for you to start pretending you're sorry with your fake concern and your big puppy eyes –'

'Gaby – come on –' Oliver half-rose. 'I've just got off a plane and driven for two hours.'

'I didn't ask you to. Think of it as a pilgrimage. I hope it' eased your conscience.'

'Jesus, that's not fair! I saved you for the last few weeks – got you here in the first place, I jeopardised my position don't you think you owe me something?'

I turned on him, shaking. 'You only saved me because you were the one who dropped everyone in it in the first place! It' your fault – how dare you tell me I should be grateful?'

'No, Gaby' – Oliver stood and thrust out a finger, his usually placid face twitching with anger. 'Edward and Pier Gaveston dropped you in it – it's their fault. And what would you have done, would you have thanked me if you'd married a man who was fucking your uncle the entire time and you didn't know? I saved you from that, because I care about you and you're too bloody stubborn and stupid to realise!'

Moira was frozen rigid, a tea-towel in one hand and a jug in the other, her face in such a rictus of shock that I almost laughed unintentionally.

382

Oliver followed me out of the room and into the library. He closed the door behind him.

'Sorry,' I said, without meaning it, slumping into a chair amid a billow of dust.

'Doesn't matter.' He walked across to the French windows, hands behind his back. 'I expect you've heard the whole story now.'

'Oh, yes. Your father and my uncle selling nerve gas illegally to Egypt and then having a man killed to cover it up. Came as a bit of a shock.'

'Piers Gaveston had him killed, Gaby. Not my father. Edward must have told you that.'

I gave a sort of half-grunt.

'Do you understand, now, why I was being so over-protective? It was nothing to do with jealousy – I know that it's not – that we're not' – he stopped and cleared his throat – 'but I think of you as one of my best friends. And you were blindly falling for this man who's prepared to kill his lover and sleep with powerful men to get his own way. Are you surprised that I wanted to protect you from that, if I could?'

'And you knew that you wanted to destroy him.'

'I promised myself that if he ever came back – I didn't know he was in Argentina – but if he ever came back, I would expose him. Not the murder – there's no evidence, and I couldn't do that without involving Dad's name. And it wasn't really Edward's fault. But Piers was so pleased with himself, he thought he was so successful – he thought he'd won, and I wanted the world to know he was an over-reaching little catamite. No better than a rent boy, whatever you thought of him.'

'You can think that. But he wasn't always –' I folded my hands in my lap and picked at my nails. Oliver turned from the window to look at me, his face shaded in the afternoon light.

'What?'

'He made me laugh. He made me feel' – I hesitated – 'alive.'

Oliver looked down. Wind tapped the Virginia creeper against the window panes.

I shook my head abruptly. 'Stupid thing to say.'

'No, not stupid.' Oliver crossed the room slowly. 'He did have – *something*, I grant you that. I can see why you would –'

'Imagine having all that and still not being happy with yourself.'

'He had a troubled conscience. Well, now I know what it's like. You're the only one who's blameless in all this, Gaby, at least you can have that comfort. None of it was your fault.'

'Except that I was too stupid to see any of it, even when it was right in front of me.'

He perched on the arm of my chair and put a hand on my shoulder. I hesitated, then leaned my head gratefully against his chest.

'Do you hate me? Do you really believe I killed him?'

'No.' I looked away. 'No, of course not. I wanted to think that because – it's easier to have someone to blame.'

Oliver nodded emphatically.

'But other people get through things and cope. He was always going to do it, some time or another. He couldn't have grown old gracefully.'

'I suppose –' Oliver moved his arm around the back of my neck and we rearranged ourselves comfortably. 'I suppose that was true of Dad, too, though I never wanted to admit it.'

'Piers thought he was in control of all this, you know. He said that some people want to have their stories written for them.'

'It doesn't work like that. You can't make a pattern out of it, it just happens. People get in each other's way. Change each other's stories without intending to.'

We sat in silence for a while, watching the dust swirling in the draught as the dusk slowly crept up on the house. The room grew cold.

'History,' I said, finally. 'That's why I do what I do – because history makes you feel safe. The stories are written,

384

hey don't change. I've been afraid of change, I suppose, because I always want to see the whole story. But you can't live in the past – you have to live with it. Experience – all the stupid little things that we blunder into – we have to make stories of it, otherwise where's the sense?'

'What are you talking about?'

'I don't know. Just thinking aloud.'

'Will you tell your story?'

'You mean, will I tell it to the *Enquirer*?' I smiled wearily.

'It doesn't matter now.'

'Is that why you're here?'

'Don't be silly. I'm here because – I wanted you to see that you're not on your own. You've got me, you've got George, you've got –'

'I've got what?'

'Edward. In a sense.'

I considered this. 'In a sense. I suppose.'

'Come back with me.'

I shook my head.

'Not just yet. Soon. I need a bit longer.'

'All right, you know best. I can stay another day, but not longer – I wish I could. But I'll be there when you get back. You know I will.'

'Yes. I know. Thanks.'

Standing among the shadows of Kilchurn Castle, the thirteenth-century ruin at the head of Loch Awe, I watch an incandescent sky reflected in the grey-green blurring shadows of the water. The castle is empty of tourists now that it's early October and the winds are fierce; below me, the dog chases its tail in ceaseless circles through drifts of fallen leaves and shouts at the gulls, as it always does.

History. It is time to go back to England. England is changing too, just as I am, and I have to learn how to live with the changes. I think I understand now that the present doesn't always come to displace the past but to build on it; that new images do not have to obscure the old but can meld with them, like layers of transparency, and life continues, sadder sometimes, but with deeper colours. This is experience, the present moment in all its confusion; this is what stories are made of. Piers is gone; he made me a part of his story for a while, and I don't regret all of it. But my story goes on, and I have to go back and take it up again. Past and future.

Patchy sunlight blinks on the loch. I will not come back here.

All shall be well, my father would have said, smiling. I can picture his face. He wouldn't have blamed me.

All shall be well.

Yes. I'm not alone.

Something, perhaps, has been salvaged.